We all have them.
The odd one. The creepy one.
The one who keeps weird
hours or who engages in an
obscure hobby.

Neighbors. Perhaps the one
right next door to you.

But what if they're something…
more?

What if they are…

THE MONSTERS NEXT DOOR?

THE MONSTERS NEXT DOOR

Edited by R.J. Carter

This is a work of fiction. All the characters and events portrayed in this book are fictitious, and any resemblance to real people is purely coincidental.

The Monsters Next Door © 2023 by Critical Blast Publishing. Individual copyrights to authors of these original works are as follows:

Mrs. McCarthy © 2023 Heather Daughrity
Midnight Deli © 2023 Mia Dalia
The Nick Victory Chronicles, Part One: Nick's New Neighbor © 2023 Paul Barile
Stanley's Last Job © 2023 L.N. Hunter
Howling Devil in the Sticks © 2023 Sirius
Shadows at Dusk © 2023 R. Gene Turchin
Man on Porch © 2023 Evan Baughfman
Captain's Last Ride © 2023 Joel Reeves
The Werewolves are Due on Maple Street © 2023 Sheri White
A Day Too Bright © 2023 Fulvio Gatti
The Dead Girl Next Door © 2023 Diana Olney
In the Pines © 2023 Ray Zacek
Welcome Mat, Five Stars © 2023 Jennifer Lee Rossman
Monster Next Door © 2023 Martin Klubeck
The Welcome Wagon of Widgeon Woods © 2023 Jean Jentilet
Good Neighborhood © 2023 Robert Allen Lupton
The Things We Do for Love © 2023 Alex James Donne
Comes a Pale Bride © 2023 Troy Riser
Mammon Estates © 2023 Ross Killey
A Night at the Zalinskis © 2023 Damascus Mincemeyer

All rights reserved. No part of this book may be reproduced in any form, including information storage and retrieval systems, without permission in writing from the publisher.

Critical Blast Publishing
1097 Preswyck Drive
Belleville, IL 62221

Book Design, Typesetting, Cover Art & Interior Illustrations by George Peter Gatsis. © 2023 George Peter Gatsis. All Rights Reserved.

First Edition August 2023

0 9 8 7 6 5 4 3 2 1

ISBN-13: 979-8-218-26312-6

THE MONSTERS NEXT DOOR

Edited by R.J. Carter

This is a work of fiction. All the characters and events portrayed in this book are fictitious, and any resemblance to real people is purely coincidental.

The Monsters Next Door © 2023 by Critical Blast Publishing. Individual copyrights to authors of these original works are as follows:

Mrs. McCarthy © 2023 Heather Daughrity
Midnight Deli © 2023 Mia Dalia
The Nick Victory Chronicles, Part One: Nick's New Neighbor © 2023 Paul Barile
Stanley's Last Job © 2023 L.N. Hunter
Howling Devil in the Sticks © 2023 Sirius
Shadows at Dusk © 2023 R. Gene Turchin
Man on Porch © 2023 Evan Baughfman
Captain's Last Ride © 2023 Joel Reeves
The Werewolves are Due on Maple Street © 2023 Sheri White
A Day Too Bright © 2023 Fulvio Gatti
The Dead Girl Next Door © 2023 Diana Olney
In the Pines © 2023 Ray Zacek
Welcome Mat, Five Stars © 2023 Jennifer Lee Rossman
Monster Next Door © 2023 Martin Klubeck
The Welcome Wagon of Widgeon Woods © 2023 Jean Jentilet
Good Neighborhood © 2023 Robert Allen Lupton
The Things We Do for Love © 2023 Alex James Donne
Comes a Pale Bride © 2023 Troy Riser
Mammon Estates © 2023 Ross Killey
A Night at the Zalinskis © 2023 Damascus Mincemeyer

All rights reserved. No part of this book may be reproduced in any form, including information storage and retrieval systems, without permission in writing from the publisher.

Critical Blast Publishing
1097 Preswyck Drive
Belleville, IL 62221

Book Design, Typesetting, Cover Art & Interior Illustrations by George Peter Gatsis. © 2023 George Peter Gatsis. All Rights Reserved.

First Edition August 2023

0 9 8 7 6 5 4 3 2 1

ISBN-13: 979-8-218-26312-6

CONTENTS

3¢
USA
MAD MANDY
665
MONSTER
VALUE STAMP
THIS IS IT!
CLIP THEM
& COLLECT
THEM ALL!

CRITICAL BLAST PUBLISHING
20¢
MRS. McCARTHY
Heather Daughrity
APPROVED BY THE READING CODE AUTHORITY
WEIRD FANTASTIC WORLDS
CRITICAL BLAST PUBLISHING
WHERE POP CULTURE GETS BLASTED
INCREDIBLE STRANGE STORIES
DO YOU DARE KNOCK ON HER DOOR?

HEAD KNIVES 100% stainless steal daggers that launch from the top of your head and kill any conversation you find boring.

FISH BOWL FULL OF WORMS Are you tired of eating meat? Get yourself a bowl full of yummy worms and feel you are saving the planet.

SUPER SECRET BOOK SAFE The special camouflage feature activates, once placed on the book shelf. You'll never find it again.

LAST MAN ON EARTH HEARD A KNOCK AT THE DOOR!

DIGITAL PUZZLE T-SHIRT Get people's undivided attention when they get engrossed trying to solve the constantly changing puzzles.

DEFEAT BLACK MYSTIC ARTS KUNG-FU Tired of getting your ass kicked every Tuesday by Black Mystic Arts Kung-Fu fighters? CALL 666-HELP to enroll in self-defense training every Hellspawn should know to survive any dark alley encounter. Become a Ninth Circle Master of Judante!

MONSTER VALUE STAMP
THIS IS IT! CLIP THEM & COLLECT THEM ALL!

RADIOACTIVE CANDY When you want to level up your personality and appear extra sweet to the people around you... and want to have a superpower over sugar... this candy's for you!

BOX OF LIVE BATS When you feel like a millionaire crime fighting hero and need to dress up your special cave, to give it that extra touch of atmosphere... a box of live bats is perfect for you. Food not included.

H.D. Daughrity loves all things macabre, dark, autumnal, and horrific. She lives with her husband, author and publisher Joshua Loyd Fox, their extended circus of children and pets, and more books than any one house can hold.

She splits her time between New England and her native state of Oklahoma, where she spends her days writing, editing, gardening, and keeping her family's head in the clouds, but feet on the ground.

For book and tour news, to purchase her varied writings, see her appearances, peruse her professional book reviews, or contact her for editing services: www.heathermillerhorror.com

The first explosion sounded like a gunshot. A ball of flame erupted into the air over Hawthorne Drive. Not a single person stirred, not one neighbor came running to see what was happening. The dead leaves still clinging to the tree in the front yard of Number One shriveled instantly in the heat, the oak which they had clung to moments before beginning to smolder as flames reached from the house and licked along its outstretched branches.

It took exactly fifty-two seconds before the second explosion sounded, across the street at Number Two, and exactly eleven minutes and thirty-three seconds before every house on the street was engulfed in flame. All along the street not a soul was to be seen. Half a mile away, the driver of an ancient van nodded, satisfied, and drove away.

A gas explosion, they would call it. The news would report a bizarre combination of deadly fumes and faulty wiring that had spread from house to house along the secluded stretch of road. This explanation was not completely satisfactory. It left more lingering questions than the police and fire chiefs of the nearby town would like, but it was the best they could come up with, and it would have to do.

But oh, how wrong they were.

EARLIER

Hawthorne Drive was an experimental neighborhood. Beyond the town limits, Main Street turned into the highway and meandered through fields and woodland a bit before the turnoff for Hawthorne appeared. Taking a left here, a vehicle would disappear from sight on a stretch of road blasted straight through the middle of a large hill, reemerging further on where the towering cliffs on either side of the road sloped back down to the level of the ground; a bit beyond that, in the middle of nowhere, would appear the neighborhood of Hawthorne, if you could call twelve houses on one stretch of road a neighborhood.

Hoping to draw in new residents, especially those in a higher tax bracket, the town had commissioned the twelve mini-mansions. Huge houses with carefully landscaped lawns had appeared in record time, and the town had waited for the rich and overworked citizens of the big city to come snatch up their piece of secluded heaven.

The town had been sorely disappointed.

After the houses on Hawthorne Drive sat empty for nearly two years, costing the town tens of thousands of dollars in upkeep, the mayor had thrown up his hands in defeat, called the realtor who represented the homes, and told her to do whatever it took to sell them.

Which is how an experimental neighborhood of vacation homes for the wealthy became a street of huge houses sold at rock bottom prices to eleven lucky families who were just glad to have enough room for all their kids for once.

Eleven lucky families, and Mrs. McCarthy.

Mrs. McCarthy was the only person to live on Hawthorne Drive that hadn't already lived in the town to begin with. She had shown up at the realtor's office one winter day as the sun was sinking in the sky and Carol Carson was just about to flip the sign on the door from OPEN to CLOSED. Mrs. McCarthy hobbled in, one hand clutching her cane, and sat herself down heavily in the chair across from Carol's desk. The realtor pasted on her best customer service smile and asked what she could do for the old woman.

Six days later, Mabel McCarthy was the owner of the final house – Number Twelve – on Hawthorne Drive.

No one saw her move in. One day the house was empty, the bare windows reflecting back the sun's winter glare. The next day when Billy Scutman, eight years old and resident of Number Ten, went outside to make snowballs to pelt his friend Jack with, the house next door, which had sat empty for months after the Scutmans moved in, was not empty anymore. Thick dark curtains covered every window, and the snow in front of the house was a mess of back-and-forth footprints. Billy stood looking up at the house pondering this strange new development long enough for Jack to sneak over from his house across the street and hit Billy square in the shoulder with an expertly packed ball of ice and snow. Billy had shouted, spun around, and dropped to the ground, his gloved hands already scooping up the powdery white stuff to form a weapon of retaliation, the new neighbor quickly forgotten.

On a street full of families whose kids ran back and forth from house to house and yard to yard as if they owned the street communally, whose parents were often found gathered in groups of four or six or more sharing dinners and drinks and game nights, whose first eleven houses were havens of happiness and muddy footprints and childish shouts and slightly drunken laughter, the resident of Number Twelve kept mostly to herself. She was a mystery to her neighbors. For three years she was rarely glimpsed, a silhouette against the fading evening sky as she pulled her tiny trash cart out to the curb or a hunched figure in the pale pink of early sunrise, hobbling out to pick up the daily newspaper when the paperboy's throw didn't quite hit its mark on her front porch.

And then one day when Billy Scutman, now aged eleven, was walking up the sidewalk after a long day of sixth grade, he heard a sound which he did not recognize. It was a sort of hissing whisper, not the dangerous sound of a snake but the sound of someone trying to quietly catch the attention of someone else. He looked around, eyes narrowed, for the source of the sound. He turned on the spot, eyes roving over Mallory and Mitch's house next door and Jack's house across the street. He saw no one. He was shrugging, turning back toward his own house, when the sound came again, louder, more insistent, and Billy's eyes shot toward Mrs. McCarthy's house. A huge maple tree, its leaves beginning to fade, shaded the old woman's house and porch, and Billy had to squint to make out the hunched form of his elderly neighbor as she held her door open just wide enough to poke her head out and call to him.

Glancing around and seeing no one else, Billy dropped his backpack on the sidewalk and approached the neighboring house, his curiosity aroused. As he stepped up onto the porch, Mrs. McCarthy moved back into the cool darkness of her front hall and motioned for him to follow. Billy stepped in, his eyes adjusting to the gloom. "Come along, young man, I have a proposition for you." Mrs. McCarthy's voice was surprisingly strong, a firm commanding voice for one so old. Billy followed her further into the house, to a sparsely furnished living room. She indicated a long, low couch, and Billy sat. She pointed to a plate of cookies, faint wisps of steam rising from them, chocolate chips still glistening with melty goodness. Billy didn't hesitate. He took a cookie and began to eat as Mrs. McCarthy began to talk.

Mrs. McCarthy was old. Not just the eighty years or so that she looked, but really, *really* old. Mabel McCarthy was a vampire. She'd been one since 1912; she'd been eighty-two when it happened. Now she was one hundred and ninety-one. The story of her conversion to vampirism was an unusual one. Her granddaughter, a beautiful girl named Maureen, had gotten herself mixed up with the wrong crowd, a vampire crowd, to be precise. Long story short, a fellow named Sean had decided he wanted to change Maureen over to his side of life, if you could call it that. Maureen had resisted. Sean had begun spiking her drink with bits of his own blood and before long she was in thrall to him. After a couple of weeks of regularly drinking Sean's blood, Maureen was more than happy to convert. Her grandmother, however, had not been so thrilled. Maureen didn't come home at her curfew one night and her grandmother, sick with worry, sat up waiting for her in the darkness. When Maureen came slinking in around four in the morning, Mabel knew something was wrong, and she had a pretty good idea what it was.

When the sun rose and daylight peeked around the curtains, Mabel entered Maureen's bedroom, where the girl was dead asleep beneath thick blankets, the dark drapes pulled tight. Mabel looked at Maureen's new paler-than-usual skin, the tiny points of unnatural canines peeking out below her upper lips, the fact that she wasn't breathing. With yards of rope and a knowledge of sailing knots, Mabel trussed her granddaughter up like a prize deer. Then Mabel got some sleep, making sure to wake long before sunset.

When Maureen awoke, there were awful howls and shrieks from the girl's bedroom and before long, an awful banging on the front door as Sean arrived to claim his newest recruit.

Mabel McCarthy stood her ground, refusing to allow him entrance, but Maureen shouted from the bedroom that Sean was welcome to come in, and then things happened fast. Sean knocked Mabel across the room, ran and untied his lover, and was going to have himself a little early-evening snack of old lady blood until Maureen hauled him backwards, appalled at the idea, screaming at him to leave her grandmother alone.

This presented a problem. They couldn't leave her alive – she'd expose them all – but Maureen absolutely would not entertain the thought of killing her. So, sighing and rolling his eyes, Sean made a cut on his own wrist, let the blood dribble into Mabel's mouth, and for the next month the two young lovebirds had a grandmother in thrall to them, following them everywhere they went. This did not make for a very enjoyable honeymoon, so one night, irritated with Mabel's blank stare and drooling mouth, Sean waited until Maureen had gone out to feed and quickly and neatly did the dirty work of making Mabel a vampire herself.

Maureen had been upset but had understood, as having her grandma sitting silent in a corner while she and Sean made sweet vampire love had been rather unnerving to her as well. So, they babysat Grandma for a few more days until they were sure she could feed herself, and then they lit out for parts unknown, leaving Mabel McCarthy, aged eighty-two, to begin a solitary century as an elderly vampire.

Most modern vampires have to move every twenty or thirty years, before the neighbors begin to get suspicious that they aren't aging, but poor elderly vampires have to move more often. Mrs. McCarthy looked like she could keel over dead any minute the day she moved into a place. If she lasted even ten years people would begin to wonder.

So, she chose Hawthorne Drive as her newest residence, moved herself in under cover of night, and settled in for another decade or so of loneliness. Once a month, when the moon was new and darkness would hide her actions, she would sneak out her back door, run at vampire speed out into the farmland and forest that surrounded her neighborhood, and find herself a meal. She had discovered that a feast once a month was more than enough to provide sustenance for her small, frail body. She tried her best to stick to woodland wanderers, hikers and hunters and hippies, because people didn't question it much when one of those idiots was found torn up in the woods. When she couldn't find a human meal, she resorted to feasting on deer or foxes or, one horrible month, a dozen plump toads, but never too close to home, and she always tried to make it seem like an animal attack or perhaps the work of a homicidal maniac. Anything was better than arousing people's suspicions that a vampire might be about.

Lately, though, a feeling had been creeping over Mabel McCarthy, and during the years she lived on Hawthorne Drive that feeling had grown and swelled until she could stand it no longer. She was lonely. She wanted companionship. And having a younger body around would go a long way toward explaining things. When a shuffling little old woman did things like lifting heavy boxes or climbing up to clean out the gutters, people panicked and tried to help and *then* people stared and started to get suspicious. If she had a younger person around as a companion, they could do all those things and people would be none the wiser.

So, Mrs. McCarthy took to watching the folks on her quaint little street, and the person she watched the most was young

Billy Scutman. He was a good-looking kid who would surely grow up to be a handsome young man. He was fast, almost always winning in the races the kids held along the length of Hawthorne Drive. He was smart. He was funny, full of jokes. He was kind to his little sister and to injured animals and hopefully, to little old ladies. He would make a good companion one day.

Mrs. McCarthy contemplated her plan for many weeks while summer turned to autumn. The kids went back to school and the street became quiet during the day. Vampires sleep in the day, of course, but little old ladies hardly sleep at all, vampire or not.

The day came when she decided to do it. No more going over it in her head, no more hem-hawing about. She pulled out flour and sugar and butter and chocolate chips and got to work, making sure to add in the special, secret ingredient right at the end: a dozen drops of her own blood.

She got Billy's attention as he came home from school, invited him into her house, and fed him the first batch of blood cookies as she pretended to ask him if he'd be willing to help an old woman out with some jobs, in return for twenty dollars and a batch of fresh cookies every week. Chocolate smeared across his fingers and chin, Billy eagerly agreed to come to her house the next day – Saturday – and begin work.

Her plan was in action. She would feed the boy a steady diet of blood cookies to keep him in thrall to her until he hit eighteen – or close enough – then turn him into a vampire himself and set off with him for a new home, where he could pose as a kind young man caring for his aging grandmother. It all seemed perfect in her mind.

Billy showed up on Saturday morning and did all the tasks she requested of him. He raked the leaves and weeded the front beds. He moved some boxes up to the attic; he swept the upstairs rooms; with a little instruction he even polished the silver. When he was finished, Mrs. McCarthy smiled and thanked him, and pressed a crisp twenty-dollar bill into his hand. She then handed him a Tupperware container full to the brim with cookies, with the instructions that they were to last him all week.

The next night, to test the effectiveness of her blood-thrall, she stood at an upstairs window and whispered into the night: "Come to me, come and stand beneath my tree and let me look at you." Within moments, she heard with her preternatural hearing the sound of Billy Scutman's slippered feet creeping down the staircase next door, saw him open his front door and come to stand in her own yard, gazing up at her. Mabel McCarthy's heart leapt with joy at her success. She whispered to him to go back home to bed and not to mention a word of this to anyone.

Monday afternoon, when Mrs. McCarthy had awoken from the few hours of daytime sleeping she could manage, she peeked out her living room window, the maple tree's shade keeping her safe from the sun. She could see Billy and a whole mess of kids playing together over at the Trenton's house across the street. She smiled.

That night, she tried again, wanting to make sure that Billy was eating his cookies regularly, keeping up the strength of her power over him. She went to the window and called once again into the night, "Come to me, come and stand beneath my tree."

A confusing cacophony of sound reached her ears as a dozen children rose from their beds, made their way out of their homes, and gathered, standing under her tree. She realized with horror that Billy, sweet, kind Billy, had shared his carefully crafted cookies with his entire group of friends. Quickly she released them all back to their homes and spent the rest of the night wringing her hands and wondering what to do.

By the time she laid down the next morning to sleep, she had decided to just wait it out. All the cookies were surely gone now, and after a few days the power should wear off and the other children should go back to normal. At least she hoped that would happen.

She did not try again that week to call Billy or the other children to her.

Billy showed up again the next Saturday and did all the chores Mrs. McCarthy could think up for him. This time, when she handed him his tub of cookies, she gave a stern warning. She looked him in the eyes, dropped her voice to a mesmerizing whisper, and said, "No sharing. Stop being so nice to your friends." She didn't want these cookies spread throughout the neighborhood, too.

She waited a couple of days before calling to him again. The weather had turned cold and rainy. She hadn't seen the neighborhood kids out playing together at all, and she took that as a good sign. If they weren't playing with Billy, then Billy wasn't sharing his cookies. She called to him.

Twelve children came.

But this time, they did not come quietly. This time they came shouting and pushing each other, pulling hair and punching. This time they stood in a chaotic huddle beneath her maple tree, shoving anyone who came within arm's reach, shivering against the cold. Mrs. McCarthy sighed. Obviously, her command to Billy to stop being so nice to his friends had gone out to all the children, still in her thrall even though it had been days since they ate the cookies. She sent them home.

She would wait until the weekend and then call them all to her at the time when Billy came to work. It would look like all the neighborhood children coming to help a little old lady ready her house for the winter. The parents would be pleased and not suspicious...she hoped.

The wait was torturous. Each day when the kids exited the school bus and made their way to their homes, she saw another black eye, another bumped head, an arm in a cast, scowls on all the faces. Luckily, the weather seemed a good excuse for the kids to not play together after school, and while individual parents were confounded by their own children's sudden turn toward bad behavior, they hadn't yet put their heads together and discovered that something was amiss in the whole neighborhood.

Saturday morning, Mrs. McCarthy resigned herself to another day of no sleep and called to the children from her living room. She could hear their shouting over the distant rumbles of thunder as they bullied each other down the street. They tumbled over one another on their way through the front door, and the old woman had her hands full just getting them all lined up along the hall.

"Now," she began, pointing her finger sternly at them, "I command you to stop..."

But she never finished her sentence, because just then Mallory Ogle, standing on one foot, lost her balance and fell into Trevor Sanderson, and at once Trevor wrapped his hand around Mallory's throat and began punching her. Within moments, every child was shouting and fists were flying; it was utter chaos and Mrs. McCarthy stood staring at it, open-mouthed and speechless.

A minute passed before she found her voice. Shouting as loud as her seldom-used vocal cords would allow she cried, "STOP!" Every child froze in mid-strike, some down on the ground with their arms up protecting their faces. Mrs. McCarthy pulled herself up to her full four-feet eleven-inches and spoke as firmly as she could. "You will all stop abusing your friends and be kind to each other!"

For a few moments, the children remained motionless. Then slowly, as if coming out of a trance, arms lowered, helping hands were offered to pull friends from the floor. Mrs. McCarthy nodded her head. Perhaps having all these children in thrall wouldn't be so bad. She was just congratulating herself on a job well done when she heard the whimpers.

She looked up sharply. Ten children were looking back at her, terrified. Two children lay on the ground, still and unmoving. Little Mallory Ogle's head was twisted at an unnatural angle, bruises matching the shape Trevor Sanderson's fingers standing out against the pale flesh of her neck. Further down, little James Harris's body was half hidden behind the other children, a puddle of blood spreading around the sneakers of his friends.

Mrs. McCarthy clutched at her heart, an entirely unnecessary but instinctual move, as she backed away from the children. Her mind was racing. What to do now? In a blind panic, she did the only thing she could think of. She pushed the other children aside, cut her own wrist open, and let her blood pour into the mouths of first Mallory, and then little James.

A tense and silent fifteen minutes passed before the bodies began to stir.

Two perfect little child vampires sat up and smiled at the old woman.

She had, of course, to command the children to keep this secret between them. She commanded the siblings of the newly made vampires to keep close watch on them. She commanded the vampires themselves to come to her each night once their parents were asleep and she would feed them. She commanded them to feign sickness in order to stay in bed all day.

Then she sent them all home and collapsed on her sofa, where she slept better than she had in decades.

She should have known it would never work. That night, it was not two vampire children that arrived at her house for feeding. It was five. And though she commanded them not to turn anyone else, the next night it was more, and the next night even more until finally twelve children were coming to her door. The children seemed to think it was all a gloriously fun new game.

Mrs. McCarthy settled the children around the TV watching late night talk shows and went running to find nourishment for them. She returned each night with freshly killed hikers and the children feasted before returning home.

Something really must be done. She couldn't keep the children's new appetites hidden for long, and once the parents realized what had happened... visions of garlic and wooden stakes made her shudder. She'd have to come up with a way to get all the vampire children away to safety without their parents raising the alarm.

Mrs. McCarthy spent all of Friday night thinking, scheming. She made up her mind.

The next day she set off down the street, a huge black umbrella and layers of dark clothing protecting her from what little sun might peek through the dark clouds overhead. She visited each house on the street, surprising the mothers who opened the doors with her sudden appearance after years of seclusion but leaving them smiling and laughing with plans underway.

There was to be a neighborhood celebration the next night. Right out in the middle of the street. An autumn harvest block party. The good housewives of Hawthorne Drive set to work organizing and planning, smugly pleased to be doing their good deed of the week in helping a little old lady realize a simple dream.

The "sick" children were not in attendance at the block party. Mrs. McCarthy had given them strict instructions not to come out. She herself spent the day baking half a dozen batches of cookies. These cookies carried a different special ingredient than the one she had given Billy. These cookies were baked with several cups-full of crushed up sleeping pills.

The party was a success. Neighbors, half-drunk and bundled against the chill autumn air, laughed and talked together. There was some discussion of the strange sickness that seemed to be sweeping through the school-age children. At ten o'clock, as the party wound down and cold raindrops began falling, Mrs. McCarthy stood to speak. She thanked them all for indulging an old woman's whim and presented each family with a plate of cookies. She encouraged them to pass them out amongst themselves and eat. Not wanting to offend the old woman, they did.

By eleven o'clock, every human resident of Hawthorne Drive had stumbled home to bed and was sleeping the deep sleep of the drugged. By midnight, Mrs. Mabel McCarthy had gathered all the vampire children in her living room once

more, fed them, and instructed them to stay put while she did some work.

Her work was to make her way methodically along the street to the end, then to enter each house and turn on the gas stoves, failing to light the flames and letting the houses fill with the toxic fumes.

All the next day, the children slept in a pile in Mrs. McCarthy's living room as their parents and teenaged siblings, too drugged to realize it, choked to death on the noxious fumes spewing forth into their homes.

At five o'clock in the afternoon, when Mrs. McCarthy's elderly tendencies combined with her anxious worry meant that she was already wide awake while the children would slumber on for another hour, she crept through the house, lifting one sleeping child after another and depositing them gently in the back of her enormous old van among piles of clothing she had pilfered from their homes.

Mrs. McCarthy set the gas to hissing in her own house while the vampire children slept on. She climbed into the van and sat in the driveway for half an hour, simply waiting. Then she drove out of the silent neighborhood. Mrs. McCarthy parked the van half a mile out, on the crest of a hill, and commanded the stirring children to stay put. Then, leaving her cane behind, she ran faster than the wind back to Hawthorne Drive, to the far end, to Number One. Screwing up all her energy, spreading her legs wide for maximum support, she leaned back and then flung her gnarled and shaky hands outward toward the house, a tiny ball of flame soaring from her outstretched fingertips and hurling with a vampire's strength through the front window.

By the time the house exploded a second later, she was already gone. Flame beget flame, explosion beget explosion, and within eleven minutes the whole of Hawthorne Drive was one giant snake of fire. At the top of the hill, Mrs. McCarthy put the van in drive, checked that the children were settled in comfortably, and drove away.

Not the best way to have dealt with things, perhaps, she thought as she watched the flames rise in the rearview mirror. But what did you expect, when you made an eighty-two-year-old woman a vampire and left her to her own devices? Oh, well. She had plenty of company now. She'd have to find a big house, out in the country away from prying eyes. She stole a glance behind her at the sleepy-eyed children coming fully awake as the last pale light disappeared beyond the horizon. She'd need to feed them soon.

She smiled to herself and hummed a little tune. She knew a secluded farmhouse just a few miles away where three curmudgeonly old bachelor brothers lived together. That would make a nice meal for her children. Perhaps they wouldn't eat all of them, though. It would be nice to have a man around to help with all these kids.

The thought made her giddy as a schoolgirl, and she giggled as she drove on into the night.

CRITICAL BLAST PUBLISHING
20¢
MIDNIGHT DELI
Mia Dalia
APPROVED BY THE READING CODE AUTHORITY
WEIRD FANTASTIC WORLDS
CRITICAL BLAST PUBLISHING
INCREDIBLE STRANGE STORIES
WHERE POP CULTURE GETS BLASTED
TERROR IS OPEN ALL NIGHT!

COCAINE FOR PETS When your pets become too excited during mating season and you don't want additional burden of feeding more pets, shot them up with some fine liquid snow and chill them out.

RENT AN ANGRY MIDGET! When you need to stop a Bully from harassing, or when you need to look like a decent human concerned for poor ugly monsters.

HYPNO-ROBOT use the special mind control eye harmonics to subdue the minds of your unwilling subjects. You'll never have to take out the trash and everyone will worship you as if their life depends on it.

1to1 MODEL PIRATE SHIP! Some assembly required. Glue NOT included. Recommend a private Island cove as the staging areo.

MONSTER VALUE STAMP THIS IS IT! CLIP THEM & COLLECT THEM ALL!

DIGITAL PUZZLE T-SHIRT Get people's undivided attention when they get engrossed trying to solve the constantly changing puzzles.

HOBO IN A BOX When your street is getting over-runned by homeless people and you need someone to speak their language and run them off to the next street down the block.

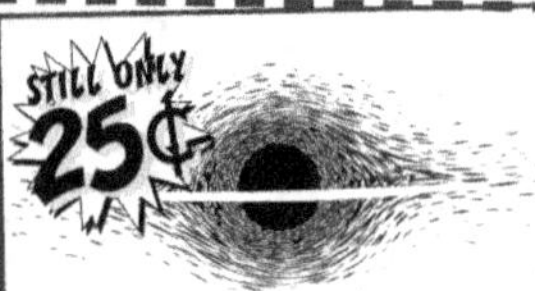

TRICK BLACK HOLE Get this special singularity and impress your friends by banishing them to other dimensions and realities.

MAKE MINE MONSTERS!

EXPLODING DRINK Sit back and enjoy the highjinks as people unscrew their drink activating the chemical reaction, causing a foamy mess.

Mia Dalia is an internationally published author, a lifelong reader, and a longtime reviewer of all things fantastic, thrilling, scary, and strange. Her short fiction has been published online by Night Terror Novels, Flash Fiction Magazine and Pyre Magazine, and in print anthologies by Sunbury Press, HellBound Press, Black Ink Fiction, Dragon Roost Press, and others. Mia's debut novel, Estate Sale, was published by Black Ink Fiction in 2023.

"I think Jeff might be a psychopath."

"Excuse me?"

"Jeff…like, have you noticed he never yawns when you yawn?"

"I honestly can't say I ever noticed Jeff's yawning patterns. Or yours for that matter."

"Well, he doesn't. Ever. And that's how you know. I saw this thing on Reddit about it."

"Oh, well, if it was on Reddit…"

"Exactly."

Chuck wanders away, distracted by something down the aisle, and I think to myself how this isn't even the strangest conversation we've ever had. Not by a long shot.

There are always things Chuck reads online, on the forums he frequents, all of them are completely random, most of them totally bogus. I can't tell if he's exceptionally gullible or extremely open-minded. What I can tell is that he's a complete stranger to critical thinking or sarcasm and categorically does not believe in daily showers.

Still, as far as coworkers go, it could be a lot worse. At least, he shows up and does the job, albeit rumpled and grumbling.

At any rate, I'm new here. And at the risk of sounding like an ass, I don't belong here, not like Chuck does. For him, this was a destination he had steadily stumbled toward before finally falling in, the gutter to his bowling ball. For me, it's something else completely.

Not that I express any of these views at work. On the contrary, I'm a model employee. I put on the same ugly polo shirt with the same ugly logo as everyone else and put in my hours uncomplainingly.

The Midnight Deli accepts no less.

Which of course is not true, but that's what Omar, the owner, says with a frequency that suggests it's his catchphrase.

I sigh and rearrange the cigarette display, forever surprised how a habit so prohibitively expensive manages to remain as popular as ever. It pays to keep busy, to move around. I've seen others doze off while standing up, sometimes with their eyes still open. They get this glazed, checked-out look.

People aren't meant to be up at this hour—we are diurnal creatures stuck in a nocturnal world. By hook or by crook, we need to get by, to make it to dawn.

It's not that large of a deli nor do we serve that large of a community, but Midnight's location does corner a certain market, shining its neon brightly across the otherwise shop-barren land.

You wouldn't know by looking around now, but the Gallows used to be a thriving neighborhood once. Before a series of poorly planned redevelopments, waves of uneven gentrification, and a flood. Before a local mill shut down and a wing of a small arts college moved across town to greener pastures.

Now, the Gallows doesn't have much left but its memories. They haunt the trash-strewn streets and whistle down its crooked alleys. The place has curled up on itself, lost in a dead dream of the past. Miss Havisham of neighborhoods. And for all my sins, I belong here.

My apartment is only a three-block walk from the deli. It isn't much, but then, I don't need much.

When I first moved here, I wandered the streets of the Gallows like a lost ghost, my insomnia-fueled brain guiding my restless feet. Then I decided I should just go ahead and monetize my inability to sleep and got a job at the Midnight Deli.

It was the weirdest job interview I've ever had. Omar just sat there and stared at me across his messy desk in blatant disbelief before finally remembering to ask me some questions.

I studied him back, politely: the too-shiny dress shirt straining at the buttons, the curly hair aggressively sprouting through at the top, looking like a furry cravat. His lower face had the bruise-like glow of someone whose five o'clock shadow came in by noon. The top of his head sported a luxurious Bollywood-style mane. But I think his most striking feature was his eyebrows, thick and lively and looking like sleeping caterpillars that were going to wake up at any moment and take off.

"Says here you went to college." He made this sound like a question. Or an incredulous statement.

"Journalism, yes."

"And you worked for a newspaper."

"Yes, nine years."

"And then..." Omar squints, "fittoprint.com."

"That's right."

He sighed heavily and—somehow—eyebrowily.

"This is a deli."

"Yes, I know."

He shifted in his chair. The chair made a shrill noise of protestation. "Look, I'll be honest with you, Nick: you're not...a typical applicant for me. Normally, they are much younger, less accomplished, less educated, all that, you know? So, I gotta ask, what is your interest here?"

I took a deep breath and released it slowly. "I still write during the day," I replied honestly. "But I can't sleep at night. And I could use some extra income."

Omar looked at me for a minute, then nodded, his face easing into a smile. "Yeah, okay, I can understand that," he said. "When can you start?"

"Anytime," I told him.

"Just one thing I should mention." Omar rubbed his hands together and loudly cracked his knuckles. "At night, we tend to get some...unusual clientele."

"I figured as much."

He gave me an almost-amused look, like 'Man, you don't know the half of it'. "Don't say I didn't warn ya."

"I won't," I told him. Then he handed me the paperwork and the stupid polo shirt.

Now here I am. Are the customers weirdos? Yeah, of course, they are. Who else would roam the streets of a bad neighborhood in the middle of the night? But so far, they seem safe enough, mostly just eccentric. Or maybe I'm not paying attention closely enough.

The shifts are twofers. No clerk's ever alone, and the deli isn't large or busy enough to merit more than a pair of us.

Usually, I work with Chuck. Sometimes Jeff. I tend to prefer Jeff, even if he is-according to Chuck—a psychopath. Jeff's quiet in that 'still waters' way. When he doesn't reign in his thousand-yard stare, it can be downright alarming. Jeff doesn't say much, but slowly I'm getting to know him. He'd been to war—two tours—and a military prison. Got a raging case of PTSD that leaves him up all night and a record that makes it difficult to find other work.

Omar doesn't care about the record and likes having a strong 'don't-fuck-with-me' presence at the counter for the after-hours crowd.

Jeff's got that vibe down to a tee. He certainly doesn't look like any Jeff I've ever met. Just over six feet tall, broad-shouldered and flint-eyed, with long tattooed arms corded with muscle and a shaved head, the man looks flat-out menacing.

And the opposite of Chuck, who mainly resembles Guy Fieri because of his tubby build and bleach-blonde spiky hair.

Chuck's real name is Lorenzo of all things. He hates it enough to have renamed himself after his favorite shoes.

These are the people I spend my nights with. Omar seldom comes in, and when he does, he looks as sleepy as we wish we felt.

Insomnia doesn't really leave you sleepy—it's an entirely different brand of exhaustion. The inability to shut down and recharge like the rest of the world makes you jittery and slightly confused, while everything around you acquires a hazy shifting aura. The rule of thumb is that if you're not questioning reality, you're too well-rested.

No one is really sure why Chuck can't sleep, but I suspect extreme ADD. The guy is constantly distracted by everything. You can practically hear his brain hopping around from one thing to the next.

There's apparently also a Jose that sometimes works the nightshifts, but I've yet to meet him. He's not part of our sleepless club, just a guy in desperate need of money for his family who chooses the shifts that pay more.

To be honest, I was kind of looking forward to seeing what weirdos roam the Gallows at night. Thought there might be a story or two there somewhere.

The thing I didn't tell Omar, the thing I don't tell anyone, is that I left journalism because I can't write anymore. I don't know why. Sure, I can still combine words into sentences and all that, but I seemed to have lost the ability to follow through. My stories go nowhere. My career took a similar direction as of late.

Hence, my move to the Gallows, a neighborhood that proudly keeps the article in its name. It sounds ominous to the uninitiated, but the reality is much more prosaic: a Scottish immigrant named Simon Gallow made a fortune in coal and decided to give something back to his adopted hometown. The neighborhood built with his money carried his name. As far as anyone knows, there had never been any public hangings.

I've questioned, though never out loud, the validity of having a twenty-four-hour open business in an area like this, but to hear the others tell it, that's when the going gets good.

"Seriously," Chuck had told me on more than one occasion, "you wouldn't guess it, but it's when we make the most money."

I guess I'm in a wait-and-see zone, being the newest hire by far.

You get your drunks who ran out of booze and your hobos who finally totaled up their begged-for coins and figured they got enough for the cheapest ticket to oblivion. You get the kids—usually early twenties, who can't afford to live anywhere nicer and stick to party-time schedules. You get the dead-on-their-feet family people who come in after long late shifts to grab milk and eggs for the next morning. Occasionally, you get a lost Yuppie who drove out to the Gallows looking for cheap thrills and realized this was a land beyond Siri's reckoning.

And then, there are the others. They tend to fall under the general 'weirdos' umbrella for the most part. Except when they don't.

There's V, who got his moniker through the double virtues of greeting people with a peace sign and having his real name be a convoluted mess of syllables. At least that's how I thought he came to be known as V.

V wanders in most nights to buy steaks and Vitamin B shots. He's a pale ugly man with an unbecoming handlebar mustache hanging like a tired horseshoe over his downturned thin-lipped mouth. An eclectic dresser, he tends to come in sporting a silk robe and matching slippers.

"What's his story?" I asked Jeff the first time I met V.

Jeff shrugged and mumbled under his breath something that sounded like, "Fucking junkie."

"For real? He doesn't look like one."

"There are many kinds of addictions," Jeff said gruffly, and that was that.

Chuck, on the other hand, was much more loquacious when asked the same question.

"V's a bloodsucker," he said, smug in the satisfaction of secret knowledge shared.

"Sorry, what?"

"You know, a vampire."

I'm sure Chuck has read something online to support that theory, but seriously? I don't know why I ever ask the guy anything.

"You don't believe me? See for yourself. Check out the reflective surfaces next time he's in."

"Why don't I just grab some garlic from the produce shelf?" I offer jokingly.

Chuck looks at me like I said something crazy. "No, dude, don't do *that*. You don't wanna piss V off."

So I don't do the garlic thing. And to be fair, I'm yet to catch V's reflection, but that's just because neither of us is that diligent at Windexing.

At any rate, the steaks are a big seller at Midnight Deli. I thought it was a weird choice for a convenience store at first, but we can't stock them enough.

The gutterpunks love them.

I don't love the gutterpunks. For one thing, they smell something awful. Like summer garbage and offal. I seldom saw them in my old neighborhood, but there's a bunch of them in the Gallows. Their clothes rusty with untold horrors and faded too far from any recognizable color, their hair a greasy matted mess, they stagger in at night for their pounds of flesh.

They seem to favor hoods or bandanas tied around their faces. Sometimes both at the same time. They look like they are about to hold us up, but they always pay with invariably crumpled dirty bills.

"Why do you call them gutterpunks?" Jeff asks me one night.

"Isn't that what they are?"

He shakes his head at me. I wait for clarification, but none comes my way.

"Oh, ghouls," Chuck explains the next night. "Yeah, there's a lot of them here. They are mostly harmless unless they're hangry."

"What?"

"Hangry, you know like hungry and angry at the same time."

"No, the other thing...ghouls?"

"Yep," Chuck nods emphatically and returns his wandering attention to the comic book he's reading.

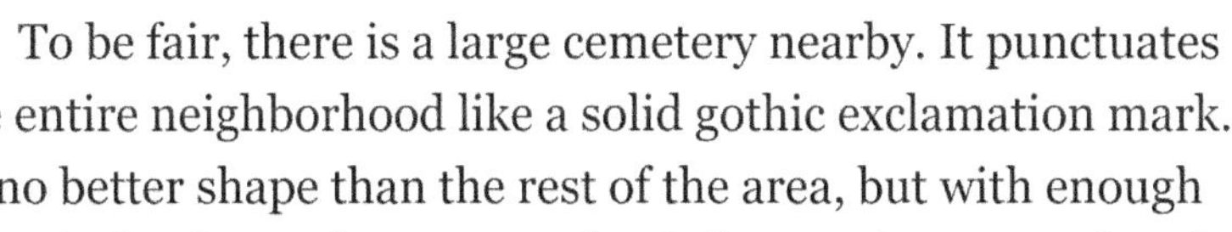

To be fair, there is a large cemetery nearby. It punctuates the entire neighborhood like a solid gothic exclamation mark. In no better shape than the rest of the area, but with enough historical value and personage buried to merit an occasional tour or two. Other than that, from what I can tell, it's been left to collapse onto itself, the same as its surroundings.

During the day, I'm largely useless. I sit in my tiny decrepit apartment and stare at the blinking cursor on my computer screen, willing the words to come. I endure fitful naps, eat sad meals standing over the kitchen sink, take walks around the neighborhood, minding the dangerously uneven sidewalks, dodging the stray cats and occasional rats. Even the pigeons in the Gallows are weirdly aggressive: they crap on you as soon as they lay eyes on you.

I look at the buildings. Count the abandoned ones, slowly taken over by nature and graffiti. I wager with myself how long it'll take their neighbors to follow suit.

I gave up my car when I moved here, but it's really not that far away from where I used to live. I can walk there in an hour or ride my bike in twenty minutes. But it feels like another universe.

The over/underpass that once seemed like such a good idea, had left the Gallows cut off from the city. The isolation bred contempt. Now it's a world unto itself.

I think I belong here, but it's tough to tell. The Gallows doesn't exactly welcome anyone with open arms. In fact, the Gallows doesn't do hugs at all.

Hob is one of the nicer customers. He likes to stock up on snacks. All four feet nothing of him. The guy's tiny. Usually, one of us has to grab him something from the upper shelves. He talks about his work, it's something custodial or janitorial. Either way, it's lots of chores. Which he says he likes doing. I enjoy his British accent, the incongruity of it.

He's not the only customer with an accent though. There's Gwyl, who looks essentially like a giant mastiff wearing a human suit, right down to the barely contained slobber.

To my shame, I can't understand a word he says. Jeff seems to get him though. They chat. I retreat to stocking shelves.

"What do you guys talk about?"

Jeff shrugs, like he does. "This and that."

"What sort of a name is Gwyl?"

"Short for Gwyllgi." Of course, it is.

"Where's he from?"

"Wales." Jeff sighs and straightens out the crossword before him with a giant mitt of a hand, signaling that the conversation is effectively over.

Every month or so, Jack comes in. The first time he came in, wearing nothing but a pair of ripped pants and a bewildered expression, I was considering enforcing the 'no shirt, no shoes, no service' sign on the front door, when Chuck waved me off.

Now it's a regular thing. Jack comes in close to the end of the shift, when the morning is at last more than a distant possibility, looking rough and tumbled. Or, more accurately, like someone who's been put through a tumble cycle. He's quite possibly the hairiest man I've ever seen. Also, the hungriest, going by how voraciously he puts away microwavable bean burritos and cheap coffee.

When Chuck first told me about Jack, I didn't believe him. And then I did, because in a way it made perfect sense.

"So, shouldn't he be sated then? From his night's… adventures?" I asked.

"No, man." Chuck shook his head the way one might when discussing some great unfairness of this world. "Jack's a vegetarian."

I fit that game piece with the rest of what I know. "Yeah, that does suck," I agree.

I wonder what people think when they see Jack in the mornings making his way home, disheveled and almost naked. Do they figure him for a man taking a walk of shame or take him for a failed jogger? In a neighborhood like this, they probably just shrug indifferently.

So, I'm getting to know the regulars. I wouldn't say I'm making friends, but it's better than nothing. Better than sitting inside my head with thoughts that won't leave and words that won't come.

Things are chugging along copasetic-like until Frank moves into the neighborhood. This giant swinging dick of a guy by all accounts. I hear about him before I see him.

Apparently, he got into it with Jose, broke the guy's nose.

Omar was going to ban him from Midnight, but Frank's got

money and isn't stingy about it either. Gave Jose enough to make the nose thing worth it.

I'm hearing all of this secondhand, so I'm not prepared for when the guy comes in one night. They said he was huge, but I wasn't expecting this mountain of a man. Frank makes Jeff seem petite by comparison. He didn't just duck, he practically origamied himself to walk in. The deli seems tiny with him in it.

His choice of purchases is reasonable, nothing crazy but the quantity of his purchases. Unlike many of our customers, he brings in his own recyclable bags. They are huge and he heaves them like they are nothing. Doesn't say much, doesn't have to. His presence speaks for itself.

I'd say I wouldn't want to meet this guy in a dark alley, but in the Gallows all the alleys are dark. And you don't want to meet anyone in them on the best of days.

Frank is the only one of the deli's night customers I also see during the day. He's renovating a row of houses near the cemetery. Seemingly singlehandedly. Shirtless in the sun, he looks like a conglomeration of muscles and scars. Easily pushing seven feet tall. Doesn't say much and when he does, his voice is low and gravelly, like a rock that's come to life.

"Let me guess. Frank's a troll, right?" I say to Chuck.

He shakes his head at me, disappointed. "Come on man," he says. "The scars…"

"Oh." Then after a moment. "Really?'

Chuck's chubby shoulders go up and down.

"Why here? Why do they come here of all places?"

Chuck looks at me like I'm the dullest crayon in the box.

"Because we're the only place open around here. Makes us the only game in town."

"No, no," I rub my chin. "I get why they come to the deli; I'm talking about the Gallows."

"Wouldn't you if you were them?" Chuck asks reasonably. "I would. I mean, why are you here?"

I don't know if anyone has ever asked me that directly. Some of my old friends were surprised or confused by my choice, but too polite or too indifferent to question it. Now I have to actually think of an answer.

"I suppose," I say slowly, "I wanted to be someplace where no one asks questions."

"Well, there ya go." Chuck grins, proud of a point landed, and wanders off.

Well, there I go.

I keep hearing about Frank making waves, making people unhappy. The gutterpunks—or the ghouls at Chuck's insistence—complain about the renovation noise. Even the taciturn V has expressed his displeasure at Frank's plan for the neighborhood. Everyone is concerned about what the changes might bring. For too long now, the Gallows have been singularly unique, and no one wants to upset this monstrous apple cart.

The neighborhood has never done well with gentrification, and it isn't likely to start now.

"Why's he doing it anyway?" Chuck speculates, while steadily making his way through a bag of Red Vines, his idea of a nutritious snack. "I mean, I would think if ever there was a misanthrope..."

"Maybe he's had a change of heart?" Jack offers, plucking stray leaves out of his stomach fur. "Maybe he likes people now?"

Chuck narrows his eyes until they all but disappear into his round cheeks. "I don't buy it."

He even builds up the courage to ask Frank directly one night.

"Just business," Frank answers in that live-rocks voice of his and that's that.

Nothing to do but wait and see.

Sometime later, a tall, gaunt, dark-skinned guy begins shadowing Frank. Eventually, Frank introduces him as, "Amun, business partner."

Amun makes Frank seem chatty. Got a glare for days too. A bird could build a nest in the caverns of his cheeks. But then again, what bird would dare?

The Gallows has never had anything resembling a town meeting, so when Frank calls for one, there are no expectations, only confusion.

The sign looks proper if officious when Frank hand delivers it. Amun, shadows him, silently.

We discuss it amongst ourselves, but curiosity wins the day. On the scheduled date, everyone's in attendance. Including some people I don't know.

The meeting is held outside the deli, appropriately enough at the Midnight Deli at midnight. When everyone's gathered, Amun slaps his hands together as loudly as a gong. An uneasy silence falls. Frank doesn't need a podium to speak, he simply stands up.

"There has been speculation," he begins looking down at the piece of paper in his hands, "about my project. Allow me to assure you, I have no intention of disrupting the lives you have built for yourselves here." He pauses as if to catch his breath. That's the most words I have ever heard out of him.

"Some time ago, I have become privy to information which means something is coming. Big changes ahead. My partner, Amun..." A glare here. "...and I have decided to address it with new construction."

Frank sighs in relief as he folds the paper in half and looks up. "Questions?"

Considering how little he actually said, questions abound. Hands of all shapes and sizes shoot up in the air.

Frank nods at the nearest one.

"What's coming? What changes"

"Revenants."

"What?" "Did he say...?" There are hushed whispers increasing in volume. The gist is that the revenants are meant to be a thing of fiction. Apparently, even a neighborhood as broadminded as The Gallows has its limits.

I nudge Chuck with my elbow. He wasn't on the schedule tonight, but he came in for the meeting. "What are revenants?"

"They are like lost souls returning from the dead," he explains in a loud whisper.

"What, like ghosts? Or zombies?"

Amun's voice interrupts the crowd. It's deep and resonant, the sort of thing that makes you think of chants and temples.

"I have been to the other side and back," he says in heavily accented but smooth English. "In my culture, death has always been viewed as a mere interruption of life, not a cessation. A soul can and does find its way back to the body, given proper conditions. That time has come now. Soon, the dead shall begin their return. I have joined forces with my colleague to ensure they have someplace to go. Other similar places are being built around the world as we speak."

"But what about the neighborhood?" someone asks. "What's gonna happen to us?"

Amun arches one of his perfect black eyebrows. It appears drawn in the same kohl that rings his eyes. "I have told you that death no longer holds dominion on souls, and you are asking me about…your real estate taxes?"

"Well yeah," the voice persists, refusing to be shamed into silence.

"Rest assured, by the time all is said and done, such earthly concerns will cease to matter," Amun declares rather pompously. "The entire power dynamic will shift. Those who've long had to hide in the shadows will become a majority. They shall rule the land."

"Don't worry, be happy," Frank says in summation. This has to be the first time he attempted a joke. It lands like a brick.

Amun answers a few more logistics-related questions in the same vague and grandiose manner. Eventually, they leave, but no one else does. There's too much to talk about. What ensues is the liveliest debate I'd been a part of in ages, especially for the hour.

"They can't be eaten," say the gutterpunks. "Can they?"

"Why not? They are not like zombies."

"Mmm…"

V smooths his mustache with long pale fingers. "I do not like it," he says, without elaborating.

Gwyl nods his giant head in agreement. A bit of spittle flies off and hits Hob on the head. Hob gets out a clean handkerchief and wipes his head without saying a word.

"Well, I, for one, am categorically against this," says a crisp peremptory voice.

I look around for the source of it.

"Hi Grif," Jeff says to what appears to be an empty space.

"Hi Jeff."

I nudge Chuck again. "Oh man, I forgot you guys never properly met. Grif, Nick. Nick, Grif."

I feel a hand reach for mine, but when I look down, I see nothing, and it's disturbing enough to make me wheeze out a rather embarrassing whimper.

"Whew. Never gets old." Chuck laughs, obviously delighting in my reaction. "Grif is a bit...well, a lot, invisible. You've probably seen him before. He favors trench coats and fedoras like some Noir reject."

"It's a classic timeless look," Grif says, huffily.

I catch on slowly. "So, if I can't see you, that means you're..."

"Yes, well, I had to sneak past my landlady, I owe her some money; besides, it is rather warm in here."

Great, here I am shaking hands with an invisible naked dude, about to discuss the impact revenants might have on my neighborhood. If you told me back in the city, this was going to be my life...

But then, back in the city I had Kate. I had my stories. I didn't care about much of anything else. Then Kate was gone, and I *couldn't* care about anything else.

And it doesn't matter how many times how many people have told me it wasn't my fault—I don't buy it.

If I had driven slower or faster that night or stayed home or...there are so many scenarios in which the crash didn't happen and only one in which it did. I can't stop thinking about it to this day.

This is how I came to be here. The city life no longer suited me; it was too new, too slick and shiny. Too happy. I wanted to be somewhere that knew the weight of sadness and history and heartbreak. In my grief I reasoned that if there was ever a place where Kate could come back to me, if only to haunt me, it would be the Gallows.

This thing with the revenants, I could hardly process it, afraid to hope, yet desperate to believe.

I had no words, choosing to surrender to the strangeness all around me. The world, after all, has always been stranger than it gets credit for.

So, I just stood there, listening to everyone trying to make sense of it all. But Kate was all I thought about.

When everyone left, I finished out my shift and walked home. I could hear the construction noises—I don't think Frank slept. I tried to imagine this brave new world Amun described and failed. My mind was just too tired, my heart too worn out. Eventually, mercifully, sleep found me at the kitchen table and, however briefly, claimed me.

I had off the next night and spent it not doing much of anything. I slapped on my noise-cancellation headphones and sat around my apartment, trying in vain to shut off my brain. I paged through a book without absorbing any of it, tried to watch a TV show that failed to suck me in.

Sad as it was, I was glad by the time my next work shift came around.

"Frank's dead," Jeff says by the way of greeting.

"WHAT?"

"Frank's dead," Jeff repeats. "Amun, too."

"How?"

"Fire."

Just this once I wish Jeff wasn't so laconic.

"What fire?"

He sighed. "There was a fire. At the site. Did you not hear the sirens?"

I flash back to my headphones. Apparently, worth the ridiculous amount of money I paid for them.

"No, I didn't hear the sirens. So, they are both dead?"

"Yes." V appears from one of the aisles with ninja swiftness. "Fire kills all."

"That's terrible," I manage. "Couldn't anyone...?"

"What? Save them? Do you know how long it takes for the fire engines to get out to a neighborhood like this?" Jeff shakes his head with disgust.

"I think they are secretly hoping for the Gallows to burn to the ground," V says, unloading his selections onto the counter. One of the meat packages has been punctured and is leaking teardrops of blood. With a long, elegant finger, V wipes it up and sucks at it greedily.

"Waste not, want not," he smiles a red smile. Then pays and leaves.

Now it's just me and Jeff. And, for all I know, Grif.

"Are you okay about all this?"

"Don't bother me." Jeff shrugs. "I've seen fire in my day. Made some too."

A stray thought wanders through the back of my mind. "Is that what landed Jeff in a military prison?"

Not that I'd ask. I wouldn't dare.

In the end, there's much talk and speculation and no one comes away any wiser. The construction has stalled, of course. Partially finished, partially fire-ravaged buildings are all that's left. It suits the Gallows aesthetic to a tee.

Things went back to...if not normal then at least pre-Frank. The revenants idea is still getting tossed around but so far there have been no sightings.

I've taken to running with Jack. Which on occasion can exhaust me enough for something resembling a solid few hours of dreamless rest. I sleep during the day, though, unwilling to give up the night shift at the Midnight Deli.

Sometimes when Jack isn't around, I run past the burned-out shells of buildings. It's dead quiet there, bleak even by the Gallows standards, a monochromatic study in greys. The only bright things I've seen there lately are matchboxes. Candy apple red with a design I don't recognize. I shudder to think that these were the things that started the fire. Or maybe they are just memorial tokens, the way people leave toys and balloons by the side of the road.

Strange to think someone would do this. Considering the appetites of some of the Gallows' denizens, the new development would have been like a food court.

I run on through a place meant for returned souls and dare to imagine; will myself to hear Kate's voice. The wind always steals it away, but I haven't given up hope.

Life goes on. Never improving, but at least having the decency to decline at a steady pace. The Gallows takes the hits, absorbs its losses, and carries on, heading nowhere too sunny, proudly displaying its scars.

One day, I find black mold in my bathroom.

"That's really dangerous," Chuck tells me during our shift that night. "Did you tell your landlord?"

I've only met the man once. He looks like an aggressively tan iguana and spends his days in tiki bars in Belize. I could tell my landlord the aliens have landed in my bathroom, and short of figuring out a way to charge them additional rent, he'd do nothing.

"Tell Hob, then, he loves this sort of thing."

This sort of thing seems like a strange thing to love, but sure enough, Hob comes over the next night and takes care of it.

"Wow, you're really good," I tell him and offer payment.

He refuses. "We're friends," he says.

"What about that hat of mine you like?" I ask, referring to the retro-style trucker number he had complemented before.

Hob looks positively offended. "No, Nick."

"Okay, how about a drink?"

"Got milk?" Hob doesn't seem to be ironic about it, so I check, and lo and behold, I indeed have some. Three days from the expiration date, no less.

"No cookies, though, sorry."

He sighs and takes a sip. "This is nice. Thank you."

He had to climb into my kitchen chair, but sitting down our size difference isn't that startling. I wonder if at home his furniture is custom-made for his diminutive stature.

We chat idly about nothing of importance when the lights flicker off.

"Another blackout," I groan.

"Get more of them in the summer," Hob nods. "Got a candle?"

I dig around the junk drawer by feel until I find one. He strikes a match and then we have some light.

It takes me a moment to register the bright red matchbox in his small hands, but once I do, it's all I see.

He notices me looking and smiles disarmingly.

"Why Hob?" I ask him quietly.

He shrugs as helplessly as a mischievous child. "I guess I just don't like changes," he says simply.

I don't know how to reply.

Hob finishes his glass and wipes at the milk mustache.

"Sorry, Nick, did I upset you?" he asks innocently.

"No, no," I wave him off. "Guess I'm just surprised."

"Well, that's life for you." Hob smiles again. "Full of surprises."

He tells me not to bother seeing him off, that he's good about finding his way in the dark.

Aren't we all? I think. Learning to, anyway.

I still sit there thinking when the power comes back on. Did I fall asleep for a moment there? Did I hear Kate's voice? Was it a dream? I guess I'll just have to wait and see.

CRITICAL BLAST PUBLISHING
20¢
THE NICK VICTORY
CHRONICLES
PART ONE: Nick's New Neighbor
Paul Barile
APPROVED BY THE READING CODE AUTHORITY
WEIRD FANTASTIC WORLDS
CRITICAL BLAST PUBLISHING
WHERE POP CULTURE GETS BLASTED
INCREDIBLE STRANGE STORIES
TOUGH HARD BOILED DETECTIVE ACTION IN A WHOLE NEW VEIN!

ATTENTION!

DEMONS!
VAMPIRES!
GHOULS!

NO MORE MONDAY NIGHTMARES!

ALL FOR $2.00

DEFEAT BLACK MYSTIC ARTS KUNG-FU Tired of getting your ass kicked every Tuesday by Black Mystic Arts Kung-Fu fighters? CALL 666-HELP to enroll in self-defense training every Hellspawn should know to survive any dark alley encounter. Become a Ninth Circle Master of Judante!

99¢

STICK IT TO YOUR ENEMIES! Real Voodoo Doll! Guaranteed Quality checked by the finest Witch Doctors! Send lock of hair and a SASE to DUDAT VOODOO, Box 9, Haiti.

10¢

SUPER SHARP PIRATE SWORD When you want to capture the hearts and minds of the people around you, this sword will cut through the muscle and bone to get to the vital organs you need to sustain your hunger.

SAVE $1.00

WELCOME MAT TRAP When you don't want people annoying you, a simple press of the button and the trap door will dispose of anyone who stands on it, while waiting for you to answer the door.

5¢

SNAKES IN A MAIL BOX Get these total mother-f$%Ken poisonous snakes and mail them with your get well gift cards.

LAST MAN ON EARTH HEARD A KNOCK AT THE DOOR!

ALL FOR $2.00

LEARN TO PLAY THE GUITAR! When you can't get a date for the weekend, rent a sexy Guitar Teacher to impress your friends and maybe you just might learn something too.

MONSTER VALUE STAMP
THIS IS IT! CLIP THEM & COLLECT THEM ALL!

STILL ONLY 35¢

HYPNO-ROBOT use the special mind control eye harmonics to subdue the minds of your unwilling subjects. You'll never have to take out the trash and everyone will worship you as if their life depends on it.

Paul Barile is a writer whose main focus is Lucha Libre books for young adults through lexographicpress.com. He also writes poetry and essays, and plays bass and write lyrics for the folk/rock duo The Grudge Brothers.

You get used to lonely when you got a job like mine. The skirts don't like the unstable income and the jacks always want to compete.

I'm Nick Victory, I'm a dick. The Midway is my beat.

Me and my sidekick Sabre had just flushed out a flim-flam artist, saving the Duchess of Central Avenue a bag of dough. They call her *The Duchess* because she owns gin joints and is very generous with her friends.

We pulled the rug out from under the rat – in the process saving her a lot of dough and even more headaches.

As the sun set over the suburbs, I found myself back in my flat soaking up the suds and some Django Rhinehart while I warmed over yesterday's grub. Sabre was at the Kit Kat Klub swilling martinis and dancing with the dames in the tiny black dresses.

There came a knock at the door. I grabbed my heater and slipped it into my belt. I opened the door slowly.

There she was – right in front of me – in all her perfection. She had legs that reached to the sky and eyes that could melt Alaska. She stood without saying a word – just towering in the doorway. Her hair piled in an impossibly high beehive – with a vibrant blonde streak. The high collar of her frock hid what could only be a perfect neck.

"I'm Mary," she said. Her voice was husky.

"I'm Nick," I replied.

My words were caught up in my chest. They thumped out of my face like a kid falling down the stairs. If she noticed – she didn't say anything.

"I just moved in next door and I haven't had time to shop."

"I got coffee and saltines and some left over take out from Maggie's."

"I'd kill for a cup of coffee."

Mary stepped into the room and brushed past me. I love a skirt who takes charge. I especially love it when that woman is nearly six foot tall – not including the hair.

"Sit here," I said, offering the less broken wooden chair.

She sat without making a sound. Her get-up was perfect – white and virginal like the nuns at St. Mary of the Waters – only she wasn't no nun.

"I don't get many visitors," I said as I filled the old percolator with water and scrounged around for some unused coffee grounds.

Soon enough I found the bright red can and put some grounds into the basket and set the percolator on the stove.

"Crackers?" I asked.

"Perhaps later."

She looked as vexed with life as I was with her. Her gaze drifted around my dingy flat. There was little there that you wouldn't find in one of those private rooms in the Cook County lock-up.

I had an ancient hi-fi and a small stack of wax, and that was about it. That and my other shirt.

"I'm sorry. I must look a wreck."

"You couldn't look a wreck if your life depended on it," I replied.

"I'm just... Oh, never mind."

I'm a world class champ at minding my own business, unless there is money – my money – involved. I pulled down two coffee cups liberated from the Steak and Egger.

Small talk has never been my thing, but I wanted to keep her at the table as long as I could. She spruced the joint up. She spruced me up. I just set the sugar in front of her.

"You're very kind, Nick" she said.

"Ah, it's nothing. Enjoy."

The phone by the bed woke me up – like it usually does. I didn't recognize the voice on the other end as I usually don't.

It was some doll squawking about her guy and why he left and what was he doing – but it all sounded like a flat trumpet solo in the key of nope.

"Please call after lunch," I managed and then disconnected.

The kitchen smelled like a tiny slice of heaven. The percolator felt like an old friend.

"Good morning, Boss," Sabre said.

He flipped this and scrambled that and had all the breakfast pistons popping on all cylinders.

"Good morning, Sabre," I said as I eased into my chair and smelled the coffee.

"We got a couple of calls today," Sabre started. "Nothing exciting and nothing that can't wait – but still, it's steady money."

Sabre lived two apartments to the east. Not buildings – apartments. I lived in 1W and he lived in 3W which would also serve as a bit of an office until I got back on my feet.

"I like steady money."

"I'll call back after breakfast."

"Have you seen your new neighbor?"

"Mary?"

"Yes. So, you've met her?"

"Yes. Poor thing" he said as he eased some grub on to my plate.

"Poor thing? What gives?"

"She just lost her husband."

"In the war?"

"No. Jail."

"What'd he do?"

"She said he didn't do anything. It was a wrong place at the wrong time type of deal."

"That'll happen."

"Eat your breakfast. We gotta beat the street and look under a few rocks. Eat up."

"Yes, Mom."

I'm a jokester.

The day turned out to be about as exciting as a yawning festival. I couldn't wait to get back to my place and relax with some Miles Davis and a highball. As the needle hit the wax, I heard the knock at the door. It was Mary.

"Hey Nick," she said. She didn't speak so much as she breathed the words out of that perfect cakehole.

I got what was becoming a familiar prickly sweat at the base of my neck. It was a combination of anticipation and gratitude. I had a matching knot in my gut.

"Come in, Mary," was the best I could do.

She did. She sashayed in and headed for the bed as if she had a plan. I started working my tie.

"Please don't get the wrong idea," she said sitting on the edge of the bed. Her spine was as stiff as I was.

I focused on that streak of blonde hair that was trying to taking my mind off of everything else about Mary sitting there on my bed. I was puzzled at how perfectly that beehive rose up from that porcelain face, and that shock of blonde did me in.

"I'm scared, Nick," she started. "And I didn't know where to go or who I could talk to."

"Is this about your husband?"

"Yes. How did you know?"

"Sabre, your other neighbor, works for me."

"He's a nice man."

"That he is, *Sister*."

"I'm afraid my husband will get out soon and I am not sure if I want him to find me. He was arrested in a cruel and barbaric way and I was helpless to do anything about it. I just stood there and watched."

"I'm sorry to hear that. How can I help?"

"Just hold me for a moment. I'm scared."

I couldn't believe my luck.

"Just hold me – nothing more. I don't want to lead you on, I am just scared."

In this world we take what we can get. I just sat next to her with my arms around her like we were doing the Ball-and-the-Jack.

She was cold to the touch. She was morgue cold, but so soft and pliable. She fell into me – resting her head on my chest – the top of her beehive tickled my chin. All was quiet.

Soon the steady thrum of her breathing let me know she was sawing wood. I was afraid to move from that spot. I didn't want to wake her. There on the edge of the bed – the room was full of energy – but the only sound was the static crackle of the needle on the wax. The record was long over.

The sun crept through my window finding me in my BVDs and little else. The room was as quiet as a tomb and nearly as cold. I was alone again – but I felt electric. I put on my robe and my slippers and shuffled into the kitchen. There was a note on the table.

"Thank you for being a gentleman," was all it said.

I put the note in my pocket and reached for the percolator. The knock that disturbed the silence made me jump.

"Who's there" I called out.

"Come on, Boss," Sabre replied. "My hands are full."

He walked into the flat with a stiff brown paper bag full of groceries from the A&P. There was bacon and eggs and English muffins. He began to unpack what would soon be our breakfast.

"So how was it last night?" he asked.

"Quiet. You know me."

"I thought I did until I saw Mary coming out of your place and heading into her own place when I was heading out to grab the groceries."

"Nothing happened between us – if that's where you're angling."

"I'm not really angling."

"Thank you."

"But you are *so* glowing."

"Stop."

"You're the boss."

"I'm gonna grab a quick shower. We got work to do."

I left Sabre in the kitchen working his magic while I went and took a hot shower. When I came back half-dressed and ready for some huevos, Mary was sitting at the table. I was amazed that her perfect beehive towered over everything without one hair out of place. I can barely run a comb through my scruff.

One small drop of coffee betrayed her otherwise perfect white tunic. One small drop just above her left breast.

"Good morning, Nick," she cooed.

"Hey, how's the kid?"

"Better now, thanks to you."

"That's aces."

"Sabre told me you had a busy day today, so I won't keep you. Would it be alright if I made you dinner this evening?"

I gulped.

Sabre smiled.

I blushed.

"It would mean the world to me," she said.

"Sure. How is 6-ish?"

"Perfect."

She stood up and headed for the door, then she stopped. She turned back to look at me, but I was frozen to my spot. She smiled.

"See you around six," she sighed. She floated out of the flat on gossamer wings.

"Nick Victory for the win," Sabre said with a laugh.

"Yeah." I smiled.

I knocked once. The flowers were wilting, but I wasn't.

"Hold on, please, Nick."

"Sure."

Just at that exact moment – there was some kind of power surge throughout the building. I thought it might be my heart – when she opened the door to let me in. She knocked the wind out of me.

She crackled with electricity. Her eyes glowed. She was more than I could have hoped for and twice what I deserved.

"Come in, Nick," she said. She gestured toward the couch. "Sit here a minute. I need to put these in water."

I tried to relax, but this doll had me all twisted up.

"Dinner is running a little behind."

When I looked up, she was wearing little more than some strategically placed pieces of gauze. I was taken aback by the map of scars that ran along her body at every joint and intersection. The stitches and the scars created a macabre tapestry on her skin enhancing the tones that worked in perfect harmony.

"Don't stare," she said. "It's not polite."

"You're perfect."

"Stop."

"You look like I feel."

She took my hand and led me to a dimly lit room that held a steel bed and a generator.

"I wasn't that hungry anyway," I said as I worked the buttons on my shirt.

The next morning, Sabre was hard at work making breakfast when I strolled in on a cloud.

"Wow, Nicky."

"Yeah. Wow."

As if he read my mind, Sabre handed me a cup of Joe.

"I guess I don't have to ask how it went last night."

"It was the cat's pajamas."

"How was Mary?"

"She's really well put together."

"Of course, she is."

Sabre slipped some grub on the plate he had put in front of me.

"You know," I said as I stuffed my napkin into my collar. "I could get used to this – to her."

"Why not?"

"Yeah, a platinum dame to share this joint with. A real looker for tripping the light on a Saturday night. She's got everything."

"But..."

"She's also got a husband and I ain't no piker."

"But didn't you just..."

"I know. I know.

We sat in silence for a while. Neither of us knew quite what to say. Seemed like one cat had both our tongues. I ate slowly. I felt as guilty as a dog and as giddy as a peacock in the same breath.

It was at that moment – everything changed. It started with slow and heavy footsteps out in the hall. They shook the room with their power – the rhythm like that of an angry metronome.

Then came the pounding on the door. Whoever had stress-tested the floor, decided to pound on Mary's door. The moans sounded like they came from another world. They were sad and ancient and deep. I looked at Sabre and grabbed my piece. He already had his in his hand. The fear in his eyes should have made me think twice about opening the door.

My blood turned to ice as I heard the primeval moans that seemed to come from the seventh circle of hell.

"I'm going out there," I said. "If Mary's in trouble, I have to save her."

"Sit down, Kid Galahad. You're not going anywhere."

Still the moaning continued. I cracked the door enough to see who was out there and to see why they were making those ghastly sounds.

There – at Mary's door – was the largest man I've ever seen. Straightaway I noticed his legs didn't match. One leg was as thick as a tree and the other was wilted. He wore one large black leather shoe on the foot of the withered leg to add height and to keep him steady.

His arms hung unevenly by his side. Both as long and thick as pythons, one was a much darker complexion. The other arm showed tattoos blued and faded with age. His skull was a patchwork of scars in between the places where hair was struggling to get out. He looked like he had just left the mission and was on his way to State Street to panhandle from the suburbanites.

The moaning subsided for a moment as the power in the building surged and Mary opened her door.

The big oaf staggered in and reached for Mary. She pulled him close to her. She didn't seem to notice me when she pulled the door closed behind them.

The next morning there was a white envelope under my door. I recognized it by the scent of sulfur and Jean Naté.

"I'm sorry, Nick. It's better this way."

Better for who? Better for Mary? Better for old Nick Victory? I wanted to reach out to her and tell her it wasn't better for me. It wasn't even going to be good. It was going to be the same old same old for old Nick Victory.

Staying the same is like moving backward. Moving backward is inching toward the grave. I wasn't ready to be inching toward the grave. I hung my head.

At that moment. the door opened and Sabre came in with a brown paper sack from A&P full of groceries. I reached for the percolator and the red can of coffee.

"We got a call today, Boss. Something about a missing diamond ring and a silver bullet."

3¢
USA
478
CACKLETAP
MONSTER VALUE STAMP
THIS IS IT!
CLIP THEM
& COLLECT
THEM ALL!

CRITICAL BLAST PUBLISHING
20¢
STANLEY'S LAST JOB
L.N. Hunter
APPROVED BY THE READING CODE AUTHORITY
WEIRD FANTASTIC WORLDS
CRITICAL BLAST PUBLISHING
WHERE POP CULTURE GETS BLASTED
INCREDIBLE STRANGE STORIES
WHEN B&E MEANS BLOOD & ENTRAILS...

HUMAN MASK When you need to walk among the humans, without being singled out as a monster. Get this mask in black, white or polka-dot, to blend right in!

SUPER SHARP PIRATE SWORD When you want to capture the hearts and minds of the people around you, this sword will cut through the muscle and bone to get to the vital organs you need to sustain your hunger.

SUPER SECRET BOOK SAFE The special camouflage feature activates, once placed on the book shelf. You'll never find it again.

BOX OF LIVE BATS When you feel like a millionaire crime fighting hero and need to dress up your special cave, to give it that extra touch of atmosphere... a box of live bats is perfect for you. Food not included.

HELIUM GAS & BALLOON SET Get away from the day to day grind of your boring life and steal a whole house while the owners are away.

LEARN TO PLAY THE GUITAR! When you can't get a date for the weekend, rent a sexy Guitar Teacher to impress your friends and maybe you just might learn something too.

RADIOACTIVE CANDY When you want to level up your personality and appear extra sweet to the people around you... and want to have a superpower over sugar... this candy's for you!

HEAD KNIVES 100% stainless steal daggers that launch from the top of your head and kill any conversation you find boring.

RENT AN ANGRY MIDGET! When you need to stop a Bully from harassing, or when you need to look like a decent human concerned for poor ugly monsters.

L.N. Hunter's comic fantasy novel, 'The Feather and the Lamp,' sits alongside works in anthologies such as 'Soulmate Syndrome' and 'Best of British Science Fiction 2022' as well as Short Édition's 'Short Circuit' and the 'Horrifying Tales of Wonder' podcast. There have also been papers in the IEEE 'Transactions on Neural Networks,' which are probably somewhat less relevant and definitely less fun. When not writing, L.N. unwinds in a disorganised home in rural Cambridgeshire, UK, along with two cats and a soulmate.

Normally, Stanley Montague wouldn't bother to break into a single occupant house, since the rewards were typically lower than family homes. However, his cash flow problems were pressing; he owed the wrong people a little bit too much for comfort.

Stanley's modus operandi was to canvas an area before picking an affluent-looking street with no CCTV cameras or Neighbourhood Watch signs. Then he'd spend a week, sometimes more, studying his chosen street. Seeing which houses were empty during the day. Looking at the people coming and going—their clothes, their cars, even the way they walked—told him a lot about what he might find inside their homes. People's social media and other online footprints betrayed additional secrets if you took the time to look; overly complex user security and privacy mechanisms worked to Stanley's advantage.

St Andrew's Terrace had been the subject of Stanley's online and offline scrutiny for the past six days. The most promising houses were numbers 5, 7, and 8, owned by parents who were both out all day.

Number 7, the Richards, had three teenagers—two girls and a boy—which would indicate the potential of a good haul of games consoles and tablets, especially given the extent of the kids' online activity. On the other hand, the car parked outside was twelve years old and he could see that it had over 120,000 miles on the clock, so door number 7 probably wasn't the one. Only a single child lived with his or her parents in the other two, but the cars outside were a BMW and a Porsche, making them more attractive.

The rest of the street was a mixture of multi-occupancy buildings, offering too much risk, and houses that were either never empty during the day or single occupancy. Number 23 fell into the last category but was his standby, with the one-year-old Saab parked outside suggesting a certain level of prosperity.

Stanley always checked the local newspapers' websites and neighbourhood Facebook groups for anything that might interfere with his intentions. Once, he'd avoided being caught up in a street party with all its potential witnesses thanks to his research. Fortunately, St Andrews Terrace seemed to be rich, boring and quiet, just the way he liked it.

At least, until the day before his planned visit, when a story appeared on the newspaper website about a family's 'disappearance' from Royston Street, adjoining the low numbered end of St Andrew's Terrace. A vague buzz of excitement was apparent in the news article comments and on the local Facebook group—no one seemed to have any concrete details of the disappearance, but were happy to share their opinions about how strange it was.

He scrolled through endless posts on his laptop, trying to decide how much was fact and how much gossip-mongering. He snorted at the ludicrous claims about lingering smells of decay, screams in the night and blood-smeared footprints. Probably conspiracy nuts making a Scandi noir mountain out of a boring London suburbs molehill. People were talking about other unexplained disappearances farther afield, claiming that they were all linked.

Stanley couldn't see much rational thinking in the speculation and concluded it was nothing more than people enjoying a foreign holiday during term time, taking advantage of lower prices, and having neglected to lock up properly or tell their neighbours. Whatever the reason, the extra spotlight so close to his target was a damned nuisance.

Usually, he would have cancelled in circumstances like this. It would be a waste to throw away all his preparation, but that was preferable to getting caught. However, he did owe some dangerous people too much money, and he really didn't fancy getting beaten up if he didn't come up with something before the weekend.

Instead of burgling number 5, close to the mysterious event, Stanley chose to watch the area a little longer. He used visits to a café and a newsagent as excuses to wander along Royston Street. The house in question looked perfectly normal—no police tape, no signs of strange goings-on. He even walked past the house inhaling deeply, trying to detect any 'smells of decay'—nothing. There were a couple of Community Officer patrols but only on the first day of his watching. 'Not even proper police,' he muttered to himself. 'Just a presence to calm the public.' Although none of those patrols strayed into St Andrew's Terrace, he decided to redirect his attention towards the higher numbers at the opposite end of the street.

Finally, at 9:27am on his chosen day, wearing blue overalls and looking perfectly unmemorable, Stanley strode up to the front door of number 23. He took a lot of care over his appearance for jobs like this: the nondescript uniform could be that of any gas man, electricity meter reader or plumber, and he carried a small toolbox to complete the outfit, though the tools inside had quite a different purpose. Thick-framed clear lens glasses obscured his face, and he'd applied colourant to disguise his greying hair.

The only anomalous accessory was his wedding ring: paradoxically this rendered him *less* visible, making him fade more into the background than if he was ringless. He didn't wear it because of that, but because of simple sentimentality. His wife had left him five years ago, taking their daughter, and he still missed them. He liked to pretend they were still waiting for him.

A stint in prison had led to the breakup of his family. His wife couldn't face the shame of it all—she'd shouted that even a fling with another woman would have been better. Stanley had been caught embezzling from his workplace. He always wanted the best for his family, even when his salary wouldn't provide, but he lost that family he'd been devoted to. He also forfeited his house, not to mention three years of freedom. However, he did pick up some new skills during his incarceration, which helped in his current endeavours.

Making no attempt to mask his approach to Jenkins' house, he was confident that any onlooker would think him a legitimate handyman. Even with the current heightened levels of alertness, he was sure no one would notice he had *not* stepped from a van that such a workman would have parked nearby.

The lock was a cheap three pin Yale, and child's play to open—it never failed to amaze him that people paid so little attention to the quality of their door locks, never bothering to replace the rubbish that came with their houses. Decent locks were expensive, it was true, but still nothing compared to the precious contents of people's homes.

Hands hidden from street view by his body, he inserted the tension wrench into the lock with his left hand. With his right, he quickly drew the hook pick back and forth to align the pins with the shear line.

Click.

Once inside, Stanley knew he had plenty of time, so no need to rush. Jenkins never returned before 6:50pm, and there were no visitors during the day.

Stanley shut the door behind him and paused. There was no security system but habit forced him to listen for the beep of an alarm. All he could hear was the hum of a fridge and the occasional rumble of a vehicle outside. While he was listening, he inhaled deeply: odours could tell you a lot about a home's occupants. A house that smelled of stale sweat was unlikely to have much worth stealing, whereas the waft of floral scent broadcast the opposite. He could detect ground coffee, though with a strange underlying hint of raw meat, as if he were in a butcher's. Assured there was nothing to hinder his work, he donned white cotton gloves—he was allergic to latex—and set to exploring.

He always systematically explored houses room by room, starting with the kitchen. Some people mistakenly believed the backs of freezer drawers to be good hiding places, or dummy cans amongst the real ones in cupboards, but those were the first places any self-respecting burglar looks. Stanley examined mains sockets, looking for fakes that concealed small drawers. He found no such hidey-holes, but did help himself to a couple of custard creams from an open packet in one cupboard. He was mildly surprised that Jenkins' freezer seemed to contain 90% meat—he guessed the guy really liked barbeques.

The living room came next. A high-end gaming PC sat under a large television, but it would be too much faff to untangle all the wires and collect the paraphernalia of controllers and power bricks. In any case, it would be a rather bulky object to risk leaving with. Why couldn't Jenkins have settled for a standard console? There was a good-sized collection of game and movie discs, but those had negligible resale value these days. The few ornaments in the room were not as expensive looking as he'd hoped. He checked the electricity sockets in the room and riffled through the few books on Jenkins' shelves—nothing worth his time.

Online searches had supplied Jenkins' name and the information that he was an accountant who had never been married. He ought to have quite a lot of money to his name, Stanley thought, and must have *something* valuable in the house. Somewhere.

Stanley peeked behind all the pictures on the downstairs walls, hoping to find a wall safe. He ignored the artwork itself—a mixture of pretty landscapes and bold, abstract art— since he didn't know what was worth anything, and had no contacts who could fence them anyway.

After completing his exploration of the ground floor, Stanley headed upstairs. The landing had doors to a master bedroom, the bathroom, airing cupboard and what must be a second bedroom or office. There was a hatch to the loft as well, but nobody hides anything valuable there without the convenience of a built-in access ladder, and the hatch was a plain wooden panel with no handle or hook that would indicate the presence of a ladder.

The meat smell seemed stronger here, or maybe it was just that he was farther from the coffee in the kitchen that had camouflaged the odour. It smelled slightly rancid, and he expected to find unwashed day-old dinner plates in one of the rooms, or leftover food in a bin.

He found a small safety box in the main bedroom's wardrobe. The lock picks came into play a second time, though getting inside took a bit longer than the front door. The box was disappointingly devoid of valuables, but did contain a passport which he pocketed—he could get a few notes for that—and an old tarnished brooch which probably had more sentimental value than monetary. Still, into his pocket it went, along with the cufflinks sitting on the bedside table. The bathroom was empty too, not even any pills he could sell on. Stanley ended up with just the second bedroom to go, hoping he'd find a home office with at least something like a laptop, but prepared for disappointment. Given his luck so far, it probably was a junk room or a space containing nothing but an exercise bike and some weights.

Thus far, Stanley had made almost no sound, no more than the pad of his soft-soled shoes. But when he opened the bedroom door, he couldn't suppress his gasp.

'What the...?'

Hand clamped to the doorknob, he stared at the girl handcuffed to the metal-framed single bed. Everything but the bed faded into the background for what felt like minutes.

Her chest gently rose and fell—she was asleep or perhaps drugged. Her eyes slowly opened and groggily swivelled toward him. She appeared to be about seventeen or eighteen, and had short black hair, sickly pale skin and piercing blue eyes. A cloth gag pulled the sides of her lips back, distorting her face into something animalistic—a too-long, pointed jawline and lips stretched wider than any normal face. Her wrists were cuffed to the poles of the headboard. She was wearing a black *Fall Out Boy* tee-shirt and light blue jeans, nothing on her feet.

After his heartrate returned to almost normal and time started again, Stanley's brain began to work: what should he do? The easiest option would be to leave as he didn't think she really saw him. But, what if she did… She might not be able to tell the police, but what about the person who left her like this? Would Stanley be in danger—what might a monster who ties up teenage girls do to anyone who discovered his secret?

A thought zapped through his mind, and he glanced around the edges of the room looking for video cameras. Jenkins, the sick pervert, might record whatever he did in this room, and could be recording Stanley right now. He checked the light fitting and scanned the walls, seeing nothing that could be the lens of a camera.

His conscience finally pushed his instinct for self-preservation into the background. It didn't matter if he was being filmed; he couldn't contemplate leaving the girl like this, could he? He needed to get her out of the house and to the police. He'd have to work out how to accomplish it without dropping himself in hot water, but he'd worry about that later.

He untied her gag, a mass of strangely shredded cloth, all the while telling her it'd all be OK and she was safe. Meaningless platitudes, but his mouth needed to do something to give his thoughts the space to sort themselves out.

She coughed, then croaked something unintelligible. He fetched a glass of water from the bathroom and gave her a sip.

After drinking, she closed her eyes and sagged back on the bed without attempting to repeat what she'd said.

Kneeling this close to her, he realised his knee was wet. The carpet near the bed was damp, and the meat stink was coming from either that or the bed. Or perhaps from the girl, a consequence of being left here for days.

Trying not to think about the cause of smell and the dampness, Stanley hunted for keys to the handcuffs. He rummaged through the bedside cabinets, then looked in the dresser, before eventually mentally kicking himself. He could pick locks, for goodness' sake, and shimming a pair of handcuffs would be a trivial task.

As he undid them, he noticed that the paint on the frame was scratched and chipped by the handcuffs, but the girl's wrists were unblemished. He shuddered—she can't have been here very long, but there must have been other victims before her to create such damage.

She didn't look physically mistreated—apart from being tied up—but who knows what she's had to endure, or what will come later? Stanley didn't want to think about it. His daughter would be about the same age as this young woman, and the idea that someone could tie her up like this sent a chill down his back.

Once the cuffs were removed, the girl's arms flopped onto the pillow beside her head. She groaned and made no effort to move. Stanley imagined the pins and needles flooding through her arms as the blood rushed in.

He tried to sit her up, but she crumpled bonelessly onto the bed. He tipped the remainder of the glass of water on the corner of the bed and used the damp sheet to moisten her face, to little effect.

He'd have to carry her downstairs. He didn't think he'd manage to get her any farther than that, so he'd just settle for getting her outside the front door. Then he'd call the police before scarpering. He'd better dump the passport—everything he'd picked up, in fact—since he wanted to leave Jenkins or the police nothing to link him to this.

He swore. This really hadn't been one of his better days.

He shuffled around the bed and slid his arms underneath the girl's shoulders and knees, and heaved. She was much heavier than he expected, as if she was somehow more solid than a normal person. Then the notion came to him that he didn't carry teenage girls very often, or anyone at all, and he almost giggled.

One of her arms fell limply around his neck. Suddenly her eyes flicked wide open, and she took a massive shuddering breath. Before he registered it, her arms were clasping him so tightly his vertebrae clicked. Her fingernails dug painfully into his back.

He half laughed and prepared to say, 'Steady on, girl,' but when he turned to look at her face, his throat seized before he could speak. Her pupils were dilated, so the vivid blue of her irises had vanished. As he watched, the black spread until no white showed in her eyes. Her lower face seemed to elongate, and Stanley caught a glimpse of vastly extended teeth in her gaping mouth as her head dived towards his neck.

She bit down. Hard.

Time stopped for Stanley again—he had no chance to cry out before he collapsed and the world went dark.

His mind raced, as if trying to squeeze as much in as possible before it was too late. The Facebook gossips were right, but he wouldn't be able to tell them. He wasn't going to be able to get the money that would save him from being beaten up, but that really didn't matter anymore. His hope of reconciling with his wife had disappeared, but he felt completely calm about it.

Then *everything* stopped for Stanley.

CRITICAL BLAST PUBLISHING
20¢
APPROVED BY THE READING CODE AUTHORITY
HOWLING DEVIL
in the Sticks
Sirius
WEIRD FANTASTIC WORLDS
CRITICAL BLAST PUBLISHING
WHERE POP CULTURE GETS BLASTED
INCREDIBLE STRANGE STORIES
ANTE UP FOR HIGH STAKES HORROR!

MONSTER VALUE STAMP
THIS IS IT! CLIP THEM & COLLECT THEM ALL!

HEAD KNIVES 100% stainless steal daggers that launch from the top of your head and kill any conversation you find boring.

RADIOACTIVE CANDY When you want to level up your personality and appear extra sweet to the people around you... and want to have a superpower over sugar... this candy's for you!

STICK IT TO YOUR ENEMIES!
Real Voodoo Doll! Guaranteed Quality checked by the finest Witch Doctors! Send lock of hair and a SASE to DUDAT VOODOO, Box 9, Haiti.

CRUISE MISSILE MODEL KIT! When you need to deliver a message across the country. Optional payload BATS IN A BOX sold separately.

BOX OF LIVE BATS When you feel like a millionaire crime fighting hero and need to dress up your special cave, to give it that extra touch of atmosphere... a box of live bats is perfect for you. Food not included.

HUMAN MASK When you need to walk among the humans, without being singled out as a monster. Get this mask in black, white or polka-dot, to blend right in!

FACE FRONT, TRUE EVILEERS!

SNAKES IN A MAIL BOX Get these total mother-f$%Ken poisonous snakes and mail them with your get well gift cards.

EXPLODING DRINK Sit back and enjoy the highjinks as people unscrew their drink activating the chemical reaction, causing a foamy mess.

BOW AND ARROW KIT! When you need to go into battle on Tuesdays and don't know what weapon to take with you.

Sirius is a queer, nonbinary and disabled author living in North Carolina, and a member of the Horror Writer's Association. Sirius's gothic fantasy novel, Swallow You Whole, will be published in September of 2023 by Curious Corvid Publishing, with dark fiction short stories The Devil's Night Grind Show and Hunter Goddess Moon having appeared in The Magpie Messenger and The Spectre Review respectively in 2022.

No one moved down to that wet strip of country road unless they had to. Past miles of trees there was some semblance of civilization, but only in the form of little white houses with sloping roofs and caved-in porches that looked like they had already seen the end times. Josiah's place was holding up better than most—only because his recent stint with unemployment had given him ample time to nail in a few boards and slap on a fresh coat of paint. Now, it was the only yellow house for miles—tucked behind twin willow trees and boasting a charming blue door. He set out a 'Welcome' mat out front. The charming feeling was almost enough to detract from the downward spiral of his failure.

A house in the suburbs would have suited him better, or an upscale apartment in the heart of New York. Not that he liked New York, or any other big city, but it was the sentiment. The idea of being so successful that he could afford to throw money straight down the tube and furnish it all with sleek, ugly modern shit. He missed a lot of things about living closer to town—not the least of which was public transportation and designer lattes. But the drive was pretty. The house was nice.

The house next door to his was in better shape. Its owners had really dug into their pockets to try and fix it up for a red-hot market. It was lipstick on a pig, as his grandmother would say—and a little hoity-toity, if you asked his opinion. Not a single living soul in what loosely could be defined as a neighborhood was going to be impressed by a bubbling water fountain in the yard or a stone pathway up to the front door. Hell, he did not even know half of his neighbors by name, and the only reason he knew even a few was because the mail sometimes got mixed up.

So when the 'For Sale' sign got pulled out of the ground, he assumed the wind had knocked it over, until he saw a *new* car in the driveway.

And it was a new car. It was cherry red and waxed to a mirror-shine. It did not even look like there was dirt on the wheels—which was impossible for anyone driving down Main County Road. Josiah tried not to stare too hard as he sipped his coffee from the seclusion of his shaded porch. There wasn't anything else—not one moving truck or a stray box floating around the yard. And nothing had been there at all, the day before.

"She is still as beautiful as the day I found her," a voice came from nearby, too close for comfort. Josiah whipped his head around and caught sight of a man standing only a few inches away on the other side of his porch railing. Josiah bit the inside of his cheek and gripped his coffee cup a little tighter to keep from dropping it.

"Oh yeah?" He almost glanced back over at the car, but something in his gut told him not to take his eyes off the man in front of him. "She looks almost new."

"That is just part of her charm," the man's smile widened. Out of a full set of pearly-white teeth, he had one gold canine, and it glistened like a jewel. "I don't think I caught your name."

"Josiah," he said, moving closer to the railing at last so he could extend his hand. "Nice to meet you. Welcome to the neighborhood."

"The term 'neighborhood' here being a fairly generous one," he had a brush of a Northern accent, just enough to set him apart. Round, purple-lensed sunglasses shielded his eyes, and he kept his hands buried deep in the pockets of his well-tailored white suit. When Josiah extended his hand, the man returned the gesture. Every pale finger bore a gold ring. He wore a Rolex on his slim wrist.

Josiah couldn't help thinking that he looked like a televangelist.

"It grows on you," Josiah said. "Getting used to the quiet is the hardest part." He looked the man up and down. Suddenly, he felt like there was a hard lump stuck in his throat. "And— your name? I'm sorry."

"Oh," the man winked, "it's Bee." He pulled his sunglasses down his nose and glanced over the thick black rims. He had eyes the color of Texas bluebonnets and his long, sinuous mouth curved into a smile. "Aren't you going to invite me in?"

"Oh, sure," Josiah regretted starting a conversation. The coffee was moving right through him—that had to be why his stomach was doing flips. He did not even see Bee walk up the three shallow porch steps, but then there they were—standing on opposite sides of the doormat. The fading word 'Welcome' rested snidely between them.

For a brief moment, Josiah could not speak. It was hard to swallow past the lump in his throat, which felt like it was growing. His heart raced behind his ribs and for a second, the blood roaring in his ears drowned out every other sound. He shook his head like the motion could clear it. "Do you drink coffee?" He asked. He nudged the storm door with his foot and pulled it open. Bee caught the door and his blue gaze never wavered.

"Sure," he said. "Why not?"

Another pause, and Josiah could feel his pulse racing so fast that it hurt. Bee slid his glasses back up his nose to cover his eyes and turned his head away. Josiah was finally able to suck in a deep breath.

"So," he said, his hands trembling a little as he almost raced to set his coffee cup down in the kitchen. "What brought you all the way down here?"

"Business," Bee said off-handedly. He moved at a more leisurely pace, peering at every curiosity and thrifted painting that Josiah had nailed to the walls. "I travel a great deal." He looked at Josiah and smiled. "Are you a gambling man?"

"Not generally," Josiah lied. He turned his back to his neighbor so that Bee could not see his face. "I never had much of a taste for it."

"That is a shame," when Josiah turned around again, Bee was sitting at his kitchen table. His neighbor had pulled out a deck of cards—sleek and glossy as if they were brand new, and jet black with laser-etched suits that were impossible to see without being tilted towards the light. He shuffled them with practiced ease and looked over at Josiah, flashing a smile that made his gold tooth gleam.

"I like Blackjack, myself," Bee said. "The rules are easy."

Josiah's mouth was dry. He swiped his tongue over the insides of his cheeks to try and find his words. "There is more of a jingle," he said, his voice weak, "to poker chips."

Bee's smile widened. For Josiah, it was an admittance of defeat. He didn't know what brought it out of him. Somehow, he felt compelled to tell Bee everything. The truth wanted to spill out of him one way or another, and his guts hurt worse than before.

"Have a seat," Bee said, as if it were his table. "Poker it is."

"Where did you say you were from?" Josiah grabbed his chair and pulled it out. Sitting down seemed like a good idea.

"I didn't," Bee began to deal. "I thought you said you didn't gamble."

"I don't, often," Josiah was still struggling with the lie. "Not anymore. I mean, I used to. A lot." There it was, the truth, bubbling out from his mouth like vomit.

Bee nodded, understanding. "It must have been difficult," he said, "when you fell behind on your payments."

Josiah didn't ask how he knew that. A lucky guess, it had to be. "And my boss had to fire me," he shredded the admittance through his teeth.

"Well, once you got caught playing on the job," Bee shrugged. "The company must share some blame though, right? They gave you access to a computer and shit else to do."

Josiah let out a breath and picked up his hand. "I need to get my chips," he said.

"Betting money is so passé," Bee said casually. "Besides, you can't bet what you don't have." Even as he spoke, something about his voice was changing. Maybe it was just his inflection or maybe he was the type of person to absorb someone else's accent like a sponge. But the Northerner was wiped clean, and there were traces of Deep South creeping onto his tongue. Then again, Josiah felt he could have been imagining it. He shook his head again, grinding his palm against his ringing ear.

"It's a good thing we're not betting decent manners then, either, because you would have nothing to bid," Josiah snapped back.

Bee laughed. He sounded like a barking fox.

"Here, I thought Southerners were supposed to be polite." He drew his tongue over his teeth. "All right, all right. I will play fair." He spoke like he was admitting defeat. "If you win, I will give you something of mine. Anything you want. If I win, you will give me something of yours."

"Anything you want?" Josiah felt like there was a hand around his heart, squeezing it like an orange.

"Of course," Bee said. "Fair is fair."

"All right," Josiah agreed with some hesitation. He didn't have a lot to give, and while he wasn't a bad player—he had lost so much during the last few games he played that he was not feeling very confident.

He didn't keep track of how long they played, but the game felt like it was over before he knew it. When he laid out a winning hand he was almost dizzy with exhilaration. Bee reached into his jacket and pulled out a thick cigar. He didn't even ask if he was allowed to smoke as he lit the blunt tip.

"Something of mine," he said, puffing out his words on an acrid gray cloud. Josiah chewed on his bottom lip and looked his new neighbor up and down, considering.

"One of your rings," he said, and then specified, "that one." He pointed to the gold ring on Bee's thumb. Bee pulled it off without hesitation and dropped it into Josiah's palm.

It twinkled in the soft afternoon light. A rush of victory he had not felt in months.

"Again?" Bee swept up the cards to shuffle again.

"Yeah," Josiah slipped the ring onto his own thumb. "I forgot how good it feels."

Bee laughed around his cigar, letting it hang from his lip as he dealt another hand. The game felt shorter than before, and

Josiah was not sure if it was the rush or the cigar smoke—but he felt even more light-headed than before. He won the hand, even though he wasn't sure how. At this point, he didn't know if his luck was changing, or if Bee was screwing with him somehow.

It didn't make sense why his neighbor would do that, but it didn't really matter, either—as long as he kept winning.

"What did you win?" Bee asked, sweeping up the cards to re-shuffle.

Josiah grinned. "Your car," he said. He didn't expect Bee to take him seriously, but his neighbor just shrugged and winked, puffing out another cloud of smoke.

"Fair is fair," he said. "I suppose I should see if I can win her back." From his pocket he pulled a car key on a metal ring and slid it across the table. Josiah's eyes widened—his tongue felt gummy and his cup was empty. He needed water, or something, but he felt rooted to his spot.

"You can't be serious," he said, even as he picked up the key.

"I'm always serious as a heart attack," Bee said. "I always pay my debts and all I ask of anyone is that they do the same."

Bee's slick black cards skittered across the table and Josiah snatched them up. The ringing in his ear formed a band around his skull, bouncing from one tunnel to the other, and he rubbed his face. His hand came back oily—he did not realize how much he had been sweating.

"Is it hot in here, to you?" He asked.

"No," Bee glanced up over his sunglasses. "You must be getting nervous."

Josiah dragged his hand across his upper lip to wipe the sweat away. His fingerprints left embarrassing smears on the black cards.

Bee laid down his hand. "Seems your luck has changed," he said. He tapped his cigar over Josiah's abandoned breakfast plate from that morning. Gray ash dribbled onto a puddle of sticky yellow yolk.

The lump in his throat was back, and Josiah ran his hand over his neck. "It's just one game," he said.

"You're right," Bee said. "I'll take back my ring."

Josiah was surprised that he didn't ask for his car, but he relinquished the ring. Bee slipped it back onto his thumb and Josiah felt anger he did not feel previously flare up in his chest. It was a sudden burst of rage that surprised even him, but he could not keep it down.

"I want to deal this time," he said hotly. Bee did not argue. He set the deck down on the table and Josiah grabbed them. They were warm from use, but still slick, and he fumbled the shuffle—losing a few that he had to pick up. Bee watched him patiently from behind his purple lenses. Josiah was grateful for the sunglasses, because the uninhibited gaze left him feeling like he had to shit.

Josiah dealt and the game went on. Bee's cigar dwindled down to almost nothing, but he kept the stump in his mouth, chewing on the butt. The game dragged on longer than the others—Josiah felt the beginning of a migraine start to form in his temple, but he only looked up to flick on the switch for the kitchen light.

Bee won again. He seemed neither smug nor surprised, and Josiah realized he was clenching his teeth so hard that his whole jaw ached.

It was dark outside his kitchen window. Had they really been playing all day?

"Well?" Josiah snapped. His stomach clenched, and he realized he must be hungry. It would probably be his last game—he had lost enough.

Bee held out his hand. His crafty fingers flicked open a thin penknife and he raised the blade towards Josiah.

For one heart-stopping second, Josiah's blood ran so cold that his sweaty skin felt clammy.

"I'll have your eye," Bee said. "You can take it out yourself or I can do it for you, if you don't think that you can."

"I'm sorry?" Josiah leaned back to try and distance himself from the blade. "You're joking."

"Nope," Bee said. "Fair is fair. Pay your debts."

Josiah drew in a shaky breath. He raised his hand and it trembled so violently that he couldn't close his fingers. "I don't think I can grip it," he said faintly.

He could have run. He could have fought back. He could have called the police—maybe. They wouldn't get there before he was dead.

He couldn't move from his spot. He felt molded to the chair. His legs and back were screaming at him and Bee's words, although they were barely audible over the din in his ears, made sense.

Fair is fair.

He had given up his car, hadn't he? And he didn't even ask for it back.

Bee's hand came around to cradle the back of Josiah's neck and his head lolled back. It felt too heavy for him to hold upright anymore. Bee stroked the corner of his eye and hummed, hovering the tip of the penknife over each one as if deciding which he wanted to take.

"Is one better than the other?" He asked.

"They're both bad," Josiah croaked.

"I noticed you squinting. Have you not been wearing your glasses this whole time?" Bee slipped his sunglasses up and caught Josiah's gaze, holding it steady with those uncanny bluebonnet eyes. "If you keep looking at me," he purred, "it won't hurt."

Josiah tried to nod, but Bee's hand on his face stayed the motion. He tried to whisper a reply, but it was suddenly impossible to speak. Everything felt numb. His tongue didn't want to move. Bee's eyes kept him paralyzed, and his breathing slowed to where it felt like it stopped altogether. He tried to swallow but his throat wouldn't contract. Josiah opened his mouth and pulled in a weak breath, choking on his own saliva as it started to eke out of the corners of his mouth.

Bee smiled down at him. Josiah felt pressure, what might have been a prick, and then half of Bee's handsome face fuzzed before all his vision shifted to one eye as the other went dark.

Bee pulled back and Josiah slumped over the table. Now that he was no longer making eye contact, a sudden stab of pain made his skull feel like it was going to split apart. It was like someone had jammed a white-hot poker through his eye socket, while blood and clear fluids ran down his cheek and splattered onto the table. He choked again and swallowed some, spitting out the rest. His throat still fell closed up, but he could breathe again. Each weak, trembling breath made his whole body ache. Josiah moaned miserably and lowered his head further. From his peripheral, he could see Bee, reclining in his chair and running the tip of his penknife down Josiah's torn eye. He split it apart and then placed the husk against his mouth, slurping up the insides like Jell-O pudding.

"You're bleeding," Bee said. "Do you want a towel?"

He popped the rest of the eye into his mouth like a strawberry.

Josiah shook his head. "I want another game," he said.

Bee howled. "Want to take pieces off me?" He grinned viciously. "It's getting late. There might not be much left of you by morning."

"Another game," Josiah said again. His own labored breathing rattled in his chest.

Bee stood up and rested a hand against the back of Josiah's head, tousling his curls.

"Rest up," he said. "I'm not going anywhere. I think I've made myself quite at home, here." He leaned over and pressed his lips against Josiah's temple. His kiss was scorching-hot and left a burn. "I'll see you tomorrow, neighbor."

With that, he put his hands into his pockets and whistled as he walked away. Josiah didn't hear him leave, but the whistle faded, and he knew that Bee was gone.

3¢
USA
466
LAFFTWIRL
MONSTER
VALUE STAMP
THIS IS IT!
CLIP THEM
& COLLECT
THEM ALL!

CRITICAL BLAST PUBLISHING
20¢
APPROVED BY THE READING CODE AUTHORITY
SHADOWS AT DUSK
R. Gene Turchin
WEIRD FANTASTIC WORLDS
CRITICAL BLAST PUBLISHING
WHERE POP CULTURE GETS BLASTED
INCREDIBLE STRANGE STORIES
...AND DOOM FOLLOWED!

COCAINE FOR PETS When your pets become too excited during mating season and you don't want additional burden of feeding more pets, shot them up with some fine liquid snow and chill them out.

RENT AN ANGRY WOLF! When you need to rip apart your competition, or when you need to look like a decent human concerned for dogs or something, something.

BOX OF LIVE BATS When you feel like a millionaire crime fighting hero and need to dress up your special cave, to give it that extra touch of atmosphere... a box of live bats is perfect for you. Food not included.

SUPER SHARP PIRATE SWORD When you want to capture the hearts and minds of the people around you, this sword will cut through the muscle and bone to get to the vital organs you need to sustain your hunger.

MONSTER VALUE STAMP THIS IS IT! CLIP THEM & COLLECT THEM ALL!

EXPLODING DRINK Sit back and enjoy the highjinks as people unscrew their drink activating the chemical reaction, causing a foamy mess.

DIGITAL PUZZLE T-SHIRT Get people's undivided attention when they get engrossed trying to solve the constantly changing puzzles.

LAST MAN ON EARTH HEARD A KNOCK AT THE DOOR!

WELCOME MAT TRAP When you don't want people annoying you, a simple press of the button and the trap door will dispose of anyone who stands on it, while waiting for you to answer the door.

HYPNO-ROBOT use the special mind control eye harmonics to subdue the minds of your unwilling subjects. You'll never have to take out the trash and everyone will worship you as if their life depends on it.

BECOME A PIRATE IN ONE WEEK! Learn to talk and kill like a Pirate. Optional hand and leg amputation. Pirate Ship sold separately. Arrrrrr.

HEAD KNIVES 100% stainless steal daggers that launch from the top of your head and kill any conversation you find boring.

HOBO IN A BOX When your street is getting over-runned by homeless people and you need someone to speak their language and run them off to the next street down the block.

R. Gene Turchin writes short stories in sci-fi, horror and toe dipping in other genres. He has just completed a science fiction novel and is working on a second book with a twisted spin on the Dracula story. A very old house occupies his time when not writing or playing guitar. Recent published works can be found in Sunshine Superhighway Anthology, Cosmic Horror Monthly and 99 Tiny Terrors Anthology, Onyx Publications, Novus Literary Arts Journal, Strangely Funny IX anthology, 365 Tomorrows and Amazing Stories Magazine.

Across the street, between the two houses, the yards converge to wide wild spot on the hill overlooking the houses. Trees and brush raise a tall barrier like a leaf fence that blots out part of the sky. In the evening as the sun slinks down behind the hill to slumber, it illuminates the leaves from above and behind making them glow chlorophyll green. Natural backlighting. There is one spot, neatly centered by nature, in the growth that forms an oval opening like a front door, letting the light pour through. The stab of brightness closes the pupil down so that the lower brush is cast in shades of black and emerald green. The colors shift and change if you sit staring too long.

It first appeared in that shadowed growth, a thing almost seen, a visual delusion appearing to move. Or perhaps it was a small breeze setting the leaves a flutter with a breath moving a vortex to shudder and shake them.

Binoculars were in the pantry, but would their use raise neighborly eyebrows? I lifted the glass of after dinner bourbon to my lips. Only a remnant of the three ice cubes remained.

The bush took on a beast shape, wide shoulders, thick head pressed between, ape-like arms hanging down. . . and wings to the sides. Bat wings stretched over a frame too large. An artist's color membrane of burnt sienna lifting and shrugging with each breath. I shook my head.

The day had been long with a thousand needles of broken things pricking my skin, thus the bourbon to unwind the mainspring coiled inside. A small college IT department with a staff of three, insufficient for the expectations of a smooth operation. Everyday everything is broken. Each term's beginning brought a hurricane of faults. A week in and the four months of the semester leaned toward the infinite. I drained the last of the glass and went inside.

Jan had flown to Minneapolis to visit her parents. A weekend turned into a week. Neither was doing well. Time had become a bogged down morass.

"Dad doesn't recognize me," she said that first night. "This may take a while. Mom is in denial and still lets him drive. One of the neighbors helped me pull the battery out of the car so they can't use it. I'm trying to get them into a home, and this may take a while."

"I can take a week," I said. "They owe me comp time. I can fly or drive out."

"No," she said. "I have to deal with this. I'm working with their doctor, and he's recommended an attorney. Can you get along without me?" Yeah, I could but didn't want to. I missed her easy warmth and laughter.

I kept my phone on the small table next to my chair in case she should call. Tonight, a cup of tea became tepid as I stared up through the yards. As the sun curled up behind the trees, I again saw or imagined the figure outlined by the bushes. It never occurred to me to glance up at the section during the day. Twilight offers half hidden figures and childhood nightmare dreams.

Faint movements of bushes or a brush of wings, I couldn't decide. The figure didn't raise the hair on my neck. It only inspired a bland curiosity. Was it real or merely that pattern recognition gene buried in the brain from the African savanna? I sipped the tea and the phone chirped.

"Things are moving along," she said. "Albeit slowly. Mom is still defiant about moving to an assisted living facility. Jake is flying in tomorrow."

Jake was her brother. Not a bad man but with three kids of his own and a shit job, he had little time for his parents. I hoped he'd be some use to Jan.

"I miss you," I said.

"Ditto," she laughed. "How are you spending your evenings alone?"

"Sitting on the porch. Drinking tea tonight," I said. "Then I go in read for a while. And I did laundry today and watered your flowers."

With the sun behind the hill, the trees were now a muted dusty green. A flicker of red glowed at head height in the bushes. Eyes? Again, the bushes moving in slo-mo on either side as if wings ruffled with each intake of breath. Rationally, there was nothing there, even the imagined red eyes had to be a twist of light, shifting the spectrum, refracting from leaf bottoms. We stared at each other, the mirage and my tired eyes until streetlamps popped on slathering the road with a harsh glow.

The refrigerator was bereft of leftovers, and choosing from an online menu seemed to be too much effort. There was enough cereal in a box to fill a bowl and a sprinkle of raisins added texture. Cold cereal for dinner was a slippery slope. Too lazy to fix a meal, end up on the couch munching a whole bag of chips. Could easily slide down that rail. Jan always did wonders preparing meals with things in the pantry. Maybe that was an unbalance in our relationship that I needed to fix. We ease into habits.

Would the creature show tonight? I had come to believe that some giant winged thing lurked in the bushes atop the hill. It patiently waited till neighbors went inside, the blue glow of screens in the living rooms faded and lights went out. Then it would continue its mission. Fear didn't enter my thoughts, only curiosity.

It was after ten when she called. I must have dozed in the chair.

"I think I can make it home by Monday," she said and sighed. "It has been hard. When did everyone get so old? I wish I'd never seen him like this. He's so frail and lost but I've made arrangements," she sighed again.

"How's your Mom doing?" I asked. "If you need help, I can fly out. I'd be glad to."

"She's angry and she cries a lot. Said I should be ashamed for putting them away like this."

"Jan. . ."

"I know," she said. "But it still hurts. The lawyer and Jake have been a great help. I just wish I didn't have to do this and it was over. Anyway, I have a reservation for a Monday flight home. Should get there around 3:30 if all goes well on this end."

I told her I loved her, and some nebulous thing ached inside me.

Inside, I put the bowl in the sink, washed over it with a splash of water and began turning out lights and locking up. As I pulled the shade on the bedroom window, the bushes on the hilltop parted and it stepped out. It stood tall for a moment and then hunched over like a soldier running between covers to dodge bullets. It moved down through the yards. The bedroom clock read 12:45. It—I didn't know what else to call it, because the creature wasn't anything in the spectra of things I knew.

Dad's old .45 sat on the top shelf in the bedroom closet in a shoe box, the loaded magazine slept in the bottom of my sock drawer. The two hadn't been together in years. Not this time either. Perhaps stupid, but I had no signs of fear. The shoe box went back on the top shelf, and I swept up the wooden baseball bat from behind the bedroom door, a remnant from youth, now a security blanket.

The basement door opened with a tired hinge creak. A three-quarter moon hung over the eastern sky. A few faint stars and luminous Venus dotted the frame of the sky. I looked away from the moon and toward the dark grass in the backyard. The going was slippery as evening dew had painted the blades.

It was sliding between the old maple trees in the yard, caution in every step. A yellow wash bucket dangled from one long arm.

The yards in back drop off with a four-foot-high bank down to the asphalt alley. It paused, I think, sensing me. It sniffed the air as it jumped down to the road. Shit, it was big. The head was the size of one of those exercise balls and the eyes glowed red. The nose was two twisted sea shells pinched above a wide mouth filled with sharp teeth. The bat hung loose along the line of my leg on my right side.

The hands and feet ended in sharp yellow talons. When it saw me thin bat wings unfurled from its back. My stupid needle was in the red zone but curiosity trumped fear. I tapped the bat against the ground.

It growled, an earthquake vibration shaking my guts. I tapped the bat against the ground again and resisted the urge to run with every fiber of my being.

"What the hell are you?" I said. It growled again and shuffled forward. No doubt its wicked appearance and terrifying face brought about shivers of fear, but it moved like an arthritic old man.

I brought the bat up to the home run position. In the dark, with one lone streetlight pushing against the night down the block and around the corner, it seemed to grow larger with each passing second. We often make decisions without playing chess with the ideas, wild hair ideas as opposed to analyzed well thought out actions and consequences. I had not been looking to confront this creature and was guilty of being blinded by curiosity.

"Move," it said. The voice came from a place deep in its belly, and it croaked the dry timbre born from lack of use.

"What are you?" I asked again. Somewhere in the back roads of my mind, a loop gif movie ran over and over, Jan coming through the front door, calling my name and I am missing, never to be found, slaughtered by a creature that shouldn't exist.

It coughed.

"Mothman," it said in a dry whisper.

"Mothman?" The image of the statue in Point Pleasant popped into my head, a silver chrome beast grasping toward visitors. Legend says the winged creature is a harbinger of doom because after it was first sighted, a bridge collapsed.

The wings folded back, and he seemed to deflate like helium balloon left floating in the living room. He became wrinkled and tired.

Then he squatted down, now hidden by the bank behind him. Anyone looking out from a window on a late-night bathroom trip might see a bush and a fool with a baseball bat.

I let the bat hang down again, weak croquet position.

"Please," he said and pointed to the yellow bucket he'd been carrying. "Water."

He pointed to an opening in the underbrush, a deer path leading through the trees down the hill. A half mile away at the bottom of our hill, a creek snaked its way in a steep valley formed by the hillside. It was difficult access, steep on both sides, covered with thick brush and slick mud near the edges. A two-lane road lumbered along 25 feet above the narrow creek. Was it going down to get water from the creek? Water riddled with empty beer cans, soggy cardboard and small roadkills kicked over the hill.

I nodded and swept my arm in the direction of path as if I owned the rights to the way down, as if I was the toll master.

It rose to a hunched crouch and scrambled down through the brush, the only sound, a ruffling of leaves touched by the wind above.

Monday morning. Television on in the background.

Something about a plane, losing an engine, crashing into a mountain side. Flight left California at noon. Cold ice dropped into my stomach.

Pushed deep into the couch by emotional weight, bloodshot eyes staring and not seeing the endless news cycle, images of a burning plane. Firetrucks. No survivors.

Numbness. Dead brain, incapable of thought. Forcing myself to breathe.

Phone ringing somewhere.

Not wanting to answer. Not wanting to hear the words.

3¢
USA
44¢   CACKLEDAZZ
MONSTER
VALUE STAMP
THIS IS IT!
CLIP THEM
& COLLECT
THEM ALL!

CRITICAL BLAST
PUBLISHING
20¢
MAN on PORCH
Evan Baughfman
APPROVED
BY THE
READING CODE
AUTHORITY
CRITICAL
BLAST
PUBLISHING
WEIRD FANTASTIC WORLDS
WHERE POP CULTURE GETS BLASTED
INCREDIBLE STRANGE STORIES
DING DONG!
TERROR
CALLING!

STICK IT TO YOUR ENEMIES! Real Voodoo Doll! Guaranteed Quality checked by the finest Witch Doctors! Send lock of hair and a SASE to DUDAT VOODOO, Box 9, Haiti.

READING IS 20 TO LIFE!

BOW AND ARROW KIT! When you need to go into battle on Tuesdays and don't know what weapon to take with you.

MONSTER VALUE STAMP THIS IS IT! CLIP THEM & COLLECT THEM ALL!

ATTENTION!
DEMONS! VAMPIRES! GHOULS!

LIVE TO SEE WEDNESDAY!

DEFEAT BLACK MYSTIC ARTS KUNG-FU Tired of getting your ass kicked every Tuesday by Black Mystic Arts Kung-Fu fighters? CALL 666-HELP to enroll in self-defense training every Hellspawn should know to survive any dark alley encounter. Become a Ninth Circle Master of Judante!

HUMAN MASK When you need to walk among the humans, without being singled out as a monster. Get this mask in black, white or polka-dot, to blend right in!

EXPLODING DRINK Sit back and enjoy the highjinks as people unscrew their drink activating the chemical reaction, causing a foamy mess.

HOBO IN A BOX When your street is getting over-runned by homeless people and you need someone to speak their language and run them off to the next street down the block.

Evan Baughfman graduated with Honors in Creative Writing from the University of Redlands. Much of his writing success has been as a playwright, with original plays finding homes in theaters worldwide. He has also found success writing horror fiction, most recently published in anthologies by Improbable Press, No Bad Books Press, and Grinning Skull Press. A number of his stories adapted into screenplays have won awards in film festival competitions. His first short story collection, The Emaciated Man and Other Terrifying Tales from Poe Middle School, is now available through Thurston Howl Publications. Visit his author page at: amazon.com/author/evanbaughfman

The following is a transcript of Chyme ™ video doorbell footage recorded from the residence located at ▮▮▮, on 07/16/2022.

\###

01:47 A.M.

Video shows a shirtless Man standing on the Resident's front porch. Man leans forward to speak into the doorbell camera. Man's eyelids are droopy. His eyes are barely visible. Man appears to be under the influence of drugs and/or alcohol. Resident speaks to Man via the doorbell's intercom system.

Man: Hello, can I get the lunch special? I know it's late, but, um, yeah. Lunch special. That's like five bucks?

Resident: I can't help you.

Man: What was that?

Resident: Sorry, I can't help you.

Man: Can't help? Why [*unintelligible*] Okay.

Resident: This isn't a restaurant. You have to leave.

Man: Hashbrowns. How much for... for hashbrowns? Two. Two, please.

Resident: This is a house. Private property. You need to leave.

Man: Just, um, two, ma'am. Only two. Thank you.

Resident: Again, this isn't a restaurant. This is where people live.

Man: And a... one orange juice. Small. No. Guava. Guava juice, yeah. Medium.

Resident: We're closed.

Man: Huh? What's...

Resident: We're closed for the day. Bye.

Man: Shit. My bad. [*unintelligible*] Cool. 'Night.
Resident: Good night.
Man: Know someplace where I can get... get grilled cheese?
Resident: No. Try the Strip.
Man: Oh? If I strip, you'll make me a...?

Man gives a thumbs-up, smiles, and begins to undo the belt on his pants.

Resident: Sir, if you remove your clothing... if you don't leave right now... I will call the police.
Man: The police? Don't... They don't... don't like me. Getting all dramatic 'cause of some goddamn [*unintelligible*]

Man extends both middle fingers to the camera before stepping off the porch. As he steps onto the front lawn, a shadowy figure tackles him, dragging Man down into the grass.

Man: [*unintelligible*]

Man struggles as he is pulled out of frame. The video ends.

02:13 A.M.
Video shows a shirtless Vampire standing on the Resident's front porch. His fanged mouth and chest are dripping with blood. Vampire leans forward to speak into the doorbell camera. Vampire's eyelids are droopy. His pitch-black eyes are barely visible. Vampire appears to be under the influence of drugs and/or alcohol. Resident speaks to Vampire via the doorbell's intercom system.

Vampire: Hello, can I come inside? Hello?

Resident: You cannot.

Vampire: I'm just... just a little... you know. Thirsty. Hungry.

Resident: Sorry, but no.

Vampire: I'll take some water. Need water. Just killed that... that guy. The one I saw bother... bothering you?

Resident: I didn't ask you to do that.

Vampire: Knew he was drunk or something. But didn't realize how drunk. Soooooo drunk.

Resident: And now you are.

Vampire: And now I am! His blood was so full of... was practically... al-kee-hall. Sorry, I don't... usually don't get like this. So wasted. Usually much more careful. Choose my prey better... more carefully.

Resident: Right. But I can't help you.

Vampire: Sure, you can.

Resident: You have to go.

Vampire: Water. H2O.

Resident: Vampires don't drink water.

Vampire: Every living thing needs water.

Resident: You're a "living" thing?

Vampire: Ha! [*unintelligible*] Got me there!

Resident: Get off my porch, please.

Vampire: Come out and... and make me.

Resident: Don't think so.

Vampire: Boo! Boooooo! No fun! Let's... Let's have fun, yeah?

Resident: Get out of here.

Vampire: Let me in.

Resident: No.

Vampire: Let me in, so I can have fun.

Resident: Leave.

Vampire: Have fun and… and feed on you… on you and your family.

Resident: We've called the police.

Vampire: Police don't scare me. I scare police. They don't know how to… how to handle guys like me.

Resident: The Monster Task Force. We called, and they're on their way.

Vampire: No, they aren't.

Resident: Yes, they are. So, you'd better go.

Vampire: If you called them… If…! Then they told you… told you that it would take a while before anyone got here. Yeah?

Resident: No, they're on their way. Right now.

Vampire: That's just [*unintelligible*] Liar!

Resident: Leave, if you know what's good for you.

Vampire: What's good for me is right here. Right behind this… this door! Inside your house! I can… can smell them. Both of them. Your children!

Resident: MTF says they're getting closer.

Vampire: No. See, what you don't know… don't know is… This weekend, there's a convention… Ghouls and goblins and every nasty thing from around the world, all right there on the Strip. So, no, sorry! MTF isn't getting closer. They're too busy keeping the peace at the hotels and casinos. You and your kids and me… We… We aren't a priority for the police department.

Resident: Just leave!

Vampire: Why do you think I'm out here? Hunting out here? Huh? Because I'm safe! This neighborhood… There's nowhere safer for me to be.

Resident: I'm not opening that door, so you can stand out there all night.

Vampire: Think I might!

Resident: And keep standing there until the sun comes up!

Vampire: [*unintelligible*]

Resident: I'm fine waiting for MTF. For morning. Are you?

Vampire: Shit. Just... I need some water! Some fucking water! Seriously! This guy's blood is all... so goddamn gross! Sticky!

Resident: There's a hose out there.

Vampire: Where?

Resident: Behind you. At the bottom of the porch steps.

Vampire: Yeah?

Resident: Yes. Use it and go. I promise you, MTF's already on their way.

Vampire doesn't immediately respond.

Vampire: O...Okay.

Vampire walks off the porch and grabs a water hose. He begins to spray himself clean.

Resident: Forgot to mention, though!

Vampire: What?

Resident: That's holy water! Our pipes were blessed by a priest!

Vampire shrieks, tossing the hose aside. Moments later, he extends a middle finger to the camera.

Vampire: Ha ha. Very funny.

Something large then zips into the frame and grabs Vampire, carrying him, screaming, up into the sky. The video ends.

02:47 A.M.

Video shows a shirtless Monsquito standing on the Resident's front porch. The insectoid's proboscis and chest are dripping with blood. Monsquito leans forward to speak into the doorbell camera. Monsquito's eyelids are droopy. Its compound eyes are barely visible. The insectoid appears to be under the influence of drugs and/or alcohol.

Resident speaks to Monsquito via the doorbell's intercom system.

Monsquito: Lost. Am lost.
Resident: You can't stay here.
Monsquito: Feel bad. [*unintelligible*] No good.
Resident: If you're going to throw up, don't do it here.
Monsquito: Eat fast. Too fast.
Resident: Better luck next time.
Monsquito: Food bad. No good.

Monsquito holds Vampire's corpse up to the camera. Vampire's body is shriveled, drained dry.

Monsquito: Food poison? Food yuck.
Resident: Look, you're just drunk. That vamp was pretty sloshed.
Monsquito: No like. Yuck.

Monsquito throws Vampire off the porch.

Resident: If you're feeling sick, I need you to move to the grass.
Monsquito: Dizzy. No more fly.
Resident: Then walk there.
Monsquito: No more fly. Danger.
Resident: Crawl. Stumble. Whatever you need to do!
Monsquito: Lost. [*unintelligible*] Am lost.
Resident: I understand, but I can't help you.
Monsquito: Help? You help?
Resident: No. Look, it's been a long night for me.
Monsquito: This hotel?
Resident: This is not a hotel!
Monsquito: Am tired.
Resident: So am I.
Monsquito: You give room?
Resident: Absolutely not.
Monsquito: Thank you. You nice.
Resident: No room!
Monsquito: Me give money tomorrow. Thank you.
Resident: God's sake...!
Monsquito: Have money. A lot. Tomorrow.
Resident: No hotel! Leave!
Monsquito: No hotel?
Resident: No!
Monsquito: Where hotel?
Resident: Not here!
Monsquito: Am lost.
Resident: I know!
Monsquito: Need friend.

Resident: I'm not your friend.
Monsquito: You no friend?
Resident: No. Sorry.
Monsquito: Am scary? Me?
Resident: Yes!
Monsquito: Am nice.
Resident: Tell that to the vampire.
Monsquito: Eat mean. Mean only. Bad only.
Resident: Only slurp on the bad guys, do you?
Monsquito: You nice. No eat nice.
Resident: Don't think I can believe that. Sorry.
Monsquito: People talk bad. A lot. No like. [*unintelligible*] Am nice. You nice.
Resident: Not as nice as you think.

Sirens approach. Monsquito turns away from the camera.

Monsquito: [*unintelligible*]
Resident: They aren't here for you. They're just late. Bad timing on your part. Sorry.

Monsquito looks to the camera. In the background, Monster Task Force vehicles arrive on scene.

Monsquito: They friends?
Resident: It really depends.
Monsquito: They help?
Resident: Just listen to them, and they'll help you.
Monsquito: You bring friends. Thank you.
Resident: Don't thank me yet.

MTF Officers exit their vehicles and take tactical positions, weapons ready. Lieutenant Unger speaks on the megaphone.

Lt. Unger: You, on the porch! Put your claws on top of your head!

Monsquito: Feel real bad. Real no good.

Resident: Listen to them, okay?

Monsquito: You real nice.

Monsquito does not comply with Lt. Unger's order.

Lt. Unger: Stay where you are! And put your claws on your head!

Monsquito still does not comply.

Monsquito: Am real sick.

Resident: Come on! Do what they say!

Monsquito: Can no sick here. No yuck here.

Resident: Claws on your head!

Monsquito: Yuck in the grass.

Monsquito turns away from the camera, toward Officers.

Resident: Hey! Don't move!

Lt. Unger: For your own safety, stay where you are! Lift those claws slowly!

Monsquito's wings buzz.

Resident: Stop! Don't!
Lt. Unger: Don't move off that porch!

Monsquito raises its claws.

Monsquito: Have to yuck! Sorry!

Monsquito moves toward the Officers.

Resident: No!
Lt. Unger: Neutralize suspect! Neutralize! Neutralize!

Officers open fire. Monsquito falls to the front lawn. Porch furniture is wrecked in the crossfire. Officers stop shooting. The video ends.

After reviewing the transcript of video footage taken on the night of July 16, 2022, it is the opinion of this Committee that decorated Lieutenant Patton Unger and other esteemed Officers of the Las Vegas Metropolitan Monster Task Force acted with sound reason and appropriate restraint and did not use excessive force when responding to the incident at ~~9688 N. Saguaro Drive.~~

It is therefore also the opinion of this Committee that no members of the Las Vegas Metropolitan Monster Task Force be charged for their involvement in the shooting deaths of the Residents at the aforementioned address. We all recognize that collateral damage is sometimes an unfortunate part of successful police work.

We send our heartfelt thoughts and prayers to the Residents' surviving family members.

CRITICAL BLAST PUBLISHING
20¢
APPROVED BY THE READING CODE AUTHORITY
CAPTAIN'S LAST RIDE
Joel Reeves
WEIRD FANTASTIC WORLDS
CRITICAL BLAST PUBLISHING
WHERE POP CULTURE GETS BLASTED
INCREDIBLE STRANGE STORIES
DEATH HAS A FAMILIAR FACE!

STICK IT TO YOUR ENEMIES!
Real Voodoo Doll! Guaranteed Quality checked by the finest Witch Doctors! Send lock of hair and a SASE to DUDAT VOODOO, Box 9, Haiti.

1to1 MODEL PIRATE SHIP!
Some assembly required. Glue NOT included. Recommend a private Island cove as the staging areo.

HEAD KNIVES
100% stainless steal daggers that launch from the top of your head and kill any conversation you find boring.

SNAKES IN A MAIL BOX
Get these total mother-f$%Ken poisonous snakes and mail them with your get well gift cards.

FISH BOWL FULL OF WORMS
Are you tired of eating meat? Get yourself a bowl full of yummy worms and feel you are saving the planet.

RENT AN ANGRY WOLF!
When you need to rip apart your competition, or when you need to look like a decent human concerned for dogs or something, something.

MONSTER VALUE STAMP
THIS IS IT! CLIP THEM & COLLECT THEM ALL!

LEARN TO PLAY THE GUITAR!
When you can't get a date for the weekend, rent a sexy Guitar Teacher to impress your friends and maybe you just might learn something too.

WELCOME MAT TRAP
When you don't want people annoying you, a simple press of the button and the trap door will dispose of anyone who stands on it, while waiting for you to answer the door.

BECOME A PIRATE IN ONE WEEK!
Learn to talk and kill like a Pirate. Optional hand and leg amputation. Pirate Ship sold separately. Arrrrrr.

Joel Reeves lives with his family and pet cat, Gray Matter, in Northwest Lower Michigan. His short stories have appeared in several anthologies, including Tales of the Unanticipated and Return to Deathlehem. Odd Birds, a collection of his twisted tales and tales with twists, was published by Scantic Press.

Rengaard, Bruckstone Castle's Captain of the Guard, ducked his head as he exited the doorway of the abbey. He stood at the edge of the convent's large herb garden, imagining the nuns in their plain gray tunics going about their daily chores, the monster having somehow infiltrated their peaceful world, ripping it asunder. Like most rumors circulated in taverns, the claim by a stranger that the creature still lurked inside the Priory of the Merciful Sisters, proved unfounded. As he walked through the kitchen, he breathed in the pleasant scents of fresh baked breads and pies that still hung in the air, though the ovens in which they were made had cooled, their fires extinguished. The other rooms in the abbey also revealed little of interest. However, the library was a different story. Here he found an embroidered rug, torn and soaked with dried blood, which warranted further investigation.

The Captain raised several loose floorboards and peered down into a tunnel filled with darkness and the lingering reek of death. Equipped with a lantern from the library, he descended a rope tied to a wrought iron handle driven into one wall. At the bottom, lying across each other as if asleep, he found the bodies of twelve nuns. Nine strangled. Three more with broken necks. The scene would have been enough to shock and disgust most, but in his military career Rengaard had witnessed plenty of death in more horrible ways. Besides, the lure of the king's reward for anyone who could rid the realm of the monster—10,000 gold pieces—was a very strong incentive. Unfortunately, after spending hours searching every room and passage of the abbey for the intruder and finding nothing one thing became clear to Rengaard: The monster, having murdered every one of the unsuspecting nuns, had moved on to perpetrate more of its atrocities.

Despite the odds against him locating the sly villain. Rengaard had discovered an important clue there in the secret passage, the scene of the hideous crime. One of the bodies had not yet stiffened in death, leading the Captain of the Guard to conclude that this victim had died perhaps as recently as a few hours prior to his arrival. Determined, Rengaard mounted his horse and urged it forward. The black steed took a few gingerly steps but then stumbled and stopped, holding one of its front hooves a few inches off the ground. Cursing his bad luck, Rengaard smacked the animal with the reins. It limped a few more steps and stopped again, twisting its head back to gaze at him, whinnying in pain. Grumbling, the angry officer slid down to the ground and lifted the injured hoof in one hand. He expected to find a stone to be the cause of his mount's discomfort, as such incidents were not uncommon, and easily resolved. But this was worse. Far worse. A rusty nail driven straight up into the sole.

Still bemoaning his ill fortune, Rengaard hurried off down the road, leaving the horse to its own resources. He didn't have any tools to remove the nail, he reminded himself to ease his conscience, and even if he somehow did manage to dislodge it, the animal would need time to heal. Time he didn't have.

🦇

"Mr. Neethling? Are you in there? I have something special I'd like to give you."

Hodge Neethling lived alone and didn't get many visitors. Truth told, it got mighty lonely with only an old pony for company. He shoved the cork back in the half-drunk bottle of ale and got his half-drunken body off the cot. Hodge groaned as he stood on spindly legs, leaving the impression of his bulbous form in the worn straw and wool stuffed mattress. The wooden cane that he'd carved out of an old hickory limb creaked under his weight as he hobbled across the gloomy interior of the tiny cottage—an opening in one wall covered by a frayed quilt. Hodge opened his "door" to find Sister Eliwys waiting patiently outside. She was attired in a grayish-white habit, tied at the waist with a leather belt, her hair hidden beneath a veil. She wore a simple wooden cross that hung from a chain about her neck. In her hands she held a covered platter. He could smell the delicious odor of baked chicken in the air.

"Hullo," he said, leaning heavily on his cane. "What brings you to my wretched hovel? Are you lost, my good woman?"

"No, Mr. Neethling," she replied. "I am not lost. I brought you a Miracle Pie."

"Miracle?" he said, chuckling. "I could use one of those alright. Let me just have a taste and maybe I'll turn from a beggar into a king."

He reached out for the covered platter eagerly, but she held it tight and slightly away.

"Not so fast now," she said. "I want to talk to you a moment. You see, the sisters held a special meeting today."

"Let me guess," Hodge said. "Another grand plan to feed the sick and clothe the poor."

"That's right, Mr. Neethling," she said, not taking offense. "There is nothing more important than making sure all of God's children are being provided for."

"In both body *and* spirit, I suppose?" Hodge sighed, guessing her purpose in coming. "That's why you're here, isn't it? To keep this simple peasant-farmer from burning in the eternal fires? Thank you, but not even the whole Church of England could—"

"In the eyes of the Lord it's never too late to—"

"Save me?" he grunted. "Sister, I don't mean to be ungrateful, but as I said, that horse left the barn years ago. So long, that I don't even remember."

Despite Hodge's protests, she refused to be discouraged. In fact, to the farmer's surprise, she pushed past him with her platter, drew aside the quilt, and entered the simple cottage.

"Hey, now," he shouted, hurrying in after her. "I didn't – come out of there right now. I ain't had time to clean the place."

The nun stood in the smoky gloom of the little hovel staring into a fire pit and watching the glowing embers of a burning log, her back to Hodge. The old farmer had carved a chair into a crude looking throne from the stump of an old maple. A set of deer antlers was mounted above it, a worn cloth made of wool hanging from one tine. Wood, chopped and split, was piled to the ceiling and covered all four walls. An ax with a broken handle lay in one corner, a smear of dried blood and tuft of rabbit fur stuck to the blade. Several mugs, fashioned by Hodge from leather or wood during the long winter months, littered the dirt floor. A hole in the far corner filled to overflowing with drinking vessels—skins and mugs that, like their owner, sometimes failed to "hold" their drink—rounded out the none too pleasant interior of the peasant's pitiful cottage.

Hodge stared at the nun's back, ashamed. There was a reason he never invited people inside. His mother, a proud woman who had toiled in the dirt all her life in loyal serfdom to a king she would never meet, had once paid him a visit. Her words still echoed in Hodge's mind. *Disgraceful. How can you live like this?* Though some thirty years had come and gone since he had committed her to a simple grave marked with a pile of stones in the field behind his loathsome hovel, Hodge never forgot her disapproving frown or her hard but honest appraisal. It was clear that she had hoped for and expected a better life for her son, and when that failed to materialize, the disappointment weighed heavily on them both.

Eliwys placed the platter containing the Miracle Pie on the table—a particularly large stump around which it appeared the cottage had been built. It was well past lunchtime and Hodge hadn't eaten anything since the three eggs he'd collected from his small flock of chickens earlier that same morning. With the nun preoccupied, the peasant farmer leaned down and picked up the platter and pulled back the piece of cloth to reveal the savory pie beneath. He ate it all, relishing the chunks of beef and potatoes, wiping the gravy from his fingers onto his stained pants.

"Please don't take this wrong, Sister Eliwys," Hodge said, stifling a belch that brought up the taste of his repast. "But I wish you hadn't come in here. This ain't no proper place for a woman, especially a servant of the Lord such as yourself."

"Oh, I wouldn't worry, Mr. Neethling," she said. "As servants of the Lord, as you call them, I've seen more than most."

Her voice sounded different suddenly. Low and raspy, like her throat was filled up with gravel. Probably just his imagination. He leaned on his cane, thinking.

"That was the best pie. Much like my dear old mother—"

Just then, she – it – lunged at Hodge, her face now his face, grabbing him around the throat. Horrified, he tried to fend her off with his cane. Her fingers, hard and sharp as nails, bit into the flesh of his neck.

"Believe me, Mr. Neethling, it's nothing personal," the thing said, squeezing against his windpipe so that it was difficult for the farmer to speak. "The fact of the matter is that I despise all of your kind, rich or poor, equally. Humanity is a blight on this world like the black mold that grows on your corn."

Hodge struggled again to break the intruder's grip, but this only caused the fingers to dig deeper like the steel teeth of a bear trap. He gasped. His eyes bugged. His heart pounded in his ears. All the while, the thing held him fast so that he could not move, while barely missing a beat of its strange testimony, droning on casually as if it were relating what it had had for breakfast.

"Where are my manners?" the thing said, interrupting its own tale. "Allow me to introduce myself. I'm a shapeshifter. Not from this plane, of course, but we'd like to add your world to ours eventually, once it has been purged of your kind. My name is Mardochaiso. It means emptiness and death." The monster paused, thinking. "Oh dear, now I've gone and told you my true name. That means I have to kill you."

"No, please..." Hodge pleaded. I—"

"Actually, I would have killed you anyway," Mardochaiso interrupted. "In any case, I thank you for the use of your likeness. It will be most useful in the carrying out of my mission."

"Mission?" Hodge choked out the words between gasps. "I – I don't understand."

"The fact of the matter is that I'm being pursued by a man named Rengaard. He's the king's Captain of the Guard. Very determined fellow, I'll give him that. Arrogant, greedy, and boastful, too. He was actually next on my list of castle dwellers for elimination, but he got suspicious—what with all the mysterious disappearances—and saw through my *disguise.* In actuality, he discovered me in a corridor of the South Tower, while I was *changing*—very embarrassing." He chuckled at his own joke. "His timing really couldn't have been worse. I had just finished choking the last bit of life out of one of the king's favorite advisors—"

Mardochaiso suddenly released his grip around Hodge's throat. Gasping, the peasant slumped to the floor and lay sprawled in the dirt, the taste of the Miracle Pie bittersweet on his tongue.

The new Hodge looked down at the old Hodge and sighed.

With his life slipping away like the last swirl of filth draining into a cesspit, Hodge watched as the monster— beer-bellied, gray whiskered, spindly-legged, and dressed in a stained woolen tunic that looked identical to the peasant's own—stuck his finger into a hole in the worn quilt and peered outside.

"Looks like a nice day to take a trip and sell some apples," Mardochaiso said, a malicious smile spreading over his face. "I'll take that pony and wagon of yours."

Hodge eyed the shapeshifter, alarmed. "No – but how did you know...how did you know of my plans to sell my apples today. I didn't—"

"It's another of my many...talents..." Mardochaiso boasted, smirking. "I can transform my appearance and I can read minds, both of which come in very handy in my line of work."

Hodge shook his head, coughing. "You mustn't—"

"Oh, but I must, and I will," Mardochaiso taunted. "It will give me the perfect opportunity to get *acquainted* with the community of Leefside and begin a new life there."

"Don't do this." The peasant farmer looked up at the monster, pleading. "Leefside has many good people. Please, let them be. Please—"

A low gurgling noise rattled in the peasant-farmer's voice. His eyes closed and he became still.

Mardochaiso looked down at the dead farmer.

"Time for this little piggy to go to market."

Outside in the bright light of a beautiful summer's day, the shapeshifter hitched the little wagon to a docile white pony he found grazing in the farmer's field. Inside the back of the wagon, he placed the seven bushels of apples that Hodge had picked earlier in the week. These he would take to the marketplace in Leefside. There he would sell some agricultural goods, trade some fine stories, and get to know members of the community, and then kill them off one by one, right down to the last man, woman, and child, as he had so efficiently done in other villages all across the king's realm.

Mardochaiso—identical in appearance, mannerism, and speech to the dead peasant farmer—climbed up into the buckboard of the little wagon, gave a whistle, then smacked the pony across the rump with one of the reins. The mare snorted and broke into a trot. The wagon bolted off down the road, hardly more than a dirt path surrounded by fields of rye and gardens of cabbages, onions, and carrots. After a few miles, Mardochaiso came to a well-kept cottage, one in much better condition than Hodge's hovel. He immediately spotted Harold Woodhame, a boy of perhaps six or seven, hopping about on his wooden hobby horse. His mother, Rowena, toiled behind the sunbaked cottage of straw, sticks, and manure, hanging clothes across bushes to dry.

"I got apples, today," the shapeshifter grinned, nodding the child over. "You can have one. I picked it fresh out'n my orchard this morning."

Harold stopped hopping about in the tall grass. He stared at the apple in the old man's hand and wrinkled his nose.

"I don't like fruit."

Looking more spry than he had in years, Hodge hopped down from the wagon like a man half his age and in much better physical health. He kneeled so he was about the same height as the boy, offering the apple to the child with a smile.

"Where's your cane?" the boy noted, surprised. "That bad hip of yours finally heal up?"

Mardochaiso stared at Harold for a moment, suddenly realizing that in his eagerness to carry out his plan to eliminate the boy and his mother, he had forgotten about the old farmer's defect. He suddenly snapped his fingers, smiling sweetly.

"You know, my lad, you're absolutely right," he exclaimed. "It is better, and I bet I know exactly what happened. You see, one of God's angels visited me earlier today and she brought me a Miracle Pie. It was delicious. I'm sure it was that heavenly dish that healed my hip."

Harold shrugged and petted the pony between the ears. The mare let out a low nickering noise and lifted its head.

"That sure is a pretty pony."

The shapeshifter thought for a moment. "Princess?" he replied. "Would you like to feed her an apple?"

"I sure would!" Harold said, dropping his pretend wooden pony in the grass and rushing up to the wagon. "Oh, boy, Mr. Neethling, thanks so much."

Mardochaiso placed the apple in the boy's hand.

"Keep your hand flat," the shapeshifter advised. "Otherwise, she might bite you by accident."

Harold drew back his hand, frightened.

"No need to be scared," Hodge said. "Princess is a good pony. She just really likes her treats and sometimes she gets a little hasty."

Harold stretched his arm out again toward the pony, the apple resting against the palm of his little hand. The pony finished off the apple and looked at the boy, licking away some of the slobber and apple pieces that clung to its whiskered muzzle.

"I think she's still hungry," Harold observed. "Can I give her another?"

Mardochaiso chuckled with delight.

"You're going to spoil the old girl."

"Really?" Harold said, worried. "I'm sorry, Mr. Neethling. I wouldn't want—"

The shapeshifter shook his head, chuckling.

"No, no, my boy, it's perfectly fine," he said, nodding toward the rear of the wagon. "It's her birthday and she's been a very good pony all year long."

"Really?" Harold said. "How old is she?"

Mardochaiso pulled back her lips and examined the pony's teeth.

"Twenty-five," he said. I guess she ain't got too many rides left in her."

Harold petted Princess' nose sadly. He looked like he might cry.

"Go ahead, give her another one," Mardochaiso urged. "Those folks in Leefside ain't going to make a fuss if a few are missing."

Thrilled, Harold climbed up into the wagon and disappeared into the back. Mardochaiso glanced toward the house and seeing the boy's mother still preoccupied with her chores, climbed aboard. The shapeshifter slipped into the back as well, sliding the curtain that covered the opening closed behind him. A few moments later, there was the sound of a brief struggle, a smothered shout, then a cracking of bone. The little wagon trembled once or twice more and then became very still. A few moments passed. Harold—or rather a startlingly realistic imitation of the boy— poked his head out, his cheeks flushed and his forehead glistening with sweat. The shapeshifter waited for his breathing to steady as he gazed in the direction of the cottage, eyes narrowing. Seeing no one out front, Mardochaiso slid from the wagon to the ground, a bright red apple clutched in one hand.

He offered the apple to Princess. The pony, seeming to sense the change, eyed him warily, snorted, rolled her eyes, and retreated a few steps.

"Ungrateful," Mardochaiso muttered, giving the pony a hard smack with the rein. "Go on. Get home!"

Princess lurched away from him, bewildered. The child's mother appeared from around the corner of the house, her arms heaped with laundry. Mardochaiso gave the pony another hard smack and it bolted off at a quick trot down the dirt road toward home, dragging the driverless wagon behind her.

"Harold!" his mother scolded. "What has gotten into you?"

"What?" the boy said, innocent.

"Don't you 'what' me," Rowena said crossly. "I saw you hit that pony. You know better than to treat the Lord's creatures like that."

Mardochaiso studied the woman a moment, then rushed to her, throwing his arms around her, tears rolling down his cheeks. He gave her a hug and Rowena winced, surprised at the strength in his skinny arms.

"I'm sorry, Mama," he said, whimpering. "That bad pony bit me."

Rowena glanced down at his arms and hands. "I don't see any marks," she said. "I hope you're not lying to me Harold. You know it's a sin to lie."

"He got me when I wasn't looking," the shapeshifter insisted with a mischievous smile. "Nipped me right in the ass."

"Harold!"

"Sorry, mother."

He rubbed the lower part of his back but stepped away quickly when she tried to lift the shirt to have a look for herself. Rowena eyed him, skeptical, then gazed down the road in the direction of the farmer's cottage. Pony and wagon had just turned into the dead farmer's driveway.

"Strange," she mumbled. "That wagon looked empty."

"No, it wasn't empty," Mardochaiso explained. "Mr. Neethling is in the back sleeping off his ale. You know how he drinks. Lucky he has such a smart pony to look after him and get him home when he's jugbitten."

"Drunk in the middle of the day?" Rowena said disapprovingly. "I'm quite sure God would disapprove of such behavior. Listen, Harold, I don't think you should talk to Mr. Neethling anymore. He's getting addled in the head."

Mardochaiso shrugged. "If it's what you want, Mother," he replied, feigning sadness. "I just thought he was all alone in the world and needed a friend and that it was, you know... the Christian thing to do."

Touched by the child's compassion, she reached down and gave him a hug. "Oh, Harold, you're such a dear, sweet, boy."

Rowena walked back toward the house. The little monster-boy, making galloping noises with his mouth, hopped after her astride his stick pony. Once inside, Mardochaiso watched the female human reach with a pair of iron tongs into a stonework oven crackling with coals and pull out a hot loaf.

"How does a nice crust of rye bread sound?"

She slid the loaf onto a trencher and laid the smoking tongs atop the oven to cool.

"You can keep your nasty old bread, Mommy." The voice was like Harold's but different, lower and full of gravel. "It smells nasty, like Beelzebub's filthy bottom."

Alarmed, Rowena turned suddenly, startled to find Harold gone. The stranger peering back at her could have been her twin. It was like gazing into a mirror. Same long ragged gray gown with a sleeveless tunic and a wimple to cover her hair. Same drawn, wrinkled face, making her look several seasons older than her thirty-seven years.

"Who – *what* are you?"

Her twin's lips twisted in an evil smile.

"Isn't it obvious," Mardochaiso snarled. "I'm Rowena Woodhame."

Rowena tried to control the shaking in her hands. "Where's my son?" she snarled. "What have you done with Harold?'

The shapeshifter started to move toward her, enjoying the moment.

Rowena snatched a heavy wooden rolling pin off the counter.

"Stay back," she warned.

The weight of the baker's tool in her hands gave her confidence. She was pretty certain she could crack the monster's skull with it if it gave her no other choice. But she had to be careful. It appeared this demon or witch, or whichever one of the Devil's servants it turned out to be, had armed itself as well. Something held out of sight behind its back. Some sort of weapon. But what?

And then she knew. The pony head. Little Harold's favorite toy.

It lay in the dirt, one of the painted-on brown eyes staring up at the thatched ceiling. The stick upon which the head rested was missing! Suddenly, the shapeshifter lunged at her, using the pointed shaft like a spear, ripping a large hole in the peasant woman's gown and piercing her shoulder.

Rowena screamed and swung the roller like a club, smashing it against the intruder's head. Furious, Mardochaiso ripped it from her hand. The shapeshifter then struck her hard across the face with a strength far beyond anything human. The force of the blow sent the peasant woman reeling backward. She fell against the stove, burning her hands, and dragging the iron tongs with her to the floor. The monster fell upon her. Rowena felt the cold hard hands around her throat, squeezing, choking the life from her until—

The shapeshifter suddenly stopped at the sound of a wagon's approach. Mardochaiso struck the peasant woman harder, this time knocking Rowena unconscious. He would deal with her later. The monster grabbed the peasant woman by the hair and dragged her across the dirt floor, shoving her into the coal hole, slamming the door, and locking it, then hurried to the window.

The old farmer's white pony and little wagon were parked outside in the road. A tall man in chainmail, equipped with a sword and crossbow, approached. It was the Captain of the Guard! Mardochaiso grabbed Rengaard by the arm, tears streaming down her cheeks.

"I beg of you, sir, you must help me!" she pleaded. "That monster has taken my only son and carried him off into the swamp."

She pointed toward a trail that started on the opposite side of the road, crossed a wheatfield, and disappeared into the thicket of cedars. Rengaard studied her face. He had dealt with peasants in the past. Most were simple hard-working people incapable of guile. To him, this one appeared to be much like any other.

"Get in the wagon," Rengaard he ordered. "You'll have to ride in the back. There's room for only one up front."

The two climbed inside, the peasant woman climbing up onto the seat, drawing aside the blanket that covered the opening, and slipping into the back. Rengaard smacked the pony across the rump with the rein and Princess broke into a fast trot, pulling the little wagon across the field toward the swamp. Rengaard smiled to himself at his turn of sudden good fortune.

He felt confident now that if he could catch the monster unawares and get off a good shot with his crossbow that all of this would be over soon. But despite his optimism, something was nagging at the back of his mind, something that threatened to spoil the pleasure of his imagined triumph. He found himself thinking of the boy whose body he had found in the back of the wagon and the corpse of the old man lying on the floor of the cottage.

"Say, Miss," he said, looking at the trail ahead. "What did you say your son looked like?"

"Oh, you know..." The voice was similar to the peasant woman's, but lower and rougher, as if her throat was full of gravel. "He was just an average boy, but he was special to me."

Mardochaiso pushed the blanket the rest of the way open, making barely a sound, his transformation from peasant woman to military captain complete. Rengaard breathed easy, resting his hand on the weapon that lay beside him on the seat. One well-placed shot. That was all. He could go home, collect his fortune, revel in his fame, and retire early, his reputation forever—

The pony tipped its ears back at the bone-snap and groan behind him, unaware that a new driver had taken her reins.

CRITICAL BLAST PUBLISHING
20¢
THE WEREWOLVES
ARE DUE ON MAPLE STREET
Sheri White
APPROVED BY THE READING CODE AUTHORITY
GRIPPING TERROR AS YOU NEVER EXPERIENCED!

HELIUM GAS & BALLOON SET Get away from the day to day grind of your boring life and steal a whole house while the owners are away.

SUPER SECRET BOOK SAFE The special camouflage feature activates, once placed on the book shelf. You'll never find it again.

CRUISE MISSILE MODEL KIT! When you need to deliver a message across the country. Optional payload BATS IN A BOX sold separately.

BOW AND ARROW KIT! When you need to go into battle on Tuesdays and don't know what weapon to take with you.

HOBO IN A BOX When your street is getting over-runned by homeless people and you need someone to speak their language and run them off to the next street down the block.

BATS, RATS AND CATS!

DIGITAL PUZZLE T-SHIRT Get people's undivided attention when they get engrossed trying to solve the constantly changing puzzles.

RENT AN ANGRY MIDGET! When you need to stop a Bully from harassing, or when you need to look like a decent human concerned for poor ugly monsters.

FISH BOWL FULL OF WORMS Are you tired of eating meat? Get yourself a bowl full of yummy worms and feel you are saving the planet.

EXPLODING DRINK Sit back and enjoy the highjinks as people unscrew their drink activating the chemical reaction, causing a foamy mess.

BOX OF LIVE BATS When you feel like a millionaire crime fighting hero and need to dress up your special cave, to give it that extra touch of atmosphere... a box of live bats is perfect for you. Food not included.

TRICK BLACK HOLE Get this special singularity and impress your friends by banishing them to other dimensions and realities.

MONSTER VALUE STAMP
THIS IS IT! CLIP THEM & COLLECT THEM ALL!

Sheri White's stories and non-fiction pieces have been published in many anthologies, including an essay included in the Notable Works for the HWA Mental Health Initiative, Flashes of Fantasy, published by Wicked Shadow Press, Tales from the Crust (edited by Max Booth III and David James Keaton), Halldark Holidays (edited by Gabino Iglesias), and The Horror Writers Association's Don't Turn Out the Lights (edited by Jonathan Maberry). Her collection, Sacrificial Lambs and Others, was published in 2018.

Once the werewolves outnumbered humans, life was never the same.

Lou pushed a button and the community gates opened outward, just enough for Jerry's car to get through.

Jerry slowed the car down to a stop at the guard's booth.

"Hey, Jerry. How are you today?"

"Oh, you know. As well as one can be these days. It's my turn to pick up this week's food and supply rations, so at least I'm out for a bit."

"Well, be careful out there."

"Thanks, Lou. Back soon."

The gates immediately closed and locked behind him.

Jerry was glad to see that the street cleaners had been through already and took care of the previous night's carnage. The mess was mostly small animals or stray pets, but occasionally you'd see a poor soul who didn't make it home in time.

Jerry clenched the steering wheel, closed his eyes, and took a deep breath.

I'll be fine. Daytime is safer. He turned right and white-knuckled the steering wheel.

He drove slowly, below the 30MPH speed limit. He'd heard rumors that cops were sometimes on the werewolves' side. He would not risk getting pulled over.

Jerry heard muffled screaming and cracked his window. The screaming was louder now, and he could see a woman up ahead getting hassled by two large men. They pushed her back and forth between them, laughing.

"We're just playing a game, sweetheart. What's the big deal?"

"Leave me alone, please! I need to get back to my kids."

Jerry slowed down, taking in the scene in front of him.

"Oh, do your kids need this?" The bigger of the two men held a carton of milk high up out of the woman's reach.

"I said give it back!" The woman was crying now. She turned her head and noticed Jerry crawling by. "Help me, Mister! Please, help!"

Jerry knew he could stop the car and unlock the door. The woman could run over and jump in fast. He considered it for a few seconds, then sped off, his tires screeching. He pretended not to hear the woman screaming the word *coward* at him.

But he couldn't take the chance those men could be monsters. Nobody could be sure who was a monster these days, whether werewolf or human.

He sped the rest of the way to the firehouse.

Jerry got in line under the A-E sign. He looked at the others waiting in their respective lines. Nobody spoke to each other, although they surreptitiously stole glances, everyone thinking the same thing.

Is anybody here a werewolf?

Jerry tapped his fingers on his leg. *It shouldn't take this long!*

He looked around to see if anyone else showed impatience and saw a man in the K-O line staring straight at him.

Jerry quickly looked away. *Who is that? Where do I know him from?* He perked up. *Oh, the "before times," maybe?*

He turned to his head to look again, hoping the guy had focused his attention elsewhere. But the man still stared at Jerry, his gaze now more of a glare, angry and piercing.

Jerry felt a little push on his back. "Buddy, it's your turn. Move up!"

"Oh, sorry." Jerry stepped up to the counter.

"Community name?" the woman behind bulletproof glass asked, her tone weary and bored.

"Um, Copperfield."

"Sir, you need to speak louder. What was that now?"

Jerry hesitated, not wanting the creepy guy to hear him.

"Copperfield," he answered a little louder.

"Do you have the Community ID card?"

"Oh, yes." He pulled his wallet from his front pocket with a shaky hand. The wallet slipped from his hand to the ground. He bent over to pick it up, and noticed creepy guy still staring at him when he stood back up.

He grinned at Jerry, showing impossibly white teeth. And were the canines just a little longer than the other teeth?

Jerry shivered. *I need to get out of here.*

"Okay, sir. Your pallet will be out back momentarily. Someone will help you load up your vehicle. NEXT!"

Jerry quickly headed to his car, daring a glance back. The man was no longer looking at him. *I bet that asshole does that just to scare people. As if we're not all living in constant terror already.*

Once volunteers filled his trunk, Jerry slammed it down to make sure it wouldn't pop open with so much stuff crammed inside. Just as he got in and turned the ignition, the creepy man jumped in front of his car and slapped the windshield with both hands. Then he moved to Jerry's window.

"Hey, man! Can I get a ride?'

Oh my god. Is he following me?

"No, sorry." Jerry pushed the driver's side window-up button, but the guy used the palms of his hands to keep it from rising.

"Come on, man! It's too far to walk back to my community."

"I saw you in line for supplies. Where's your car?" *Why are you talking to him you idiot? GO!*

"I came here with a friend from my community. I held his place in line while he took a leak. We forgot there wouldn't be enough room for me to ride back."

"Sorry, man. Can't help you. Good luck, though." Jerry tried raising his window again, but the guy still held the glass down.

"That's not very neighborly of you, Jerry."

"What? How... how do you know my name? Have we met before? At a barbecue or something?" OH MY GOD.

The guy stood up and flashed the terrifying grin that chilled Jerry earlier. He reached into his shirt pocket and pulled out a thin card.

"You dropped your Community ID." He flicked it into the car. The edge cut Jerry's nose as it whizzed by his face and landed on the passenger-side seat. "You should be more careful, you know. It's *dangerous* out here."

And then Jerry recognized him—he was the larger of the two men harassing that woman earlier.

Jerry sped off, wheels screeching, not caring if he hit the freak.

"Maybe I'll see you around, *Jerry from Copperfield!*" the man yelled after him. "Woooo!"

Jerry looked in his rearview mirror and saw the creep pumping a fist in the air. Jerry would have sworn the man just howled.

###

"Jesus, was he one of them? No. No, don't freak yourself out. They haven't intimidated people during the day. Or at least not until now. Could this be a new tactic to get access to us?"

Jerry talked out loud, hoping to calm himself down. It wasn't working.

"Okay, we'll have a town meeting this afternoon to figure out what to do. Everything will be *fine*."

A few minutes later, he passed the woman from earlier. She was on the sidewalk, covered in milk and blood. Her throat had been slashed and her torso ripped open, her intestines and other viscera next to her. Jerry took her open dead eyes as an accusation.

He pulled up to the gates and waited for Lou to let him in.

"Welcome back, Jerry."

"Glad to be back, that's for sure."

"You okay? You look stressed."

"I *am* stressed, Lou. Listen, can you get on the loudspeaker and announce a town meeting for 4:00 this afternoon?'

"Sure thing. Something serious going on?'

"Maybe. But we'll figure it out together as a community. Like always."

Jerry drove home after dropping the supplies at their community center. He heard Lou announce the meeting as he entered his house.

By 4:15, most neighbors had arrived at the park. Children played on the swings and slides, oblivious to the grown-ups' discussion.

Jerry explained what happened at the firehouse earlier that day and told them about the two men harassing the now-dead woman as well.

"So everything is *probably* fine," he concluded, "but I think we should put a few extra precautions in place. That one guy could be dangerous."

"Such as?" Eleanor asked.

"Okay, well, we should take turns at the gate booth in twos and threes. From sunset to sunrise. That's a start."

Eleanor scoffed. "Oh, please. What good will *that* do? Those things will be over the fences before you could sound an alarm!"

Jerry clenched his jaw. Good old Eleanor, always with a problem to every solution.

"Listen, the fence is pretty high and fortified with razor wire." Jerry gestured to the six-foot-high concrete fence with circles of sharp wire on the top. No werewolves allowed! and Fuck werewolves! were graffitied with spray paint, along with other crude sayings.

"The old lady's right!" Marvin called out. "That won't stop those things from getting in if they're determined. I'm surprised they haven't tried to get in before now!"

"They *have* tried," Olivia said. "You've just been too chickenshit to take a nighttime watch shift."

Marvin spun around and glared at Olivia standing behind him. "*Excuse me?* You know I have health issues."

She rolled her eyes as others snickered at the man. Aside from laziness, he had no real medical issues.

"Yeah, we know all about your *issues*, Marvin," another neighbor spoke up. "That's all you ever talk about!" Anytime he was asked for a favor, to do a task such as loading up supplies in the community center, or to help someone carry something, he would suddenly crouch as if just standing were hard and say he hadn't taken his meds yet and his body couldn't handle the stress.

Marvin looked around but couldn't determine who had just spoken. Then he shook his head. "This is how you all feel about me?"

"Everyone, please!" Jerry called out. "We're getting off track here!" The neighbors ignored him. He glanced around at the park and the kids playing in the sandbox. He clenched his hands in frustration that nobody would listen.

"Maybe if you cleaned up after your dog when you walk him, you wouldn't piss everyone off so much!" Eddie, only 17, puffed out his chest and practically got up in Marvin's face.

"Don't you dare talk to me like that, you little punk! I can't help that my back hurts too much to bend over and pick up Charlie's...uh, leavings. Show some respect!"

Eddie not-so-gently poked Marvin's chest with his finger. "Go to hell, you lazy old man." Murmurs of agreement and light clapping followed.

Jerry finally blew on a whistle he always kept in his pocket for luck. When the noise finally faded into a few whispers here and there, he spoke again. "Please, everyone! This needs to stop. We can have another meeting to address neighborhood issues, but right now we need to pull together in case we're attacked tonight. Okay? So listen—"

"Wait a minute!" yelled Eleanor.

Shut up, you old bat! "Yes?" Jerry responded through clenched teeth.

"How do we know this really happened?" The woman crossed her arms and looked around at the neighbors with a smug look.

Jerry's jaw dropped open. "What the hell? You're accusing me of lying?"

"Oh, hey! You know what I heard?" Eddie interrupted. "There are people who actually *work* with the werewolves." He spread his arms in an *I'm-just-sayin'* gesture.

"Everybody knows that, Eddie." Jerry sighed. "What's your point?"

"It's just…I don't know!" Eddie said in a flustered voice. "My dad told me after he got back from a supply run a few weeks ago."

Jerry shook his head. "Where *is* your dad, Eddie? He's the one who should be part of this discussion."

Eddie laughed with a cynical edge. "He's sleeping one off, dude. What else?"

"Okay, Eddie. Thanks for your input." Jerry clapped his hands for attention. "Folks, we don't have a lot of time left until dusk. We really need to—"

"No, first you need to *answer* Eleanor's question!" Jerry's friend Sean spoke up, anger in his voice.

"Are you kidding me, man? We've lived next door to each other for years! You've invited me to join your family for Thanksgiving and barbecues. How can you think I'm lying?"

"Here's how." Sean stepped closer to Jerry, almost nose to nose. "Where do you go at night, Jerry?"

"What? I'm home every night! Where could I go?"

"I've seen you leave your house and walk down the street, Jerry. Sometimes it's almost daylight when you get home."

"You've been *spying* on me? Why?"

Sean just stared at Jerry in silence.

"Look, what I do at night is *my* business, Sean, and it has nothing to do with this situation."

"You know, my kids have woken up in the middle of the night crying. They hear howling and are terrified werewolves are coming to eat them," Lucy said. She was a single mom, having lost her husband at the beginning. "Now I wonder if they're right."

"Oh, for crying out loud," Jerry said in exasperation. "That's Marvin's dog Charlie! I hear him too. Everyone does."

"Nope, Charlie don't howl," Marvin said. "He's old and deaf. Sleeps all night."

All eyes turned back to Jerry.

"There *are* other dogs around, you know." Jerry felt the command of the situation slipping away from him.

Nobody uttered a word. They just kept staring at him.

"I can't believe you people!" Jerry burst out. "Some creep harassed me today and could be one of *them*. We need to figure out together how to handle this!" He looked at the sky, realizing the sun was about to set. Hues of purple, pink, and red painted the sky. Jerry wanted to cry at the juxtaposition of beauty in the heavens and the hell they were living on Earth.

"But you can't prove it, Jerry."

His eyes met those of the speaker. "Really, Olivia? You too? You think I have something to do with what is happening?"

She blushed and looked away.

He sighed. "Then I don't know what else I can say to all of you." He shrugged, his palms up, beseeching. Then he saw Lou walking towards them. *Oh, thank God.*

"Look, here comes Lou. He'll back me up."

"Is this the meeting you had me announce?" asked Lou. "I wanted to be here earlier, but Alex relieved me late."

"Help me out, man. You saw me after my supply run earlier. I was obviously terrified, right? These people," he said, gesturing to the neighbors, "think I'm lying."

Lou shifted his feet and avoided meeting Jerry's eyes. "I mean, I noticed you were stressed out, and you said that you were. But you didn't seem terrified or anything. You didn't even tell me *why* you were stressed, just told me to announce this meeting."

More murmurs sounded from the group. Jerry covered his face with his hands and shook his head in despair.

"Oh, by the way—this note was left for you at the gate." Lou pulled a folded piece of white paper from his jeans pocket and held it out to Jerry.

Sean intercepted the note out of Lou's hand.

"Hey, that's private!" Jerry protested. He tried to take it from Sean, but Sean had already opened it. His eyes widened at what he read.

"Tell us what it says, Lou!" called out Eleanor. "He seems pretty nervous about you seeing it."

He read it aloud: "*Great seeing you today, Jerry. Thanks for your help. Everything is all set.*"

Immediately the group erupted into shouts and gasps.

"Oh, my God!"

"He's one of them!"

"Jerry's a werewolf!"

"He's setting us up to be slaughtered!"

Jerry furiously shook his head back and forth, beads of sweat flying off his forehead.

"No! No, I'm not! Please, you all know me!" Jerry tried to bolt, but Sean yanked him by his upper arm. Jerry screamed. "You dislocated my shoulder, you asshole!"

Before Sean could respond, menacing howls surrounded them from outside the high fences.

"Oh, my God! They're here!"

"The sun went down! How did we not notice?"

"Because the streetlights are on. And Jerry distracted us!"

Parents screamed for their children to run home as the parents raced behind them.

It was too late. Werewolves sprinted through the streets on all fours coming from the direction of the gates. They growled with teeth bared, spittle and foam flinging from their mouths, long sharp claws clicking on the pavement.

The wolves took the children down first. They screamed for their mommies before their throats gushed blood from the tears inflicted by the creatures. One child tried to run away, carrying his own arm in his opposite hand. The anguished wails of parents along with shrieks of horror and pain from the children combined into a cacophony of terror that filled the night air.

Blood spattered the swings and slides. Torn little bodies lay strewn about on the playground, blood and organs soaking the spongy safety mats, body parts everywhere. Some children lay clutched in their parents' tightened arms in their futile attempt at protecting the kids.

"Why did you do this to us, Jerry?" Sean gripped Jerry by the shoulders and shook him hard. "Why?"

Jerry screamed at the pain in his dislocated shoulder, then he sobbed. "I didn't! I swear!"

"Rot in hell, Jerry." Sean shoved him to the ground. Sean took off running as fast as he could but didn't get far before a werewolf leapt on him. Sean had no time to even scream before the creature ripped his throat out.

Jerry lay there, not even trying to get away, making himself listen to the carnage happening all around him. He turned his head and saw Eleanor pinned to the ground a few feet away from him. She made eye contact with Jerry and stared at him, then he realized Eleanor had been decapitated. The werewolf continued ripping away at her face, until the light in her eyes finally dimmed.

Olivia was already dead. He closed his eyes and whispered a prayer of thanks for the small mercy of not having to watch his lover die a horrific and painful death.

Then he felt hot breath on his face and sharp claws penetrating his chest. Jerry looked into the eyes of the creature about to kill him and knew. "It's you," he said before the teeth tore into his body.

By the time the sun rose, the werewolf pack had scattered, leaving behind death and destruction throughout the community.

A lucky few survived by hiding in their locked basements or closets until daylight, waking up to a new world for a second time.

A little boy who had hidden under the body of his best friend finally gathered the courage to emerge. He was covered in blood and gooey stuff from when his friends were killed. He walked around, staring at the dead people everywhere, slipping occasionally on the carnage on the street.

"Mommy! Mommy, come get me!" he called out, but got no answer. He looked at the grown-ups on the ground, looking for her. He found her a few minutes later, her eyes open but not seeing him. He saw blood on her too. He lay down with her, his back against her front, and put her arm around him. He didn't notice it wasn't attached to his mother's body. He cried softly until he fell asleep.

Two men walked through the neighborhood, stepping over bodies and limbs and making sure they didn't step in blood or other slick fluids. Here and there they noticed traumatized faces peeking out from behind curtains and blinds. Eventually they arrived at the front gate, still open wide from the previous night.

A man lay on his stomach, face down in a pool of blood spreading out from underneath him.

One of the men pushed the body over with the toe of his shoe.

"Ah, damn it. I didn't mean for Lou to get killed. He was a good guy."

"So, was it worth it?"

The man didn't respond. He stared down at Lou's bloody face, his eyes frozen forever in agony and terror.

"Dad! I need to know! Was all this worth it?"

A black SUV with tinted windows stopped at the gate. A back door opened, but it was too dark inside the vehicle to see the waiting passenger.

"I guess we'll find out soon, Eddie." He put his hand on his son's shoulder. Together they walked into the unknown.

3¢
USA
JOKULUXE
361
MONSTER
VALUE STAMP
THIS IS IT!
CLIP THEM
& COLLECT
THEM ALL!

CRITICAL BLAST PUBLISHING
20¢
APPROVED BY THE READING CODE AUTHORITY
A DAY TOO BRIGHT
Fulvio Gatti
GENERATION GAP CAN BE MURDER!

ATTENTION!

DEMONS!
VAMPIRES!
GHOULS!

SURVIVE TUESDAYS "YOU" DAYS!

DEFEAT BLACK MYSTIC ARTS KUNG-FU Tired of getting your ass kicked every Tuesday by Black Mystic Arts Kung-Fu fighters? CALL 666-HELP to enroll in self-defense training every Hellspawn should know to survive any dark alley encounter. Become a Ninth Circle Master of Judante!

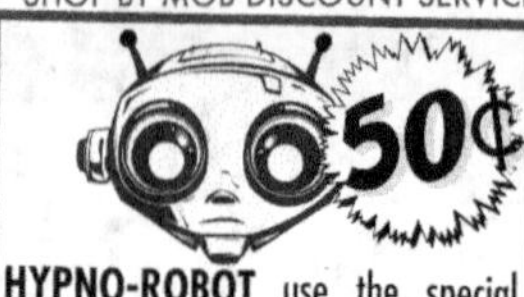

HYPNO-ROBOT use the special mind control eye harmonics to subdue the minds of your unwilling subjects. You'll never have to take out the trash and everyone will worship you as if their life depends on it.

MONSTER VALUE STAMP THIS IS IT! CLIP THEM & COLLECT THEM ALL!

SNAKES IN A MAIL BOX Get these total mother-f$%Ken poisonous snakes and mail them with your get well gift cards.

FISH BOWL FULL OF WORMS Are you tired of eating meat? Get yourself a bowl full of yummy worms and feel you are saving the planet.

HELIUM GAS & BALLOON SET Get away from the day to day grind of your boring life and steal a whole house while the owners are away.

RADIOACTIVE CANDY When you want to level up your personality and appear extra sweet to the people around you... and want to have a superpower over sugar... this candy's for you!

BOX OF LIVE BATS When you feel like a millionaire crime fighting hero and need to dress up your special cave, to give it that extra touch of atmosphere... a box of live bats is perfect for you. Food not included.

YOU ARE NOT THE THING!

Fulvio Gatti is an Italian speculative fiction author writing and publishing in his native tongue for 25 years. He has been writing in English for the global market since 2018. His stories can be found in Galaxy's Edge, and magazines and anthologies published in the US, UK, Canada, Northern Europe and Australia.

He's been a student of Kevin J. Anderson and Rebecca Moesta's Superstars Writing Seminars and part of Dave Wolverton's Apex Writing Group. He's also been a panelist at Worlcon/Discon III. An associate SFWA member, he lives with his wife and daughter on the wine hills of the Northwestern Italy.

You can only hide from your parents for so long. A few centuries, a millennium if you're lucky. Then, even if you've last seen her during the Italian Renaissance and you have clear memories of her spending too much time with Leonardo Da Vinci—enjoying his personality, his blood or both—the day will come when your mother comes knocking on your Brooklyn apartment door.

"Don't pretend you're not home, Nadia, my dear," she says, straightening up her pre-French-Revolution hat, same color as her dress and her umbrella. An almost-living ad about how you don't need to reflect in a mirror to be posh. "I can smell you."

I punch the door to unlock it—I had a key, during the Great Depression, then one of my cats swallowed it or something—and yank it open. I haven't changed it since the peephole is exceptional, and there's nowhere I can still find any glass as good as the one they made in the Republic of Venezia.

"Come in," I bark, checking the surroundings. Besides the bachelor Wall Street broker living two stories above, walking his dog, there's no living being around. The guy is quite fit, and mostly straight, so I considered seducing him once, just to drink some fresh blood. Then I remembered how bad those finance dudes taste.

Also, I don't do that anymore.

"Sorry for the mess," I tell Mom as she analyzes my humble abode, counting every speck of dust. She double-checks the stacks of vinyls all over the hallway; new tech, for her. "I've been trying to figure out for days how many of these twenty-first century albums will let me make some bucks fifty years from now, and whose are just trash fodder."

She pushes a fanged teddy bear away from the chair and sits by the living room table. "Saving for the future," Mom nods. "That's good."

I push away a bang of black hair then scratch my forehead as I debate whether to sit with her or to offer her something to drink. Yes, I'm pretending I'm just nervous—it's way worse.

"Please, Nadia, ignore the formalities and sit here with me," she says. "We have important matters to talk about."

This is so sudden, especially from her, that my discomfort peaks. "I *could* get some decent plasma from the fridge for you, in fact."

"You're kind, but I have already eaten." The way her gray eyes shimmer, probably thinking about assaulting some poor soul in a dark alley, gives me the creeps, just like it did back when Ramses was a living pharaoh to gossip about.

I give up and take my seat to her left. I can only wonder if this is some kind of metaphor, and she wants to put the pack back together. At the moment, the way she's stalling, anything is possible.

"So... I heard you and Dad are back together," I say, as an immediate thought.

A smile so subtle that she barely moves her lips. "You two keep in touch, don't you?"

In fact, I only consult him from time to time. Having been the secret Lynyrd Skynyrd band manager back in the day makes his network of underground music collectors probably the best on the planet. Too bad they all convinced him to turn them, and then for the stupid bloodsuckers-population-control rule he had to kill them all, faking accidents.

"He's a good man," Mom continues. "You're definitely more like him than you are like me." She puts her hand over mine. And I thought I was cold. "I have bad news for you, my dear." She ponders. "Bad, and some good."

"Go on, make my day," I weakly joke. "If we're creatures of evil, we must enjoy bad things."

Melancholy invades her flawless features. "You won't enjoy this one, I'm afraid," she begins, and I'm uncertain whether to find it promising. "You're not, truly, our child."

I burst into a laugh. She pulls back, upset.

"What's so funny?" she wonders.

I stand and walk around the table five times before the hilarity fades.

"I'm sorry, Mom," I manage to say, sitting back. "It's quite a no brainer that bloodsuckers can't reproduce the traditional way. You just turned me, back in Ancient Egypt. I was a street urchin or something."

"How do you know?"

"About being a street urchin?"

"No, about us not being able to reproduce like humans."

"Stephen King?"

She stiffens. "I don't know what you had to do with that old farmer in Boston before even the railway was built, but let me say it was very rude of him to tell you."

I've lost her. "Not *that* Stephen King." I have no idea who she's referring to, but she does have a good memory, and must have met many people with the same name.

"Who, then?"

"Never mind, Mom." I frown. "What's the good news, then? Now I'm worried."

"I'm not sure it's the right time..." she wonders, eyes wandering.

"We can wait until this civilization collapses, indeed," I reply, framing my vinyls with a concerned look. "It'd all be quieter. It might also get harder to travel, though."

Those gray eyes of hers shimmer again. "You believe it, too, right? That this human civilization is concluding its cycle, I mean."

"I wish I didn't," I say. "There are a lot of comforts I'd miss. Fast food and digital downloads. Not to mention how many hundreds of years it would take to afford a Brooklyn apartment again." I grimace. "But signals are signals and I've lived too long to ignore them."

She hammers her fingers on the table. Some kind of death sentence Egyptian drum rhythm betraying her excitement. "So, you'd agree with this," she says.

"Guess so."

"Your Dad and I are going to hibernate," she announces. "I won't go into details, but a scientist of our kind found a way to do it with little energy spent and perfect results."

I wonder whether being a shadow people that gathered most of their knowledge before electricity was even invented makes it easier to find low-impact solutions. Then I realize she's been waiting for my reaction with an unearthly benign expression painted on her face.

"Great," I say. "I guess."

"No surprise?" she asks.

"Living so long makes it quite an easy bet you'll change your mind about anything, one century or the other," I muse out loud. "I myself spent a full decade pretty convinced Abba were good."

She flashes a helpless grin. "You know, Nadia, my dear, sometimes you utter words and names way beyond my comprehension."

"It's mutual, Mom, don't worry." I stifle a giggle. "So, are you throwing a party or something?"

"Why should we?"

"Mom and Dad stop being dirty-minded people-eaters and go freezing into the future!" I suggest, feeling silly. "Or something like that."

"Oh." She suddenly looks hurt.

"What?"

"You still begrudge us for following our true nature, don't you?" She holds her gaze in that motherly, supernatural way that makes it impossible to lie to her.

I wave a hand. "It's not like that, I don't judge you," I ramble. "I love you both in my own quirky way. Hey, don't blame me for being a sociopath. You're the one who brought me up like that. Also, maybe having an adolescent body for thousands of years let me preserve some extra teenage angst, for all I know."

She relaxes. "What if I suggested you join us in hibernation?"

I chuckle, find the fanged teddy bear and start toying with it. "Come on, you know I won't do it."

"Why?"

I shrug. "Just, no."

"All right, then." She takes a business card from her purse. I'm surprised it's not a papyrus or something. "This is where you can find us if you change your mind. There'll be a few layers of security and bureaucracy, but you will get through."

I take the card, briefly reading the address. California. I wouldn't be surprised to find Jerry Garcia behind all this.

"Thank you, Mom."

She stands. "Will you be all right, on your own?"

I hold back a joke about having gone through colonialism, industrial revolution and two world wars without even knowing where she was. "I will, thank you."

"And what if... human civilization..." After her big speech, now she's back to being too polite to finish such a sentence.

"I try to keep optimistic." I grin. "They have all the smarts to go through the pandemic, climate change and, I guess, anything else."

"Good for you."

She's ready to walk back to the entrance, but she waits until I follow her.

"One last thing, my dear," she says, at the door.

I nod in expectation.

"The blood you drink to survive, the one you so eagerly label as 'cruelty-free.'" I picture my reserve down in the cellar freezer.

"What about it?"

"Your Dad wants you to know it's stolen," she explains, words as sharp as razors. "Organized crime has set up an underground distribution network that starts with stealing from blood donor organizations." Her lips twitch. "Sick humans die because they don't get their transfusion on time. And it's your fault."

I close the door behind her and barely keep from screaming. I forgot she'd been having the last word since Socrates ate his hemlock. Why did he owe a rooster to Asclepio? Because he'd just lost a bet with my freaking bloodsucking adoptive mother.

CRITICAL BLAST PUBLISHING
20¢
THE DEAD GIRL NEXT DOOR
Diana Olney
APPROVED BY THE READING CODE AUTHORITY
A BEAUTIFUL TALE OF LOVE AND DEATH!

HEAD KNIVES 100% stainless steal daggers that launch from the top of your head and kill any conversation you find boring.

FISH BOWL FULL OF WORMS Are you tired of eating meat? Get yourself a bowl full of yummy worms and feel you are saving the planet.

SUPER SECRET BOOK SAFE The special camouflage feature activates, once placed on the book shelf. You'll never find it again.

DIGITAL PUZZLE T-SHIRT Get people's undivided attention when they get engrossed trying to solve the constantly changing puzzles.

MONSTER VALUE STAMP THIS IS IT! CLIP THEM & COLLECT THEM ALL!

DEFEAT BLACK MYSTIC ARTS KUNG-FU Tired of getting your ass kicked every Tuesday by Black Mystic Arts Kung-Fu fighters? CALL 666-HELP to enroll in self-defense training every Hellspawn should know to survive any dark alley encounter. Become a Ninth Circle Master of Judante!

RENT AN ANGRY WOLF! When you need to rip apart your competition, or when you need to look like a decent human concerned for dogs or something, something.

BOX OF LIVE BATS When you feel like a millionaire crime fighting hero and need to dress up your special cave, to give it that extra touch of atmosphere... a box of live bats is perfect for you. Food not included.

Diana Olney is a Seattle based fiction writer, but she is most at home in the shadows, wandering the dark paths between nightmares and dreams. She has authored many twisted tales, which can be found in such chilling tomes as Drawn & Quartered, The Devil You Know Better, Dark Horses Magazine, Shallow Waters Vol. 9 (Crystal Lake Publishing), and the upcoming anthology, To Hell & Back. She is also the creator of Siren's Song, a horror themed comic series soon to be haunting bookshelves near you. Currently, she is writing two novellas and a leaning tower of short stories. Visit her at dianaolney.com for updates on her latest releases.

There's always been something irresistible about the girl next door. Maybe it's her smile; the sly smirk that glitters with the unspoken secrets of a modern Mona Lisa as she passes in the hall. Or her laugh, cascading like a gentle breeze through white picket fences and paper-thin walls. Maybe it's her figure; the curve of an hourglass hip in the window as she peels a brightly colored blouse off a diaphanous lower back tattoo. Or maybe it's just the proximity of all those pheromones, filling the air with the sweet, succulent scent of forbidden fruit. Maybe it's all of the above.

David James Fischer, struggling twenty-something and lifelong hopeless romantic, had no clue. But the fact remained, night after night, day after day, that Dave was falling—head over heels and entirely ass-backwards—for his girl next door. And he knew he was destined for a crash landing. The second he saw her, cupid's arrow hit him like a sledgehammer, sending him spiraling into a sinuous rabbit hole where the only possible way out was down.

This wasn't the first time, naturally. But in Dave's heart, it might have been the last. His hometown was a never-ending parade of temptation—it was Los Angeles, after all—but Violet, his tantalizing new neighbor, wasn't just eye candy. She was his dream girl, the daylight embodiment of every late-night fantasy he'd had since he was thirteen years old drooling over his mother's Cosmo magazines. Platinum blonde hair: check. Diamond-bright eyes: check. Seductive, come-hither smile: check. Au naturel figure with a hint of Wonder-Bra-enhanced cleavage: check and check. Thus, all Dave's lovestruck senses were in agreement: on paper, Violet was perfect.

There was only one problem: she might have been dead.

Dave couldn't prove it, of course. Not even to himself. His heart was set on Violet, but his mind was perpetually divided, caught in a dichotomous debate over the mortality of his mysterious love interest. On the one hand, she was beautiful; too beautiful, his enamored neuroses insisted, to possibly be suffering from decomposition. But there was something suspicious about her beauty too. Something sharp and serrated, like the blade of a lazily buried murder weapon waiting to be unearthed. Even behind closed doors, Dave could sense it haunting the halls, lingering beneath the allure of her exotic perfume. His ex-girlfriend had worn a similar fragrance. Similar, but not the same. Violet's scent was unique, a miasma of heady aroma far more potent than any of the expensive bottles his ex had in her vanity. It was sweet, yet abrasive, as if she'd mixed her latest Macy's purchase with a cocktail of heavy-duty chemicals. Drain cleaner maybe. Or something stronger. Lancôme with a pinch of paint thinner. Gucci Bloom cut with bleach. Chanel Number Five with a splash of formaldehyde.

Whatever her secret was, Dave got the feeling it was past its proposed shelf-life. Which was a bad sign. And yet, his infatuation continued undeterred. He wanted Violet. Wanted her so badly, he would have followed her anywhere. Even to the morgue.

Who knew, maybe he would. But in the meantime, he was taking notes. So, that was one check in the Soulmate column, one in the Living Dead Girl section, adding another shadow of doubt to the deep, dark grave his crush may or may not have crawled out of.

But—there was always a "but"—Dave had no reason to believe Violet was dangerous. Like every girl next door, she seemed far too warm to be a cold-blooded killer. In the short time since she'd moved into the apartment beside his, they'd exchanged less than twenty words, but she always smiled when she passed him in the halls, and in her glossy Cosmo girl visage, there wasn't a single hint or twitch of hostility. Or hunger. The dead were supposed to be ravenous, bloodthirsty cannibals, but the closest Violet had come to mauling him was the time she'd grazed his arm in the laundry room. He had a loose thread on his shirt, she'd told him. And when she reached for it, Dave's composure came undone, unraveling into a heap of tongue-tied heartstrings at her feet. Fortunately, Violet didn't seem to notice. She just kept smiling that picture perfect smile of hers, then sashayed around the awkward outpour, leaving him to clean up the mess.

He didn't blame her. Dave was quite a ladies' man, once upon a time, but his smooth-talking days were behind him. Or perhaps it was he who was lagging behind. In life. In love. In everything. As cliché as it sounded, Dave was a shadow of his former self, a man chewed up and spit out by the saw-toothed jaws of heartbreak. And ironically, the owner of those lethal lips wasn't even a cannibal. That he knew of.

But she was a man-eater. Gina, the aforementioned ex-girlfriend, was a predator of the deadliest caliber, a sultry serpent with a bite as toxic as a diamondback rattlesnake. The only difference was, she killed her prey slowly—and painfully—leaving her victims to drown in the rivers of venom she left in her wake.

That was another story, though. A tragic tale Dave was sick and tired of telling. Right now, all he wanted to do was turn the page. Ideally, to a chapter featuring his crush as the centerfold. She didn't have to be nude (not in chapter one, anyway), but every story needed a love interest, and dead or alive, Dave couldn't help but imagine a happy ending with Violet. The kind that unfolded between the crisp, white covers of king-sized bed.

But—yup, there was another one—not all love stories ended that way. The "best" ones, the ones people remembered (*Antony & Cleopatra, Romeo & Juliet*—hell, even *Titanic*), had a much darker twist, reminding cupid's victims of the dangers of the phrase "till Death."

Not that Dave was an expert on the subject. Despite his proximity to the mass graves and overcrowded cemeteries that lined the bad part of town—the only part Dave could afford to rent in—he had very little experience with death. Even the living variety. Thanks to the atomic gusto of the military, the terror of the outbreak fizzled back when he was a kid, counting screams like sheep from his fortress of security blankets. It wasn't an ideal upbringing, but those sleepless nights were just a bad dream now, locked away with the rest of the monsters in his childhood closet. The same went for all Dave's friends. This was a *post*-post-apocalyptic world they were living in, a city rebuilt on the bones of the dead.

And as far as anyone knew, they really were dead. The cannibals, or zeds, as the media called them, since no one had the guts to utter the word in its entirety, were long gone, with the exception of an unlucky few that were kept for research—in the hopes of finding a cure, supposedly. These creatures, according to the government, posed no threat to society. Dave believed that, most of the time, but like everyone else in the country, he'd heard the rumors—all of them. He'd heard the ones about zed experimentation, whispers of walking corpses sizzled into submission by shock therapy à la Frankenstein's laboratory. He'd heard the ones about genetic modification, viral mutation, and grave robbing; the top secret breeding of underground armies of darkness. And he'd heard the ones about dead escapees, fleeing the research labs to "live" among humanity. Granted, none of those theories were particularly plausible, save for the last one. Zeds were deceased, technically, but they weren't brain dead, and it was possible that eventually, some of them would get smart enough to blend in.

Meanwhile, Dave had been doing some investigating of his own. Though he wasn't the greatest detective. He had never been the type to buy into conspiracies, but after meeting Violet, he'd spent more than he cared to admit on copies of the *Dead Enquirer*, the latest issue of which featured a cover story entitled, "Killer Strippers Exposed: Ten Signs Your Next Lap Dance Could be Deadly." A ridiculous title, made significantly less ridiculous by the fact that even fully dressed, his girl next door exhibited five signs out of ten. She was pale, mysterious, soft spoken, and despite her ability to maintain balance in six-inch heels, her body language was a little stiff, a sure warning of rigor mortis. Oh, and there was her strange scent, obviously. Though in the magazine, this odor was simply described as the smell of "decay and/or rot." Apparently, the alleged femme fatales didn't bother with formaldehyde. They preferred to bathe in blood.

Yup. Actual fucking blood.

That was all hearsay, of course. From a not-so-reliable source (the *Enquirer* now had three imprints: the *Dead Enquirer*, *Alien Enquirer*, and *Monstrous Enquirer*, a behemoth periodical devoted entirely to "I saw Sasquatch—jerking off in the backwoods!" type stories). But the zine's propensity for bullshit aside, the cannibal stripper exposé was enough to give any guy nightmares. According to an "anonymous inside source," today's living dead girls were regular Elizabeth Bathory's, staving off decomposition by literally soaking up the life of their red-blooded victims.

Dave shivered, envisioning his dream girl slipping into a candlelit bloodbath, milky skin slathered in a hemorrhage of scarlet death as she picked slivers of bone from her teeth. Not exactly his teenage fantasy.

BUT—this was a big one, printed in all caps—he was still crazy about Violet. And much as he hated to admit it, Dave knew what that meant. It meant she would eat him alive—even if she wasn't dead.

On the porch, Dave fired up a cigarette, staring across the street through the center of an evanescent smoke ring. Beneath the midday sun, LA foot traffic simmered, beads of sweat sparkling like gems on the bodies cruising the sidewalk. And from where he was sitting, they looked ripe for the taking. The city was in full bloom today, filled with home-grown gardens of earthly delights, but thus far, there was no sign of his shrinking Violet.

Dave's breath shuddered as he exhaled, pouring a thick, mercurial fog onto the hazy glow of his cigarette. This was his third one since arriving home, a last-ditch attempt to cool his deep-fried nerves. It wasn't working very well, but for the time being, he had nothing better to do. He was waiting, not very subtly, for the arrival of his girl next door, which according to his watch, would be any second. Dave didn't know much about Violet, but as her neighbor, he was privy to the ins and outs of her schedule. She worked in the hive of anonymous office buildings down the street, and often came home shortly after he did, filling the hall of the cramped apartment complex with the tell-tale *click-clack* of her platform heels. Dave took comfort in that sound, even though all he usually did was listen, pausing his post-work routine to nod along to the rhythm of her gait.

But this time, he wasn't hiding. In the interest of self-preservation, Dave needed to put his mind at ease, a task which, insane as it sounded, required him to check for signs six through ten from the *Enquirer* article. His subject, though, had yet to arrive, and as he waited, his anxiety level had gone from manageable to manic. Granted, some of his jitters were self-induced. He'd had a long day at the "office"—aka Disc Junkies, the preferred record store of the city's finest DJs, hipsters, and stoners—and to stay alert, he'd upped his caffeine intake, a choice he was now regretting. Dave loved a good latte as much as the next guy, but that last double espresso had his pulse pounding in triple time, ruining any chance of peace or quiet.

Meanwhile, the LA beauty pageant carried on as usual. On the street, another flock of fallen angels sailed by, sun-kissed skin and balletic limbs gliding with feather-light grace over the pavement. But Dave didn't bother checking them out. He was a firm believer in monogamy, even when it came to courtship. Unfortunately, the objects of his affection weren't always as devout.

Especially the last one...

Dave shook his head, hoping to cast his duplicitous ex out of it. Too late. Gina may not have been dead, but the ghosts of her betrayal continued to haunt him, crowding his mind with the skeletal overflow of her exploding closet. And the worst part was, they were still rotting. According to the media, Dave was lucky to live in a time free from infectious corpses, but those peppy newscasters would have pissed their pantsuits if they'd seen the disease in his bloodstream. A disease that, if left unchecked, would run rampant, twisting like barbed wire through his brain until he begged for a lobotomy.

Unless he managed to find an antidote. But even then, there were no guarantees. For most romantics, heartsickness was incurable.

Dave frowned at his shrinking cigarette, ruminating on the risks of rushing into a rebound. It was a treacherous road, following the beat of a broken heart. Especially with the architect of its ruin so close to home. Adding insult to injury, his ex lived just a few blocks away, right in the middle of his route to work. So, it was no wonder Dave was a wreck. The second he stepped outside, he was Dante to her inferno, sweltering in the heat of his old flame. But on the bright side, that blaze would go out. Soon. Gina's vacation to Paris was coming up—a trip originally planned for two—and once she was gone, Dave would be free to play the field on his own terms. No more defense, no more games, no more looking over his shoulder every time he left the house.

But Dave didn't want to wait. Why hide from an old flame when there was a five-alarm fire burning next door?

I'm sensing a pattern here.

That's what Dave's therapist would have said, if he could afford a session. Then, he'd launch into a very pricey round of twenty questions, a game which Dave habitually lost. His shrink, a pretentious Ivy League type with a penchant for equally pretentious observations, turned every session into an interrogation, salting wounds and twisting knives. Dave's ex had left a lot of those, arming her skeletal legions to the teeth, and over the last month, the blades had rusted enough to necessitate a tetanus shot.

The result wasn't pretty. Not to Dave, anyway. Gina had a thing for pretty boys, bad boys too, but in his head, they were depraved, rawboned wraiths; hundred-watt grins and chiseled jaws spreading Glasgow-wide as they slunk out from the shadows of his memory. The mere thought of these lascivious spectres made Dave's skin crawl, particularly when he was pressed to recount the various states of X-rated coitus in which he'd found them. His shrink, on the other hand, seemed to find those gory details fascinating, scribbling frantically in his chart as he mapped out the stains of Dave's dirty laundry. Then, at the sound of the buzzer, he pushed his hapless patient straight to the reception desk, leaving Dave with a head full of old, angry wounds and a brand-new hole in his wallet.

Bastard.

There was a silver lining, however. Since he'd already wasted several paychecks on torture masquerading as therapy, Dave could now skip the interrogation and shoot right to the finish line, completing the Q and A singlehandedly. He didn't have a grad degree, but he'd snuck enough peeks at his chart to know what kinds of questions Dr. Yale was asking about him.

Number one: Is the patient capable of change? His pattern of poor decisions does not inspire confidence.

Dave cringed. That sounded familiar.

Number two: Or (and this is an intriguing notion), is the patient so traumatized by his past that his neuroses are prone to sabotage, turning every fear into a self-fulfilling prophecy?

Dave cocked his head.

That's a new one.

It was a good question. So good that the second he tried to answer it, his mind flooded with a dozen others, unleashing an rising tide of What Ifs. What if he was wrong about Violet? What if all this worry, all this stress, all this agonizing over the girl next door and her hypothetical lack of a pulse was just paranoia talking? What if he was so jaded, his own mind had turned against him, disguising his dream as a nightmare? And what if, despite what the *Enquirer* had to say, all he really had to do to make his dream come true was...

Wake the fuck up.

Dave slumped in his seat on the porch, sinking deeper into the notion. This wasn't a Dr. Yale hypothesis, not verbatim, anyway, but it was the type of educated guess an Ivy League psychiatrist would come up with—more educated than any half-cocked rebuttal his wounded pride could impart. And maybe that was part of the problem. Maybe...Dave's issues were all in his head. Maybe...after twenty-six years of failed jobs, goals, and relationships, he was finally losing his grip.

Sucking down the last of his cigarette, Dave furrowed his brow, searching the smoke for additional insight. He didn't have any, but thankfully, he knew someone who might. And based on the briskness of her pace, she would arrive in:

Five...

Across the street, a pair of platform heels struck the pavement, sky-high fanfare rising above the murmur of the milling crowd.

Four...

The crowd parted; swells of pedestrians split like atoms by the approach of a blonde bombshell.

Three...

Two...

The blonde looked his way, smiled. Dave's heart skipped a beat.

One.

"Hey, neighbor," his dream girl purred, her cadence smooth as the spotless ensemble sheathing her ethereal silhouette. She smelled like the fragrance counter at a strip mall in Hades, but looked like an angel. An angel of mercy.

Dave stiffened, clenching his jaw to keep it from dropping. "Hey," he croaked.

Violet tilted her head, scanning the smoldering heavens, and her diamond eyes softened to rose gold, gilded sparks divining the impending sunset. Then she shifted her gaze, glancing from Dave's dumbfounded expression to the burnt-out cigarette in his hand. "Got another one of those?"

Do the dead smoke?

Dave stepped up to the mirror, then paused, waiting for his reflection to chime in. For once, his answer came quickly.

Maybe. It's not like they have to worry about cancer.

Dave chuckled softly to himself, and his mirrored twin joined in, echoing his amusement at what could only be called a very private joke. Finally, he was feeling okay. Not good, not great, but distant enough from the weight of his heavyset ennui to enjoy a little breathing room. And he didn't look too bad either. While unlucky in love, Dave was blessed in other areas, and surprisingly, his history of heartbreak had yet to put a dent in the display of good fortune staring back at him from the vanity. Even in the smoky haze of the dimly lit bathroom, his reflection made an attractive portrait, shadows framing his features in soft twilight.

You, sir, are a work of art.

That's what Dave's first girlfriend used to say, anyway. Mandy, his high-school sweetheart, was a big Renaissance buff, quoting art history lectures whenever he needed a compliment. She wasn't a saint, of course—none of his exes were—but to this day, Dave still cherished his memories of her. Particularly the ones where she compared his scruffy likeness to the immaculate Rembrandt's and Caravaggio's in the pages of her textbooks. He was no masterpiece, but given the scarcity of surviving art in a post-apocalyptic era, Dave happily accepted the compliment. And he kept it, even when Mandy's affections moved on to the rising star of the school's drama department, a chiseled he-god who bore a striking resemblance to the statue of David.

But at least she'd had the decency to break up with him first. Unlike a certain two-timing serpent he knew.

Dave leaned into the tepid sixty-watt light of the vanity, washing out the encroaching dark of melancholia. Today was not about the past. Today, tonight, and each and every moment therein—however many Dave was allotted—was about moving forward. And that was all thanks to his girl next door.

Though whether he'd be thanking her or begging for mercy was still up for debate.

Reining in his bundled nerves, Dave cracked a timid smile, testing the integrity of his charisma. His mojo needed a lot of work—the meandering procession of fumbles that nearly derailed his conversation with Violet proved that much—but if he smiled enough, perhaps she would be more inclined to kiss him than eat him. Less than an hour ago, as they'd shared that fateful smoke on the porch, she seemed to be leaning more towards the former than the latter. Especially when she'd taken the second to last drag, wrapping her cherry red lips around the end of Dave's cigarette before tenderly placing it between his own. At the taste of the secondhand kiss, his heart soared, even when he detected a hint of decay beneath the fruity flavor of her lip gloss.

But Dave never got a chance to analyze the content of his cigarette. Before the smoke cleared, Violet was already closing in, eyes gleaming with diamantine radiance as she asked him if he'd like to come over. Tonight. She had a new bottle of white wine she'd been waiting to open, a housewarming gift better enjoyed with two glasses than one.

Dave was surprised, completely shell-shocked actually, but for once, he didn't hesitate. The second the question left Violet's enticing lips, he snatched it out of the air, rescuing the invitation before awkward silence could ruin the moment. Yes, he said, he'd love to have a drink. Hell, if he'd been honest, she had him at "come over."

Not that Dave wasn't scared shitless. He was. Of many things. At the top of the list were his date's as-yet undisclosed appetites, and his inability to sate them, between the sheets or otherwise. In his defense, Violet was terrifying, in more ways than one. Her beauty and kindness and sudden, unsolicited interest in him were just as intimidating as the spiderweb veins delineating her too-pale-for-LA skin and the way she never seemed to blink. But—there was that "but" again—all his insecurity aside, Dave couldn't let the girl next door be the one that got away, now could he?

When he saw Violet, Dave screamed.

But no one heard him. Not even his doe-eyed date. Fortunately, Dave's cries were all internal, for the time being. In the silence hanging between them, his pulse cranked up the volume, blood-rush echoing between his ears like a built-in metronome. Next, his lungs chimed in, rasping staccato breaths above the backbeat. His heart, though, was the loudest by far, rattling his bones like the reverb of a blown-out stereo. Or the new Metallica album, which incidentally, was still stuck in his head after a long day of hawking records at work.

Dave shook himself, trying not to lose his cool in front of his crush. But his lovestruck system wasn't making it easy. It was cupid's arrow all over again, only this time, that devious little cherub was waving his weapon like a baton, turning Dave's body into his own personal orchestra.

On the bright side, his date was quite adept at stealing the spotlight.

"I'm glad you made it," Violet said, sizing him up from beneath a veil of dark, feathered lashes. Her tone sounded nonchalant, but the glint in her eyes told him she meant it.

But...

He swore she still hadn't blinked.

"Yeah, me too..." Dave fumbled, already tripping over his words. When he'd left his place, he'd had an entire list of lines ready, practiced them even, just to ensure he was prepared. But no amount of preparation could have defended against the disarming bombshell standing in the doorway.

And her outfit wasn't helping. Violet always dressed well, Dave had noticed that the first time he saw her, mixing classic girl-next-door chic with a subtle flourish of LA glamor. But tonight, his dazzling crush was dressed to the nines, despite the fact that she was technically only wearing two articles of clothing, neither of which came close to covering her voluptuous frame. Crafted from a fabric that had the appearance of leather and the translucency of gauze, Violet's little black dress was practically microscopic, dwarfed by the sky-high heels strapped to her slender ankles. Meanwhile, Dave's hormones were having a spike of their own. He didn't have to think hard to picture Violet naked, but thanks to his post-break-up dry spell, his imagination was running wild anyway, racing straight from foreplay to the steamy, sweat-soaked finish line.

"...hey, anyone home?"

Dave leapt to attention, roused from his stupor. Before him, Violet's coquettish expression tilted quizzically, slanting at an angle that suggested she'd repeated the question more than once.

"Yeah, of course." Dave smirked, praying his devilish grin would save him the embarrassment of admitting his sins. Lust being number one, as usual. He hadn't taken his eyes off Violet, but thanks to the plunging neckline of her dress, his attention had dipped lower than he'd intended.

"Is something wrong?" Violet followed his gaze, eyeing her pint-sized outfit. "Sorry, I totally overdressed." An ironic choice of words.

"No, you didn't!" Dave laughed, a little too loudly. "I mean...you look great. Amazing, actually."

"Yeah?"

"Yeah," Dave echoed.

"Thank you," his date replied, beaming with a refined surety much more convincing than Dave's half-assed attempt at charm. Her pose was polished, practiced; a snapshot of airbrushed allure ready to print on the cover of *Maxim*. Her scent, though, reeked of *Enquirer* material: florals—lavender, or jasmine maybe—wilting in a chemical bath. The funerary bouquet of an open casket.

"You're very sweet," Violet added. She ran a hand along the taut waistline of her dress, smoothing out an imaginary wrinkle.

"Is that a Vivienne Westwood?" Dave ventured, shifting focus away from the odor. He was starting to remember his lines now, and his date's daring attire was a great place to start.

Violet smiled thoughtfully. "Umm…"

Dave smiled back, assuming he was on the right track. His break-up may have cramped his style, but the infidelity severance package was full of parting gifts, including an aptitude for fragrance and a newfound (and usually useless) eye for fashion. His ex was a textbook shopaholic, meaning her idea of a romantic evening was to blow his date night budget at Nordstrom, then quiz him on all the trends in the latest issue of Vogue. If he scored well, her new wardrobe would end up on the floor. If not, he went home alone. So, Dave did his homework. Until she dumped him. After he caught Gina modeling Victoria's Secret for one of his coworkers, her back issues of Vogue were the first thing to go—straight to the dumpster—but six weeks later, his fashion sense was still a solid B average.

In the doorway, his date looked completely lost. "Honestly, I have no idea." She paused and raised an expertly manicured eyebrow. "Is that a designer?"

"Oh..." Dave flushed, abashed by his failure to impress. "Yeah. But it doesn't matter. My...my ex was really into fashion—"

Shit.

Dave stopped himself, biting his tongue before it could betray him any further. He'd just broken the golden rule of the rebound: never, ever mention an ex-girlfriend.

"Sorry..." he added, shrinking back in anticipation of being given the boot. Or stiletto, as it were.

Thankfully, his crush didn't seem offended. "It's okay," she assured him. "Really." Violet broke into a girlish giggle, sweet as birdsong, honeyed intonations beating like wings against the air. But she didn't seem to be laughing at Dave's expense. Her laugh was an invitation, a tease, a dare to come closer. When the flutter of mirth subsided, she reached out, playfully smacking him on the shoulder. Her touch was like frostbite.

Jesus.

Dave shivered in silence, clapping a hand over the goosebumps crawling down his arm.

"Hey, maybe we could go shopping sometime!" his companion chirped. "But I'd love a drink first. Why don't you come in, and we can open the wine?"

"Sounds good." Dave squared his shoulders, straightening himself out. He wasn't sure how to read Violet's below average temperature. Paranoia pointed straight to the postmortem, inciting chilling visions of stiff, frozen limbs bending and cracking, creeping like tendrils from a frost-burnt morgue drawer. But there could have been a simpler explanation. It was July, after all, and the California heat had everyone's air conditioning cranked. So for all he knew, his date just needed to warm up. As did he, clearly.

"You coming?" Violet turned and glanced over her shoulder, leading the way into the apartment. On her lips, promises glittered, embers of a secret fire waiting to be fed. A fire untouched by fear or death, by pain or tears, blazing as if to spite to the harsh winter cold of her skin.

But—this was the last one, Dave hoped—that didn't mean the fire wouldn't spread. In fact, he was already starting to sweat.

The moment Violet kissed him, Dave knew he was done for. He'd known that for a while, if he was being honest with himself, since before he even walked in her door. He was a hopeless romantic, after all, which in this disenchanted era of one-night stands and incurable STDs and careless, crooked love triangles-turned squares and quatrefoils, made him a damned soul, flesh and bone forever tethered to the crushing gallows of heartbreak. So, it was no surprise to Dave when the night took a dark turn. Not when, during a *Dawn of the Dead* adjacent make-out session, his lover's lips started to wander, trailing suddenly from his neck onto his chest. Not even when her soft, tender affection sharpened to razors, sinking jagged canines into his skin.

But what did surprise him was how much he enjoyed it.

Dr. Yale—and Freud, and Jung, and Darwin too, probably—would have had thoughts on the subject. They would have wanted to study him, to crack him like an egg and inspect every neuron, every vein, every pulse of hard-wired pathos, dissecting desires like the anonymous innards of a new species. Anomalies like these had to be researched, examined, classified, in the name of science, before the subject could make a run for it.

But Dave didn't want to run. Not when he was looking at her.

Beside him, Violet's quiet countenance hovered in thoughtful repose, Mona Lisa smile painted scarlet by the sheen of bloodlust. But Dave didn't move. Didn't flinch. Didn't even recoil from the cold hands that were exploring his anatomy, charting constellations from the pour of his heart. Instead, he looked down, following the crimson web back to its inception, into the dark, gaping mouth of the wound. The sight of it scared him, yes, shook him to the depths of his very core, but as Dr. Yale would have pointed out, there was more to this equation than fight or flight. Which was probably why Dave hadn't tried to get away. Or defend himself. Beneath all the blood and gore, his heart was wide open, swelling like a rose in bloom. And in the hot, red center of those ripened vessels, something new was starting to grow. Something that had twisted his mortal terror in vines of ecstasy, smothering the fear of death in a sweet, sanguine embrace that refused to let go.

And it felt good. So good, he hoped she never would.

At Dave's side, a sigh slipped between ruby red lips, soft and gentle as a summer breeze brushing his skin. Then, slowly and with an air of melancholy worlds apart from the cold, lizard-brained stigma of her species, the creature attached to the sigh began to pull away, sinking into the arms of the plush leather sofa. And as she moved, Dave felt himself fall—all over again. But he saw no need to resist. In his eyes, she was a goddess worthy of worship, worthy of blood.

Violet raised a slender hand, tracing the claret streaks staining her lace bra, one of the few garments to survive the evening's violent foreplay. With the other, she took Dave's hand in hers. Then, she spoke.

"I know you must have a lot of questions," Violet said, lacing her fingers through his. "So, I'm going to make this easy. I'm going to give you all the answers. You don't even have to say anything. Not unless there's something I miss."

On the other side of the loveseat, Dave plucked his discarded t-shirt from between the cushions and pressed it to his chest, hoping to stifle his weeping wound. But he didn't say a word. He'd been speechless for a while already, since around the time Violet took her top off, and the thrill of near-nudity was enough to leave him stunned, let alone the savage passion that followed.

Remarkably, there wasn't much pain—that must have been the virus working its magic, killing off nerves behind the scenes—so Dave never bothered to scream. But if he opened his mouth now, he feared he'd wind up speaking in tongues, or moans, or groans, or more likely, all of the above; adopting the slurred, blood-drunk speech of the legions of dead he would presumably soon be joining. Which would be embarrassing. It was too late to impress his date, but if these were his final moments, he'd rather spend them in silence, preserving the crumbling vestige of his dignity, than blathering like an extra from a Robert Romero movie.

His deceased lover, on the other hand, never seemed to get tongue tied. So, that was one more mystery to add to the books.

"That sound okay?"

Dave turned to his date and nodded, head lolling in acquiescence.

"Okay, cool," Violet said, cover girl smile beaming red-carpet bright. The blood on her lips was beginning to dry, framing her words in what to the untrained eye could have been nothing more than red lipstick. If it hadn't been for her signature scent—that tell-tale mix of florals, decay, and formaldehyde—she would have been ready for her close-up. "First off—don't worry, I'm not going to kill you. But I think you already knew that. You're a sharp guy. Though you might not know that, contrary to popular belief, I don't kill people. Not anymore." She paused, giving Dave's hand a reassuring squeeze. "I used to have...problems with aggression. Violence. Impulse control. But that's all over now. I've been...rehabilitated."

Dave's eyes went wide, shock glazing his dilated pupils. The rumors were true, then. The grave robbing, the experiments, the escaped test subjects, all of it. In the back of his mind, he wondered how many injections and electrodes and toxic chemicals had given life to the angel of death in front of him. A fuck-ton, probably.

"I still have to eat, of course," she explained, noting her companion's surprise. "But I'm not a monster. Or an animal. I'm still human, you know."

Dave glanced at his blood-splattered chest, quietly counting heartbeats. So was he, for the time being.

Violet shifted in her seat, extending a long, fishnet-clad leg out from the sofa. As she stretched, a series of loud cracks shot out from the slender limb, like the sound of kindling being snapped into pieces. Yet on her face, there was no visible sign of discomfort. "Sorry, rigor mortis is a bitch," she laughed, lowering her spiked heel down to the floor. "But the rest of it isn't so bad. Not for a Jane Doe, anyway. Between you and me, my life before this...well, it wasn't much of a life. That's how I ended up in the morgue. I know this sounds crazy, but..."

"Oh..." Dave started to speak, then thought better of it. He didn't see the need to tell Violet, but from where he was sitting, they'd passed crazy a while ago.

"For me, death was like a second chance. I mean...if this hadn't happened, I wouldn't have even been buried. Girls like me don't get funerals." Still clutching Dave's hand, Violet sighed and leaned back, receding deeper into the sofa. "But after they picked me up, I was embalmed right away. So, I don't have to worry as much about decomp. A little formaldehyde goes a long way, if you keep up with it."

Dave narrowed his eyes. He was right about that too, then. Apparently, he'd been right about a lot of things. Even the gory details of his date's beauty regimen. Her checkered past, though, was news to him.

"The dietary requirements aren't ideal, obviously. It used to be tough, trying to get a decent meal without making a mess. But I've got it worked out now. A few months ago, I landed a part-time gig at South Med—you know, the school where they send the organ donors?"

Dave nodded. He knew. South Med was infamous for cutting corners. Literally and figuratively. Rumor had it that when the school reopened after the outbreak, half the bodies they used for anatomical instruction were overflow from the mass graves of zed victims. That was before his time, though he vividly remembered his parents talking about the protests. The city was more than happy to free up space in the cemeteries, but the bereaved families didn't take it so well.

"Anyway," Violet said, sweeping a hand through the cascade of platinum locks curled around her shoulder. "You wouldn't believe how laissez-faire their security is. No one notices if I stay after hours...or if a few cuts of meat go missing."

"Wow," Dave whispered. He had more to say, but at the moment, words were lost to him. Among other things. The pour of his wound was turning inward, submerging his senses in a well of catharsis that from the inside, seemed bottomless— which was strange, given everything he'd heard about the infection. After the bite Violet had taken out of him, he should have been crawling the walls by now. Instead, he felt stoned; high as a kite and still totally love-drunk. Not that Violet's post-mortem confessional wasn't shocking. Had he been more lucid, he'd be feverishly debating which was crazier: human remains being referred to as "meat," or a member of the living dead using the term "laissez-faire." He'd always thought Violet was too well spoken to be a zed (that was a big check on his Soulmate list), but whoever was responsible for her version of the virus was owed a Nobel prize.

"...the pay is a joke, but the professor is a total pushover," Violet was saying, skirting her gaze across the room as another laugh roiled from her lips. It wasn't very convincing though. The glimmer in her eyes was distant now, a star eclipsed by a tempest of rolling fog. "Long story short, I'm not going to eat you. I ate already. And like I said, I'm not going to kill you, either. Unless..." she lowered her voice, slipping into a hushed, throaty timbre that would have been sexy, under less dire circumstances. "Unless you want me to."

In the wake of her words, Dave's heart snapped to attention, rattling the bars of its cage so hard, it was as if the love-struck muscle was about to finally, after twenty-six years of solitary confinement, break loose. And it was breaking, he knew. But this time, it wouldn't bounce back.

Unless...

Unless he gave it to her.

Violet shot him a sympathetic look, unspoken apologies written in frantic scrawl across her face. "We don't have much time. Before you...change. But you can choose. You can choose to be like me...to be with me," she paused, sighing into the empty space between his face and hers.

Dave scooted closer, urging her to continue.

Violet squeezed his hand tighter. "But you'll have to make a decision—soon. And I'm sorry for that. I'm sorry for...for everything. The truth is, I've just been so lonely. I'm still getting used to this, and I haven't found anyone else who...who..." she trailed off, and the storm in her eyes started to swell, pooling with silver rain as a teardrop diamond slipped onto her cheek.

Without a second thought, Dave reached out and caught it, cradling the tear like the precious gem he knew it was. "It's okay.... I get it," he whispered, straining to speak over the hammer of his heart. "You just needed some company."

Beside him, Violet's million-dollar smile made a tentative twenty-buck comeback. "You're not upset?"

"No." Dave shook his head. "I was...but..." he gazed into Violet's eyes, watching himself mirror her smile, "Not anymore."

Dave pulled a knife from the open drawer and held it aloft, inspecting the integrity of the blade. In his hand, the stainless steel gleamed eagerly, florescence refracting into hungry sparks along its serrated edge. Yes, this one would get the job done. He lowered the cleaver as he turned and crossed the kitchen, making his way to the chopping block.

With every step, Dave stiffened, tightening his grip on the razor-sharp implement. Truth be told, he was overdue for some new cutlery, but this one was practically brand new. It was a gift—the kind he would never ask for—from Gina, reigning Queen of the Man-eaters, for their six-month anniversary, and he'd made a point never to use it. Aside from one night of drunken post-break up self-loathing, whereupon he'd considered testing the blade on himself. He didn't do it, though. Like his love for the aforementioned succubus, the urge to self-mutilate was fleeting, waning like stale moonlight into the long, dark hours of inebriation before finally burying itself below the mind-numbing hangover that followed. So, the blade had remained in its drawer, lonely and forgotten.

Until now.

Dave stood over the chopping block, cleaver in hand, eyeing the evening's fare longingly. Dinner wasn't for another hour or so, but the sight of the main course was already making him salivate. Which wasn't surprising. He'd had a light lunch, but even if he'd gone for the T-bone he'd been craving, he'd still be ravenous. No matter how much he ate, his appetite was never truly satisfied. Night and day, the hunger remained, gnawing at his insides like an extra set of teeth. This made waiting for dinner an uphill battle. The old Dave never complained if his meal was late—or if he had to skip a few to pay the rent—but these days, patience wasn't the easiest virtue to come by. But he would wait, because she was worth it. She was always, always worth it.

Keeping a firm hold on the knife, Dave reached into the pocket of his Levi's and retrieved his cigarettes. He'd been trying to cut back in the hopes of improving his oral hygiene, which hadn't been looking good lately, but if there was ever a time for an appetite suppressant, this was it. Plus, a little smoke might enhance the flavor of the meat.

Two drags later, Dave felt a little more at ease. Cinching his cigarette between his lips, he raised the knife, then sunk the steel blade into the meat, making the ceremonial first cut of the evening. The cleaver did not disappoint. Beneath the edge of the blade, fat and sinew melted like butter, falling away to reveal the smooth shape of what would soon become tonight's special. Dave flushed, suspense simmering in his cold veins. Plus a few other areas. He couldn't wait to dig in, but deep down, he was more excited for dessert than anything else on the menu. That was his favorite part of every evening.

It took a long time to prepare the meal. So long, Dave not only burned through three more cigarettes, but completely forgot to check the clock. And just as he was making the final cut, hyper-focused on the symmetry of the supple size-four tenderloin, the knock at the door made him jump so hard he nearly lost a finger.

"Damn it!"

Dave abandoned the knife and raised his hand, checking the damage as he went for the door. The cut wasn't deep, but it still stung. He winced, automatically pressing the wounded digit against his t-shirt. It wouldn't bleed much, he knew that, but old habits die hard. Among other things.

A lot had changed over the past few weeks—that was the understatement of the year, of his lifetime, really—but more than anything, it was the pain that got under Dave's skin. So to speak.

Shouldn't all these fucking nerves be dead already?

That was a question he'd have to save for later. It was almost time for dinner.

Dave opened the door to a dream; an arresting vision of ivory skin and flowing silk so fine and delicate, it was as if he was gazing at a falling star, or a wisp of cloud, clocking the shifting shape of a mirage that could vanish at any moment. But she didn't, of course. The girl next door was starving, too. He could see it in her smile, in her posture, in her eyes, in the flicker of smoke signals that spoke only his name. She had been waiting for this night all day, waiting for her love to sate the hunger no one else could.

"You okay, babe?" Violet asked. She tossed a wave of golden hair over her snow-white shoulder, part fairy-tale, part Gene Juarez commercial.

"Yeah, of course," Dave whispered, shrinking into an umbra of humility. No matter how much time he spent bathing in Violet's limelight, he was still taken aback by her radiance. Since he hadn't known his sweetheart when she was alive, he couldn't help but wonder if she'd always had this kind of glamor, or if, by some serendipitous twist of fate, death had given it to her.

She reached over, trailing her fingers down his left arm. "You sure? What's going on here?"

"Oh, right," he chuckled, glancing at the injured hand still tucked in the hem of his shirt. "Just a little kitchen scrape. No big deal."

"Hmm..." Violet bit her lower lip. Next to her immaculate attire, the lipstick she'd chosen looked like an accident, a painful one; like she'd somehow mistaken a switchblade for her go-to glossy Revlon. Dave knew she hadn't, that was just the light—*her* light—playing tricks on him, but nonetheless, the dark, wet red on her lips didn't seem like make-up. It was the red of disasters: of highway hit and runs, of wine stains on satin, of slit wrists in a bathtub. But with Violet, there were no accidents. Everything was intentional. Before Dave could say another word, she reached out and took hold of his arm, drawing him closer. "Let me see."

Dave let his arm go slack, watching while the girl next door slowly uncurled his fingers. In her grasp, the wounded digit pulsed, the lingering echo of a beat he'd already given up. "It's fine, really."

"I'll be the judge of that," she insisted. She held the afflicted hand up to her face, studying the injured flesh. Along the edge of the cut, a single drop of blood glistened, wet as a fresh dew drop. "Aww," she tittered playfully. "You're bleeding."

Dave raised an eyebrow. That was a surprise. He'd cut himself shaving this morning. No blood. Plenty of sweat, though—all those extra chemicals had to go somewhere.

He was sweating bullets now.

"This might be the last time, you know. So that makes this a special occasion." Violet zeroed in, gaping at the droplet hungrily. Then she parted her blood-red lips, slipping the tip of his finger between them.

"Oh," Dave murmured, freezing like a deer in headlights as Violet ran her tongue along his lacerated fingertip. His heart was still, silent as the grave he should have been buried in, but in the stiff, frozen branches of his bones, he could feel a pulse, coursing electric through his rigid frame until it reached his loins. He may have been dead, but there was one part of his anatomy that still worked.

Thank God for rigor mortis.

Violet beamed as she released his hand, satisfied with her work. "Hey, now," she teased. "Let's not get ahead of ourselves."

Dave crossed his arms, folding into himself. "Sorry."

"Hey, I'm just playing. You'll get yours." His date giggled, laughter sending minute shivers down her hourglass silhouette as she stepped inside. She shut the door behind her. "After we eat."

"Oh, yeah..." Dave glanced over his shoulder and into the kitchen, where a lavish feast was ready to be served. For a second there, he'd forgotten how hungry he was.

"So," Violet said, following his lead, "what's for dinner?"

Dave grinned. As if she didn't know.

"*Holy shit.*" Violet licked her lips, knife clenched between bone white fingers as she sawed off another sample of tenderloin. "This is to *die* for."

Dave chuckled, soaking up the praise. "Thanks, babe."

He downed a quick sip of merlot—the cheap stuff, poured ostensibly into his best glasses—before taking a generous bite of his own. In the clash of his teeth, the meat ruptured, flesh and tendons and spiderweb veins pureed by primal hunger. Dave inhaled the morsel and dove right back in, plunging his cutlery into the rare delicacy on his plate. He'd given his date the tenderest cuts, so his steak was a little tougher, but he didn't mind. They'd already split the rib-eye—Dave's culinary *pièce de résistance*, hand rubbed and marinated in imported olive oil—and he didn't want to be greedy. Plus, his carving skills were getting pretty good. With expert precision, he worked his knife through the flank, seamlessly severing flesh from bone. As he cut, the meat bled in rivers, staining the polished face of the pale China.

Across the table, Violet was quickly devouring her entrée. She looked up with a laugh, her lilting giggle a choral crescendo over the metallic scrape of steel against porcelain. Her eyes were wide as saucers, like she'd just slipped through the pearly gates and snuck a peek at God. "What did you season this with?"

Dave leaned forward, admiring the familiar flesh on her plate. "Just garlic...and a pinch of Johnny's."

"Hmm..." Violet swallowed another bite, then set down her fork, pausing the feast. "Johnny's *is* great on everything," she admitted, pursing her hemorrhage-red lips. "But that's really all you did?"

Dave nodded. Despite how much time he'd spent in the kitchen, the meat didn't need much seasoning. Or cooking. Vengeance, he had learned, was a dish best served medium rare.

"Well, you must have the magic touch, then. I mean..." his date swooned, "there's no fucking way she could have tasted this good *before*."

"No, she didn't," Dave agreed. "But..." he added with a smirk, "she's still not half as good as you." He reached over the table, taking his lover's hand in his. At his touch, sparks flew between them.

But the real magic was just beginning.

The girl next door smiled, and her gaze ignited, engulfing the room in the glow of burning diamonds. And in that moment, Dave knew he was right. Because this girl wasn't just good—she was his saving grace, his goddess, an angel incarnate. And even in the City of Angels, halos like Violet's were hard to come by. But as luck would have it, hers was big enough for two.

3¢
USA
MIRTHQUAKE
MONSTER
VALUE STAMP
THIS IS IT!
CLIP THEM
& COLLECT
THEM ALL!

CRITICAL BLAST PUBLISHING
20¢
IN THE PINES
Ray Zacek
APPROVED BY THE READING CODE AUTHORITY
WHERE NOBODY WILL SEE YOU DIE!

COCAINE FOR PETS When your pets become too excited during mating season and you don't want additional burden of feeding more pets, shot them up with some fine liquid snow and chill them out.

HEAD KNIVES 100% stainless steal daggers that launch from the top of your head and kill any conversation you find boring.

1to1 MODEL PIRATE SHIP! Some assembly required. Glue NOT included. Recommend a private Island cove as the staging areo.

MONSTER VALUE STAMP THIS IS IT! CLIP THEM & COLLECT THEM ALL!

HYPNO-ROBOT use the special mind control eye harmonics to subdue the minds of your unwilling subjects. You'll never have to take out the trash and everyone will worship you as if their life depends on it.

DIGITAL PUZZLE T-SHIRT Get people's undivided attention when they get engrossed trying to solve the constantly changing puzzles.

HOBO IN A BOX When your street is getting over-runned by homeless people and you need someone to speak their language and run them off to the next street down the block.

BECOME A PIRATE IN ONE WEEK! Learn to talk and kill like a Pirate. Optional hand and leg amputation. Pirate Ship sold separately. Arrrrrr.

MAKE MINE MONSTERS!

LEARN TO PLAY THE GUITAR! When you can't get a date for the weekend, rent a sexy Guitar Teacher to impress your friends and maybe you just might learn something too.

Ray Zacek is a retired fed living in Tampa, Florida. An inveterate scribbler, he writes dark fiction, horror, satire, and crime/noir. His work has been published by Critical Blast, All Due Respect, Shotgun Honey, Out of the Gutter, Denver Horror Collective, Deadman's Tome, Allegory Ezine, Sirens Call, and Tule Fog Press, among other venues. His fiction is available on Amazon. At present Ray is finishing a Florida Gothic novel, Don't Be Cruel, about a north Florida Elvis cult.

> *In the pines, in the pines*
> *Where the sun never shines*
>> Traditional American folk song

The bamboo laughed at Robert Jordan's efforts to eradicate it. He cut down a patch with Sawzall and machete and the bamboo grew back almost overnight.

Robert and Marcie Jordan worked like demons to renovate the house in rural Pungo, south of Virginia Beach. They followed an established plan. To wit, buy a distressed property for hard cash, renovate, and resell. They worked fast, living on-site in their Fleetwood RV, and doing most of the work themselves. New floors and countertops, cabinets, plumbing, paint, and landscaping.

On the Pungo property, landscaping proved the obstacle. The bamboo behind the house had grown monstrous and wild. It towered, emitted creaking noises as it swayed in the breeze, and inundated the yard with a thick carpet of yellow, blade-shaped leaves. Robert glared at it.

"Maybe we could harvest it and sell it," said Marcie.

"That's too much trouble," said Robert. "We're property fixer-uppers not farmers. I want it gone!"

Things that Robert Jordan wanted gone, generally, *went*. He contracted a crew and conducted a total scorched earth campaign on the bamboo. A squad of men chattered in Spanish and worked while Latin pop music blared. They chopped the bamboo down to ground level and hauled the branches to a dump truck. Then a stump grinder rolled in on tank treads; a roaring, turbo diesel-powered beast with a razor wheel that slashed bamboo roots and a scraper blade that finished the job, raising a suffocating cloud of dust.

Robert Jordan exulted. He won. But with the thick screen of bamboo gone, Robert and Marcie Jordan owned a perfect view of their neighbor's property. Rural Virginia scenic vista it was not.

Under scrawny, spear-like pines sat a ramshackle grey clapboard house with a rusty tin roof and satellite dish. A red brick chimney clung to its side. A ragged, limp Confederate flag hung from a dormer window. Junk had accumulated in the lee of the sagging porch. Trash. Tattered lawn furniture. A concrete lawn jockey, its shiny ebony head smashed. A disassembled lawn mower. Rusty oil drums and plastic detritus. Piles of scrap metal and discarded machine parts. A blackened stone fire pit and piles of empty beer bottles. In the gravel sat a mud-splattered Ford F-10 pickup truck, old jalopies of indeterminate make, and a blazing red Mustang GT on cinderblocks without tires, rims, windshield, or upholstery.

"Hideous," said Marcie.

"Yeah, absolutely," said Robert. He calculated. "That's a fifteen percent reduction in After Repair Value."

At twilight they sat in foldable lounge chairs under the canopy of their Fleetwood RV and drank Bloody Mary's while chunks of porterhouse roasted on a hibachi. The dismal tableau across the property line chilled their spirits. They knew nothing about their neighbor. Hadn't even caught a glimpse of whomever lived there. The dilapidated house remained quiet as a tomb.

"We ought to be celebrating," said Robert. "We've been here a month and we're ahead of schedule."

"We were better off with the bamboo curtain," said Marcie as she glugged Bloody Mary.

Robert removed the steaks from the grill. Rare, red, and juicy, the way they preferred it. He dropped the meat on plates with sliced beets and wild mushrooms. They ate in silence. Robert chewed, thinking, grinding his molars.

"I'll pay them a nice, neighborly visit," said Robert. "I'll make an appeal to reason. Maybe I can induce them to clean up the place."

Marcie scoffed. "Think about a privacy fence."

A road designated Featherbed Loop branched off from Princess Anne Road, the main artery through Pungo, Virginia, and meandered for several country miles, unpaved, rutted and cratered, past Robert and Marcie's house, past pine and hemlock strands and Virginia DOT signs Swiss-cheesed with bullet holes, and along the edge of a tannin-stained creek the color of lapsang souchong. Eventually Robert reached the grey clapboard house with a galvanized tin mailbox on a rotting wood post, lettered Fernfox.

Robert Jordan rode his bike. Upon arrival he removed his helmet and walked to the house, calling hello.

"Hallo!" Someone answered. A man's voice. A bearded man in coveralls emerged from behind the canvas flap covering a lean-to shed on the side of the house. A stout man about sixty years of age, long straggly grey hair under a greasy baseball cap, rolled up sleeves showing hirsute arms bristling with dark hair thick as steel wool. A fierce body odor preceded him.

"Can I he'p you?" his voice a deep bass.

Robert tried to sound as plummy and positive as possible. "Hello! I'm your neighbor, Robert Jordan. I live over there." He pointed across the weedy field to his house and RV.

The bearded man looked at the house with heavy-lidded eyes, and looked at Robert, as if trying to make the connection. Finally, he nodded. "That place. People name of Carmody lived there. They was bankrupt, I believe."

"Yeah, it was a foreclosure sale," Robert replied. "Never actually met the owners."

The old man guffawed. "Nor did I. Until now, that is. Privilege to meet you, sir. Pardon me for not shaking hands." He held up his hands, palms wrapped in dirty bandages, fingers gnarled, knuckles like a rock formation, nails long and black.

"That's okay," said Robert.

"I'm Monroe Fernfox," the man announced. "I'm retired on disability, and this here is my home and my haven." With a sweeping motion he indicated the premises.

"Nice, very nice," Robert lied. "You live alone?"

"Nossir, but times I wish I did." Fernfox put two fingers in his mouth and whistled, a high-pitched screech that made Robert cringe. Then Monroe yelled at the house. "Bring it on out and be sociable. We got company."

The screen door slammed as three people emerged from the house and stood on the porch. Two younger men in ragged jeans and t-shirts, as stout and grizzled as Monroe, both squinting in the daylight. Sleeves of dark tats unfurled under their beefy, furry arms. A slender young woman in a tank top and cut off denim shorts accompanied them. Her green eyes remained wide open, and feral, scared, Robert noted, as if she might dash for cover at any moment. One of the men crooked his arm around her neck and tugged her to his body, petting her hair as if she were a skittish cat.

"I'm a widower," announced Monroe. "The missus died years ago. Of lupus." He shrugged. "Save the condolences, for I'm over it. These here rascals are my sons. That's Fo'c'sle, Folk for short, named in honor of his great great granddaddy who was a clipper ship captain and ran the Union blockade. That other is Jimmy, and his wife Lilybeth."

"We're not married," Lilybeth blurted out.

"Shut up," Jimmy told her. He gripped her by the neck and pulled her to his shoulder.

The old man fixed her with a stern scowl, as if to reprimand her for speaking out of turn. "Lilybeth, go in the house and get some tea for us and our guest." He turned to Robert with an accommodating smile. "Perhaps you'd like some sweet tea?"

"Sure," Robert replied.

Monroe's bushy eyebrows elevated. He chortled. "Maybe something stronger? Eh?"

"Oh, no, thanks." Robert demurred. "Tea is fine."

"Squeeze some lemons into it too," Jimmy said and reached out to squeeze one of the girl's breasts. Lilybeth slapped his hand away and scurried into the house. The screen door slammed again. The brothers exchanged wolfish grins; their teeth were yellow as corn. They gawped at Robert holding his Allez-Allez ten-speed, clad in black nylon bicycle shorts and a bright orange polo shirt, with an undisguised mixture of amusement and scorn.

Monroe finger-wagged them. "Wipe those smirks off your stupid faces. I will not tolerate rude behavior toward a guest and Mr. Jordan is our guest. Are you hearing me?"

"Yes, daddy," Folk and Jimmy said in unison. They ceased grinning.

Monroe turned to Robert. "I apologize for my boys." He turned to his sons, raising his voice, growling. "Forget'n their fuck'n manners! Shame!" Folk and Jimmy cowered, hangdog, contrite, and silent.

"That's okay," Robert said, conciliatory, hoping the peevish old man would be placated. He needed Monroe Fernfox to focus.

"Nossir," said Monroe. "Ill-mannered and uncouth is never okay. Fernfoxes have lived in Tidewater Virginia since 1789 and was once a right proud family. I lament how our lineage has forfeit its dignity and become sluggards." He glowered at his sons.

Robert nodded. "I see," he said, trying to project earnest sympathy while suppressing a grin. The bathos amused him.

"Now, sir," Monroe's mood shifted to quizzical, a rheumy eye twitched, and his attention focused on Robert.

"Call me Robert." He smiled. His cheeks ached.

"Alright, Robert." Monroe furrowed his brow and rubbed the bridge of his nose with two fingers, black half-moons of grime under each fingernail. "Well, Robert, believe me or don't, but Monroe Fernfox possesses right extraordinary powers of divination."

"Uh-huh." Thinking *what weird shit is this?* Was Monroe Fernfox one of those rural savants who claimed to find water with a dowsing stick?

"You are not here on a social call," said Monroe, eyes wide open, studying Robert. "Tell me what the nature of your business is. Be blunt. I admire a man who speaks his piece plainly."

"Okay," Robert replied, abashed, but deciding, what the hell, cut to the chase. "I want to discuss your property. It is your homestead and haven, I know, and I respect that, of course. But I'll be candid. It's a mess."

"A mess?" The old man mulled this over a few moments, pursing his lips, and letting his dark eyes survey his homestead. "I suppose, yes, since you mention it, the place could stand some improvement." He pointed at Robert and Marcie's house. "Is that what you and your missus are all about, fixing up the Carmody place?"

"Yes, and let's talk property values." Robert fell back on a handy bromide. "Your home is your single most important investment."

Monroe nodded as if in agreement. He laughed, suddenly jovial. "Well," he drawled. "We Fernfoxes never been aces in the art of gain. But you, Robert, now, you I take for what they call a flipper. A house flipper, that is. I've seen them on the cable TV channel."

"HGTV, daddy," said Jimmy.

Monroe snapped at his son. "Shut up! I am talking!" He resumed speaking to Robert, calm but sly, grinning. "You and your missus are going to fix up and sell that Carmody house, are you not? Reaping a quick profit thereby?"

"I see nothing wrong with that," said Robert, a bit defensive. "My wife Marcie and I work hard and make a good living improving real estate."

"Once you finish here," Monroe said, "you will mosey along to somewhere else and do it again. Is that so?"

Robert nodded. "Precisely. And we are good with that."

"But it ain't rooted," Monroe asserted. "You traipse about in that big caravan of yours and you put down no roots." He shook his head. "There's something not right about that."

The screen door slammed again. Lilybeth carried a tray with a plastic pitcher and tumblers and a paper plate of cookies, piled high.

"You sure took your time, little bitch," Jimmy said to her. He reached for cookies.

"Guests first!" Monroe barked, and Jimmy shuddered and removed his paw from the cookie plate. "What did I tell you about *manners?* Like talking to a damn block of wood!"

Lilybeth placed the tray on the spool jar by the tarp and poured a tumbler of sweet tea for Robert. He said no thanks on the cookies. When Lilybeth handed him his tea, she slipped a small, folded piece of paper surreptitiously from her pale white hand to his. Robert tucked it beneath the elastic of his cycling shorts without any of the Fernfox males noticing. The sons shambled from the porch and attacked the cookies.

"I see nothing wrong with what my wife and I do," Robert said to Monroe. "I'm sorry you think otherwise."

The old man shrugged. "Well, we all got to live according to our own light." He slurped tea and emitted a dry cackle of a laugh. "Or by the darkness that forsakes the light."

"Uh-huh." Robert pondered whether that remark was profound or simply nuts and leaned toward the latter interpretation. He sipped his tea. Sicky sweet and lemony, awful, puke-inducing. He placed the tumbler on the spool table and put on his biking helmet. "If you'll excuse me, I need to get back and get to work. Think about what I said, Monroe. About cleaning up this place. Putting things in order. It's to your advantage, I assure you."

"I will think upon it," Monroe said, in a tone of voice that convinced Robert the man would neither think upon it nor make any serious effort to improve the property. "Oh, by the way, neighbor, we are fixing to have us a sort of get-together tonight and I expect things will get a mite raucous."

Jimmy and Folk laughed, splattering crumbs like gravel. They grinned, as if savoring a private joke at Robert's expense, munched on cookies and poked one another in the ribs. Jimmy put his hirsute arm around Lilybeth. She squirmed. She stared at Robert, her lips quivering, her blue eyes intent. Pleading?

"Sorry for any disturbance," Monroe said. "I'd invite y'all but it's kindred only. No offense meant."

"None taken," Robert said. "Have a good evening. Enjoy your get-together with, uh, your kindred." He strained to sound sincere. "Nice to have met you and your family."

The old man responded with a slight bow. "Same here and goodbye to you, sir. May the Ruler of Demons never snatch your soul."

"I'm not worried about that," replied Robert, after staring for a few gobsmacked seconds at the old man.

Monroe retreated behind the tarp. The brothers, like wary canines, and the girl stared at him as Robert walked his bike back to the gravel road. Robert heard them chuckling and whispering. He mounted the bike, pedaled a safe distance, out of their sight, and stopped to unfold the note Lilybeth had handed him.

Help me pleese Ima prisner, it read in a jittery scrawl. *There aminuls.*

"They're assholes," said Marcie that night after Robert told her about his visit and showed her the note. "Just listen to them out there!"

They sprawled on the lush queen mattress in their RV bedroom, both exhausted after working on the house the afternoon and evening. Peeking through the curtains of the side window, they could see the bonfire by the Fernfox house, orange flames licking at the night sky, and hear the serenade— a cacophony of banjo plucking, screeching fiddle, whoops, shouts, chittering, and strident voices. They sang a doleful rendition of *The Night They Drove Old Dixie Down.*

"This is a cry for help," said Robert, holding the note in his hand, Exhibit A. "The girl's scared. The fear, the abuse, the desperation, are palpable. She's vulnerable, a damsel in distress, and you know I have a penchant for damsels in distress."

Marcie rolled her eyes. "They are morons and nothing but trouble. Don't, I repeat, *don't* get entangled in their sordid business. Give this note to the sheriff's office or social services and let the authorities deal with... whatever." She flailed her hands as if to flick away something mucous, nasty, and sticky.

"Alright," Robert replied. He slipped the girl's note into a clear plastic envelope and sealed the envelope, as if securing evidence, and deposited it in a cabinet drawer.

Marcie approved. "Good. Now, we have property to improve and resell and we have an unholy fucking mess on the periphery. Let me say it again: privacy fence."

"Aha," said Robert.

"I hate it when you say *aha.*" Marcie sighed. His keen aha always signified that Robert Jordan had an inspiration, or had devised a scheme, or was about to indulge some devious whim.

"I searched property records," said Robert, tapping his Acer laptop. "Guess who owns the Fernfox property."

"Monroe Fernfox," Marcie said.

"No, the City of Virginia Beach for all intents and purposes. They haven't paid property taxes in a dog's age. We can buy it at auction for the unpaid taxes."

"No." Marcie twisted her face into a disapproving frown and shook her head. "That's additional time, trouble, and expense and will require an eviction. No! That's unwise. Privacy fence instead."

"No, I prefer my plan," said Robert and he waved his hands as if engaged in prestidigitation. "*Vulpes expello*."

"No." Marcie insisted. "Privacy fence, privacy fence, privacy fence."

"Wait! Listen!" Robert sat up suddenly, alert.

"What?" said Marcie, alarmed. "I don't hear anything."

"That's what's strange!"

The utter, minatory silence, fraught with dread, unnerved him. Something primal in Robert's brain stem flared and sent shivers of apprehension through his body. He took a deep breath. Then another. A series of deep breaths centered him. Marcie nodded, her eyes narrowing, pupils dilated; now she felt the same sharp sinister vibe. Robert leaped from bed to the window, lifted the curtains, and peered outside. Clouds had parted and moonlight streamed, rendering the landscape pewter. A full moon dominated the night sky. Across the no-man's-land between properties, only a wreath of smoke remained of the bonfire. He spied no one, detected no movement; no glimmer of light came from the Fernfox house.

Then—*like that*—the howling started.

Robert and Marcie crouched by the window, petrified. They held each other's hands. The howls increased, blending into a mad chorus, punctuated by growling, snarling, barking, guttural cries, angry woofs, yelps, yips, and long, mournful high-pitched whines. A woman -- Lilybeth? -- screamed, babbled, and moaned, in agony or sexual ecstasy, and then she howled with the others.

Inside an hour, clouds concealed the moon and silence reigned again.

Robert removed a bottle of Fireball from the cabinet and took a hefty swig. "Well," he said, breaking the tension. "Our first full moon here. Wow. Wasn't that fun?"

"Shit." Marcie crawled back into bed and rolled the duvet over her. She declined the Fireball. "I realize now why we got this place for so cheap."

Robert nodded and drank more Fireball. The whiskey and cinnamon ignited in his mouth, blazed on his tongue, and sizzled down his gullet, warming his heart and belly. Fireball felt good. Restorative, but not quite. "Yeah," he said, his voice rueful, "and there goes the neighborhood."

"We need to reassess our plan," said Marcie in her bland, inarguable, matter-of-fact voice.

"Pronto, for sure." Robert kept a tight grip on the bottle and parted the curtains again to survey the area. A heavy blanket of silver cirrostratus drifting westward played peekaboo around a haloed moon. Darkness enshrouded the Fernfox premises. Nothing stirred. Robert looked at his wife. She lay supine and pulled the comfy, warm duvet up to her chin.

"I suspect," Robert said, "that we have Old Virginia lycanthropes for neighbors."

"Correction," Marcie said. "Werewolves. Those people are too fucking stupid to be lycans."

###

The next day Robert Jordan was installing the bidet in the master bath when the girl materialized like a wraith in the bedroom. Wild-eyed, barefoot, disheveled in a ragged pink nightie, its fringe barely reaching her knees.

"Hello!" said Robert, startled. He saw the scratches on her skinny legs.

"Help me," Lilybeth pleaded, her voice a hoarse whisper. "Save me from them. Please!"

Robert abandoned the bidet. He stood. "Are you okay?"

"No," she choked out. "I ain't fuck'n okay!"

Hearing their voices, Marcie strode in from the kitchen where she had been tiling the backsplash. She spied the girl and frowned. "Hey, hey! What are you doing here? What do you want?"

"I run away," Lilybeth replied. "Look at what they done to me!"

She stripped off the cheap polyester nightie, wearing nothing underneath but a G-string. Her breasts were the size of pears and she covered them demurely with her hands. With a grimace she swiveled and challenged Robert and Marcie to gaze at her body. Fresh scratches, abrasions, and bright red weals marked her shoulder blades, back and supple little butt.

"See what they done! You see? They're monsters! Save me from them! Please please please!"

She collapsed on the floor, sobbing. Pleading, babbling. *Help me help me pleeese.*

"It's okay." Marcie threw a paint-stained sheet over the girl and grasped her shoulder, lifting Lilybeth from the floor. "You'll be safe. We'll protect you. Promise. Your ours now."

"You said you didn't want to get entangled in their business," said Robert.

"I didn't but she dropped in our lap," Marcie replied. "We've no choice."

They brought Lilybeth to the RV and gave her one of Robert's shirts to wear. Marcie made her a cup of chamomile tea with honey and gave her an antibiotic ointment to rub on her skin.

"They don't know yet that I run off," said Lilybeth. "They was dead asleep when I snuck off. Sleeping off the big drunk from last night. They going to be hoppin' mad! Don't know what they might do. We ought'r take this big fancy caravan of yours and flee for our lives!"

"We'll manage them," Robert assured her.

"No! No, you can't! Y'all don't have no idea how crazy and mean they are!"

"Oh, we have them figured out," said Marcie. She sat next to the girl on the couch in the RV.

"It's okay," said Robert. He held up his cellphone. "I called the sheriff's office. A deputy's on his way. You have nothing to worry about now. This'll all be sorted out and, in the meantime, you're safe with us."

"Thank you, thank you." Lilybeth sobbed. She sniffled. Clutched Kleenexes from the box Marcie offered and blew her nose, dropping the snotty tissue on the floor. She slurped her tea. "Jimmy ain't my husband, you know."

"Yes," said Robert. "You tried to tell me yesterday."

"And blabbing like that that earned me a good whupping from Jimmy and Monroe!"

Robert shook his head. "How did you ever fall in with these brutes?"

She lowered her face, sheepish, and sipped her tea, as Marcie encouraged her to finish the cup. Then she took a breath and turned to Robert again. "Jimmy and me was going out. Met him when I was working at Shorebreak Pizza. Jimmy used to come in a lot. I liked him at first. He was sweet. He, like, lured me to their house. I got sorta drunk and stoned and Monroe said he married us. Monroe says he's a minister but he ain't no way. They wouldn't let me leave. It got ugly. Jimmy hurts me. He's real rough-like. So's his brother." She broke off, choking up, and sobbing.

Marcie shook her head and clicked her tongue with disgust. She draped her arm around Lilybeth's shoulder and patted the girl's hand. "That's over now. You're safe. You're not going back to them."

"If you say so, hon," said Lilybeth. She rocked back and forth, feeling dizzy. "I sure hope not. I got a sister I can go live with in Roanoke. That's a good long way off."

Robert spoke up. "What about the howling?"

She stared at him dumbly. "Huh? Last night you mean?"

"Yeah, last night," said Robert. "The full moon. What the hell was that all about?"

"It's their thing-like," Lilybeth replied. "They drink a snootful and put on stinky old pelts and cavort about and make out like wolves. Because, crazy old Monroe says, the wolf is their ... um ..." She paused to recall the word. "Their *totem*. Is that the word? You know, like, a spirit animal. From the injun side of the Fernfox family what mixed with the Pungo tribe in colonial times."

"You were howling too," Robert pointed out.

"They made me do that," she admitted. "After they fucked the daylights out of me."

"Uh-oh," said Robert, his attention diverted. He grinned. Pointing out the window, he said, "Looks like Fernfoxes are on the trail."

Lilybeth shuddered, dropped her empty teacup, shrieked in panic, and wriggled around to look out the window. Marcie casually glanced out the window, then recovered the shards of the shattered bone china teacup and deposited them in the trash.

In the distance Monroe, Folk and Jimmy paced about their house, scrutinizing the ground, like hounds searching for a scent. They sniffed the air, hunkered down, looked for signs, and sniffed the dirt too. Then Monroe discovered some trace, called his sons to his side, and pointed in the direction of the RV. The three of them froze for a few seconds, forming a menacing tableau. Monroe turned to speak to his sons. Jimmy dashed off into the house and returned with a shotgun. He nodded to his daddy, ready. Then, on Monroe's command, the three of them marched.

Lilybeth whirled about, aghast, flailing her arms. "Shit shit *shit shit shit!*" Robert and Marcie remained preternaturally calm. She gawped at them.

"They're coming! They're riled! They got a gun! I told you we should've taken off!"

"Not to worry," said Marcie. Confident, almost blithe. She smiled. "I will deal with them."

"You can't! They won't listen! They'll hurt you! Maybe even kill you!"

Marcie sniffed. "Unlikely."

She opened a cabinet and removed a coiled, black strand of wire and nodded at Robert, who nodded back his assent. Marcie donned a broadbrimmed straw sun hat and designer shades, looked in a mirror to adjust the hat and tuck a strand of her hair under its brim, then stepped outside with the insouciance of a beautiful woman going out for a noonday stroll on a sunny day.

Lilybeth remained in panic mode, fretting. She staggered, losing her balance. She grabbed Robert and pleaded. "Stop her! You got to! She don't know what's going to happen!"

Robert sat the girl down. "No, I think she does. Perfectly. Wait and see. Watch."

Marcie stood where the bamboo had been and waited as the Fernfox men approached. She beckoned them closer. They halted just a few feet from where Marcie stood. Dour Monroe stepped toward her. He eyed her. Scowling.

"You're Mrs. Robert Jordan, I take it."

"I am," Marcie said. "And you are trespassing."

Fernfox remained resolute. "We're chasing a runaway. She snuck off and went thisaway. And I am sure you got my son's wife here with you and we are here to take her home."

"That is partly correct and partly wrong," said Marcie. "She's here, yes, but she's not married to that pathetic dickhead son of yours."

"How dare you!" Monroe bristled. "I married them my own self!"

"Really?" Marcie laughed. "In what legal capacity?"

The question enraged old Fernfox. "In what legal capacity? I will tell you what fuck'n capacity, woman! As paterfamilias and elder of the Fernfox clan and de facto Pungo justice of the peace!"

Amused, Marcie shook her head, patronizing and bubbling with laughter. "My, that is quite a mouthful. But it means absolutely nothing."

The old man tensed, fuming, screwed up his face, sucking his cheeks and spat copiously at Marcie's boots. His sons, sensing Monroe's anger, sharing it, also tensed, and leaned in. They also spit. Jimmy's hairy hand covered the trigger guard of the 12-gauge, and his grimy forefinger wormed its way over the trigger.

Monroe hollered. "She run off. Shame! You got her here. You got to give her up. She got to go back to Jimmy. You people got no right to stand between us and her. That wayward wench got one hellacious chastisement coming to her. You had best not interfere. You hear?"

In response, Marcie continued to smile at the malicious old man. She held up the black coil. She could feel it awake now, feel it throbbing. "See this? Do you know what it is?"

"'lectrical cable of some sort," replied Monroe, dumbfounded by the question.

"No," said Marcie. "It's your death."

Marcie snapped her wrist. The coil unfurled. Like a serpent, obsidian black, with a razor-sharp edge. Marcie sprang-whipped the coil in the air and snapped it across Monroe Fernfox's shoulders. His grizzled head went flying with a geyser of crimson. Monroe's body tumbled.

Jimmy and Folk, both agog, screamed. Jimmy fumbled with the shotgun. Marcie snapped the coil again like a whip, severing his arm above the elbow and slicing a chunk of his chest to the ribcage. The shotgun, clutched by a dead hand, discharged. The blast, both barrels, toppled Folk. Stepping forward and twirling the serpent blade like a lasso, Marcie lashed Jimmy where he knelt screaming and gushing blood. His sallow blonde head soared. Marcie caught it in the air with the toe of her boot, like a soccer player. With another easy snap of her wrist, Marcie recoiled the serpent. Harmless now. She stroked and praised it. *Good diabolical little serpent.* She knew from experience, aeons of experience, that familiars required regular blandishment.

Lilybeth gagged, heaved, and then fainted at the sight of the first decapitation. Couldn't stand the sight of blood, Robert figured. Of course, the potion Marcie added to her chamomile tea no doubt added to the girl's wooziness, as meant to, rendering her helpless.

Robert gazed at the massacre on the property line. Had to admire his wife's resourcefulness; she dispatched the Fernfox men with ruthless efficacy too. Robert grinned. The yokels never saw it coming nor knew what hit them.

Marcie sauntered back to the RV. Once inside she replaced the serpent in its cabinet and gestured toward the unconscious girl on the floor. "Wake her up."

"Of course," Robert replied. He took a cup of cold water and splashed dainty drops on Lilybeth's face until her eyelids twitched and she opened her eyes and focused on Robert standing over her. She sat up, groggy, saw Marcie, and gasped.

"Omigod! What you done! How you gonna explain that to the sheriff when he gets here?"

"Confession," said Robert. "I didn't really call the sheriff's office." He sneered. "We don't need them. Marcie and I have matters well in hand. Don't we, love?"

"Uh-huh," said Marcie. She wet-toweled Fernfox gore from her clothes, annoyed. "Hurry it along, will you? I want to get back to the kitchen tile."

Lilybeth recoiled and started crawling away from Robert and Marcie, but her wooziness increased, and her limbs became heavy as paralysis set in. "Who are you people?"

"Good question. I'll show you, girl meat." He peeled off his skull-fitting Robert Jordan mask to reveal, under the skin suit, his daemon face. Ancient, reptilian, malevolent, monstrous. The glistening green scales, the sharp ridges of his cheeks, the jagged teeth when he spit the prosthetic from his mouth.

"Hello," he said to the terrified girl. He didn't disguise his voice now or withhold his brimstone breath or bridle his ferocity. He belched sulfurous fumes as he told of the horrible things he would do to her, and clutched Lilybeth's soft, lilywhite throat to silence her screams ...

Their remains boiled in the rusty, 55-gallon drums that had been part of the clutter in the Fernfox yard. Acquiring enough lye without arousing unwanted suspicion had required trips to three different Walmart Supercenters in the area.

Robert and Marcie followed an established plan in disposal of victims. Boil overnight and in the morning pour the sludge into a fresh grave and cover with dirt. That meant a vigil and a sleepless night tending the fires under the drums. Robert had Salvadorean contacts, his *brujo* bros with heavy tats, who would descend the next day to take the Ford pickup truck and whatever else they could scavenge from the Fernfox premises, no questions asked.

Robert tended the fire under the drums while Marcie wielded the shovel and dug a deep and oblong hole.

"Why must I be the one to dig the hole?"

"Because you're far superior at it," replied Robert. "You have a burrowing instinct I lack."

"One of these days," said Marcie, pausing to confront him, "you might find yourself in a hole, swimming in sodium hydroxide."

Robert tsk-tsked the threat with harsh clicks of his tongue. "Oh, now, where would you ever find another me to partner with?"

"Tinder," Marcie replied. "There's a darknet Tinder, the dating app of the damned. I'll search for *daemonium virum* and see what responses I get."

At sunrise they sat under the unfurled canopy of the Fleetwood RV and grilled their breakfast of Fernfox morsels on the hibachi. Chunks of livid red meat, strips of hypothalami, tenderized lymph nodes, and cauliform pieces of grey matter.

"Tastes gamy," said Marcie.

"They were rustic types," said Robert. "Wild in the country. Southern-fried lycans. Or werewolves, which was it again?"

Marcie scoffed. "No, no, no! I've told you before! Lycanthropy is old sorcery and has its ethos. Lycans are astute, practice arcane rites, and change into wolves at will. Werewolves are bumblers. Randomly bitten and subject to lunar phases, with no control over transformation. But it's moot." She dismissed the topic with an elegant wave of her hand. "The Fernfoxes were neither! Hicks playing at being the Big Bad Wolf, that's all they were, foolish furries. I'd call them atavistic. Primitive throwbacks."

"Oh?" Robert chuckled. "And we aren't?"

"Apples and oranges," replied Marcie, biting and chewing. She gestured toward the former Fernfox home. "Now that the wretched Fernfoxes are disposed of what will we do about that ugly monstrosity? Privacy fence?"

"Reduction to an inferno," Robert said. "One of my Salvadoreans does arson too."

"Oh, that is excellent," said Marcie, genuinely thrilled at the prospect. "I love fire and a good raging inferno. They are so cleansing."

"Yes, me too, I love an inferno," said Robert. A wistful sigh escaped his lips. "Reminds me of home."

CRITICAL BLAST PUBLISHING
20¢
APPROVED BY THE READING CODE AUTHORITY
WELCOME MAT, FIVE STARS
Jennifer Lee Rossman
WEIRD FANTASTIC WORLDS
CRITICAL BLAST PUBLISHING
WHERE POP CULTURE GETS BLASTED
INCREDIBLE STRANGE STORIES
YOUR FEEDBACK IS VITAL!

ATTENTION!
DEMONS! VAMPIRES! GHOULS!
NO MORE MONDAY NIGHTMARES!

DEFEAT BLACK MYSTIC ARTS KUNG-FU Tired of getting your ass kicked every Tuesday by Black Mystic Arts Kung-Fu fighters? CALL 666-HELP to enroll in self-defense training every Hellspawn should know to survive any dark alley encounter. Become a Ninth Circle Master of Judante!

STICK IT TO YOUR ENEMIES! Real Voodoo Doll! Guaranteed Quality checked by the finest Witch Doctors! Send lock of hair and a SASE to DUDAT VOODOO, Box 9, Haiti.

SUPER SHARP PIRATE SWORD When you want to capture the hearts and minds of the people around you, this sword will cut through the muscle and bone to get to the vital organs you need to sustain your hunger.

WELCOME MAT TRAP When you don't want people annoying you, a simple press of the button and the trap door will dispose of anyone who stands on it, while waiting for you to answer the door.

SNAKES IN A MAIL BOX Get these total mother-f$%Ken poisonous snakes and mail them with your get well gift cards.

FACE FRONT, TRUE EVILEERS!

SUPER SECRET BOOK SAFE The special camouflage feature activates, once placed on the book shelf. You'll never find it again.

MONSTER VALUE STAMP
THIS IS IT! CLIP THEM & COLLECT THEM ALL!

RENT AN ANGRY MONSTERS! When you need to stop a Bully from harassing, or when you need to look like a decent human concerned for poor ugly monsters.

Jennifer Lee Rossman (they/them) is a queer, disabled, and autistic author and editor from the land of carousels and Rod Serling. Their work has been featured in dozens of anthologies, and they have been nominated for Pushcart and Utopia Awards. Find more of their work on their website http://jenniferleerossman.blogspot.com and follow them on Twitter @JenLRossman

[Editor's note: The following document contains product reviews compiled from various online retail sites, from accounts owned by Lucy Morris, the person at the center of the incident in question. The reviews are arranged in chronological order beginning on March 3, just after she and her husband moved into their house on Quincy Street and concluding just before the massacre.

Please read them with an open mind, putting aside for the moment the official story about the cult, and perhaps read up on certain folkloric motifs relevant to Lucy's experiences.

It is my hope that the story contained within these reviews will shed some light on the incident in question.]

Non-Slip Outdoor Welcome Mat (Floral)

★★★★★

My husband and I recently bought our first home and, call me corny and old-fashioned, but I just think there's something about a welcome mat that makes any house feel homey. It lets the neighbors know they can pop by to borrow some sugar whenever they need to. (As long as they share some of the cookies they're making lol)

Well made, and a decent price.

Although my husband says I should've bought the blue one, but what does he know? The floral one goes better with the yellow siding anyway.

Reusable 12 x 12 Plastic Stencils For Wall Painting
★★★★★

Recently moved into a lovely old house and while it was almost suspiciously budget friendly, the previous owners seemed to favor a darker, Gothic design scheme. It's beautiful, but not really our style, so I have been trying to spruce it up a bit buy [sic] painting cheerful floral borders on all of these dark walls.

Very impressed with the quality of these stencils, the paint does not bleed past the edges at all!

Wondering what else I can stencil…

Outdoor Seasonal Flag Assortment
★★★★

They seem to be a good quality fabric, very durable, and there's one for every month.

One small thing: a couple of the flags are different from the ones pictured. We got a Cupid instead of the pink hearts, and the Christmas one has a cross in addition to the tree and ornaments. I'm not particularly religious but I don't mind it, just thought I would mention it because I know it would bother some people.

(My neighbor across the street, for instance. She was outside when the package came, so I thought I would open it and show it to her, trying to be friendly. She seemed deeply offended at the Christmas one. I don't know what faith she practices; I hope I didn't offend her.)

3 Pack Plastic Flyswatters
★★★★★

It's a fly swatter, not much to say. It has a nice little loop for easy hanging.

Haven't had a chance to use them yet, but I hear giant moths fluttering around my house almost every night so it's only a matter of time...

Gardening Gloves
★★★★★

Never been much of a gardener, so I don't know how these compare to other gloves on the market. They fit rather nicely though, and I'm looking forward to sprucing up my front yard with some flowers.

(If I'm being totally honest, I mostly want an excuse to be outside more often so I can strike up conversations with our neighbors. I don't think they like us very much, but I'm not sure why. They seem friendly with each other, it's a very close-knit community. I'm hoping I can make some friends here.)

Ceramic Frog with Mirrored Gazing Ball
★★★★★

I've always wanted something like this, and maybe it's a little tacky, but it makes me happy.

Bigger than I was expecting but that's probably my fault for not understanding metric measurements.

[Editor's note: attached to the review is a close-up photo of the item, a smiling green frog statue with a pale yellow house visible in the background. The frog is holding a dark purple ball with a mirrored finish.

Zooming in on the gazing ball, one can see the reflection of a young woman taking the picture—Lucy Morris. Also visible is her husband, who appears to be having an animated conversation with someone, despite them being the only two people present in the reflection.]

All In One Travel Toiletries Set

Bought for my husband, who is going on a work trip.

It's a cute little set, with a toothbrush and various bottles of shampoo and such, and all in a handy carrying case. He likes that it came in blue.

Glass Mason Jars (10 Pack)

Needed a cute container for some barbecue sauce. My neighbors have finally invited me to a cookout and my mother taught me to always bring a gift. She also taught me that presentation matters—this was not a job for my old dollar store Tupperware!

I just wish I could buy a smaller package. Oh well, I'm sure I'll find some use for the extras.

Garlic Powder

Decided to bring some of my Uncle Bob's barbecue sauce to a cookout my neighbor invited me to. I don't eat meat, but it's always a big hit and I thought my neighbor would like to try it.

Worst decision ever!

I don't know if the garlic powder is expired or what, but everyone who had my sauce got violently ill so there must be something wrong with it. (And I know it's the garlic powder because that's the only ingredient I didn't already have on hand, and my husband used the rest of the ingredients just last week before going on his work trip so...)

I am so embarrassed. One star, never buying from this company again!

Meat Thermometer

Bought it for our neighbors after noticing the steak at a recent barbecue was not cooked thoroughly. I'm a vegetarian, but still, meat should not be that bloody.

(I am secretly hoping they will think it was the steak that gave them food poisoning, and not my barbecue sauce.)

[Editor's note: this item was returned soon after posting the review, with the reason stated as "bought it as a gift, but I am afraid it will be seen as passive aggressive."]

Personalized Charcuterie Board

★★★★★

I bought this as a gift for our neighbors to apologize for accidentally giving the entire neighborhood food poisoning at their barbecue [cringing emoji]

The seller was awesome and answered all of my questions (and even taught me how to pronounce "Charcuterie"!). Will definitely buy from here again, although fingers crossed it won't be an apology gift next time!

Ultrasonic Bat Repellent

★★★★★

Ever since moving into our new home, my husband and I have been hearing "moths" fluttering around in various rooms throughout the night. Imagine our horror when we finally saw one, and it was actually a bat!

(I know they are good for the ecosystem and we don't have vampire bats in our area. But I still don't want it in my home! I didn't even think we had bats in this area? I've also been hearing what sounds like wolves howling at night, so maybe we are closer to the wilderness then [sic] I realized.)

Animal control said they can only help if the bat is injured, or we need help to relocate one that is nesting in our house. Since it only happens occasionally, we are assuming they are getting in and out somehow but have yet to find exactly how.

This product was suggested as a harmless way to repel the creatures.

Have not had a chance to use it yet, but it was very easy to set up. Took off one star because the box was a little damaged.

Xtreme Caffeine Midnight Oil Blend Instant Coffee
★★★

Boy howdy, this is some strong coffee! It'll peel the skin right off your bones, as my dad would say.

I really don't care for the flavor, no matter how much creamer I add, it tastes extremely bitter and burnt. But I've been feeling rather fatigued lately—well, more than usual—so I thought I would try a little extra boost in the morning.

"My Memories" Photo Album
★★★★★

I was cleaning the attic the other day, and I found a box of photos that must have belonged to the former owners of our house. The real estate agent doesn't have any information about who they were, so I can't return them, and I didn't think it was right to just throw them away.

[Editor's note: attached to this review are several images. Each shows the album, with six photographs on each stark white page. They depict holidays and everyday events of a family of five, though the eldest son disappears abruptly between pages. Soon after, the photos show only nature scenes and architecture; the rest of the family does not appear in any of the photographs.]

Iron Supplements, 200 Capsules

★★★★

Taking off one star because of the awful metallic taste when I burp (I know, TMI). But they are easy to swallow and apparently I am anemic. HMM... now that I think about it, that's probably why I've been so tired recently.

Hopefully this will help.

11-Piece Garden Tool Set (Pink)

★★★★★

It's getting a bit late this summer to do much gardening, but now I will be prepared for an early start next year!

It's such a fulfilling experience, I feel kind of... connected to the dirt, almost? I don't know. Silly first-time homeowner syndrome, probably lol.

Women's Black and White Sun Hat With Ribbon

★★★★★

The sun has been giving me migraines lately, so as someone who just discovered a love for gardening, the extra wide brim is a life saver!

Personalized Decorative Wooden Spoons

★★★★★

This is my second time buying from the seller, and once again, I am incredibly pleased (and I got a discount!)

These are an engagement gift for my sister, and not only did the seller put her and her future husband's initials on them, but they even engraved little rabbits on the handle as an inside joke between me and my sister!

I wish this app would let me give more than five stars!

Glass Cleaning Spray

★★

While I appreciate that it doesn't have that strong chemical odor many cleaning sprays do, that's about all I can say in its favor because it just doesn't work very well.

No matter how many times I go over it, my windows are still so streaky I can't even see my own reflection!

3/4 Length Sleeve Navy V-Neck Sweater

★★★★★

Early birthday present for my husband. He usually goes for turtlenecks, but I think he looks very handsome with an exposed neck.

Full Length Mirror (Cherry Finish)

★

Arrived on time, packaged securely. The frame is beautiful. The only problem is, it doesn't work!

I have never had an issue with mirrors before, certainly not one this bizarre. It reflects the room behind me just fine, but not me.

My husband has a reflection; maybe it's because I am so much shorter? Maybe the light is refracting differently? I don't know. I'm not a scientist, but I'm going to do some research, see if I can troubleshoot it. If not, well, at least this site offers free 90-day returns...

Three Dozen Cellophane Favor Bags

★★★★★

As the maid of honor (matron of honor I suppose) for my sister's wedding, party favors are one of my duties. These are very cute little bags, with pre-applied blank labels that are easy to write on.

White And Cream Drapery and Artificial Roses For Outdoor Weddings

★★★★★

This will be perfect for my sister's wedding, which we are holding in my backyard this weekend! I can't wait to have my entire family visiting, maybe we will invite the neighbors for the reception...

[*Editor's note: That is the last review left by Lucy Morris before the massacre at the wedding.*

Please note, I make no declaration as to what actually occurred that evening on Quincy Street, nor do I claim that the official story—involving a cult and blood sacrifices—is anything less than accurate, though I do have a personal theory and would be willing to discuss it with anyone who will take it seriously. I simply ask that you read about Lucy's experiences in her own words and come to your own conclusion.

And perhaps consider the ramifications of purchasing a welcome mat.]

3¢
USA
GIGGLECRUNCH
$10
MONSTER
VALUE STAMP
THIS IS IT!
CLIP THEM
& COLLECT
THEM ALL!

CRITICAL BLAST PUBLISHING
20¢
THE MONSTER NEXT DOOR
Martin Klubeck
APPROVED BY THE READING CODE AUTHORITY
WHAT LURKS ACROSS A MIDNIGHT STREET?

HUMAN MASK When you need to walk among the humans, without being singled out as a monster. Get this mask in black, white or polka-dot, to blend right in!

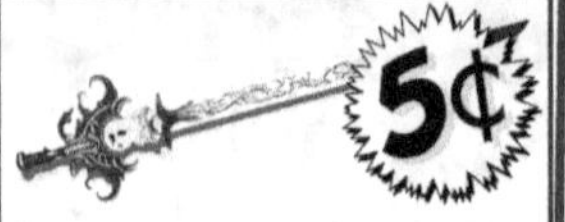

SUPER SHARP PIRATE SWORD When you want to capture the hearts and minds of the people around you, this sword will cut through the muscle and bone to get to the vital organs you need to sustain your hunger.

SUPER SECRET BOOK SAFE The special camouflage feature activates, once placed on the book shelf. You'll never find it again.

LAST MAN ON EARTH HEARD A KNOCK AT THE DOOR!

BOX OF LIVE BATS When you feel like a millionaire crime fighting hero and need to dress up your special cave, to give it that extra touch of atmosphere... a box of live bats is perfect for you. Food not included.

COCAINE FOR PETS When your pets become too excited during mating season and you don't want additional burden of feeding more pets, shot them up with some fine liquid snow and chill them out.

HELIUM GAS & BALLOON SET Get away from the day to day grind of your boring life and steal a whole house while the owners are away.

RADIOACTIVE CANDY When you want to level up your personality and appear extra sweet to the people around you... and want to have a superpower over sugar... this candy's for you!

HEAD KNIVES 100% stainless steal daggers that launch from the top of your head and kill any conversation you find boring.

EXPLODING DRINK Sit back and enjoy the highjinks as people unscrew their drink activating the chemical reaction, causing a foamy mess.

Martin is the author of six Organizational Improvement books; Why Organizations Struggle So Hard to Improve So Little: Overcoming Organizational Immaturity, Metrics: How To Improve Key Business Results, Planning and Designing Effective Metrics, The Professional Development Toolbox, Success Metrics and his latest Don't Manage…Coach! He is a recognized leader in Organizational Development. He is also the author of the series, The Adventures of Sir Locke the Gnome, as well as the YA adventure, The Time Warp King. He is working on The Goode Knight, a mystery-thriller.

Janelle stood by the door, waiting for her husband.

He had returned, as he always did, from a business trip. She checked her dress, her hair, and her modest make-up in the hallway mirror. She checked her fingernails and toenails. Barefoot was how he liked her. Everything was in order.

She didn't know why she checked. If something was amiss, she definitely didn't have time to fix it. Perhaps she could've tried to hide it. But that never worked. He noticed everything.

She prayed this time would be different. This time he wouldn't notice everything.

She watched through the small glass panels beside the door. As he approached, suit jacket over right arm, suitcase in his left hand, she swung the door open. She bowed ever so slightly.

"Thank you," he said with no hint of gratitude.

She closed the door behind him. No reply required.

He didn't seem to look at her, but she knew he had done a visual inspection. He saw everything.

He walked down the hall to their bedroom.

She followed a respectful distance behind. Not close enough to crowd him, not too far that she was out of his reach.

"It was a good trip. I'll likely make Division Sales Rep if it keeps going at this rate." He handed her his suit jacket and she walked it over to the closet. She hung it on a wooden hanger.

"Then we can get a decent house," he said. He picked up the unopened pack of cigarettes from his nightstand. He never smoked on business calls, some clients didn't like it. He wasn't addicted to them, they were just a guilty pleasure. One with benefits.

She hurried over to the suitcase he had lain on the bed. She began unpacking it.

He played with the pack, manipulating it like a magician with a new deck of cards. He seemed to be contemplating if he wanted to use them.

"What's for dinner?" he asked.

"Lasagna with garlic bread and a side salad," she recited. It was what he had every time he returned. She had to monitor his itinerary, specifically his return flights to make sure she had dinner ready when he arrived. If any of his flights were delayed, she had to wait. Timing was everything.

She finished putting away his clothes. She deposited the ones needing laundering into the hamper, picked up the hamper, and waited.

"I'll be out in a second," he said.

She bowed slightly again, more a nod than a bow. She was glad to see him put the cigarettes back on the nightstand, unopened.

When he came out for dinner, he was dressed in jeans and a polo shirt. He had on boat shoes and argyle socks. He had showered, fixed his hair, and shaved.

She wondered what plans he had, he never dressed up for her benefit. She knew better than to ask, she'd find out when he was ready to tell her.

"We had a very successful trip. We'll be going places," he said.

Instead of wondering why he used we instead of I, she busied herself setting the dining room table.

In the beginning, she had tried having everything set before he came home. But that didn't work. He had slapped her hard enough to loosen two teeth.

He said he liked to watch.

"Did someone move in next door?" he asked.

Not part of the script, but not unexpected. He noticed everything.

"Yes," she said. She dreaded this more than the beatings, at least those she knew what to expect, she knew what was coming.

He opened the drapes and looked at the house next door. She could see the lights were on. She had stood at that same window each day and night for the last two days. The new neighbor never seemed to leave the house.

"Hmm."

She got the food out of the oven and plated the meal. From the kitchen she heard him ask another question. She stopped moving so she could hear.

"... a family?" was all she could make out. She had missed the first word or two.

"Just a lady, no family," she said loud enough he could hear. She waited. After a few moments, she resumed putting the bread on the plates.

When she brought the food to the table, he was still standing by the window.

"Did you visit her? Take her a housewarming gift?" he asked. At least it was an easy question.

"No..." she wanted to add something, but the more she said the higher the risk.

"I think we should introduce ourselves, don't you?" he asked as he sat down.

She didn't know how to respond. She hoped he didn't want an answer.

He took a forkful of lasagna.

She sat frozen, looking at him, waiting.

He finished the bite and chased it with a swallow of water. He never drank alcohol. Not beer, or wine, or any hard liquor. He didn't do drugs. He worked out regularly and read voraciously. He said he liked to be healthy in body, mind, and spirit.

By spirit he didn't mean religious mumbo jumbo. He hated organized religion almost as much as organized government. By a healthy spirit he meant something totally different.

"Yes. I think we should take her a housewarming gift. A woman alone in such a big house would probably appreciate some company," he said.

She nodded. She would say she found it funny how he continued to use we when he definitely didn't include her in his plans. She would say funny, but she hadn't found anything in her life to be humorous. At least not since they were married. Their anniversary was coming up soon. She didn't want to think about how he would want to celebrate.

"Eat your food," he said.

She had about half the portions she had given him. She had to clean her plate or it would be added to her personal debt. Her husband abhorred the concept of debt. But that didn't keep him from selling people things they didn't need. It was okay if they went into debt to pay for what he was selling. He would never fall into that trap.

And he liked teaching his wife about avoiding debt.

Especially personal debt. The kind of debt she accrued by doing the wrong thing or not doing the right thing. Saying the wrong thing. Not saying the right thing. Her debt would add up until he decided to collect payment.

In the first year of their marriage, she accumulated so much personal debt that he collected daily. As she learned to adapt, it dropped to weekly. Now, after three years, he only collected monthly. Of course, any small thing could earn her a slap, punch, or kick. Those unexpected ones were worse.

He liked her afraid. But she couldn't cringe or wince. He didn't like her acting or looking afraid. He said it made him look bad, as if he was a monster, when in reality all he was trying to do was help her be the best version of herself she could be.

He repeatedly told her he loved her, without the slightest hint of affection.

"I made a pie, you could take it for her." She said this while looking down at her plate. It was a large gamble. She didn't normally take risks.

He seemed to think it over.

She knew it would depend on his cravings. It was an easy excuse to punish her for speaking before spoken to. That in itself was worth at least a punch to her thigh or stomach. Or he could add it to her debt.

Or he could, as he did on rare occasions, use it to appear human.

"Good idea."

She knew not to smile.

"Now finish your food."

After dinner he put on his best cologne.

She was waiting by the front door with the pie in a covered pastry dish and his jacket.

"Don't you want to come and meet our neighbor?" he asked as he put on the jacket.

Back to the script.

"I have dishes to do," she said, not looking him in the eyes. She knew she wasn't invited.

She wondered if he'd try to seduce or intimidate the neighbor. It probably depended on how attractive he found her.

From what she'd seen of her, she figured he would try to seduce her.

In the two days since the neighbor had moved in, there had been five different men over there. At first, Janelle thought she was a call girl. But she had never heard of one who worked out of her home. The men all came by taxi or Uber. They all came bearing gifts. She would watch from behind her drapes. Her neighbor entertained them, sometimes feeding them, giving them drinks, and talking. Eventually they went upstairs. All of them.

She thought she must be wrong. Perhaps the most expensive call girls did work out of their home. Then, one time, the upstairs drapes were slightly askew and she saw more than she was supposed to.

Janelle counted to ten.

She ignored the dishes. She walked over to the window and watched her husband saunter up the front steps of their neighbor's house. He didn't use the doorbell. Like the good salesman he was, he knocked confidently, as if he were an old friend or relative coming to visit.

Janelle smiled. She reached up and nervously touched her face.

He hadn't noticed. She hadn't given anything away.

The neighbor's door opened, and Janelle could see her husband's smile. It was the same smile he used when he had courted her. The same smile she was sure he used on countless women to make a sale or get in their beds.

Janelle watched as her husband and neighbor crossed in front of the window. She saw her husband sit at a table, the pie and neighbor were out of view.

Then the neighbor returned with a large slice of pie, topped with whipped cream. She put the pie in front of Janelle's husband. She bent over to place the fork and napkin in front of him, showing a lot of cleavage. She was wearing a dress with a low-cut top, high slit hem and no sleeves. She looked like she was expecting company or planning to go out.

Janelle touched her face again. She was still smiling. She couldn't remember the last time she smiled. She glanced once toward her kitchen, to where the dishes were waiting.

After some animated conversation, her husband ate the pie. He leaned back in the chair as if it were his home; comfortable, relaxed. He was in control.

The neighbor got up and walked around behind Janelle's husband. She reached around him and picked up his plate. Her breasts pressed against his back, and she turned her head as if to whisper something in his ear. When she pulled away, Janelle could see, just for a second, that she had pulled at his ear with her mouth.

Her husband grinned like a school boy.

He took the plate from her and stood up abruptly. Even from that distance, Janelle could see that her husband was excited. The stupid grin on his face and the bulge in his pants left no doubt. The neighbor offered her hand and he took it.

They walked out of Janelle's view and the light went off.

Janelle waited.

A light on the neighbor's second floor came on. The shades were drawn up there. They always were. Except that one time, when they were askew.

Janelle waited.

The light went off.

Janelle checked the smile was still on her face. It felt strange.

Then she heard the scream. It was louder than the others she had heard. It was a shriek. It was shorter than the others she had heard. It went on for only three seconds. It seemed like minutes.

Janelle closed the drapes and laughed. She actually laughed. At first very quietly. The sound surprised her. She didn't recognize it. Then she realized what it was and laughed again. This time louder. She decided it felt good.

She turned out the lights and went to bed.

The dishes could wait.

CRITICAL BLAST PUBLISHING
20¢
THE WELCOME WAGON OF WIDGEON WOODS
Jean Jentilet
APPROVED BY THE READING CODE AUTHORITY
WEIRD FANTASTIC WORLDS
CRITICAL BLAST PUBLISHING
WHERE POP CULTURE GETS BLASTED
INCREDIBLE STRANGE STORIES
SPINE TINGLING CHILLS! HOT OFF THE GRILL!

MONSTER VALUE STAMP
THIS IS IT! CLIP THEM & COLLECT THEM ALL!

HEAD KNIVES 100% stainless steal daggers that launch from the top of your head and kill any conversation you find boring.

RENT AN ANGRY MIDGET! When you need to stop a Bully from harassing, or when you need to look like a decent human concerned for poor ugly monsters.

RENT AN ANGRY MONSTERS! When you need to stop a Bully from harassing, or when you need to look like a decent human concerned for poor ugly monsters.

READING IS 20 TO LIFE!

SUPER SECRET BOOK SAFE The special camouflage feature activates, once placed on the book shelf. You'll never find it again.

BOX OF LIVE BATS When you feel like a millionaire crime fighting hero and need to dress up your special cave, to give it that extra touch of atmosphere... a box of live bats is perfect for you. Food not included.

HUMAN MASK When you need to walk among the humans, without being singled out as a monster. Get this mask in black, white or polka-dot, to blend right in!

SNAKES IN A MAIL BOX Get these total mother-f$%Ken poisonous snakes and mail them with your get well gift cards.

EXPLODING DRINK Sit back and enjoy the highjinks as people unscrew their drink activating the chemical reaction, causing a foamy mess.

WELCOME MAT TRAP When you don't want people annoying you, a simple press of the button and the trap door will dispose of anyone who stands on it, while waiting for you to answer the door.

Jean Jentilet was born in Annapolis, Maryland. She attended law school next to Edgar Allan Poe's grave, which was her favorite thing about law school. She has stories featured or forthcoming in ParaABnormal Magazine and Cry Baby Bridge: A Collection of Utter Speculation. Jean currently resides in North Carolina at the whims of a miniature pinscher and a Shih Tzu. They occasionally grant her leave to write dark fiction and take long walks.

SOLD

Maybe she would go to hell for it but seeing that word on the sign in the yard across the street made Marilee Duncan smile. She had spent months watching Doug Mailor (whom she had said two dozen words to in their five years as neighbors) hustle contractors in and out of the house and hoping that the Mailors weren't just making improvements for the sake of improvement. She got nosey and checked out the online listings. (For all that traffic, it appeared that the only thing the Mailors had done was replace a single bathroom counter.) She maneuvered around the cars of prospective buyers that clogged both sides of the street during the open house.

PENDING

That this sign appeared the day after the last scheduled day of the open house came as no surprise. The market was tight, and the house across the street was one of a quickly draining pool within the financial grasp of actual people.

FOR SALE

This sign reappearing two days later settled under Marilee's thoughts like a pebble in a shoe. It was the flipflopping of fortune, right on her doorstep.

PENDING

Back again, four days after its disappearance. She dared not get her hopes up, and then—*SOLD*

PENDING was temporary. *SOLD* was forever.

From her front porch, Marilee waved at Morgan Wolfinger as the unofficial realtor of Widgeon Woods tossed the old *PENDING* card into the back seat of her car. Morgan lived two streets over on Duckling Drive. Marilee didn't know anyone who hadn't bought their home under Morgan's guidance.

"Ding dong, Meanypants is gone," Sarah Stanton said with her usual smug half-purr, from her usual post next to the rosebush at the corner of Marilee's front porch. Sarah had the type of voice that always seemed to be implying something. "Are we having a party?

Marilee blew steam off the surface of her coffee. "Wouldn't it be...untoward? Their mail probably hasn't even caught up to their forwarding order yet."

"Untoward? Mmmm...." Sarah sipped from her own mug and narrowed her eyes. "Well, the only people that would get the vapors from such a breach of decorum officially don't live here anymore, so I say we go for it."

Marilee shrugged. "You're the party-planner."

"We'll just go all out on the Fourth."

Marilee grunted. The Fourth meant Marilee spending a day making a big batch of her jalapeño spread. There would be potato salad and corn and melons from all corners of the neighborhood. Case Trudeau would smoke a whole pig and everyone would drink too much and wake up on the fifth with at least one regret. Marilee hadn't knowingly eaten a pork product since college, but the smell of Case's smoker going on Memorial Day and the Fourth and Labor Day always stoked her appetite. Of course, she stuck with the non-meat options, once or twice giving in to a real beef burger when she was drunk and feisty, but she never partook of the pig. There was something feral about the idea of cooking an entire animal, head and all, in a giant metal can. It was a thing that shouldn't happen in a world where all the human knowledge about every disease the pig could possibly carry could be accessed in fractions of seconds. Still...it smelled so good. And the smell would linger all day and into the night, even after everyone had picked their share off the carcass, even over the hazy brimstone residue of fireworks. Fingers would be lost. Cats' tails would catch fire. And still, the smell of smoked pig would be the last vestige of the day.

Marilee didn't want to know what Sarah's "all out" vision entailed.

Sarah knocked on one of the pickets of the porch railing. "By the way, Riley said that Leigha said that you said she could stay over tonight."

"Sure," she said. Marilee couldn't tell who was spending the night where but it didn't matter. They were a hundred feet away either way.

Sarah started across the lawn, stopped halfway between the Duncan and Stanton houses, and lifted her mug. "Think you can bring that back this morning? If Riley gets home from swim camp and her tea is in a different mug..."

"Heads roll, got it." Marilee raised Riley's mug. "I'll have it back before noon."

She looked back towards the Mailor house.

SOLD

It was the end of an era.

The Mailors were the last of their kind in Widgeon Woods. They had bought their house when it was just a floor plan and a lot number, had moved in when its hedges were knee-high and its shade trees were still being staked. Their kids were small and their cars were new and their lives were just getting going. But then they turned around and their kids were grown and their cars were rusted and fences sprung up in place of diseased hedges and the shade trees took over the front lawn and lost branches in storms. One by one, all the families that had moved into the neighborhood with them left, replaced by the Duncans and the Wolfingers and the Stantons and Case Trudeau and all the rest. Maybe the Mailors had always been grumpy, but Marilee didn't think so. Mrs. Mailor hadn't always been patrolling the street with her tape measure at night, making sure that street parkers were the city-mandated distance from curbs and mailboxes. Mr. Mailor hadn't always been posting surly essays about proper leaf-blowing etiquette to the community discussion forum. They had shared coffee mugs with their neighbors at some point, too. It's just that their neighbors had mostly gone and been replaced by a bunch of strangers.

At least that's what Marilee thought when she was feeling generous.

She was still happy them gone.

Marilee had always started her day in earnest before Ryan even woke up so she would have a good half hour to sit in quiet and think about nothing. Since her layoff, her days started later and later. Every day it was a little harder to make herself sit down and send out resumes. The morning chats with Sarah slowed her momentum; on those days when she somehow avoided her neighbor, she was as productive as she'd ever been. But most of the time she found herself in precisely her current position: waiting in the hall outside the spare room that had become Ryan's office, listening to the mumbles and groans and odd chuckles sneaking past the door. The weekly departmental meeting. Ryan never came out of those in a good mood. Marilee listened for a few more minutes, then went to return Riley Stanton's mug.

The first van pulled into the driveway across the street a week later. The grumbling engine and squealing brakes cluttered the air for five minutes before Marilee realized what she was hearing. She grabbed her mug—her own mug—and scurried out to the front porch just as a stubby moving van was backing up to the Mailors' open garage door, giving her a glimpse of empty shelves and bright white walls. Her own garage had looked like that once. Once. With a few back-up beeps, the van blocked her view. The engine cut off. Something moved inside the cab.

"What'd I miss?" Sarah whispered from the rosebush.

Marilee caught her breath. Sarah was stealthy.

"Nothing, yet," Marilee whispered back.

Sarah stepped around the rosebush but made no move to climb the porch steps. Just as well. Marilee had a lot to do and not much to say. Still, both women stood watching the van, its doors and sides a perfect blank white. Not even a trace of mismatched paint where an old logo had been.

"Think they see us?" Sarah asked.

"Yeah." Marilee tossed the last of her coffee over the side of the porch, into the hydrangeas. "But I have to walk Clarence."

"Need help?"

Marilee thought about how dawdling the old Shih Tzu's walks could be, and how much of a morning person Sarah was.

"Nah, I'm just going up the block." She jerked her chin at the blank van. "Just a quick one."

Sarah winked, lips slipping into a knowing smile. "Got it. We'll talk later."

Back in the house, Marilee leashed up Clarence and filled his little travel water kit. The old boy wasn't what he used to be, and for every shrub and mailbox he raised a leg at, he needed a long drink. Outside, she let him lead. He put his snout to the ground and sniffed his way along, swerving wide of some unknown puddles of goop, getting far too close to others. He led her halfway down the street in the opposite direction of the Mailor house before u-turning. All was quiet but for Clarence's snorts and the hollow metallic warble of the van's sides shimmying with footsteps. Nearby, cheers rose up from someone's television and drifted out to Marilee. From further away—maybe the next street over—a dog barked. Clarence took no notice but sat down and put his snout in the air, his eyes closed. Marilee waited a ten count.

"Clarence?"

He gave no signs of hearing her. This was what Ryan called a "senior moment." More and more frequently, Clarence got stuck in corners, or forgot how to use stairs, or forgot he was on a walk.

"Come on, boy." Marilee tugged the leash. Clarence shuffled after her.

The van was pulled tight up to the Mailor garage; so tight that Marilee had to squint to see where the van ended and the house began, so tight that if the van had been a couple feet higher it would have been pressing against the gutters. It wasn't completely blank after all. On the van's fender near the headlight, no bigger than Marilee's hands side-by-side, were black letters following the contour of the wheel well. She drifted in closer to the driveway until she could make out the letters.

*Welcome Wagon Rentals * "Move It Yourself"*

The footsteps from inside van stopped. Had someone seen here? She knew she was being obvious, but she couldn't look away. Something tickled her intuition. Her skin didn't crawl with eyes examining her from some hidden spot in the bushes, or prickle with some unaccountable cold breeze, but something was there. Something.

New people.

The dog on the next street over barked again. Clarence, still oblivious, continued along on bouncy paws towards his favorite bush.

The van had disappeared by the time Leigha and Riley deboarded the bus from swim camp. Marilee hadn't seen it go, hadn't even heard it, but gone it was, and the Mailor house stood with its garage door shut against curiosity. Still, Marilee caught herself glancing out windows on that side of the house more than she had any reason to. There would be another van, eventually. Surely. Even if the new neighbors had managed to pack all their worldly possessions into one single van, there would be furniture deliveries, there would be new appliances. There would be something.

"Didn't we have pasta last night?" Ryan asked, squinting at the plate of noodles in front of him as if puzzling out the meaning of an ancient artifact.

"Did we? You cooked."

"We had sweet and sour soup last night," Leigha said, her fork already entwined with spaghetti. "And a salad with too many cucumbers."

"We did. That's right," Ryan said around a garlic knot. "What's going on across the street? We have new neighbors yet?"

"I don't know." Marilee pushed a vegan meatball around the edge of her plate with the tip of her knife. "There was a van there earlier, but I didn't see anyone."

"It takes a minute to move in, I guess."

"It was weird. It was one of those little, short moving vans, and they backed it all the way up to the garage door." Marilee popped the meatball into her mouth and went to winding her own forkful of spaghetti. "Like, all the way. Like they didn't want anyone to see what was coming out of the van. Or going into it."

Ryan speared a meatball of his own and sat with it poised over his plate. "Are you serious? I can't tell."

"I don't understand what you're asking me."

"Are you really this worried about other people's moving techniques?" Ryan set his fork down onto his plate, his face tight with annoyance. "Just the fact that you've noticed all this about them and haven't even met them yet I think justifies what's probably them being worried about nosey neighbors making judgments based on the way they fold their moving boxes or whatever. Does Sarah have an opinion, too?"

Marilee contemplated the space between their plates. The whole thing was ludicrous. Patently ludicrous. Ryan was right. The new neighbors didn't want everyone to see their underwear. Her bad feeling was just the toll of months of getting second and third and fourth interviews but no offers. Blaming it on the new neighbors felt better than what it really was.

"You're right," she said, and picked up the last garlic knot. "Wild imagination, I guess."

Ryan's shoulders relaxed and his face softened.

"Do they have any kids?" Leigha asked.

"We don't know yet," Marilee said. "But I guess we'll find out eventually."

Headlights swept across the ceiling and back wall of the bedroom and winked off the mirror in the en suite. Marilee thought she had been in a deep sleep, but her eyes opened and she was aware and oriented at the first cry of brakes. Her brain had been lying to her. Nothing new there.

When the headlights disappeared and the engine cut off, she slid out from under the covers and went to the window, nudging aside the sheer curtain. Sure enough, the van was back, pulled tight against the garage again. She held her breath watching for movement in the slice of the cab that she could see under the streetlights, but the shadows were still too thick to tell anything from anything else. She let herself breathe. There were a hundred explanations for this midnight moving. A thousand. After all, between traffic and loading and breaks, they didn't have to be coming from too far away before two big trips in one day were all that made sense. And still she found that she couldn't drop the curtain, couldn't leave the window. There was something...there was something...

No lights.

Not a single light on at the Mailor place, not a flood light, not a porch light, not a bedroom light refracting from the heart of the house, not even running lights on the van.

That's not...

She let the thought linger, looking for its end. From behind her, the slippery sound of limbs moving under sheets tugged her attention away from the window. Ryan had turned on to his side and faced her now. If he opened his eyes, she would be the first thing he saw, and he would ask her what she was doing (even though it would be obvious) and she would never hear the end of it.

One more look at the Mailor place. No lights. Just the blank white sides of the van and the dark cave of its cab. Movement closer to the house caught Marilee's eye. For a second, she thought she could make out a man-shaped shadow standing at the top of the Mailor driveway. Close to the house, under the eaves, just off the crushed marble path that led from the driveway to the front door.

But it was just a trick of the light. There was nothing there after all.

The woman appeared in a blink, as if manifested by the simple act of Marilee looking towards the Mailor place. From the bay window of the Duncan living room, the woman's instantaneous materialization next to the moving van was the only interesting thing about her. She wore black yoga pants and a clingy pink t-shirt. Her dark hair was tied in a jaunty ponytail that jigged when she moved. She stood in the Mailor driveway, hands on hips, back to Marilee, tilting her head from side to side and occasionally pacing the width of the driveway only to return to center and resume tilting.

Marilee was not in the mood for the task at hand. She'd spent the morning reading the latest batch of automated rejections, and mostly just wanted everyone to go away so she could lay on the couch and die or drink or binge watch something terrible or all three. But if she didn't get to the woman soon, Sarah would, and anything Marilee could ever know about her new neighbor would be forever tainted by Sarah's first (and probably unfair) impression. So, Marilee closed her laptop on all of its hateful news, put on some fresh deodorant, and crossed the street.

"Hello," she called from next to the Mailors' mailbox.

The woman turned around. Her face was open, and her smile was bright and easy. Sweat had beaded on her upper lip and across her forehead.

"Hi." She started toward Marilee, hand extended, ponytail jigging. "Shawna. Shawna Cabrisi."

"Marilee Duncan. We're right there." Marilee returned Shawna's light shake, then gestured towards her own house, where Clarence was paws up at the bay window, watching whatever he could see with clouded eyes. "Welcome to the neighborhood."

"Oh, thank you." Shawna swiped at her forehead with the back of her hand. "The past few weeks have just been insane. I don't think I've talked to anyone but lawyers and realtors. And my husband."

"Well…" Marilee glanced back at Clarence, then up at the window above the bay window—Ryan's office, where even now a meeting was in full swing. "I was just thinking about lunch. If you need a break, we'd love to have you."

"Go ahead." A deep voice resonated from the brief wall of box hedges that delineated the last few feet of the crushed marble path leading from the driveway to the front door. "I don't want to miss the HVAC guy." The man that stepped out from behind the hedges was tall and broad-shouldered, with a thick sweep of dark hair combed back tight, and a five o'clock shadow ticking near six on his cheeks. The sun hit his face just right to deepen the ridge of his brow and obscure his eyes.

Shawna stepped to the side. "This is my husband. Dan. Dan, this is—"

"Marilee Duncan. I heard." He flashed a quick, lifeless smile and cocked his head towards his wife. Marilee could only assume that his eyes followed. "I'll just pick up tacos or something once he gets here. Go ahead."

"If you're sure?" Shawna's voice seemed to wobble. Marilee wished she could take back the invitation.

"You've got to eat." Dan took a step back behind the wall of hedges. "And make nice with our new neighbors."

Shawna shook her head. "Nice, nice, nice," she muttered. Then, to Marilee: "Just let me get cleaned up and I'll be right over."

After some exploratory sniffing, Clarence planted himself under Shawna's chair at the breakfast nook. Marilee had tried to invite Ryan to join them, but he had shooed her out of the room.

"Another hour. At least."

Now as the two women spoke over sandwiches and tomato salads. Clarence licked his lips shamelessly and watched Shawna with his most pitiful eyes. He knew better than to beg any more aggressively.

Marilee gave him a quick pat. "So, what brings you to our little corner of the world?"

Shawna sighed and shifted in her seat. "Unfortunately, my father-in-law passed a few months ago and left a mess. We now have four car dealerships and zero automotive knowledge between the two of us. Just a big mess. Our mess now, I guess." She speared a stack of tomato slices and dragged them through the puddle of dressing on her plate. "Some opportunities opened up, so here we are. Shuffling our entire lives. Fingers crossed, right?"

"Fingers crossed. Yeah. Wow. Wait—Cabrisi Imports?"

That's where she and Ryan had gotten their last car. Marilee felt stupid for not recognizing the name right away. Shawna nodded and chewed.

"Well, the HOA president is right next door." Marilee pointed her fork in the direction of Sarah's house. "So just watch the lawn."

A beat of worry crossed Shawna's face.

"I kid," Marilee said. "Everyone around here is super easygoing. Just don't have tigers in your front yard and we're cool."

Shawn smiled and swallowed her mouthful of tomatoes. "That's great to hear. I mean, we're actually going to live in Big Dan's house after we finish some renovations. Place is way too big for two people, but it's the house Dan grew up in, so it's special for him. Then we're going to rent this one out. We might not know what to do with a car dealership, but I think we can handle an investment property or two. And this one was a great one to start with. What a deal."

"Oh." This information caught Marilee by surprise. The house had been listed at a market price—maybe even a smidge more—the last time she had looked at the listing to mock the single new bathroom counter with Sarah. "That seems very unlike the Mailors. They were...they were inflexible."

"Don't know about that," Shawna said, and picked up half a sandwich. "We never met them. I just know we put in a bid after the open house. Ten percent over asking. Got rejected. Next thing you know, a couple of days later, we get a call from the realtor to see if we're still interested. All our red flags go up, so we counter with this stupid low number. Nothing to lose, other irons in the fire by then. And they take it." She took a gulp of sweet tea. "Believe me, I was braced for an entire floor of black mold on the inspection, but nothing. Place is perfect. Except for that wallpaper from the eighties."

Marilee nodded. "Let me tell you about the subway tile on the counters that this place came with."

"Yeah, but you've got that conversation pit." Shawna pointed towards the living room. "I'd keep the terrible wallpaper if it came with one of those."

"Until the first time you forget it's there and fall straight on your ass."

Shawna threw her head back and laughed. Clarence stood on his hind legs and rested his front paws on her lap. Shawna patted his head.

"Good boy, Clarence," she said, "but you're not getting any of my food."

Clarence settled back onto his haunches and swept his tail back and forth across the floor. He liked her.

Maybe the new people weren't so bad after all.

The Cabrisis' driveway was empty again, of vans and people. The house stared with its blank, uncurtained windows at Ryan and Marilee sipping beers on their front porch as they waited for Leigha's camp bus to return. Ryan didn't want to talk about his day—his meeting had gone until four—so Marilee talked about her lunch with Shawna Cabrisi. Ryan stared off at some point in the sky, nodding and grunting, until Marilee mentioned the Cabrisis' plan for their house.

"It's a thought." He twisted off the cap from a fresh beer and tossed it into the little flowerpot in the corner of the porch, next to the rosebush. He would start missing after a couple more beers. If they ever had to pull the rosebush out, they would find enough bottle caps to supply a brewery.

"A far-off thought." Marilee put her own bottle cap on the little table between her and Ryan. "The only thing my parents are going to leave me is thirty years' worth of newspapers to take to the dump. And your parents are going to slice and dice their estate between churches and long-lost relatives until you can afford a nice new spittoon for your bottle caps or something."

"Pfft." Two sips in and he was already loaded with dismissiveness. The meeting must have been worse than usual. He might start relaxing around the same time he started missing the flowerpot. "We have equity in this house. The rainy-day account isn't looking too shabby. Leigha's—"

"Stop right there. We're not dipping into our child's college fund to invest in real estate. Get it out of your head."

"I'm just thinking out loud." He reached across the little table and swiped a bottle-cold fingertip along her jaw. "Look, if I run the numbers and can show you how we can make the money back in five years, *and* catch up Leigha's college fund, could we at least agree to consider opening up the dialogue? As a possibility? Just have it out there?"

"Have what out where?" Sarah's voice slid from behind the rosebush with its usual feline sibilance. The woman herself appeared a half-second later.

"Damn ninja," Ryan sighed.

"Met the newbs." Marilee nodded across the street. "I met the wife. They own Cabrisi Imports. Well, they inherited it, I guess."

"A car salesman?" Sarah blinked.

"Oh, I don't think so," Marilee said. "Just the father-in-law. I don't remember if I asked about her husband."

"This is why you're not on the social committee, Mar. You have to ask questions. Get information. Give me dirt."

Marilee shrugged. She had never wanted to be on the social committee. Every time there was an HOA election, the social committee needed to be fully restocked, probably because *nobody* wanted to be on it.

"We had lunch," Marilee said. "I mean, you can't get dirt without laying the groundwork. Right?"

Sarah shook her head and turned away. "Impossible."

An engine rumbled. The nose of the white and blue camp bus rolled up to the corner. Brakes hissed. Bus doors thunked opened. Riley and Leigha and two other kids— Case's son, maybe, and a little boy Marilee didn't recognize at all— tumbled out in a puddle of giggles.

"There they are." Ryan stood and stretched, then started down the porch steps. "Thank God."

Ryan's hangover was going to be vicious. He drank too much before dinner, then didn't eat enough, then drank even more. All Marilee could do was get Leigha settled in for the night, then creep downstairs for a sports drink and some preemptive headache powder. These things were Ryan's only hope.

The first floor was too dark. In his drunken zeal, Ryan had turned off every light, even the light over the stove that they never turned off. Marilee—a beer or two too deep for her own good—patted the wall at the bottom of the stairs until she found the bank of light switches that commanded the entire first floor. She flicked each one up and down until the breakfast nook light came on.

Even after all these years, there were things about the house Marilee had never gotten used to, like the light switches at the bottom of the stairs. Besides forgetting which switch controlled what, she still forgot their exact location, and still reached for the opposite wall more often than not. And then there was the way the creak of the stairs traveled to places in the house it shouldn't have. The worst was how standing in the kitchen with the wide window in the breakfast nook and the high window over the sink always felt like someone could watch her entire life from her own backyard and she would never know. Like all such things, the feeling was worse at night. So, she moved quickly, filling two glasses with ice and grabbing a sports drink and the last envelope of headache powder from the pantry, leaving the lights on as she jogged past the bank of switches and up the stairs with more purpose than she ever had during the day. She was halfway up and rounding the landing when a shadow slipped across the entryway in the corner of her eye. Bright alarm pinged across her beer-dulled mind. Just like the creaking stairs, just like the stupid big windows.

She pivoted and slinked back down the stairs.

Dollars to donuts Clarence forgot where his bed is.

"Clarence? Where are you bud?"

"He's with me, Mom," Leigha called from above.

Alright, then.

Marilee took one more step down. Another creak. Another shadow, this time with matching movement outside.

"Shit."

Headlights passed on the street. Something else. She went to the bottom of the stairs, to the dining room window, and hooked the curtain back just enough to see. In front of the

Cabrisi house, the Cabrisis and Sarah and Shane stood in a loose circle near where the crushed marble walkway to the front door met the driveway. Marilee could see their shapes, the night-blurry thumbprints of their faces, but their eyes were lost to distance and darkness. Smiling. Chatting. Sarah casually touched Dan Cabrisi's shoulder. He didn't seem to notice. Marilee wondered if Shawna did.

Shane started down the driveway first, streetlights bouncing off his glasses with each wobbly step so that he looked like a confused owl. Sarah staggered close behind. Halfway across the street they remembered to look both ways. They waved over their shoulders and called something towards the Cabrisis in a slurry sing song that pressed softly against Marilee's windows. The Cabrisis waved back, then looked at each other. After a moment the thumbprints of their faces seemed to tilt slightly, and Marilee tried to follow what she imagined their line of sight would be, but she couldn't be see anything but stars and quiet rooftops where their eyes could focus or rest. Surely, they couldn't see Marliee. Surely.

"What's going on?" Ryan asked from the landing.

Marilee started, tipping an ice cube onto the floor.

"Nothing. Coming up." She snatched up the cube and gave one more look out the window. The Stantons reached their driveway, and seemed to finally compose themselves.

The Cabrisis were gone.

The next morning found Marilee queasy but not completely hungover. She poured cereal for Leigha, then made herself toast and coffee, which she took out to the sunroom, away from whatever loud thing Leigha was watching on her phone. It was still too early for the sunroom to live up to its name, but not too early for Sarah to emerge like a lost forest nymph from the hedges separating the back portions of their lots. She was mugless.

"Do you need coffee?" Marilee asked by way of greeting.

"Yeah. I guess."

"Toast? Anything else?" Marilee meant to add an edge of sarcasm to the question, but she just sounded tired to her own ears.

"No." Sarah yawned around the word. "Thanks."

Ryan was at the stove, pouring his own mug when Marilee went back inside.

"How're you feeling?" he asked.

She shook her head.

"Same," he said, handing her the pot. "We're officially not young anymore." He watched her pour Sarah's mug and add one sugar and just a splash of half and half. "I'm going back up. Don't let me sleep past ten. I think."

"Yep."

Back out in the sunroom, Sarah was stretched out over the hammock that Marilee never laid on because it always ended in spiders. "Here." Marilee handed Sarah the mug, then eased into her own spiderless chair.

Sarah took a deep, noisy drink and sighed. "Shane and I had an interesting visit with the new neighbors last night."

"How interesting?" Marilee bit down on the urge to say that it had looked interesting, at least from her end.

"They're both vets, by the way. See how easy it is to get what you need?"

"Army?"

Sarah rolled her eyes. "Cats and dogs."

An anemic revelation, coming from Sarah. It hardly supported the late-night gathering in the driveway. Of course, Marilee couldn't say it *quite* like that.

So she said, "That doesn't sound very interesting."

"Mmm...I mean, they're just interesting people in general. I've invited them to the Fourth." Sarah took another animated gulp. "Case is making a whole pig again. I think you should make a triple batch of your jalapeño spread. Last time, there almost wasn't enough for me to have leftovers."

Marilee's stomach turned at the thought of smoked pig and spicy cheese, sitting on open plates, soaking in each other's flavors.

"Can I think about this...later?"

Sarah relaxed back into the hammock, mug in her lap. "You're right. It's too early to think about anything."

The novelty of new neighbors faded into the background as Marilee sent out more resumes every day. Responses dwindled, as if the recruiters could smell her desperation over the internet. She was only able to keep track of the days by the rhythm of Leigha's camp schedule. When Leigha was gone and the only sounds in the house were the clacking of Ryan's keyboard and the puffy sighs of Clarence's farts, Marilee felt like a ghost, doing laundry when there wasn't enough for a load, cleaning things that were already clean, all for nobody to notice. Sometimes, she would listen at Ryan's office door during his meetings, just to hear other people's voices, just to make sure that she hadn't fallen into one endless day. Other times, if his door was open just a crack, she would peek in to see that he wasn't even at his desk but staring out the window, across the street, towards the Cabrisi house. They began to have the same conversation every day, usually during lunch.

"We could cover the mortgage, and the property management, and still have money left over."

"Where will we live? The tool shed?"

"We move some place cheaper. I keep my job, you have a different market to look in—"

"Do you think other places are cheaper because people want to live there? And where does Leigha go to school?"

"She's going to a different school next year whether we move or not."

"But she has friends here."

Round and round they went, over and over, wearing grooves into her will until it started to feel right. Inevitable. Even as the interviews without callbacks piled up, even as messages to recruiters went unread. Anything different had to be better. She mentioned it to the only person she knew that would give her unvarnished candor.

Sarah listened intently from the rosebush's side, mug sending wisps of steam up past her face. "I guess that's the thing about being married to a risk manager. You lose your sense of adventure. Shane just doesn't have the stomach for anything we didn't map out and color code when we got married."

"I didn't think Ryan did, either. We've nickeled and dimed everything for so long. It's like a dam burst as soon as he heard the idea. And honestly? I'm starting to think he might...not...be wrong?"

Sarah wagged her head side to side. "If you can make it work. I mean, you two are down a job and you don't have an inheritance. There's a lot of variables. What if Ryan gets laid off, too?"

"I don't know." Marilee had given that exact scenario one sideways thought. Any more than that set anxiety to a low churn in her stomach.

"Mar, you should do what makes you happy. I'm just telling you why I would have misgivings. I don't think our situations are that different."

There was a tone in Sarah's voice, a condescension that reminded Marilee of the way she spoke to Leigha sometimes when she was tired of fighting and ready to let her daughter learn a lesson the hard way. It raised Marilee's hackles. Time to divert.

"Well, you know, it's all just talk right now. I just needed to vent." Marilee cut her eyes across the street. She hadn't talked much to Shawna since that first day. There had been waves from their respective mailboxes and quick greetings, and even a few polite exchanges with Dan, even though he never seemed to leave the crushed marble walkway. Nothing more. It had been days since she'd seen either of them, or their car. There hadn't even been any more vans. "What time do you plan to have people start showing up for the Fourth?"

"Sixish, I think. Time to eat before the fireworks. Is Leigha doing the overnight thing with camp?"

"What overnight thing?" Marilee balanced her mug on the porch railing.

"They're taking them out to the cabins at Keyes Lake to watch the fireworks, then they're doing the whole gross campfire and marshmallows thing."

It all rang a distant bell. "Yeah, of course. Brain fart." The dim memory of signing a permission slip fluttered across Marilee's mind.

"Oh!" Sarah slapped her hands together and smiled. "I forgot to tell you—Shane's going to the border for fireworks this year, so we'll have the good ones. Fair warning for Clarence."

"Of course." A fly dive-bombed into Marilee's mug. She tossed coffee and fly into the hydrangeas. "Fair warning about fireworks from the risk manager."

Marilee awoke on the morning of the Fourth with a groan. Her mind had a habit during the night before holidays of tricking her into thinking she didn't have to be anywhere. She would play along until one alarm snooze short of officially sleeping late before getting up and dealing with all the things she didn't have to deal with on non-holidays. Today, there was the jalapeño spread that she was beginning to wish she had never let out of her kitchen, and making sure Leigha had everything for her overnight.

While Ryan went out on an early run, she took Clarence for a walk. She intended to make it an extra-long one, hopefully tiring the poor old guy out enough that he slept through the fireworks. He didn't hear much these days, but he'd at least hear some of those fireworks, and he wouldn't be right for the rest of the night, and a few days afterward.

"Alright, Clarence. Let's try to act right."

Marilee pulled the dog's harness tight and scratched behind his ears. He pulled her towards the door with his usual frail enthusiasm. Out on the sidewalk, he made a right turn. They were nearly out of sight of their house when the realization reared up in Marilee's consciousness in full, undeniable view: she was being watched. The feeling was as palpable as another person pacing her and Clarence.

She glanced over her shoulder. There was a van in the Cabrisi driveway again. Were they still moving in, or moving back out again? Had they really gotten everything in order so quickly? There were no signs declaring the house for rent, though Marilee supposed she could check online later. It must have been easier to be a nosey neighbor in the days when educated guesses about a person's status could be made by the size of the pile of uncollected newspapers on their porch.

She let Clarence walk until his steps slowed with exhaustion and his tongue lolled out of his mouth with heat. The feeling of eyes on her had become heavy, intrusive, and she kept walking despite Clarence's condition just to get away from it, but the feeling didn't pass. She picked Clarence up and turned around, back the way they had come. They would just go home, where he could cool off and she could take a shower and get Leigha ready and make jalapeño spread. But the closer she got to her house, the more intense the sensation became, until she wouldn't have been surprised to glance towards the Cabrisi windows and see Dan standing there, and probably with binoculars.

Clarence stopped panting and tilted his nose at the air, sniffing. She put him down.

"Just a little farther, buddy, then we're home. Promise."

His sniffs grew louder, frenzied. He tugged at his leash to press his nose hard against the sidewalk.

"Clarence, there's nothing there."

Clarence didn't care. His head popped up and his body straightened with the determination of a dog still able to hunt. Even his ears perked up under their shag.

"What's going on, puppers?" Marilee stooped and touched the top of his head; it was as if she had flipped a switch. He took off, straining so hard against the limit of his leash that the loop of its handle chafed Marilee's hand. Clarence only pulled harder, until his front paws lifted off the ground, and then he exploded with a hail of barks so loaded with fury that his back paws skipped forward with each cry. The barks turned into growl-howls, noises Marilee hadn't heard from Clarence in years.

"Buddy, what—"

His jaws snapped shut and he fell back onto his haunches.

"Come on. Let's get home." She tugged his leash. Clarence rose to all fours and planted. She tugged harder. "I'm serious, bud. Let's go." He still resisted, tried to sit down again, but she tugged him, harder, almost too hard. Enough to make twelve obstinate pounds scuff paw pads across asphalt in protest.

They passed the Cabrisis' driveway and were nearly past the hedges that separated the Cabrisis from the Martinezes when the sound started: a high, shrieking whine, too sudden and fierce to make sense of what or where it was. Clarence jumped and broke into a jog; Marilee followed. On the other side of the Martinezes' lot, Marilee's brain settled enough to try to name the sound. Animal? Person? Machine? Too full to be someone's dying brake pads. Too loud and long to be a person. If it was an animal, it wasn't one she wanted to see. Unease dug back in when she realized that the sound could be coming from anywhere. The dip in the terrain and the trees thick with leaves were enough to fool any ear. Sweat ran down her spine and pooled at the top of her shorts. Clarence's tongue was out again.

"Come on, boy." She reached down and scooped him up. He licked her cheek. "Love you, too, bud."

The whine went on as they cut across the street. Clarence tightened into a ball of muscle in her arms. It was only when she was almost to her front door, where the rosebush and the hydrangeas and even the sides of her house killed the misdirecting echo, that she could tell that the sound was coming from the Cabrisi house. She watched for a moment, waiting, but there were no people, motion, just the unidentifiable sound.

Marilee shook her head. It was too hot. It was none of her business. And anyway, she could just mention it to Dan and Shawna at the party that night.

Or she could just forget about it.

After breakfast, Ryan fell asleep in the recliner with Clarence in his lap. Marilee took her own nap after the triple batch of spread was done and Leigha's bag was packed. She woke up in the quiet blue of the afternoon to her phone vibrating with a text from the swim camp that the bus was running late but would be there within an hour. Marilee called the news up to Leigha, then worked up into a sitting position to get her bearings. Even with windows closed, the air was lurid with the scents from Case Trudeau's smoker. She roused Ryan, and once they were both awake, they packed up the spread, saw Leigha and Riley and Case's son and the other unknown kid from down the street onto the bus, then headed across the lawn to the Stanton house.

The crowd was thin. No sign of the Cabrisis. Marilee checked the time on her phone. Maybe it was still a little too early to expect everyone there, but it felt less like a party and more like a regular day, and a handful of friends had all happened to drop in at the same time. The only thing that told the tale of the occasion was the picnic table set out on the back patio with a red, white, and blue tablecloth, and the assortment of cafe tables and stools and folding tables and chairs spread out around the yard. Case's smoker sat in the midst of it all, oozing tendrils of meaty air from its vents. The fire pit squatted next to it, cold and jealous.

So much for my triple batch.

It wasn't even dark by the time she ran out of people to talk to and things to say. She found Sarah in the kitchen, standing at the island, rearranging appetizers with one hand and taking down a glass of wine in one gulp with the other.

"What's going on out there?" Marilee asked.

Sarah put down the glass and looked up from what was left of the jalapeño spread. Thin crowd or not, it was all but demolished. Sarah wouldn't be getting her leftovers.

"What do you mean?"

"I didn't know my spread was going to be the whole show. I would have made a quadruple batch."

Sarah snatched up a cracker and plowed it through a strip of the spread, then popped it into her mouth. "I just didn't invite a lot of people. Last year was a little too much, even for me. Quality, not quantity."

"Okay. Sure. I guess I'm flattered to be considered quality.

Sarah's half-drunk smile was too big. "You should be."

Marilee left Sarah to finish the spread, and found Ryan in the living room, where Shane had trapped him next to the fireplace.

"Can I borrow him?" she asked.

"Of course!" Shane bowed his head and flourished his hand. "Anything for you."

It was Shane's weird, drunk attempt at charm. Marilee hated it.

"What's up?" Ryan asked once they were out of Shane's earshot.

"Nobody's here," she said. "I'm tired, Ry."

"Give it another hour." He jerked his chin towards the sliding glass door. Night had begun draping itself over the Stantons' backyard. "We'll watch the fireworks and then we're done, okay? I mean, he went all the way to the border, right?"

Marilee bit her lip. Nothing like fireworks to turn men with jobs and families into pre-teen boys.

"Okay," she said. "Yeah. I guess."

"Everyone!" Shane bellowed, so close to Marilee's head that her hair moved. She hadn't realized her was so close. He was as stealthy as his wife. He reached past her shoulder and flipped on the floodlights to the back. "Time to eat!"

"Finally," Ryan sighed.

"Well, come on." Shane pushed the door open wide. The handful of neighbors scattered around the living room drifted towards the open door. "Main event, y'all. Let's get some cue and watch the works."

"That is the most dad shit I've ever heard," Ryan said in Marilee's ear, and she smiled, and laughed.

She would remember that moment for a long time. The happy buzz in Ryan's voice. The smell of the smoker. The grin on Shane's face. She would remember it all forever.

On the patio, everyone passed around plates, and heaped them with potato salad and corn and watermelon as fast as Sarah could bring the food to the table. People found their spots. Case fiddled with dials on the smoker. Shane patted him on the shoulder, mumbled something, then hopped up onto the edge of the fire pit and raised his hands over his head until all eyes were on him. Only the crickets objected.

"Everyone, welcome. As always. Plan is to eat, then show off these fireworks, then make a bunch of bad decisions. Right?" A few weak chortles shuffled around the gathering. Marilee managed a smile. "I think Sarah has something," Shane said.

Sarah declined climbing atop the fire pit, but her voice projected all the same.

"Everyone knows how much I love a good party." More scattered laughter. "Any excuse for a batch of Marilee's jalapeño—"

"Ooooooooooooooooo!"

The entire scene froze at the sound. There was desperation in that sound, deep and clawing.

"What the hell?" Shane's grin faltered. "Coyotes so early?"

"OooooOooooOooooo!"

Marilee knew that sound. It seared into her brain like a baby's wail.

"Clarence!" She was up and halfway across the lawn before anyone else had a second reaction.

"What is it?" Ryan called, his voice shaking with the jog to catch up to her.

"Something's wrong with Clarence!" Marilee called back, barreling straight for their side door, even as Clarence let out another long, high howl.

"OoooooooOooooOoooooooooo!"

"Okay. Okay." Ryan was at her side, out of breath, smelling grassy and boozy and sweaty all at once. "Let's see what that little nerd's up to. Let me go first. Alright?"

He pushed open the door.

There was Clarence, sitting in the middle of the kitchen floor, watching the door as if he knew that's where his humans would come to his rescue. He popped up onto all fours and licked his chops, then pressed his nose against Marilee's knee.

"He just misses us. You." Ryan squatted down and ran a hand down the dog's back. "It'll just get worse as he gets older. Maybe we should talk to those Cabrisi people about helping his stress levels or whatever. They're vets, right?"

"Yeah. Yeah, maybe." Maybe it was the lackluster night, or Clarence's plaintive cry, but the sound of her new neighbors' name made Marilee's shoulders and neck tense up, the same way Clarence had balled himself into her arms after their walk. She thought about the still house, the van pulled tight to the garage, Clarence's lupine outburst. She thought of being watched, and of that terrible noise. "Can we just check the house first, though? Please?"

"Of course. Of course."

They went from room to room, Marilee a step behind Ryan, Clarence in her arms and licking the back of her hand nervously. Ryan turned on the light in each room, checked behind each door and under each piece of furniture big enough to conceal a person.

"Nothing," he said finally, as they stepped out of their bedroom. "Nothing on any of the cameras, either." He shook his phone at her. "Just give him a treat and put him in his anxiety shirt. Maybe we should cut out before the fireworks, too. So you can be with him."

Marilee nodded. "Yeah. I mean, you can stay there if you want to. I understand."

"Nah," Ryan said. "The whole night's been a bust, I think."

He started back down the stairs. Marilee took a step to follow. Something flashed from Ryan's open office, from where its window looked out over their front lawn and across the street. From deep in the Cabrisi house, a light flickered.

"Someone's home," she said.

"What?" Ryan snapped from the landing.

"Make sure we locked all the doors. I'm bringing Clarence. We'll make our apologies and come right back."

Ryan sighed.

"Like I said, you can go back and watch the fireworks if you want," she said.

He shook his head and said nothing, but did as she asked.

The part of the Cabrisi house that Marilee could see from the side lawn was as dark and still as always. She might have imagined the light, but she didn't think she had. Their apologies would be quick. She wanted to be home, behind locked doors, Clarence safe and calm at her side.

When they made it back to the Stanton backyard, Case Trudeau still stood by his fuming smoker, and Sarah and Shane were still in their spots by the fire pit, as if everything had paused while the Duncans tended to Clarence. Marilee and Ryan slid back into their seats. Clarence grunted and nuzzled into the crook of Marilee's elbow.

"Everything alright?" Shane asked.

"Clarence just being a grumpy old man," Ryan said, taking the fresh beer that Sarah stepped forward to offer him. "But we'll probably head out soon. Before the fireworks. Just to be safe."

"Oh, of course," Sarah said. "But not before we finish the toast. Marilee? Do you have a drink?"

Marilee lifted Clarence.

"Good enough, I guess." Sarah said to a ripple of laughter much more genuine than the polite titters Shane had gotten.

Everybody loves Sarah.

"So, anyway, I just want to make a toast to the best neighbors a girl could have. That goes double for the Duncans and the best damn jalapeño spread ever. Cheers!"

Glasses and bottles and cups and Clarence rose into the air.

"Cheers!" came the chorus from around the fire pit.

"To our health!" Case Trudeau drank deep from his own bottle, then knocked on the top of the smoker. He reached down and pulled a lever, then pulled open the top jaw of the smoker. It opened with a creak. Case stepped back and took another drink.

Marilee recognized Dan Cabrisi right away by the thick shock of black hair and the quarter to six shadow that stood out even against his browning skin. Shawna was not so easy to tell; her face was mostly obscured by the smoke rising from the racks of cuts beneath their heads. All of this information Marilee's brain took in, but refused to collate. Refused to process. It was a joke. It wasn't real. Couldn't be real.

Ryan grabbed her hand. She opened her mouth to scream but Sarah was there, pressing a finger to Marilee's lips.

Shane hopped off the fire pit and stood in front of Ryan and Marilee. He was suddenly towering, suddenly broad in the shoulders the way Dan Cabrisi—Dan Cabrisi—had been. Broader. He looked down on them, eyes wide and unblinking behind his glasses.

"This is our neighborhood. We have to keep it that way," he said, his voice thin and high and sharp, like a…like a…

Eagle. Owl. Bird of prey.

Sarah moved in closer, squatted to Marilee's level and gripped her knee. Her nails were sharp. When she spoke, her too-long incisors glistened in the blue-white floodlights. "You know, Morgan went through a lot of trouble to make sure we covered the loss the Mailors would take from rescinding their acceptance of the offer from the investment company. Almost wiped out all the HOA accounts and even then…well, look, I think Cindy will enjoy her retirement a little better now without Stan. He was never happy anyway."

Memorial Day…Memorial Day…Memorial Day…Oh…not Memorial Day….

Sarah jerked her head back in the direction of the smoker. One of Dan's eyes had begun to slide down his cheek. "These two. They lied on their paperwork. Some loan scam to get a better interest rate, when they knew the whole time they weren't going to live here. Weren't going to be one of us. You let that kind of thing go, and next thing you know, the streets are lined with plastic mailboxes and discount store lawn ornaments. That's not what we all worked for. Saved for. Right? You two…" Sarah shifted her weight and took the same hand of Marilee's that Ryan had taken. "We watch each other's kids. We drink each other's coffee. We mow each other's lawns. Check each other's mail."

Marilee lifted her head and scanned the backyard. The rest of the party gathered in a semicircle around the smoker, but none of them were right. They were all too big, too tall, limbs too long, joints at all the wrong angles. Their eyes flickered as if there were fire in their skulls. Even when she looked away, she could feel their stares on her. That feeling. She knew that feeling.

She should have seen it earlier in the night, not that it would have mattered, because she still wouldn't have known what it meant: the crowd was so thin because it was the board of the HOA and their spouses. No one else.

"You weren't one of us, but it was okay for a long time, because you're a good neighbor, Marilee. Truly." Sarah's voice rasped and fizzled. Purred. "That's why we're giving you a chance now. To be one of us. Make it official. Make it *permanent.*"

Morgan stepped forward, holding several thin cuts of glistening, crimson meat on red-white-and-blue paper plate towards Marilee and Ryan. Sarah picked up a slice of meat and held it to Clarence's nose. He snapped it out of her fingers and chewed. He yelped when Marilee dropped him, but kept chewing.

"I can't...I can't..." Ryan's hand had gone slick with sweat. Marilee could feel the tremble coming from deep inside him. Gut deep. Bone deep.

"We know you're vegetarian," Shane said. "You might have a stomachache for a few days since your body isn't used to meat, but it'll pass."

"Leigha..." Marilee croaked.

"It takes a village, Marilee, but we don't tell you how to raise your child. We wouldn't dare. We're sure you'll do what's best for her. And when it's time she'll make her own choices. That's the end of good parenting, right? They make their own choices." Shane nodded as his wife spoke. "You know, you buy a house, but you build a home, and we've built something special here. We're just asking you to appreciate that. That's all. I mean, what are your choices, Mar? Really?" Sarah patted Marilee's hand and stood up. "We always need someone for the social committee. As much as I pick, I think you'd be perfect for it. You know how to make people feel at home."

Marilee's mouth opened and closed without a sound. She had no words. There were no words anywhere.

"Right," Shane trilled. "In the meantime, we're going to have a house to get out of foreclosure and a lot of paperwork to do. We can count on you two to pitch in, right?"

Marilee felt herself nodding. In the corner of her eye, she saw Ryan do the same.

"All work, no play, huh?" Case said. "Come on. Let's save business for tomorrow." He stood over the smoker. Slicing. Slicing. Slicing. How could he hold the knife with his hands like that, with his fingers like claws, with his wrists that bent the wrong way?

"Not all business." Shane slapped his scaly talons together and rubbed them. "Now—let's eat."

3¢ USA
261 LAFF GOBLIN
MONSTER VALUE STAMP
THIS IS IT!
CLIP THEM
& COLLECT
THEM ALL!

CRITICAL BLAST PUBLISHING
20¢
APPROVED BY THE READING CODE AUTHORITY
GOOD NEIGHBORHOOD
Robert Allen Lupton
THE JOHNSON GIRLS WERE DIFFERENT!

COCAINE FOR PETS When your pets become too excited during mating season and you don't want additional burden of feeding more pets, shot them up with some fine liquid snow and chill them out.

WELCOME MAT TRAP When you don't want people annoying you, a simple press of the button and the trap door will dispose of anyone who stands on it, while waiting for you to answer the door.

EXPLODING DRINK Sit back and enjoy the highjinks as people unscrew their drink activating the chemical reaction, causing a foamy mess.

HYPNO-ROBOT use the special mind control eye harmonics to subdue the minds of your unwilling subjects. You'll never have to take out the trash and everyone will worship you as if their life depends on it.

RENT AN ANGRY MIDGET! When you need to stop a Bully from harassing, or when you need to look like a decent human concerned for poor ugly monsters.

LEARN TO PLAY THE GUITAR! When you can't get a date for the weekend, rent a sexy Guitar Teacher to impress your friends and maybe you just might learn something too.

BOX OF LIVE BATS When you feel like a millionaire crime fighting hero and need to dress up your special cave, to give it that extra touch of atmosphere... a box of live bats is perfect for you. Food not included.

LIFE IS A BIG CHALLENGE, SO LET IT GO!

FISH BOWL FULL OF WORMS Are you tired of eating meat? Get yourself a bowl full of yummy worms and feel you are saving the planet.

SUPER SHARP PIRATE SWORD When you want to capture the hearts and minds of the people around you, this sword will cut through the muscle and bone to get to the vital organs you need to sustain your hunger.

HEAD KNIVES 100% stainless steal daggers that launch from the top of your head and kill any conversation you find boring.

BOW AND ARROW KIT! When you need to go into battle on Tuesdays and don't know what weapon to take with you.

Robert Allen Lupton is retired and lives in New Mexico where he was a commercial hot air balloon pilot. Robert runs and writes every day, but not necessarily in that order. Over 200 of his short stories have been published in various anthologies, magazines, and online magazines. He has three novels in print, Foxborn, and the sequel, Dragonborn. His third novel, Dejanna of the Double Star was published in the fall of 2019 as was his edited anthology, Feral, It Takes a Forest. He co-edited the Three Cousins Anthology, Are You A Robot? in 2022. Visit him on Amazon at amazon.com/author/luptonra

This was a good neighborhood until the Johnsons moved next door. They didn't take care of anything. Weeds speckled their unmown grass, the house paint was faded and peeled, and their backyard was a dumpster fire waiting to happen. It seemed like every pigeon, crow, sparrow, and grackle in town lived in their trees. There was enough bird poop in their yard to fertilize a small farm.

I rode the school bus with the Johnson girls, Iris and Azalea. Their clothes were worn and dirty, they wore shoes that would fit circus clowns, and they smelled a little like wet dogs. Iris and I were a year older than Azalea. They were both taller than me.

My dad said, "Connie, you stay away from them Johnsons. Something's not right about those girls."

Mom said, "Brian, you were young once. Remember, there's nothing like forbidding a twelve-year-old to do something to ensure that she does it."

I just smiled, nodded my head, and did what I wanted whenever Mom and Dad weren't around. At first, I was afraid of the Johnson girls. They did smell funny and like I said, they were big, really big.

Our bus broke down one Friday and we were stuck at school until another one could come and pick us up. Kids with time on their hands is a recipe for trouble and Carl Baron was trouble incarnate. He lived right across the street from me. His parents owned the biggest house in the neighborhood, drove really expensive cars, and people said that they didn't have a washer and dryer. They were so rich they threw away their clothes after they wore them one time. Mrs. Baron never drove herself anywhere. Her driver was big enough to pick up the car and carry it to the mall.

We didn't know where the Barons' money came from, but it was fun to speculate. Gloria, my best friend, said, "My dad's a detective. The police got nothing on Mr. Baron, but Dad thinks he's some kinda mobster from Boston or New York City. His electric bill is really high. Could be making drugs. Maybe the Barons kidnap girls like us and sell them as slaves to other countries. It'd be exciting to be sold into the harem of some really rich sheik, who'd fall in love, marry me, and make me a sheikess or something."

I punched her in the shoulder. "Glo, you gotta quit reading those bodice-rippers your mom buys."

That's when Carl shoved me against the school building. "You got any lunch money? Give it to me."

The rough brick building scratched my elbows when I tried to squirm away. "Lunch money? Why you want my lunch money, you got more money than all of us put together."

"Gotta keep in practice. My dad makes me ride the stupid bus with you people. I hate it, I've gotta do something to entertain myself. So lunch money, now!"

He twisted my arm and my eyes watered. I fell on the sidewalk and scraped my knees. Iris grabbed him by his hair and jerked his head back. He let me go and took a swing at her, but Azalea caught his fist in her right hand. He stepped back and raised his hands like a boxer. "What the hell," he said. "I don't fight girls, especially girls who smell funny. The circus called. The clowns want their shoes back."

Iris shoved him. "We fight boys, especially boys that pick on people smaller than them. What's the matter, Carl? Are you afraid to fight someone your own size?"

"There's two of you and you're both bigger than me."

Iris shoved him again. "Just me. Azalea won't help. Let's go. Fight me or give Connie your lunch money."

Azalea helped me up and handed me her faded dirty scarf to wipe the blood from my knees. I blubbered through the sting of the sidewalk scrape. "I don't want his damn money. I just want him to leave me the hell alone."

Iris punched him in the chest. "He has to pay something. If it doesn't cost him something, he won't learn nothing."

"If Connie doesn't want his money, make him tear it up. That'll teach him," said Gloria.

"You better stay out of this, Gloria Westervelt. I know where you live. I know where you all live. I'll tell my dad."

Iris grabbed his ear and twisted it until he cried. "I hate you. I hate you all," whined Carl, but he took out his money clip.

"Tear it up," laughed Gloria.

Carl's eyes glistened, but he ripped up his money and tossed it into the air. "Happy now?"

Iris gave his ear one final twist. "We will be. No bus for you today. Start walking."

Azalea followed him across the street. He yelled, "This ain't over." He took his cell phone out of his backpack and made a call. After he hung up, he walked to the nearest corner and waited. He was still leaning against a streetlight when the substitute bus picked up the rest of us.

That night after dinner, I told my parents that I was going to the neighborhood park to play hide-and-seek with my friends. Mom smiled absently and said, "That's nice, dear. Be home before dark."

I met Gloria and we walked together. Azalea and Iris were already at the park. They sat under a large oak tree and at least a hundred birds flocked around them. A squirrel slept in Azalea's lap and three baby rabbits played with her shoelaces. I asked, "Are you guys related to Dr. Doolittle? Can you talk to animals?"

"I'm gonna tell them," Iris said to her sister. "Yes, and no. No Dr. Doolittle, but yes, we talk to animals."

"Looks just like a scene from Snow White," said Gloria.

"Naw, we aren't princesses. Princesses aren't as tall as we are."

I said, "Princesses got little feet, too!"

"Yes, Connie, they do. That's what I'm going to tell you about, but you can't tell anyone, cross your heart and hope to die. The animals like us, because we're more like animals than we are regular people. Our dad says that folks like you, humans that is, folks like you lost the ability to talk to animals thousands of years ago. We aren't animals, but we aren't exactly humans. Mom and Dad left the north woods when they got married about fifteen years ago. They keep themselves shaved pretty good, learned to speak English, got jobs, bought a house, and had us."

I said I didn't understand.

"People are destroying the forests and soon there won't be any woods where our kind can live. Men hunt us all the time and our parents decided that if you can't beat 'em, join 'em. Azalea and I will be well over six feet tall when we grow up. Professional basketball here we come. You talked about our shoes earlier. Big shoes mean big feet. Bigfeet! That's one of our names. Bigfoot, Sasquatch, Yeti, and Manitou are different names, but they all mean us."

Glo laughed, "Crap. That's crap. No such thing as Bigfeet."

I backed away. "Monsters! Bigfeet are monsters. You eat people, especially children."

Azalea petted one of the rabbits. "Don't be stupid. We're vegetarians. Why would you think we're monsters? No human ever even took a clear photograph of us, let alone joined one of us for lunch."

Gloria petted a rabbit. "I bet Carl thinks that you're monsters."

Iris growled and the animals moved away from her. "Carl's a shit. Don't care what he thinks if he leaves us alone. Protecting you and ourselves doesn't make us monsters."

"Iris," replied her sister, "There'll always be someone who thinks you're a monster."

"Don't give me that mumbo-jumbo, I'm not a damn monster. Carl's the monster and so are his parents. They're trolls. I can smell trolls from a mile away."

"Slow down, girls. I can't speak for Glo, but I'm not ready to believe in monsters. I don't believe my neighbors are Bigfeet or trolls. Iris, stop teasing us."

Iris moved her arm in a gentle circle that encompassed the birds, rabbits, and squirrels. She made a clicking sound and three chipmunks ran from the bushes and climbed in her lap. "Believe your eyes."

"Okay, the animals love you. I get it," Glo said. "Being Peter Cottontail's best buddy doesn't make you a Bigfoot, even though you do have some big feet. Connie and I aren't ready to believe we're living in a Saturday morning cartoon come to life."

Azalea cracked and ate three acorns. "Carl and his parents smell like trolls, a mix of greed, decay, violence, and mold. It's hard to get the stench of living under a bridge out of your hair no matter how many times you wash it. Trolls are about making money and eating things. They're hoarders, the same as dragons. The animals hate trolls because trolls eat them. I betcha Carl and his parents would eat us if they thought they could get away with it. Their jaws are like snake jaws and they can open their mouths really wide. Trolls eat everything!"

"First, yuck to eating acorns. I know Carl is an ass," said Glo. "But you're telling us that he's a troll and a cannibal."

"Not a cannibal," replied Azalea. "Cannibals eat their own kind. Trolls don't eat other trolls, but they do eat people."

Iris chimed in. "You'll notice that the coyotes don't come into our neighborhood since the Barons moved in. No rats or stray cats around either."

"So, we're supposed to believe in Bigfeet and people-eating trolls. How about vampires? You haven't said anything about vampires."

Mrs. Johnson whistled for Azalea and Iris to come home. That woman could whistle. There was no way the girls could pretend they couldn't hear her. "We gotta go," said Iris. "Of course, we didn't say nothing about vampires. The closest ones live about three miles away. Mr. Dark is the all-night disc jockey on KOMO."

The next few days were like an armed truce at school. Carl sat by himself on the bus and the four of us sat together, but as far from him as we could. We pointedly ignored him in class and he behaved as if we didn't exist. His dad picked him up during lunch on Friday. Gloria laughed and said, "I'm glad he left early. He looked sick. I was afraid he was contagious. I'd hate to catch trollio."

Azalea emptied her water bottle over Glo's head.

All in all, it was a good week, but things went to crap when I got home on Friday. My mother wasn't in the house. I looked in the backyard and the garage. She wasn't in either place. I opened the garage door and her car was there. I opened the overhead door and walked outside. Azalea and Iris stood in the weeds they call a front yard. "Our mom's not home. The house stinks like trolls."

"My mom's not home either. Maybe they're both at Glo's house."

Gloria ran around the corner. She had tears in her eyes. "My house was unlocked and my mom's not home. There was a pot of soup on the stove. It was almost boiled dry. Mom would never leave the burner on."

Iris hugged her. "Our mom isn't home either. Our house smells like trolls."

Azalea sniffed my garage. "Trolls. I bet Carl and his parents took our moms."

I'd like to say that I was brave, but I wasn't. A week ago I didn't believe in trolls, bigfeet, or vampires, and I was overwhelmed to learn that not only did monsters exist, but they'd kidnapped my mom. I blubbered, "They took our moms because we stood up to Carl. What'll they do with them?"

Glo punched my shoulder. "Don't you remember anything? It's gonna be bad. Trolls are people eaters. They damn sure won't make them sheikesses."

"Pretty sure sheikesses isn't a word," said Iris.

"Shut the hell up," shouted Glo. "Just because you got a good razor and learned to speak English don't me crap to me. I want my mother, not a vocabulary lesson."

I tried to be the voice of reason. "Chill. They want us to fight with each other instead of trying to save our moms. We should call our fathers."

"What're we gonna tell 'em? Hi, Dad. This is Gloria. Mom's missing and the Johnson girls say that our house smells like trolls. What's that? How do I know? Well, Iris and Azalea are actually baby Bigfeet and they can smell trolls."

I thought about it. Glo was right. Our dads would figure that our moms had gone shopping or were sharing a bottle of afternoon wine. They were at work and wouldn't appreciate a fake fairy tale emergency from a twelve-year-old. The four of us were in this together. The Baron house loomed across the street. It was silent, deathly silent. Not a bird chirped. No bees tended the blooming flowers and there wasn't a cricket or grasshopper to be heard.

"Do you think the Barons are home?"

Azalea nodded. "Must be. It's too quiet. Birds and bugs stay away when the trolls are home."

"If we're gonna save our moms, we're gonna need a plan," said Iris. "I feel them watching us."

"How can you feel someone watching you?"

"I can't explain it, but we can. It's why no one ever took a good photograph of us."

We went into my garage and closed the door. Azalea said, "Iris and I can sneak into the house. I don't know how we'll get you and Glo inside."

"I'm pretty damn sneaky," shouted Glo.

"Sneaky is usually quieter than that," observed Azalea. "Sneaking is mostly about not being noticed. We're good at that. Being still and blending in is one of the things Bigfeet do best. Iris and I can show you."

Iris reached into her jeans and pulled out a handful of coins. "Watch," she said and she scattered the coins on the concrete garage floor. I watched and listened to the coins clatter for a few seconds. I looked up and Iris and Azalea were gone. The doors were still closed and they were gone.

"Son of a bitch!" exclaimed Glo.

After a minute, Azalea waved her arm. She was in a corner by the garden tools. Iris whistled softly from the shadows next to the refrigerator. "We can hide in plain sight. It's a gift. We can walk right into the Baron house if we can get them to open the door."

"I got a plan," said Glo. "Everybody likes Girl Guard Cookies. Connie and I will put on our uniforms, grab six or seven boxes, and knock on the door."

"That'll work. We got a dozen boxes in the freezer."

Azalea opened the freezer door. "You got Skinny Mints? I love those."

Iris slapped her hand. "It's a poor fisherman who eats his own bait. You two put on your uniforms. We'll put the cookies in the sun and let them thaw. Hurry, who knows what those assholes are doing to our moms?"

Ten minutes later, Glo and I knocked on the Baron's front door. Carl answered. "Isn't this nice? We didn't order any cookies."

Glo said, "Your parents always buy a dozen boxes. We've got Skinny Mints, Raspberry Rockers, and Caramel Cannoli."

"Yeah, I'd buy them all if someone hadn't made me tear up my money." He slammed the door.

Glo and I looked for the Bigfeet girls, but we couldn't find them. They were gone and so were two boxes of Skinny Mints. "I hope they got inside. Should we wait here or go back to my house?"

The door opened before Glo could answer. Azalea said, "Leave the gun, bring the cannoli."

I whispered, "What gun."

Azalea smiled, "I know you don't have a gun. I just wanted to say that."

Glo and I followed Azalea into the kitchen. Iris stood next to a locked basement door. "Our mothers are in the basement. I can smell them. They're afraid, but I don't think they've been hurt. I don't smell blood."

"Where are the Barons?"

Iris inhaled deeply. "Mrs. Baron is in the basement. She smells afraid, too. Carl's down there. Mr. Baron is upstairs."

Azalea nodded. "Carl first. Once we free our moms, they can help us with Mr. Baron. We'll figure out what to do with Mrs. Baron once we've taken care of Carl."

"What are we gonna do with Carl?"

"I don't know, Connie. We've never fought a troll before," replied Iris.

Azalea concentrated and a dozen roaches scampered out from under the stove. The disgusting little beasts crawled up the basement door and into the lock. A moment later the lock clicked open. We closed the door behind us and crept downstairs.

"You talk to roaches. That's just wrong," I whispered.

"Hush," whispered Iris.

I hushed and looked around. Our mothers and Mrs. Baron were gagged and tied to chairs bolted to the floor. Clearly, they weren't the first people to spend some quality time in the basement. Carl sat in the corner reading a comic book. If he was supposed to be on guard, he was doing a damn poor job.

"Iris," I whispered. "Why's Mrs. Baron tied up?"

"She's not a troll. She smells human."

"I heard that," screamed Carl. "My dad's monitoring the room. I knew you guys were planning something. How nice of you to just waltz in. Saves us the trouble of hunting for you."

Carl picked up a club and stepped between us and our mothers. The door opened and Mr. Baron stomped down the stairway. He chanted, "Fe Fi Fo Fum. I smell the blood of human scum."

Carl groaned, "Dad, you're embarrassing me."

"That's my job. Let's get these young ladies tied up. I'm sure we'll find someone to buy them. If not, the stew always needs more meat."

Iris stepped toward the stairs. "I got the old man. Azalea, you take Carl. Connie, you and Glo untie our mothers."

It was a good plan, but like most plans, it didn't work. Azalea was able to restrain Carl, but Mr. Baron was more than a match for Iris. Glo and I left our mothers tied and jumped on Mr. Baron. The four of us rolled on the dirty floor. Mr. Baron was fast and he fought dirty. He bit and scratched and kicked and hit. He tore off my sash. I wrapped it around his head so he couldn't see. Iris wailed, "He's biting me. Stick something in his mouth."

Glo had Mr. Baron's left foot. He'd lost his shoes in the scuffle. She pushed and pulled it toward his mouth. She yelled for me to help her and I did. I dropped my sash and grabbed his ankle. We forced his big toe into his oversized mouth. We kept shoving and his other four toes followed and then his whole foot. Whenever he tried to stop swallowing, Iris pinched his nose and every time he inhaled, we shoved a little more leg down his gullet.

Iris pinned one arm with her left hand and his other with her legs. "His other foot. Feed him his other foot."

Glo pried and I shoved. One toe at a time disappeared until both feet were in his mouth. We made him swallow his legs, but his hips were really big. He'd stopped fighting and Iris let him go. "We're gonna need our moms to help us. You two keep shoving and I'll cut them loose."

"What about Mrs. Baron," I asked.

"That's up to Mrs. Baron," said Iris and she untied our moms. She took the gag out of Mrs. Baron's mouth. 'Are you with us or not."

"With you. Stop calling me Mrs. Baron. I'm not his wife and I'm not that little shit's mother. They caught me, but didn't sell me or eat me, at least not yet. I'm nothing more than a house slave. I hate them."

Things went faster with four adults helping us. Glo's mom and my mom weren't quite ready to accept the whole troll and Bigfeet thing, but they weren't too happy about being bound and gagged. Mrs. Baron and Mrs. Johnson were pretty convincing. After Mrs. Johnson used her Bigfeet powers to vanish and then order a trio of mice to sing about Cinderella, our moms were believers. My mom said, "I always thought this house smelled funny, funny peculiar, not funning amusing."

My mom and Mrs. Baron helped Iris and me force Mr. Baron's hips into his mouth. Next, we started on his arms. Finger by finger, wrist after wrist, and one elbow at a time, we pulled, jerked, and shoved his arms in past his shoulders. "Iris, he's getting smaller all the time. How can that happen?"

"Connie, who cares. Just keep feeding him to himself."

We all shoved and pushed until Mr. Baron was the size of a beach ball, and then a basketball. When he was the size of a baseball, Mrs. Baron rolled and rolled him on the concrete floor. The more that she rolled, the smaller he got. Smaller than an apple, smaller than a grape, and then, she held a dirty pea-sized ball between her thumb and forefinger. She sang, "Bye-bye baby, goodbye," and rolled the pea between her palms until there was nothing left except some greasy slime. "I'll need to wash my hands."

Azalea and our moms were busy feeding Carl to Carl. His face was red from lack of breath. Glo's mom shoved Carl's left arm in his mouth. "You girls gonna just sit there, or what."

Glo said, "What!"

"Bring your Be-Prepared Girl Guard cookie-selling butts over here and help me. My hands are getting tired."

With eight of us to feed Carl to himself, it didn't take long to make him vanish into his own mouth.

Mrs. Baron laughed, "Serves him right. He never could keep his damn mouth shut."

We went upstairs, washed up, and ate all the cookies. I bet we drank a gallon of milk. Mrs. Baron, who wasn't really Mrs. Baron, told us all about how she'd been captured by Mr. Baron and Carl. If there'd ever been a real Mrs. Baron, she didn't know anything about her.

Mom and I got home before Dad came home from work. We never told him about Bigfeet, trolls, or vampire disk jockeys. I just did my homework and took the bus to school on Monday.

People quit asking about Carl and Mr. Baron after a couple months. When the school called Mrs. Baron, she said that Carl's dad had run off with his secretary and he'd taken Carl with them. She hired a good lawyer, got an expedited divorce for abandonment, and was awarded the house and all the money. She bought a washer and dryer right away.

Azalea and Iris made the high school basketball team as freshmen and led us to a state championship. Glo was the point guard and I was the team manager. I never could hit free throws.

We've started dating. Azalea gives all the boys the sniff test. "Can't have my BFFs dating trolls, or gremlins, or goblins. Vampires just want one thing from a girl and orcs are downright mean."

Life's pretty good. This was a good neighborhood until the Johnsons moved next door. Now, it's a great neighborhood.

CRITICAL BLAST PUBLISHING
20¢
the THINGS We Do For LOVE
Alex James Donne
APPROVED BY THE READING CODE AUTHORITY
WEIRD FANTASTIC WORLDS
CRITICAL BLAST PUBLISHING
WHERE POP CULTURE GETS BLASTED
INCREDIBLE STRANGE STORIES
MEET THE NEW NEIGHBOR

STICK IT TO YOUR ENEMIES!
Real Voodoo Doll! Guaranteed Quality checked by the finest Witch Doctors! Send lock of hair and a SASE to DUDAT VOODOO, Box 9, Haiti.

BATS, RATS AND CATS!

HELIUM GAS & BALLOON SET
Get away from the day to day grind of your boring life and steal a whole house while the owners are away.

MONSTER VALUE STAMP
THIS IS IT! CLIP THEM & COLLECT THEM ALL!

ATTENTION!
DEMONS! VAMPIRES! GHOULS!

LIVE TO SEE WEDNESDAY!

DEFEAT BLACK MYSTIC ARTS KUNG-FU Tired of getting your ass kicked every Tuesday by Black Mystic Arts Kung-Fu fighters? CALL 666-HELP to enroll in self-defense training every Hellspawn should know to survive any dark alley encounter. Become a Ninth Circle Master of Judante!

HUMAN MASK When you need to walk among the humans, without being singled out as a monster. Get this mask in black, white or polka-dot, to blend right in!

EXPLODING DRINK Sit back and enjoy the highjinks as people unscrew their drink activating the chemical reaction, causing a foamy mess.

HOBO IN A BOX When your street is getting over-runned by homeless people and you need someone to speak their language and run them off to the next street down the block.

Alex James Donne is a lifelong resident of West London, an unrepentant hoarder of books, and a writer of dark fiction. His short story 'Fun and Games' can soon be found in the forthcoming anthology Doors of Darkness (Terrorcore Publishing), with more to be announced. 'The Things We Do For Love' is his first story accepted for publication.

Here's the truth: I never really liked that cat.

Not that I have a problem with cats in general; we had a lovely little tabby called Chaz when I was growing up who used to curl up on the corner of my desk while I was doing my homework, purring merrily away, occasionally walking across a half finished essay on *The Go-Between* or the importance of the Spinning Jenny to the development of manufacturing during the Industrial Revolution to demand attention with an affectionate headbutt. I loved that little guy. But I didn't love Jackson. I, at best, tolerated Jackson, because Jackson came as part of the deal with Alice, and I definitely did love her.

But to be fair, Jackson was there first. He was Alice's moving in present to herself when she became the tenant of 45B Haddon Gardens, Ealing, W5, a good two years before I even met her. So by the time I did meet her at Roland's birthday party in April last year, both of us friends of a friend and consequently not really sure what we were even doing there at all, Jackson had his adorable little paws firmly under the table. He was resolutely an Indoor Cat, content to enjoy the view of quiet, tree-lined Haddon Gardens from behind the ground floor window, on rare occasions deigning to enter the Great Outdoors as defined by the drab patch of ill-fitting paving slabs that constituted 45B's sorry excuse for a back garden. He'd never stay out there for long, showing no interest at all in the potential of a wider world beyond the creosoted fencing, instead opting to sniff and, every now and then, nibble at the contents of the various plant pots arranged to add some actual colour to the otherwise uninviting space. Then it was back inside, where he reigned unchallenged, the sole male about the house.

Until I moved in, that is.

Of course, he was somewhat used to me by then. The first time she invited me round there for dinner, Alice and I were three months in to what we both strongly suspected was developing into an actual sustained, long-term relationship. A love of cooking, and food in general, was high up on the list of things we had in common; the previous week it had been my turn to play host, and a damn good job I'd done of it, if I do say so myself. Bearing a very good Pinot Grigio (as instructed via text earlier that afternoon) I arrived twenty minutes early to the delicious smells of pasta carbonara and the equally delicious sight of the woman I was undoubtedly falling in love with dressed in a vintage *Ready Steady Cook* apron, apparently a genuine souvenir from her late Mum's appearance on the programme back in nineteen ninety-seven. Alice kissed me, thanked me for the wine, and warned me that she'd feed me through the pasta maker if I went anywhere near the kitchen.

And then she told me to go through and introduce myself to Jackson.

Take my word for it, he was definitely expecting me. Stretched out across the middle of the sofa's three forest green cushions, tail swaying nonchalantly back and forth, he was a pale, almost bluish-grey British Shorthair whose bright orange eyes watched me stroll into the front room, shrugging out of my coat, and finding the warm, cosy little space very much to my liking. His ears twitched briefly at the clatter of a pan lid coming from the kitchen, but those eyes remained fixed on me. They narrowed ever so slightly as I approached, tail swishing with noticeably more energy, but he made no move to stop my hand as I reached down to give him a friendly little stroke. He allowed me no more than two seconds of contact before easing his head firmly out from under my fingers in a manner that communicated loudly and clearly *That is all, Human. You are dismissed.*

He didn't hiss, he didn't growl, he didn't so much as lift a paw in enmity, but nevertheless our brief first interaction made it perfectly clear to me that we would never be friends. When Alice briefly joined us to hand me a beer – Tynt Meadow no less, which I'd briefly mentioned as a particular favourite on one of our earlier dates – Jackson took that as his cue to relinquish the sofa. He strolled over to his cat bed in the corner by the radiator, curled up, and went to sleep. Alice may not have noticed that he did so with his back turned to the pair of us, but I did.

The tone was set. As Alice and I grew closer I spent more and more time at her place in Ealing, which was considerably nicer than my comparatively drab little flat in White City. When our relationship reached the stage where vague musings about moving in together became serious discussions, me boxing up my possessions and moving them the roughly six miles west was the obvious conclusion. So that's what I did.

Four months later, Mr. Conover moved in next door.

Two weeks after that, the pets started disappearing.

Neither me nor Alice really noticed it at first. The odd poorly photocopied 'Have You Seen My Cat?' poster stapled to a tree or Sellotaped to a lamppost isn't a particularly unusual sight, especially in built-up suburban areas with plenty of traffic. That's how we lost Chaz in fact, and I grew up in a near-rural corner of Essex that was practically the middle of nowhere when compared to densely populated Ealing W5. And when the subject did crop up in conversation, in the wake of a fifteen-minute natter Alice had had with Donna Best from 56A, which she only mentioned in explanation for why it took her twice as long as usual to nip down to the co-op for a pint of semi-skimmed, Alice certainly didn't seem overly concerned. This occurred three days after Donna's own cat Midas (apparently so named for its golden orange colour) had gone missing, the fourth local pet to do so in as many weeks. As Alice pointed out Jackson was a certified indoor cat, so the risk of him running out blindly into traffic was better than zero.

Only it wasn't just cats. The second pet to go walkabout was a dog, the seemingly inexhaustible little terrier from up the road at number 43. Then, a week after Midas, the list of species prone to go missing went up by one, when a rabbit named Patches (no doubt for obvious colour-related reasons) vanished from its hutch in the back garden of number 60. And that's when the residents of Haddon Gardens really started to wonder if there wasn't more going on than unfortunate run-ins between domesticated animals and road traffic (or foxes, a theory particularly popular with Donna's other half, Anwar).

Like many neighbourhoods up and down the country Haddon Gardens and its environs was subject to a local neighbourhood watch scheme. What this amounted to, in reality, was occasional posts to a little-trafficked WhatsApp group, the majority of which originated with the scheme's instigator, Nevill Cross from 38a. According to Alice there had been a spate of burglaries and attempted burglaries a few years previously and Nevill, a victim of one such attempted break-in, had "gone a bit vigilante" and just about managed to garner enough half-hearted support to make his dream of keeping the hallowed streets of Ealing crime-free a reality.

With the disappearance of Patches however, activity on the WhatsApp group saw a marked upturn. Because Patches had clearly been taken, as one look at the picture of the hutch's twisted, torn away door undeniably demonstrated. Steve Kemper, Patches' erstwhile owner, followed up his photographic evidence with several posts detailing the reactions of his seven-year-old daughter Betty (inconsolable), eleven year-old son Howie (mild indifference) and wife Maggie (furious, primarily at Steve, which explained the multi-post venting). Several other residents, including owners of now missing pets, contributed to this sudden burst of activity, and it was during the hours-long exchange of theories, complaints, and speculations that attention was first directed at Haddon Garden's most recent arrival.

Now because I happened to be home on the day Mr. Conover moved in, and what's more because I'd actually spoken to the man, I was apparently now an expert on the subject of our new neighbour. When Alice, who'd been keeping one eye on the group chat all afternoon and periodically updating me on progress (much to both our amusement), let me know my "expertise" was being called upon, I thought at first she was joking. But, no, she showed me her phone and they were genuinely trying to decide amongst themselves who was best suited to popping over and asking me to dish the dirt on The Mysterious New Resident of Number 47. But there was no mystery, not as far as I could see. In the three or so minutes of interaction I'd had with Mr. Conover, he struck me as nothing more sinister than a quiet, polite, fifty-something single gentleman who would quickly vanish into the fabric of Haddon Gardens until it seemed as though he had always been there. I thought he was altogether rather dull and forgettable, though catching a glimpse of the *Greatest Safety Battles in Snooker 1980 – 1989* DVD in the box at his feet may have had something to do with that.

As far as I could see they were making far too much of what was undoubtedly a simple coincidence: namely, the pets only started disappearing after Mr. Conover moved in. Which, while true, in and of itself proved nothing. Add to that the fact nobody had yet established that any of the pets (with the possible—fine, highly likely—exception of Patches) had actually been taken and not run over or simply even run away, and all you had was a group of no-longer-pet-owners clutching at straws. Alice, because she's smart, level-headed, and sensible, agreed.

If Jackson were to disappear, however, it might be a very different story.

As was the case when Mr. Conover moved in next door, I happened to be working from home that day. It was a particularly warm day as well, and as I'd set up my temporary office - laptop, pen (for some reason), glass of non-alcoholic cider, TV remote – on the dining room table in the main room, the back door was open to allow in what you could just about describe as 'cool' air. For most of the morning Jackson had been content to occupy his usual spot on the middle cushion of the sofa, occasionally deigning to turn his yellow gaze in my direction but for the most part dozing away the hours before someone (usually Alice) fed him. A few days had passed since The WhatsApp Vigilantes had conducted their group chat, and as yet the proposed fact-finding mission to our front door hadn't come to pass. And, at least as far as I was aware, nobody had been round to bother Mr. Conover either.

At about one o'clock that afternoon, when I went through to the bedroom to grab a USB stick in order to secure a non-cloud-based backup of my morning's work, Jackson roused from his doze, no doubt thinking the only possible reason The Inferior One (as I sometimes imagined he thought of me) would be up and about was in order to feed him. While he did jump down from the sofa with the intention of following me into the kitchen, as soon as he saw me head off towards the bedroom instead, he sauntered towards the open back door as if that had been his plan all along.

When I opened the bureau drawer where I kept assorted phone chargers, tangled-in-knots earphones, aux leads, loose batteries and USB sticks, I made the usual mental note to one day label the damned sticks so I'd know what was actually on them before spending the next minute – at most two minutes – selecting one I was reasonably sure had some space on it. Returning to the front room and noting the sofa's empty middle cushion I assumed Jackson was still outside. When I happened to glance towards the garden it wasn't out of concern or even curiosity about what the cat might be up to, but rather to identify the origin of the odd, rather unpleasant smell that definitely hadn't been present a few minutes ago.

It certainly seemed to be coming from outside. There was a spoiled meat, blocked drain quality to it that didn't entirely rule out someone's nearby barbecue but probably made it unlikely as the source (I've been to some shockingly bad local barbecues in my time). It grew stronger as I stepped out onto the paving slabs, and stronger still the nearer I came to the seven-foot-high fencing that separated our drab rectangle of yard from next door's.

On that particular side, next door meant Mr. Conover.

There was no sign of Jackson. For the moment ignoring the strange smell and the implications of where it seemed to be coming from, I went back inside and thoroughly searched the flat. As I did so, I concocted an elaborately paranoid fantasy in which Jackson, a hyper-intelligent alien being and not an ordinary cat at all, had orchestrated the entire pet-nabbing saga himself. His fiendish, Machiavellian plot would culminate with his own staged disappearance under circumstances where I would be blamed for it, and once the inevitable happened and Alice, no longer able to trust me, kicked me out (naturally it would be raining when this happened), Jackson would make his miraculous return, once again the unchallenged master of his domain.

It seemed about as likely as the nice old man next door being an actual pet-nabber.

But there was no sign of Jackson inside the flat, which left me little choice but to seriously consider the possibility of Mr. Conover's involvement.

The question was, what exactly was I supposed to do about it?

Pondering that question, I headed back outside. Though fading, the smell still lingered and was still strongest the closer I came to the fence. I had no idea what was on the other side of it, and pictured everything from a perfectly ordinary suburban back garden to a junk-littered mess where, in amongst the bald tyres and ancient Zanussi washing machines, could be glimpsed a series of small, pet-sized gravestones. Still waiting for an actual idea to occur to me, I went right up to the fence, turning my head to try and peer through any potential gaps between the slats. As I did so, I heard the faint but

...mistakable sound of a cat's meow. It was followed by a deeper yowl of utter consternation; the exact same sound Jackson had greeted me with the one and only time I'd made the mistake of trying to pick him up.

The sounds were distant enough to be coming from inside the house rather than from the garden itself, which made my next act seem slightly less risky. Taking a firm grip of the top of the fence, and without pausing to ask myself what the hell I thought I was doing, I hauled myself up until I could peer over into Mr. Conover's garden. There was nothing either quiet or dignified about this, and I fully expected that the first thing I'd see was an alarmed Mr. Conover rushing out through his back door to see what all the noise was about. Instead what I saw was, as imagined, a perfectly ordinary patch of lawn, a bare strip of earth along the opposite fence ready for planting, and the back door leading in to Mr. Conover's house. At first glance, the back door appeared to be closed, but before my strength gave out and I had to lower myself back down, something told me to look again. There was a tiny gap between the edge of the door and the frame, as though the last person to go through it hadn't pushed it quite hard enough for the mortice lock to engage.

If I hadn't spotted the back door was open like that, I don't think I would have done what I did next. I would, instead, have done the sensible thing, and popped round to Mr. Conover's front door, rung the bell, and asked him politely if by any chance he had seen our cat. Which was, in actuality, Alice's cat, and that was the point. I knew she would have run out into traffic in order to save Jackson. And me? I knew I would have run out into traffic to save her.

The second time I grabbed the top of the fence and heaved myself up it was with the intention of hauling myself all the way up and over into Mr. Conover's garden. It was, if anything, even noisier and more undignified than my first effort, but I just about managed it, and moments later found myself standing on my neighbour's neat patch of lawn. I stood there for a few seconds, perfectly still, and listened. I have no idea how I might have gone about explaining myself had Mr. Conover stepped outside at that moment, but he didn't, so once I'd let another thirty seconds pass, I crossed the short distance to the back door. It was open an inch or two, no more, and whatever the source of that awful, spoiled meat and blocked drain smell actually was, it definitely originated inside the house.

The Voice of Reason in the back of my head threw everything it had into its demands that I stop at once and get the hell out of there, but I ignored it and carefully eased open the door.

Thanks to the heavy, dark blue curtains closed across the inside of the door and the room's single window it was gloomy enough that I struggled to make out much detail beyond identifying several vaguely furniture-shaped lumps. It was very warm as well, and practically humid once I'd slipped into the room and eased the door almost shut behind me. I couldn't hear a sound, which was both comforting and worrisome given the not-at-all-happy yowl I'd heard from Jackson just a few minutes before. My eyes adjusted quickly to the gloom however, so I carefully crossed the carpet towards the closed door directly across the room from me.

Because number 47 (where the increasingly desperate Voice of Reason pointed out I was now TRESPASSING!) retained its status as a house, the layout would naturally be different to number 45 next door which, like a good third of the houses along Haddon Gardens, had been converted into two separate flats. I had no idea what awaited me beyond the closed front room door, and tried to picture nothing more sinister than an ordinary suburban hallway, with no doubt a door through to the kitchen at one end, the front door at the other, and a staircase leading up to the first floor between them. The source of that increasingly foul smell was beyond that door as well, which didn't help, but I was all in now, so I eased it open and hoped for the best.

Hallway, front door, stairs, exactly as predicted. Peering round the door and looking to my right revealed the kitchen, the door to which stood open. It appeared to be as gloomy and empty as the front room I currently stood in.

That just left upstairs.

Blasting the mental equivalent of a dozen air horns The Voice of Reason put in one last, mammoth effort to get me to see sense, but I went on ignoring it and crept carefully along the hallway to the foot of the stairs. With each step the smell grew stronger and more terrible. Joining the bouquet of spoiled meat and blocked drain was an underlying reek that was unpleasantly faecal. In that moment I wanted to be anywhere but at the foot of those stairs about to climb them, but climb them I did. Slowly and carefully, expecting the creak of an old floorboard to give me away at any moment. A deeper, darker gloom awaited me, but there was something else too, a feeble shuffle of sound I dimly recognised. It made me think of

Chaz, he of the corner of my desk naps and distracting headbutts, and as I reached the top of the staircase the memory came to me.

What I could hear was the sound of a small creature – a cat, say – moving around inside a wire cage, perhaps one very similar to the cage I'd lifted a weeks-old, nameless tabby from on the day my dad took me along to a local off-the-books breeder to pick myself out a pet.

There were three closed doors leading off the landing. The smell, approaching eye-watering levels of foulness now, was coming from the closest one to my left, but the sound of the caged animal I had to assume was Jackson seemed to be coming from the next room along. Despite that, the temptation to open the closer of the two doors, to know what on earth Mr. Conover had going on in there to produce what was unquestionably the worst smell I had ever experienced, was almost too tempting to resist.

But resist it I did, creeping past the first door and listening intently for the slightest hint of movement behind it, then pausing outside the second room to listen for any additional sounds inside it as well. All I could hear was the sound that had drawn me to it, the sound of something shifting within the confines of a wire cage. So, with a deep breath, I opened the door.

Lined up at the foot of the opposite wall were eight wire cages of various sizes. I don't know what specific animal, domestic or otherwise, the largest was built for, but it did occur to me that it was more than large enough to accommodate a small child. The room was as gloomy as the rest of the house, but I could see that all but one of the cages was empty, though two others appeared to contain what looked suspiciously like small heaps of bones.

Behind the closed wire door of the last-but-one cage, Jackson, true to form, stared at me with what I can only describe as mild interest. He sat there perfectly calm, seemingly content to wait for me to cross the room and let him out. Before doing that, I peered around the door to check the rest of the room, and, finding it empty, made my way forward. After just a few steps I felt something soft beneath my left shoe. Looking down as I lifted my foot, I saw what appeared to be the ragged, bloody, top half of a rabbit's ear.

As I reached Jackson's cage and crouched down, I did what in the moment felt like the single stupidest thing I'd done so far that day: I placed a finger against my lips in the universal signal for *shhhhh*. Jackson simply sat there watching me. His cage was secured with a simple slide bolt, which I opened as quietly and carefully as I could, before adopting a similar cautious approach to pulling open the wire door itself.

If it was any other cat, I might have expected an immediate bolt for freedom, the terrified animal throwing itself down the stairs secure in the knowledge that it's legendary ability to always land on its feet would see it safely to the bottom. But this was Jackson. He simply stepped forward out of the cage and strolled towards the open door, pausing to sniff at the ragged slice of rabbit ear on the way. When he paused in the doorway, it took me a moment to realise he was waiting for me to follow him. From there he led the way back to the top of the staircase, moving at the same perfectly silent, unhurried pace, and only started down the stairs once I was directly behind him.

I didn't follow him back to the ground floor, however. Instead, I paused to look at the remaining closed door on that side of the landing, once again struck by the overwhelming temptation to open it. Only this time that temptation was too great, and knowing I was almost certain to regret it, I stepped forward, placed my hand on the doorknob, and turned it.

It might have been minutes or an hour later that I finally stumbled through the back door of number 47 Haddon Gardens and once again found myself in Mr. Conover's back garden. As calm and inscrutable as ever, Jackson sat by the fence waiting for me. On some level I understood that he wanted me to lift him onto the top of the fence, and as soon as I did he leapt nimbly down into his own domain without sparing me a second look.

I didn't think I had the strength left to join him. I stood there and wondered if the reason I felt so calm was because I was simply too exhausted to feel anything else. I hadn't run back down the stairs; in fact I'd made my return journey at a pace leisurely enough to rival Jackson's. But seeing what I'd seen behind that door had drained me, and I was dimly amazed that I was somehow able to remain standing up.

And as for what I did see behind that door ... I don't think it's something I'll ever be able to put into words. In one respect it *was* Mr. Conover, I recognised him just as I would were I to pass him outside on the street; but on a much more fundamental and terrifying level, he was something else entirely. Something vast and monstrous, something that should not have fit within the four walls of a bedroom in a terrace house in Ealing, something so abhorrently vile I think part of me simply refused to fully comprehend it.

Still, as weak and insubstantial as I felt, I somehow managed to grip the top of the fence, haul myself back up, and scramble over. As I stepped through my own back door, I was greeted by the familiar sight of Jackson laid out across the middle cushion of the sofa, tail swishing gently, bright yellow eyes regarding me with his usual lack of anything even remotely resembling affection.

But that was fine. That was as it should be. It didn't stop me sitting down at my laptop and opening my browser, it didn't stop me typing 'wedding rings' into the search bar and spending the next hour and a half browsing through options, and it wouldn't stop me asking Alice to marry me as soon as she got home from work.

Jackson or no Jackson, I was pretty confident she'd say yes.

And Mr. Conover?

Later that night, as Alice slept beside me, I heard some very strange noises coming through the wall from number 47. One of them sounded almost like laughter, and one of them sounded like a door-sized tongue dragging itself along the wall above my head, though I'm perfectly willing to accept that was just part of the dream I suffered through once I finally managed to get to sleep myself. And the next morning as I opened the bedroom blinds, it was just in time to watch a van labelled Sanjeev's Quality Van Hire pull away from outside the house next door, driven by a rather dull, forgettable fifty-something gentleman who it seemed would very soon be somebody else's problem.

I wished them luck, whoever they were, and then went through to the kitchen to cook breakfast for my fiancée.

And yes, while I was there, I fed Jackson too.

3¢
USA
223
SHARKFLY
MONSTER
VALUE STAMP
THIS IS IT!
CLIP THEM
& COLLECT
THEM ALL!

CRITICAL BLAST PUBLISHING
20¢
COMES A PALE BRIDE
Troy Riser
WEIRD FANTASTIC WORLDS
CRITICAL
BLAST
WHERE POP CULTURE GETS BLASTED
INCREDIBLE STRANGE STORIES
APPROVED BY THE READING CODE AUTHORITY
THE HUNTER BECOMES THE HUNTED!

RENT AN ANGRY MIDGET! When you need to stop a Bully from harassing, or when you need to look like a decent human concerned for poor ugly monsters.

SNAKES IN A MAIL BOX Get these total mother-f$%Ken poisonous snakes and mail them with your get well gift cards.

BOX OF LIVE BATS When you feel like a millionaire crime fighting hero and need to dress up your special cave, to give it that extra touch of atmosphere... a box of live bats is perfect for you. Food not included.

FISH BOWL FULL OF WORMS Are you tired of eating meat? Get yourself a bowl full of yummy worms and feel you are saving the planet.

RADIOACTIVE CANDY When you want to level up your personality and appear extra sweet to the people around you... and want to have a superpower over sugar... this candy's for you!

HOBO IN A BOX When your street is getting over-runned by homeless people and you need someone to speak their language and run them off to the next street down the block.

WELCOME MAT TRAP When you don't want people annoying you, a simple press of the button and the trap door will dispose of anyone who stands on it, while waiting for you to answer the door.

HEAD KNIVES 100% stainless steal daggers that launch from the top of your head and kill any conversation you find boring.

COCAINE FOR PETS When your pets become too excited during mating season and you don't want additional burden of feeding more pets, shot them up with some fine liquid snow and chill them out.

Artist and writer **Troy Riser**'s work has most recently been published in Cirsova magazine with his science fiction/horror story, "Starring Hedy Lamarr", and in The Devil You Know Better horror anthology with his short story, "The Kingman Deal", itself a horror and neo-noir genre blend. He's currently working on a picaresque novel entitled 'Target Girl', about one stabby chick on a mission of vengeance and discovery.

Alana Von See took lunch nearly every weekday in the Biology Department's conservatory. Seated at a ledge by the big windows, Alana liked the smell of the banana tree nearby, the varied splashes of colors in the verdant green, the heat through the glass after a long winter, the view of 3rd Street and the people on it. Alana played a private game while she watched the street, a game where she would pick people out as individuals, read their body language and expressions, take in the way they dressed and walked and moved, and then guess at their thoughts, imagine their lives.

Outside looking in, she thought.

Most days Alana ate alone, but sometimes colleagues in the Art History Department would join her. Arthur Chu sat beside her today, and she was troubled by the weak, jerky stop-start, stop-start, arrhythmic beating of his heart. Alana had been noticing it for weeks and had struggled to find a way to urge him to a doctor without sounding unnaturally specific, her awareness of his condition begging potentially compromising questions, but Alana liked Arthur. She would try.

"My father died of a heart attack," she said abruptly. This wasn't true. Alana had no father in the true human sense, no mother either, but the lie came easily enough.

That much of me is human, she thought.

Arthur, eating a meatball sandwich from a cheap and greasy deli down the street, stopped chewing, confused and taken aback.

"So sorry for your loss, Alana," Arthur said, peering at her closely.

He's surprised I brought up family, she thought.

She and Arthur were close as colleagues, even friends, but Alana rarely spoke of her family—wait, no, she thought: never.

She had never spoken of her family, which would be an entirely fictional family in any case, and she had no wish to make one up, which would force her to maintain yet another teetering stack of carefully constructed lies.

"My father's color was off as yours is off," Alana went on, pressing, driving it home. "I remember him complaining how tired he was. You are tired, yes? I have heard you say it. You mentioned it the other day."

This wasn't true either. Arthur was the stoic sort who rarely complained, but Alana could read him as a predator could read sick or crippled prey, sense his frailty so deeply it was as if she could feel it herself.

"I look that bad?" he said.

Alana caught the worry in his voice, and this pleased her. Worry is the seed she wanted planted.

"Perhaps I overreact, imagine things," she said, "It's just that..." She trailed off.

"The death of a parent can be traumatic," Arthur said. "My own father died comparatively young, at fifty-five." He noted the arch of her eyebrow. "And yes, a heart attack."

"I am truly sorry, Arthur. I did not wish to bring up hurtful memories. My social skills are notoriously lacking. I can be like a child when dealing with people."

Arthur chuckled softly, brightening the mood. "Agreed, you do come across as—"

"—Too direct?" Alana said. "I don't mean to be. It's just that I don't like talking around things. I like it to-the-point, no beating around the bushes."

Smiling, Arthur said, "*Bush* singular, Alana: 'No beating around the bush'. To-the-point is good, yes, and that's okay. I appreciate directness in people."

"Some don't," Alana said.

"No, some don't."

Alana gave a slight shrug. "I spend too much time alone, Arthur. I am good with solitude, but too much time alone can make one weird." She straightened her spine and threw her shoulders back, striking a proudly heroic pose. "I embrace my weirdness."

"I embrace your weirdness too, Alana," he said, smiling gently. "And no, I'm not upset. All you've done is force a doctor's appointment. I've been meaning to make one but kept putting it off."

"Not any longer, I hope."

"No," Arthur said, rising to leave. "Not any longer, and thank you."

Alana rose with him, standing to her full height. Usually with men Alana would bend slightly at the waist and hunch forward at the shoulders to make herself seem *less* to men intimidated by formidable women, but not with Arthur. With Arthur (and a precious few others) she could be herself—not entirely herself—no, never entirely, not her true self, her real face, but close enough.

"Are they all like you in Switzerland?" Arthur said. He was looking up at her, smiling. "I've never been."

"Yes, Arthur, we are all like me in Switzerland. Ours is a land of tall, lanky giants with too-big hands and too-big feet. We hatch from boulders and live in caves and come down from the Alps every so often, yodeling our battle cry, raiding villages, making off with the occasional tourist."

Arthur laughed. "As long as the made-off tourist is only occasional."

"The medical appointment," Alana said, suddenly serious again. "Promise me, Arthur."

"I promise, Alana, first thing."

After Arthur had left, Alana thought ahead and debated going back to her office but decided against it. Lectures were done for the day and Leon, the graduate student she was guiding through his dissertation, had begged off their usual Tuesday afternoon appointment, the second time he had done so, and Alana had begun to question his commitment. She didn't like Leon personally, finding his arrogance off-putting, but quickly dismissed the idea of *like* from her personal equation. *Like* doesn't matter, Alana reminded herself. What matters is the work and the value of it. His theory regarding Kandinsky's alleged synesthesia merited exploration. Leon was, she thought, a perceptive young man with a fine analytical mind.

And poor hygiene, Alana added as an afterthought.

On impulse, Alana absently reached in her bag and took out her antique, silver-plated clamshell compact, a gift from a long-ago lover, and checked her makeup in its ornately framed oval mirror. Alana used a heavy base to hide the unnaturally translucent skin beneath, and checked her face frequently for smudges and gaps. The makeup she wore was an artfully applied mask, not to make her beautiful (I can never be beautiful, she thought) but to pass for human or at least appear *human enough* to not cause that frisson of unease real humans feel when what they see is indefinably amiss, close to but not quite what it should be.

When something is off, she thought.

And then she stopped moving, going suddenly still. She had long ago learned to listen to her body, and it was talking to her now, a whisper building to a shout.

Alana quickly put away her compact and focused. Seeing her there, her head canted quizzically to the side, an onlooker would think the tall, striking, raven-haired woman was having a momentary lapse, reading on her frozen face the sudden realization of something lost or forgotten, a woman retracing her steps, her body motionless but her pale blue eyes roving from side to side, searchlights hunting a fugitive memory.

Human beings filter stimuli. Their minds unconsciously winnow and glean, seeking that which is significant and discarding that which isn't, but Alana Von See had no such filter. Alana's perception of time slowed to a crawl and in that captured moment she could see, feel, hear, taste, and smell all within range of her senses: children's laughter nearby (kids on a field trip), the hum of an overhead air unit, the flutter of a finch turned loose in the arboretum by staff, the chitinous skitter of beetles on a rock. She could also feel...something else, a tension at her midriff, a vise-like squeezing pressure at her temples, a prickling of the tiny hairs on her arms and at the nape of her neck. She knew that feeling. She had been trained to trust that feeling decades before during the war by hard, ruthless men at the SOE Finishing School in Beaulieu. She had called herself Elsa Gray then, presenting herself as a patriotic Manchester schoolteacher with an uncanny facility for languages, which those cold, deadly men had found useful. *If you feel as if you're being watched*, you're likely being watched, her instructors had told her.

I'm being watched, Alana thought, and my watchers are very good.

She had instantly assumed *watchers* plural. No one who knew enough to surveil her would be so foolish as to try it alone.

Alana brought herself back to the moment, shaking her head as if remembering what she had forgotten or misplaced. She made a show of opening her purse and looking inside, nodding slightly as if to say *Oh look there it is*, snapping it closed and shouldering it, moving on. No more than a few seconds had passed.

Alana had sensed no threat close by, but the walls of this place were greenhouse glass and where she stood was easily visible from one of the shops and restaurants along 3rd Street or—she broadened her search—from Greek Row with its cluster of fraternity and sorority houses. Alana scanned the windows, looking for movement—and there: second floor, second house from right, a man at the window. A sense of unreality washed over her. The man at the window was dressed in a dark suit with a navy and yellow Oxford striped tie. Alana had known Oxford men. She recognized the tie. He was sporting a bowler hat. His face was slightly rounded and cleanshaven. He was smiling at her as if faintly amused. He looked, she thought, exactly like a figure in a Rene Magritte painting, down to the bowler hat, as if he had just stepped through the picture plane and into the real world. At first she explained it away as a cardboard prop celebrity silhouette, the kind people stand beside for those photographs at conventions and the like, a fun and kitschy trick. But then the man in the bowler hat waved at her. Unable to help herself, Alana gave a wave in return, cupping her hand and turning her wrist, a beauty queen wave at a parade.

He's fixing me in place, she thought, and quickly backed away from the glass. If this was a hit, her possible would-be killers' avenue of engagement showed poor tactical judgment. Hitting a target through thick, reinforced glass requires a large, penetrating caliber and painstakingly precise calculation to account for angle of deflection. Few could reliably make that shot.

In the few seconds it had taken her to back away and assess the threat, the man in the window had disappeared.

You don't know anything yet, she told herself. Don't make assumptions. Think it through.

Alana forced an inward calm and played out various *if I do x then y* alternatives. She imagined herself storming the frat house (where she would have no justification to be), going room by room and seeking them out by scent because if those watching her had been fully briefed beforehand then they would be afraid, and Alana would smell the pheromones emitted by that fear, pinpoint its source, and...then what? she thought. Interrogate them in front of witnesses? That wouldn't do. What would? She could use a pretext to gain entry but talking her way in would take too much time. Victory, she had been taught, rarely comes from the single, decisive battle however dramatically climactic and gratifying such a battle might be; rather, it came from the patient, gradual accumulation of small advantages.

This is me gradual, she thought. This is me patient.

No viable option presented itself. No plan coalesced. Any move she made against them from her current position would risk exposure, and Alana wasn't yet ready to give up her life here. She liked this life.

"I'll just go home then," Alana said, unaware she had spoken aloud.

Home for her was a small, single-story bungalow two kilometers south of campus, a block west of the B-Line Trail. Living close to campus, Alana walked when the weather was fair and drove when it wasn't.

Like any normal human person, she thought.

It was nice out today, one of the first comparatively warm days of early spring, and so she had walked to work and now she would be walking home, out in the open, vulnerable and exposed. Alana didn't like the idea but there was nothing for it. She slipped on her coat, a black down jacket, and set out. Alana carried no distance weapons but dearly wished for one now. A gun was rational. A gun could be explained. If they came at Alana now she would need to take them hand to hand and there would be no hiding it then—no hiding *her*, who and what she was.

Alana thought bitterly, I've grown complacent. This time around has gone all too smoothly, with no old life complications, all enemies dead or out of the picture. Stupid, stupid, stupid, she thought, two hundred years a fool. There will *always* be enemies, she thought. There will *always* be complications.

Once off-campus and on the B-Line, Alana walked at a brisk, confident pace, her face outwardly calm, even serene, exchanging nods and smiles with oncoming passersby on the trail, some of whom she knew, all the while feeling a burning sensation at her back, between her shoulder blades, the stare of hostile eyes upon her.

Alana decided to talk while she walked, taking out her cellphone and dialing Hargrave & Fitch by memory and touch so she could keep her eyes on the trail. Ambushing her here would be public and risky but they would have cover and concealment in the tree lines on either side. On the phone, a friendly automated-sounding voice asked for her name.

"Codename Plain Jane," Alana said. "I spell: Papa Oscar Lima India Delta Oscar Romeo India."

Alana heard an audible click as the call transferred to a human operator. Had she not responded with proper codename and password sequence, the call would've been directed to a software help desk in Des Moines, Iowa.

A woman's voice answered, pleasant and professional, with a clipped, not-quite-posh BBC British accent. Alana could hear faint background static, the kind common on plain old telephone service. The woman asked for her order number and Alana responded with a sequence of five numerals. Hargrave & Fitch employed quantum cryptography. Several seconds of silence passed. Neither spoke while they waited.

She isn't good at small talk either, Alana thought.

"We have a match, Jane. Trouble?"

"I need Clive Hargrave," Alana said. "Is he available? He knows me. I'm an old friend, and this is urgent. I want priority."

There was a pause at the other end. Finally, the voice said, "This is Lynn Hargrave, Jane. Clive Hargrave is—was—my father. He passed recently. I do know who you are and how important you were to him, so yes, you have priority, no need to ask. What can we do? What do you need?"

Alana said, "I need a reaction team on my location immediately, code yellow, level two. I need full eye-in-the-sky coverage this point forward. Transfer whatever it takes from my primary account."

Lynn Hargrave said, "The closest we've got is our man in Chicago, ETA two hours plus or minus. Can you hold out until then?"

"Not a team? Just one man?"

"Carlo is very good." The understated, matter-of-fact way Hargrave said it was reassuring. Alana pictured Carlo, Lynn Hargrave's man in Chicago, as a dark, stealthy, stony-faced assassin moving silently and unseen through the grimy back alleys of the city—probably not true, probably an innocuous gray man clerk-type no one notices (the best of them are), but the fantasy gave her confidence.

"Movement is life," Alana said. "I might need to displace."

"Understood, Jane. Tracking actuated. We've got you."

Alana said, "I'm terribly sorry about your father, Lynn. Clive was truly one of a kind. He saved my life that time in Istanbul."

There was another pause on the line. Alana could feel the weight of a daughter's grief on the other end. Grief was one of a handful of human emotions Alana could fully experience and understand, but she wasn't good at sharing it.

Lynn Hargrave said, "I know that story. According to my father, it was the other way 'round. You saved him, for which we're all grateful here, myself especially. He even talked about you at the end. He said he never understood why you gave yourself nom de guerre *Plain Jane*. He said he thought you were beautiful."

Alana ended the call. She wasn't good with emotions. Emotions eroded her sense of self-control, making her weak when she needed to be strong. Self-doubt crept in, as it always did when she experienced inner turmoil.

What if you're wrong? she thought. What if this is all paranoia on my part? Some kind of dementia unique to my strange physiology, the degradation of age?

Not wrong, not crazy. I saw what I saw. He's real.

You imagined Dapper Man. You saw the wave of a curtain blowing in the breeze and your freakish and paranoid mind obliged with a paranoid hallucination.

I saw a man in a dark suit and tie. He wore a bowler hat.

You're describing Magritte's *Son of Man*. You teach Art History. You're immersed in it. It would make sense if you were to hallucinate, you would hallucinate famous paintings.

"If I were to hallucinate, I would hallucinate paintings by Peter Paul Rubens or drawings by Andrea del Sarto," Alana said aloud. "Never Magritte. I don't even like his work, the sameness of it, its endless redundancy. So trite and gimmicky. Surrealists bore me."

"The Magritte thing was my idea. I figured it would discombobulate you, throw you off," said the man on the trail, seated at one of the few benches lining the trail a hundred meters south of the Switchyard. "I love the word *discombobulate*. It almost rates as an onomatopoeia, don't you think? That sense of disassociation? Dis-com-bob—bobbing along, bobbing along...yes? No?"

The man dressed like a painting was still in costume, she saw, down to the distinctive bowler hat, but he spoke with a flat, midwestern American accent, spoiling the jarring, otherworldly effect he strove to achieve.

The dog doesn't fit either, Alana thought. A massive black dog on a leash was on its haunches at the man's feet, appraising her warily, a Neapolitan mastiff and Rottweiler mix, she guessed. It bothered her too that she couldn't read the dog, pick up on its mood and personality through its scent, nor did she understand how this man could be ahead of her on the trail. Although warmer than usual, the air was still cold enough to see his breath. Dapper Man was real. So was the dog.

"I was briefed on your capabilities but wanted to see for myself," Dapper Man said. "You fixed on a distant, undefined threat in seconds. Impressive."

When Alana didn't respond, Dapper Man gave her a smug, knowing grin. "You're wondering why you didn't see me or smell me or whatever it is you do," he said. "It's a dampening field attuned to human senses, something about wave suppression, yadda yadda. I don't follow the science behind it, and I frankly don't need to. I leave the techie stuff to the techies. I only know it works. The best part is it works on *you*, which was a matter of some debate between the boys in the lab since it only affects human beings and you're not exactly human, are you?"

Dapper Man was right. His voice had a tinny, distant quality, and the colors of her surroundings were somehow suppressed. Alana also noticed this usually busy part of the B-Line Trail was empty of people but for the two of them. She assumed civilians on the trail had been deftly diverted, funneled into other points of entry and egress. This measure of staging and control spoke to careful planning. This elaborate scenario didn't just happen. This took money and trained personnel. There was power behind this.

"And the dog?" she asked.

The dapper man dressed like a Magritte painting tugged playfully at the leash. The huge dog growled in response, a menacing rumble coming up from deep in its belly. "To discourage you," the man said.

"From what?"

"From doing to me what you did to Ivan Tarasov in Berlin thirty-five years ago—points for originality, by the way, one professional to another: messy and brutal but effective. I mean, damn, you tore that Russian's arm from its socket and beat him to death with it. I always thought it was just an expression, something guys said to sound badass. Never thought anyone would actually, you know, do it."

Alana said, "I gave fair warning. I told Tarasov what I would do if he went through with his operation. Those were civilians. We don't do civilians. He should've listened." She shrugged her shoulders dismissively. "He made the wrong choice."

"You are one cold, literal bitch."

"And you stink of Langley."

Dapper Man said, "Not anymore, Alana. This is all strictly private sector."

Alana kept her affect flat, her voice measured and calm. "To the point, please. You have a dozen or more men with eyes-on right now. Why are we even talking? What is it you want?"

Dapper Man gave her his sly, Cheshire grin again. "We want you, Alana. Here's the deal: come with me of your own volition. From here, we fly to Belize—lovely place, Belize. Upon arrival, you submit to an in-depth examination conducted by our team of experts, the best men money can buy. After the examination, you receive one billion USD deposited in that centuries-old Swiss bank account you think no one knows about—and get this, this is the best part: we will gladly share the test results with you. I mean, come on, aren't you the least bit curious to find out what you really are?"

"I know what I am," Alana said. She struggled to hide her surprise. The account's existence went back to her oldest name, her first identity on paper.

Dapper Man smiled again. "Oh, do I have your attention now? Yes, we know about the account. We know everything."

That grin again, Alana thought. She imagined casually reaching out and taking hold of his lips between her thumb and forefinger and—with an abrupt snapping motion too fast to follow—pull his lips loose from the ligaments and tissue that held them to his face. The pain would be sudden, violating, and tremendous. The shock would probably kill him.

"I've been examined before," Alana said. She didn't elaborate.

"We know," he said. "Nazis were good at record-keeping, so meticulous that way, but the Ahnenerbe's methods were crude back then, as you know: more magick than science. We're way beyond that now, trust me. Our people are doing some real cutting-edge work."

"Best men, cutting edge," Alana said mockingly. "You sound like a brochure."

Dapper Man shifted his mass on the bench, eager to close the deal. "Look, we can go over all this later, but for now the big takeaway is we mean you no harm. We're not monsters, okay?" Dapper Man abruptly stopped himself and held up his hands with his palms out in mock contrition. "Whoops, so sorry, I was told you might be sensitive to the M-word. My bad, won't happen again."

Dapper Man looked, she thought, supremely confident, fully in control.

Alana said, "Do you have a name, Dapper Man?"

"Dapper Man?" he laughed, lowering his hands. "I like that. You can call me Bob, Bob Gaines. That's what I'm going by now, anyway."

Without preamble, Alana said, "A Scots laird once hunted me with hounds, Bob."

Bob tried to cut her off. "I'm not lying about the money, Alana. That's a billion, with a B. You could dump it in a pool and swim in it. All you've got to do is lie back and dream of Switzerland or whatever while our people do their thing. A billion dollars. I wish I had a billion dollars, but I'm not special. Like you.

"By the way, Alana, how old are you, really? The boys've got a pool going on back in the cubes. Some say two hundred, others more. What with the scanty documentation back in those days, you could've conceivably gone a thousand years undetected. It's mind-blowing, really."

Alana ignored him and went on: "The Scotsman and his dogs chased me for days, Bob. I tried everything to throw them off but it didn't work and they finally had me cornered, my back against the face of a sheer, unscalable cliff, nothing for it but turn and fight.

"I was naked and new then, Bob: savage and primal, armed with nothing but fingernails and teeth, desperate and afraid. I was always afraid in those days, Bob, acting on instinct like an animal—I was an animal—and it was that instinct that made me reach out, not to the man but to his hounds, a few of them nearly as big as this adorable angel at your feet."

She smiled at the dog, which whined and rolled onto its back, showing its belly.

"You know what I did then, Bob? I flooded that pack of baying brutes with the belonging scent bitches release to soothe their pups. That's their real language, Bob, and I know that language, Bob. I speak that language.

"I made that laird's pack my own, Bob, and together we took that Scotsman down like a deer, and because I was starving I ate his heart and liver, cracked his bones and sucked the marrow. The rest I gave to the pack, my pack now."

Alana smiled, baring her large, even, white teeth, teeth that could bite through a skull like an apple, giving Dapper Man Bob a glimpse of her true face, the one she kept hidden from all but her enemies. "Look down, Bob."

Bob looked down. The huge attack dog at his feet was eyeing him carefully, growling softly, its hackles up and its ears back. Alana had emitted a flood of pheromones signaling the presence of a threat. Alana could catch a quizzical note in its growl. The dog appeared to be wondering if Bob was the source of that threat.

"No sudden moves, Bob. Don't speak. Nod if you understand your situation."

Bob nodded, his terrified gaze switching from her to the dog and back again.

Hard place meets rock, Alana thought.

Alana chanced a glance down the trail. No one she could see but she could faintly feel their presence—two teams, at least. She imagined these armed and armored men moving in file in the treeline on each side of the bike trail, coming her way in parallel. It's how she would move them, what she would do.

"You are wired, yes? Call them off, Bob. Do it now."

Bob pressed behind his ear and muttered a code, nodding shortly at Alana when he had finished. She liked the fear in his eyes. She needed to feed it.

"I have this thing I do, Bob. I drive the heel of my palm under the sternum, pulling the blow slightly at point of impact rather than driving through as I usually do. If I do it while your heart is between beats and generate just the right amount of force, you go into cardiac arrest. If I do it right, there won't even be a bruise. It would be as if none of this ever happened, as if you never happened."

Although she only killed when necessary, Alana very much wanted to follow through on her threat and remove this smarmy little blemish from the skin of the world. She fought that urge, stifling it, ramrodding it down to the core of her being like a round ball of lead still hot from the mold.

Alana felt a flush of self-satisfaction as the murderous red wave receded. Earlier, fiercer versions of herself would've killed Bob badly, horribly, painfully. This is me climbing the high tower, she thought, each tiny, incremental step taken one step closer to the acquisition of a soul, the door at the top imperceptibly open.

Alana beckoned give it to me to the leash Bob held loosely between his pale and pudgy fingers. Taking the leash, Alana reached down to the dog to scratch the scruff behind its ears. Its soulful brown eyes, locked on hers, were adoring.

"You have no idea what's coming," Bob said. "People like him, they're like gods." Bob was on his feet now, shifting his weight from side to side, one foot to the other, back again, like a child needing to pee.

Alana nodded at the dog. "What's her name, Bob?"

"I don't know its name," he said. "It's a dog. The dog's a prop, okay? Call it whatever you want."

To the dog she said, "I'll call you Bella, I think: such a pretty name. I've always liked that name. A big, beautiful girl like you needs a pretty name."

Alana turned to Bob.

"I'm going home now, Bob. Relay my decision to your employer."

"He already knows," Bob said. "The man owns satellites. Look up, wave, say hi!" Bob giggled, as some do when afraid.

Alana had known love once, four lives before. They had even married—a foolish move, she knew, but love had made her stupid. The French Army corporal who came to her door with news of her husband's death in the Siege of Paris, he had giggled like that, his oafish face filled with fear when the strange new widow's features momentarily writhed and shifted in the dingy light of the hallway.

He was right to be afraid, she thought. They all are.

Alana looked up. The sky was blue, cloudless, and empty. Like talking to God, she thought.

"Your employer, can he read lips?"

Dapper Man Bob said, "Machines do that, AIs, but yeah, sure. He can read lips."

Still looking skyward, Alana said, "I give you fair warning, Mister Eye-in-the-Sky. Hunt me and I hunt you back. We can end it here. Your choice."

Alana lowered her gaze. "Give me a name, Bob. Tell me—" her mouth an O as she shaped the word who.

But Dapper Man Bob was dead, shot through the head, with her new friend Bella sniffing disdainfully at his corpse. Alana hadn't heard the shot or the drop-thud of his body, so the suppression field Bob had boasted about was still operating, dulling her senses. Alana briefly wondered why she hadn't been shot yet but decided Bob's mysterious billionaire boss was probably right now weighing his options, formulating a next move. For now, he wanted her alive.

The man owns satellites, now-dead Bob had said.

Alana had encountered his kind before, this Mister Eye-in-the-Sky, the kind defined by a cancerous, all-consuming greed. The one before this one had been a Gilded Age railroad tycoon, a slobbering, sweaty, uncouth behemoth of a man whose agents had chased her for almost a decade. In the end, Alana had flayed the fat man alive, brain-tanned his hide, and made of him a coat.

"As I told him I would," Alana said, through gritted teeth.

Father Mark Dougherty was waiting on Alana's porch when she arrived home with Bella. At first Alana thought her friend was there on food pantry business. Alana had a knack for logistics and volunteered time to expand the supply channels for the two food pantries her church operated in the city. But then she saw Father Mark's expression, knowing him well enough to read him. He looked pensive, anxious.

Not here to talk supply chains, she thought.

Bella growled menacingly but Alana cut her off, signaling not-threat, part of our pack, one of us to the big, fearsome-looking animal.

"Stay, girl," Alana told the dog. "Guard the house."

Even in her private moments, Alana strived to stay within the human range, a woman of easily observable routine, habits, and pattern. Aside from the time she devoted to her church, Alana made tea upon waking, fed the cat, tended her roses and orchids, swept the porch, took out the trash, mowed her lawn, signed petitions, graded papers on her porch when the weather was nice, and knew by name the neighbors on either side and across the street. It wasn't an act. This was the life she had always wanted, ordinary and boring and beautiful, and the look of apprehension on the face of her priest—even more so than Dapper Man Bob dead on the trail—gave her the sense it was all slipping away.

Alana didn't bother with a smile. "We can talk inside," she told Father Mark. She inserted a key in the door but it wasn't the key that unlocked her door. A hidden biometric whole-body scanner confirming her identity served as the locking mechanism, not the key. She turned the key counter-clockwise. Turning the key counter-clockwise armed the house's more lethal defenses, all controlled using alpha brainwave pulse technology employed in advanced fighter jets in lieu of overly complicated manual controls. When the system was armed, Alana could kill an intruder with a thought—a bullet in the head, a flechette in the neck, a mist of acid in the face. The system was armed.

Alana and Father Mark crowded into the narrow, cramped foyer—narrow and cramped because she intended it as a chokepoint in case the door was breached. She noticed the priest's hesitancy, his frown, the way he averted his eyes.

He's anxious, uncertain, she thought. Suspicious, maybe, of me?

That Father Mark might know the truth of her made Alana ineffably sad. Mark had been one of her precious few. She considered offering him a drink—Mark liked his rye neat—but decided against it. She needed him sober. As for herself, Alana occasionally drank to be sociable, but it was all for show since her body neutralized the effects of alcohol and other poisons as soon as they entered her system.

"The living room, Father. Please."

Father Mark Dougherty moved like an ageing linebacker, a large man in his mid- to late-thirties who spoke with a thick, indefinable Eastern accent—Pittsburg, Alana thought, but she couldn't be sure. Father Mark listened more than he talked but she had picked up enough pieces of his story to put together a picture: a steelworker's son from a big Catholic family, a rough-and-tumble upbringing, a full-ride football scholarship. Father Mark had received his calling late, a few years after college, surprising everyone. The premature lines on his face spoke to struggle and hardship, which was good. She liked her priests grounded.

Father Mark broke the awkward silence. "I have a confession to make," he said. "The irony kills, I know."

"Tell me everything, Mark," Alana said.

The priest nodded and settled heavily into her leather easy chair, her guest chair. Alana remained standing. Men with guns were close by, watching her home, possibly prepping for an assault. She wanted to be ready and on her feet should they try it. Most of all she wanted Father Mark out of her house. She wanted him safe.

"Make it quick," she added, without explanation.

Father Mark nodded and tiredly wiped his face with his hands before going on. "Three days ago, I was approached by a very strange man. He just showed up. I was working alone in the rectory, looked up, and there he was. I won't go into it but the experience was…" Father Mark trailed off, at a loss.

"Surreal?"

He nodded. "So odd, unsettling, something you'd see in a weird dream, dressed like a fantasy book cover—"

"—the Dapper Man," Alana said. "We've met."

Father Mark seemed bemused, out of his ken, his ordered world neatly bound by ritual and tradition about to be reduced to smoking ash and rubble by a visit from a malignant human cartoon. Alana worried for her friend. She was glad Dapper Man Bob was dead.

"Go on," she said.

"He wanted to know about you, Alana, everything about you—everything I know, anyway, which isn't really much. I figured him for a crank. We get them, people with mental health issues. They get fixated, you know what I mean? We're trained for it, of course. Half this job is Psychology 101."

Alana said, "And then he offered you a ludicrous amount of money."

"You wouldn't believe," Father Mark said. "The bribe was real. He had it on him, a black nylon gym bag filled with cash, large denominations. I'd guess a million dollars, easy. Like something out of a gangster movie."

"Dapper Man wanted details," she said. It wasn't a question.

Father Mark nodded. "Of your confessions, yes. I refused the money."

"You should've told me right away, Mark, first thing."

"I am telling you. That's why I'm here."

"You're holding back," she said. "There's something else."
She could feel it. She could read it in his face. Finally, it came
to her. She put it together.

"Blackmail," she said. She didn't ask what lever they had
used against him. It didn't matter. What was odd is she hadn't
sensed it, smelled it on him, his secret sin. Rapists, murderers,
schemers, child molesters and the like all have a distinct aural
flavor, a stink. She could feel no such evil emanating from
Mark; the only stink emanating from Mark was a cheap, lime-
smelling aftershave, but she could see in his eyes the self-
flagellating guilt he endured. Guilt over what, Alana didn't
know. Whatever it was, she decided, she wouldn't judge him
for it.

"Did you give me up, Mark? That's the question."

Father Mark shook his head. "No, but I wanted to, I
considered it. I was told warning you is one of the release
triggers—that's the term he used: release triggers. Who talks
like that? Right now, the Monsignor is receiving an email in his
inbox. That email will have a link. If he follows that link, then
I'm no longer a priest."

Mention of the Monsignor gave Alana an idea, another
piece of a plan she had been putting together since speaking
with Lynn Hargrave. She couldn't perceive its details, not yet,
but she had a glimpse of its outlines.

"Wait right here," Alana said. "Under no circumstances go
outside."

A few minutes later Alana returned to the living room,
holding an envelope, its paper yellowed with age, an expensive,
hand-made, cream-colored vellum, the name on the face of the
envelope written by hand in a delicate, flowing cursive.

Mark reached out and took the sealed envelope. "Marie Clerval," he read aloud. It had been over a hundred years since Alana had worn that name. Hearing it spoken flooded her with memories.

"This isn't your name," he said. "Is this your name?"

Alana looked at Father Mark. "This is a Writ of Jus Sanctuarii, Right of Sanctuary. It means—"

"—I know what Right of Sanctuary means, Alana."

"I'm invoking it," Alana said. "Take this to the Monsignor and ask him to send it up the chain. Tell them to contact the Knights of Malta—the real Knights of Malta, not its public face. They can confirm my bona fides."

"Your bona fides?"

"I saved a Bishop once who later became a Pope. The Church has a long memory, so maybe they'll remember my one good deed and the promises they made for the sake of it. I need an ally right now. I need an out."

"What can I do, Alana? How can I help?" he said. Father Mark had gathered his wits. Helping others is what he did best, how he defined himself, and he was desperate to do it.

I want you to leave here—out my front door for all to see— and then I want you to pick a parishioner, any random member of our church, and stay there for the night—several nights, if you can swing it."

She wrote down a sequence of numbers on a piece of scratch paper and gave it over. "Call this number," she said. "The person who answers will not be me, but you can trust them. They will give you a set of instructions. You can choose to follow those instructions or not, your choice. Everyone should have a choice."

"Can you tell me anything, Alana? The more I know, the better I can serve."

She shook her head. "The more you know, the more likely the men after me will erase you. You are a rounding error to such men."

"Tell me anyway," he said insistently. "I know we're short on time. Just tell me what might be useful in the here and now."

Alana considered for a moment. She said, "I have a fallback ID in case this one is compromised, but those after me have enormous resources. They can tear through my backup like tissue paper.

"But I am not without resources, myself," she went on. "Given time, I can disappear, my trail such a tangle it would take them decades to unravel. Fifty years or so go by, and it ends with them dead and me free. I've done it before.

"I need time, Father Mark. Time is my friend. And time is what the Church can give me, the time it takes to build a new, impenetrable life."

His gaze was steady, level with hers. She had always liked that Father Mark was so tall. It was nice looking someone in the eyes without slightly crouching or bending down.

He asked, "Forget who. What are you, Alana? Are you some kind of, I don't know, immortal being? Angel?" He paused. "Demon?"

Alana shook her head at both. "All flesh is grass, Father, even mine. I can be killed. Fire would do it, I think. Fire can kill anything. Blowing me to tiny bits, maybe. There just hasn't been anyone yet up to the job."

She ushered Father Mark to the door. He stopped in the foyer and turned to speak. "One more thing," he said, "although I know you're sick of questions."

"Ask me anything, Father. I'll answer if I can."

"What was your crime? The Church extended Right of Sanctuary to certain criminals—"

"—The artist Caravaggio," Alana said, interrupting. "He was hot-headed. He liked to drink. He liked other men's wives. He killed a man in a fight over a woman and the Church gave him sanctuary."

"Everyone knows about Caravaggio, but what about you, your crime, Alana?"

Alana thought about it. "Existing," she said.

⁂

After Father Mark had gone, driving off in his sensible gray Volvo sedan, Alana stayed on the porch with Bella the dog, partly to further bond with the big animal and partly so she could survey the street to gauge the skill of those watching her. Bella would be a useful ally, more weapon than pet, but Alana needed time to cement the bond between them. As for those watching the house, Alana could feel her watchers out there, right now probably wondering how she was jamming their listening devices and blurring the feeds on their cameras, why satellite imaging showed her home as a vacant lot in real-time. They didn't know the full extent of her capabilities, and this she knew gave her a definite edge. She glanced skyward again, knowing the psychopath hunting her couldn't see her under the porch roof but calling him out anyway.

Do your worst, little man.

Alana went into the house, taking Bella with her. Perdy, her calico, was nowhere to be seen. Smart cat, she thought.

Lynn Hargrave called while Alana was in the kitchen, tending the dog. After authenticating the line, Hargrave said, "My people have been noodling a solution. We've made some headway. I'm sending an intercepted video file...now."

"You've seen it?"

"I've seen it, Jane. You need to watch it right bloody now. Timestamp puts it at twelve days ago."

"What am I looking at?"

"You're looking at the dayroom of Shortridge Polar Station, a drifting station in the Arctic Circle they claim conducts oceanographic research. Its location isn't fixed since it's designed and built to move with the ice floes."

"They claim?" Alana said. Mention of the North Pole imbued her with a deep sense of foreboding. Alana knew what still wandered those icy wastes. Her mind whirled at the implications. She wasn't yet ready for what she knew was coming.

It would make sense they would come for us both, she thought.

"I know this might be hard for you," Hargrave said, as if she had anticipated Alana's train of thought. "Watch first, then we'll talk."

Growing impatient, the not-knowing grating on her nerves, Alana said, "I see pool tables, card tables, a pinball machine, some chairs. No sound. No people."

"Wait for it," Hargrave said. "Almost there."

At one minute, twenty-six seconds, a headless, limbless human torso was hurled in front of the camera, flung across the width of the dayroom from left to right. A human being would not have recognized the object for what it was unless they slowed the rate and tracked it frame by frame. Alana knew immediately, her worst fear confirmed.

Two masked, helmeted men bundled in futuristic-looking cold climate environmental suits entered the frame at top left, backing into the dayroom, both firing automatic weapons Alana recognized as US military-issue M27s. The two men were panicked, wildly spraying their fire, a fatal mistake.

He took their leader first, she thought, as I would have done. He tore the man apart in front of the others to terrorize them and muddy their response.

"As I would," Alana said aloud.

It ended quickly, with the creature moving almost too fast for even Alana to follow. The ceiling fell in above the two men and through it dropped an enormous, vaguely human, fur-wrapped form.

"Smart," Alana said. "Practical-tactical."

"What do you mean?"

"He drapes himself in a polar bear pelt and no doubt moves like a polar bear on the ice, hiding in plain sight. It keeps him warm, and he is a polar bear when seen from above."

The creature closed with the first man, punching through his body with his massive fist and then yanking out the man's organs, disemboweling him, leaving him standing over a heap of entrails until the man's brain registered he was dead. In the single second before the body dropped, the creature had turned at the waist in a turret-like motion and grasped the other, his huge hand closing on the second man's neck, his talon-like fingers completely encircling it, and then raised the man high to eye level. Alana felt a grudging admiration for the second man, who continued resisting with kicks and strikes against his hulking, freakishly large attacker even as he was being lifted from the floor. Finally, the man gave up and clasped both hands on the iron bar of a wrist holding him up, looking like a hanged man fighting the noose. At this point, Alana expected a straightforward snapping of the neck—no need for a show without an audience—but the creature held the man in place for nearly a minute. They were clearly conversing. The man was masked and the camera feed came without sound, but he nodded several times, shook his head once. The creature was in profile so she couldn't read its lips, but she saw its massive jaw working as if it were talking. When their conversation ended, the creature snapped the man's neck (as she had anticipated) and threw the lifeless sack of a body at the security camera, disabling it.

Cut to black, Alana thought.

Alana asked, "Do you know what they're saying, Lynn?"

"Subject B, the man interrogated by the being I'll refer to as Subject A, has a protective mask on, so his responses can only be inferred from context and approximated. Subject A we can read readily enough."

"Go ahead."

Hargrave clears her throat. "Subject A asks, 'Who sent you?' Subject B replies, 'Shortridge'. Subject A says, 'Tell Shortridge to leave me alone'. Subject B says (approximately), 'Tell him yourself, he's watching us right now' and points directly at the camera. Subject A says, 'So I keep you alive why, little man?' Subject B realizes his mistake and apparently tries to bargain with his captor."

"Bargain how, with what?"

"He gave the monster your name, Jane. The name you're using now: Alana Von See. Based on context and implication, we don't think he knew your location."

"Mister Eye in the Sky at Shortridge knows my location, and now 'The being we refer to as Subject A' knows he knows. Subject A doesn't get tired. He never stops. He will find this man and make him talk."

Hargrave said, "I can muster an army of professionals, Jane. We can be at your door in a day—and don't worry about the expense. Hargrave & Fitch will do it for free, pro bono. It's what my father would've wanted."

Alana shook her head and then smiled in spite of herself, realizing Lynn Hargrave wouldn't see her do it. "You're too kind, Lynn, but no. He's far faster and stronger than I am—probably smarter, too. He would kill you all. Besides, there would almost certainly be civilian casualties, innocent people. I can't live with that. I won't. So no, tell your man in Chicago we won't make a stand here. Tell him the mission is extraction. And we'll need the house sanitized after we're safely away. Too many questions otherwise."

Alana tried hard not to picture in her mind's eye the incineration of her home.

Of this life I've grown to love, she thought.

Hargrave said, "I've seen the file, you know, the detailed report compiled by my father, but even after reading it and talking with him—talking to you now—I still find it hard to believe the story true and the monster real, that you are real." Hargrave hesitated before going on. "The mind balks, Jane."

Alana replied, "You are wrong to call him a monster. Mary never thought of him that way. Whenever she spoke of him, she called him The Being. She was very specific about it. That tortured, twisted thing out there is what a madman made him, the same madman who made me, who chopped me into pieces and threw me into the sea. We are not the monsters here! We never were!"

After a slight pause, Hargrave said, "What do you propose we do, Jane? I am bereft of ideas."

"This company, Shortridge, what do we know?"

"Everything," Hargrave said. "It's a massive, multi-billion-dollar investment firm owned by the man who founded it, Robert 'Bobby' Shortridge, a narcissistic snake-in-a-suit by all accounts. A few years ago, Shortridge heavily invested in a laboratory researching life-extending biotechnologies. The research was premised on biologically reprogramming the body at the cellular level. That line of research dead-ended—or was never legitimate in the first place. Con men congregate wherever the rich and gullible gather."

"The longevity studies, that's how you found him," Alana said.

"Yes, that's how we found Shortridge."

Alana asked, "Do you know where this Bobby Shortridge lives?"

"Shortridge owns properties all over the world. Please forgive me for stating the glaringly obvious, but all of those sites are heavily fortified even by our measure. I won't say impregnable, but close."

"Shortridge knows he is hunted. Based on what you know so far, where would he go to ground, best guess? Where would he feel safe?"

"His mansion in Medina, Washington," Hargrave said. "It even looks like a medieval fortress. Sending you its security profile now."

Alana asked, "Does Hargrave & Fitch still have its Ukrainian contacts? I'm thinking specifically of heavy ordinance—high explosive, thermobaric, nothing NBC—ideally something small, in a suitcase-sized package."

"Yes, we still have those contacts, and yes, what you describe is in their product line, a next-gen plastique, I believe."

"Reach out to them. Also know I'm authorizing use of the remainder of my balance, which should be enough to cover expenses."

Hargrave started to protest but Alana cut her off. "I knew your father, Lynn. Clive and I were very close once. Your use of the words free and pro bono would wound his dark, mercenary heart. I pay my debts."

"You have a plan, Jane?"

Alana said, "We can't know where my other is, but we know where he soon will be. All lines converge. My plan is to be there when and where those lines intersect. All I need do is show up."

"With a bomb," Hargrave said.

"All good plans should conclude with a fiery explosion—or so my teachers told me," Alana said. "It's written down somewhere. In a book. Or should be."

After killing all aboard, the creature had left the drifting station at twilight and set out at a run across the thick, shifting ice of the Arctic Sea, its long, loping strides effortlessly eating the distance, moving faster than any man-made machine on the hostile, unforgiving terrain. The creature wasn't impervious to the tearing bite of the wind and sting of the tiny needles of ice driven by it; the creature's body knew pain but it could withstand that pain and draw from it and use it to go even faster. The computers on the station had been useless to it but there had been paper maps. It took the maps. It could use maps. The stars gave it direction.

Two weeks after its attack on the drifting station, moving always and only by night, the creature killed a man for his dogsled and team twenty kilometers southeast of Utqiagvik. A week later it broke into a house for food in Tanana, killing no one. The terrified Inuit family, shocked awake by the noise and cowering in closets and under beds, mistook it for a bear newly awakened from hibernation and made reckless and wild by hunger. It crossed the Denali Range a few days later and eventually made its way to the outskirts of Anchorage, finding itself dazzled by the lights, the first city it had seen in over two centuries. Adapting quickly as it always had, the creature made its way unseen to a railyard and stowed aboard a freight train heading south. From there, it traveled by semi-trailer truck and rail, following the coast.

Close now, the creature thought. Shortridge, Medina, Alana, the man at the drifting station had said.

It approached the Shortridge Estate by stealth from the north, through the wooded golf course bordering its grounds, moving at a low crawl, slithering through the grass on all fours. Like Alana, it could blend seamlessly into its environment and raised no alarms. No neighborhood dogs barked at its passage. No birds broke from the cover of the trees. The creature wasn't aware it was making a sound itself, a soft, low and continuous hiss. It was eager. It was close.

The creature instinctively knew clearing a building is best done starting at the top and working down, so it scaled the castle-like stone walls of Bobby Shortridge's manor and used the immense strength of its fingers to prise open the frame of a third-story window, its supple, double jointed limbs allowing it to squeeze its massive bulk through the seemingly impossibly small and narrow opening. It didn't occur to the creature to wonder at the silence when it breached the house since it was still very much of its time. No electronic sensors existed when the creature had last been in the world of men, but the lack of guards gave it pause. It had expected bodyguards, servants, retainers, but the mansion was inexplicably empty.

It stopped and listened, sniffed the air. It sensed a single human being in the house, just ahead, in what it presumed to be the master bedroom at the end of a long, classically arched, high-ceilinged hallway. It could smell the fear from here.

The heavy, reinforced double doors were unlocked. The creature knew traps and knew this was a trap but entered anyway. It was a being of pure will. No trap could kill or hold it. Nothing could stop it. It would crush and kill with savage fury any who dared stand in its way.

"Hello, lover," Alana said.

She stood by the bed, a massively portentous four-poster complete with a silk floral canopy. On the bed was Bobby Shortridge, the billionaire investment wizard and entrepreneur who had hunted her, who had hunted them both. Shortridge was still alive and relatively untouched, but his hands and feet were bound, his mouth taped shut. The sight of the gigantic, misshapen creature looming in his doorway—the sheer wrongness of its presence—caused him to desperately squirm and whimper and moan. His bladder and bowels emptied, the stench filling the room. Alana thought the man might have gone mad, and found she didn't care.

"Alana," her other said, its voice a croak from disuse, speaking the name the man at the drifting station had said was hers. It moved forward—to hold her, to kill her, she didn't know which.

Alana held up the remote detonator. "Touch me and we die," she said, and the creature stopped moving, becoming utterly and instantly still, intuitively grasping the nature of the threat, if not the means. She imagined it could probably stay motionless like this for days, weeks if need be.

"Together...forever," the creature said simply (so like a child, Alana thought), its long, gangling arms and huge hands dangling at its sides.

"Not today," she replied. "Maybe one day. Let's talk, you and me."

"And then it just walked away?" Lynn Hargrave asked. "It didn't say anything, do anything?"

The two women stood on a knoll two hundred meters from the main house. Daylight soon. A helicopter waited. They needed to leave.

Alana shook her head, striving to hide her annoyance at Lynn's use of it to describe what she had come to think of as her other. "He's barely verbal, Lynn."

"You took an enormous risk."

"You saw how he is," Alana said. "No guarantee our bombs and bullets would stop him. He could kill us all. Talking, just talking, seemed the sensible approach."

"Yes, I saw," Hargrave said, her tone subdued. The up-close reality of this impossible being had shaken her.

More to herself than to Hargrave, Alana said, "I showed him another way, letting him know he could be more than a mindless murder machine, a child's nightmare. He didn't know he had a choice."

"Is that it, then? Are we done?"

"You're done, Lynn, not me. There will always be another Bobby Shortridge. History bores me with its repetition."

"You should try something new, break the pattern," Hargrave said.

"What do you mean?"

"You could sell your secret, Jane. Make yourself so fantastically rich and powerful none of them can touch you."

"Oh, right, my secret. My secret is there is no secret, Lynn, only a simple truth: that which was never alive can never truly die. My other and I were sculpted from corpses. We shouldn't be, yet here we are: undead anomalies cursed with pure cogito ergo sum. We exist and will probably go on existing in one form or another until the very end of things. I try not to think too much what that means."

Lynn Hargrave interrupted. "You say, 'probably'. You can't be certain of any of this."

"I have faith," Alana said. "With faith comes hope."

"What is it you're hoping for?" Hargrave asked. "What is it you want?"

"An explanation," Alana said. "I have questions."

CRITICAL BLAST PUBLISHING
20¢
APPROVED BY THE READING CODE AUTHORITY
MAMMON ESTATES
Ross Killey
CRITICAL BLAST PUBLISHING
WEIRD FANTASTIC WORLDS
WHERE POP CULTURE GETS BLASTED
INCREDIBLE STRANGE STORIES
SPINE-CHILLING SUSPENSE IN SUBURBIA!

■ HELIUM GAS & BALLOON SET ■ Get away from the day to day grind ■ of your boring life and steal a whole ■ house while the owners are away.

SUPER SECRET BOOK SAFE The special camouflage feature activates, once placed on the book shelf. You'll never find it again.

RENT AN ANGRY FISH! When you need to stop a Bully from harassing, or when you need to look like a decent human concerned for poor ugly aquatic monsters.

SNAKES IN A MAIL BOX Get these total mother-fS%Ken poisonous snakes and mail them with your get well gift cards.

HOBO IN A BOX When your street is getting over-runned by homeless people and you need someone to speak their language and run them off to the next street down the block.

IT'S JUST A TUESDAY!

DIGITAL PUZZLE T-SHIRT Get people's undivided attention when they get engrossed trying to solve the constantly changing puzzles.

SUPER SHARP PIRATE SWORD When you want to capture the hearts and minds of the people around you, this sword will cut through the muscle and bone to get to the vital organs you need to sustain your hunger.

FISH BOWL FULL OF WORMS Are you tired of eating meat? Get yourself a bowl full of yummy worms and feel you are saving the planet.

EXPLODING DRINK Sit back and enjoy the highjinks as people unscrew their drink activating the chemical reaction, causing a foamy mess.

■ BOX OF LIVE BATS When you feel ■ like a millionaire crime fighting hero ■ and need to dress up your special ■ cave, to give it that extra touch of ■ atmosphere... a box of live bats is ■ perfect for you. Food not included.

TRICK BLACK HOLE Get this special singularity and impress your friends by banishing them to other dimensions and realities.

MONSTER VALUE STAMP THIS IS IT! CLIP THEM & COLLECT THEM ALL!

Ross Killey says, "Mom would tell you my Father got me hooked on horror movies at too young an age. Although a 90's kid, I had a steady diet of everything from Abbott and Costello Meet Frankenstein to Dawn of the Dead. I work security full time and read and write when my daughter is taking naps. I live in central Indiana with my wife, daughter and two fur babies. I'm the author of Full Moon Highway which was published by Raven Tale in 2023."

Nicholas staked the "FREE" sign in his front yard and looked at the pile of assorted junk near the curb. Satisfied, he wiped sweat out of his eyes and went inside to get a cold glass of water. While stretching his back over the sink, Nicholas looked out the back window and saw Christine raking up some of the leftover leaves from Fall. Houdini was out there with her, wagging his tail and rolling around on his back, making a mess of her work.

The sputtering cough of an engine sounded in the driveway.

Nicholas peered out a front window and saw an old blue Chevy. The truck had to have been twenty years past its prime and the same could be said about its driver. The old man got out of his truck in grease-covered overalls and walked over to examine the pile of junk next to the curb. Nicholas had hauled out many items from the homes previous owners that were either damaged or undesirable. The man looked at a skimpy lamp and couch with torn upholstery, then moved on to a dresser missing half its drawers. His gaze fixed on an old washing machine lid.

By the time Nicholas got outside to help, the man had just dropped the scrap metal into the bed of his truck. "Hey, need a hand with anything?"

He looked at Nicholas.

"I guess you got it covered," Nicholas said and reached out his hand in greeting. "My name is Nicholas. My wife and I moved here in January. I'm guessing you live in the neighborhood?"

The older man ignored his friendly gesture and looked at him as if sizing him up. After a few awkward seconds of silence Nicholas put his hand down. The man had grease marks all over his skin and the unusually hot spring day made it run down his face as if from his pores. The man got back into his truck and shut the door. The engine revived itself and the truck slowly backed out of the driveway. Nicholas watched the Chevy get smaller and smaller and eventually turn down another street.

If the man did live in the neighborhood at least he wasn't close. Nicholas and Christine had just moved to Mammon Estates in January and had only met their direct neighbor, George Herman. He was a bachelor that Nicholas had quickly considered a friend. He was glad he lived next to George and not the greasy man.

Nicholas turned but heard another vehicle stop on the street. Looking back, he saw the window roll down on a police cruiser and a friendly face peered out.

"Hey, is that a bookshelf?" The officer wore a smile.

"Yeah, you want it?"

"Oh man, my kid loves to read. He'll love this!" Officer Friendly put the cruiser in park and got out. Nicholas grabbed the bookshelf and carried it to the trunk, where the officer stood propping it open. "You think it will fit?"

Nicholas strained to answer as he did all the lifting. "Well, you might have to leave the trunk open a bit. You have any bungee cords?"

"No, but that's okay. I don't live too far from here." His smile never faltered as he watched Nicholas put the shelf in the trunk; he didn't once offer to help. The bookshelf stuck out of the trunk and Officer Friendly carefully lay the lid down over it. "I'll just take it slow from here. Hey, thanks again!" Officer Friendly took Nicholas' hand, shook it almost violently, and got back into the car.

The cruiser was already pulling away when Nicholas realized he hadn't gotten the officer's name.

As the day went on, more and more people came to take the junk that sat in the yard. Nicholas guessed most of them lived in Mammon Estates. Either way Christine was happy the items were no longer of their concern and that made him happy too.

The hot afternoon faded into cool evening, and Nicholas pulled the FREE sign out of the ground. But as he did, he thought he could smell a garbage truck coming. However, it was a lone, disheveled man walking down the sidewalk that he smelt. His clothes were more akin to dirty rags, and he wore a torn cap on his head from which long, dirty strands of grey hair fell. As the homeless-looking man got closer, he eyed the sign in Nicholas' hands.

"It's all yours, if you want it," said Nicholas. He held it out and the smelly man took it with arms so frail Nicholas thought they'd break. He left the man to it and started back up the drive until he heard shuffling feet. The man was right behind him, following him up to his house. "Um, did you have a question?"

The man merely looked at him, his face expressionless, totally content. Before Nicholas could say anything else, the man spoke. "You said it was all mine?"

"Excuse me?"

"You said it was all mine, if I wanted it…" The man's words trailed off as he arched his head to the side and looked past Nicholas. "Do you have any more?"

"No, that was the only one. Sorry."

The man's smell festered in the air as he continued to look past Nicholas. His eyes rolled around in his sunken sockets, continuously scanning the house and yard before they stopped and fixated on something. Christine came around the side of the house to place a glass ornament in the front garden and Nicholas realized what the man was staring at. To say it made him uncomfortable that this man starring at his wife in a stupefied gaze of desire was an understatement.

"Like I said, that's all I have. Sorry." Nicholas could have been rude, but the man hadn't said anything, and he didn't want to create a scene in front of his wife. Luckily, the man's gaze drifted back to Nicholas and a moment later, he was walking back down the sidewalk with his prize.

Nicholas made sure to watch the man until he was completely out of sight. It took a few minutes, but eventually the man turned the same bend the cop had turned down earlier, and Nicholas couldn't be sure, but thought he saw him turn and look back. Eventually he walked out of sight and Nicholas relaxed.

Nicholas woke up to Christine shaking his shoulder. He'd fallen asleep early and was having nice dreams about raising children in their new home, but now Christine stood over him looking awfully worried. Their Bull Terrier sat next to her, wagging his tail. He asked her what was wrong, and she told him she'd seen someone in the backyard.

"Are they still there?"

"I don't know. Come look."

At the back door, Nicholas peered around the corner so if someone were out there, they wouldn't see him. Christine stood behind him with Houdini. He could see the deck and the table set that sat upon it. A tree loomed over a quarter of the yard and the fence could be seen for a few feet beyond that, but the darkness swallowed it up as if the fence suddenly ended.

"I'm going to turn the lights on." He flipped the switch and light flooded the area. Now they could see half the backyard and a little beyond the fence.

Christine pointed to the right. "There. On the other side of the fence."

"I'm going to step out and have a look."

"Take Houdini with you."

Nicholas stepped out into the cool night with Houdini. Christine stood in the open doorway, looking in all directions. Nicholas stepped up to the fence and looked to the side of the house and then the neighbor's backyard. He couldn't make out any movement or person-like shapes. "I don't see anything Honey."

"I could've sworn I saw someone. Maybe I'm just too tired and I'm seeing things." She didn't seem too frightened or worried anymore. She went back into the house, Houdini and Nicholas right behind her. Before stepping in, however, Nicholas felt a gentle breeze, and with it came a smell of rotten garbage.

He double-checked all the doors and windows to make sure they were locked before going to bed.

A week went by, and life couldn't have been better. There had been no signs of anyone snooping around the yard and they wrote the incident off. Nicholas blamed the garbage smell on the neighbor's trashcan; a coincidence, the draft had brought the smell. No worries.

The weather was magnificent, and the couple decided to walk Houdini around the neighborhood. It was noon and they'd worked up a descent sweat walking half the neighborhood. Houdini was panting and the couple stopped to pour some water in a small bowl. Houdini lapped up the water and Nicholas looked at the dog jealously.

Christine noticed and said, "Don't worry, he'll share."

Nicholas laughed. "Yeah, I suppose we should have brought some for ourselves." They continued walking and within minutes they spotted a little girl running a lemonade stand in front of a house all by herself. "Look at that," said Nicholas with a gratifying smile. "Just what we needed."

The couple approached the stand and as they got closer, they noticed what must have been the girl's father, slowly rocking back and forth in a rocking chair on the porch.

By the looks of it, the stand had been hastily nailed together and painted yellow all over. The front read "LEMONADE 50 ENT" in bright pink paint. The little girl, who wore her best Sunday dress, sat in a chair and was drawing in a coloring book. She looked up and smiled when they approached.

"Hi there, can we buy some lemonade?"

Her smile widened, exposing a missing front tooth. "You want two cups?"

"Yes please," answered Christine. The girl poured the lemonade into plastic cups. Nicholas dug out a dollar bill from his wallet and handed it to the girl.

The girl turned the dollar over in her hand as if she were confused at what it was and then looked back at her father, then back up at the couple. "Do you have any more?"

Nicholas chuckled. "Well, your sign says fifty cents for a cup, and I gave you a dollar." He looked towards the porch where the father had stopped rocking and watched them.

Christine elbowed Nicholas in the side. "Honey, just give her another dollar."

The last thing he wanted to do was to argue a point to the girl in front of her father, so Nicholas retrieved another dollar and handed it to the girl. She examined it just like the first, and then smiled at them. "Thank you."

"You're welcome," Christine said as they walked away with their cups. Nicholas turned to look back at the house; the father went back to rocking in his chair and the girl gave Nicholas that missing-tooth smile.

A few days later Christine noticed a glass ornament had disappeared from the garden. She told Nicholas as soon as he had come home from work, and they talked about it over lasagna.

"Which one?" Nicholas asked.

"The one that looked like a sunflower."

He remembered it. The ornament was blown from glass of many colors and, when the light hit just right, looked dazzling.

"Who would have taken it?"

Christine looked defeated. "Kids maybe?"

Nicholas didn't have an answer for her. Why would someone steal an ornament that you could buy at any lawn store? He promised to buy her a new one.

The sun had set, and the couple were loading the dirty dishes into the washer when they heard a small crash outside.

"What was that?" Christine sounded wary.

"Sounded like the trash bin falling over."

Christine continued loading the dishwasher while Nicholas walked back into the dining room and looked out the window. He was right. The trash bin had caused the noise, but it hadn't fallen.

Three people stood at the end of the driveway, rummaging through the garbage that had spilled onto the street. It was dark out and Nicholas couldn't tell who it was, but he had an idea of who it might be. Nicholas went into the kitchen and grabbed a flashlight from a cupboard.

"What was it?" Christine asked.

"I think some homeless people are going through our garbage." Christine said something, but in his haste, he didn't hear what. He was out the front door and across the lawn before he knew it and turned the light on the curb.

He expected to see the homeless man and maybe some of his buddies going through the trash, but the people Nicholas saw didn't look homeless at all. One was a woman who looked to be in her late thirties, another was a man of the same age and wearing a ball cap, and the last person was a kid who could have been as young as sixteen. They looked like a family.

"What are you guys doing?" His voice was curious yet stern; Nicholas wanted to know why they were going through his trash. His question went unanswered, for as soon as the words left his mouth the three scavengers bolted in different directions. "Wait!"

Nicholas thought about running after them, but which one? What would he do if he caught them? After all, they only knocked over his trash. That wasn't exactly a criminal offense. Before he could decide, the trio disappeared into the night.

Dumbfounded, Nicholas went back inside. Christine stood in the living room looking worried. "What happened? I saw people running off." He told her all of what happened. "Should we call the police?"

"They aren't going to do anything. Once garbage hits the curb its public property. Plus, I didn't get a great look at them and have no idea where they ran off to. The police will see it as a waste of time."

"Well, we should do something. I mean, I saw someone in the backyard, then someone stole an ornament right out of the yard and now we have people going through our trash."

"You *thought* you saw someone in the back yard." Nicholas knew she was becoming agitated. "But if it makes you feel better, I'll buy a bat or something."

"A bat?"

"Yeah, a baseball bat."

Christine folded her arms and looked unimpressed. "How about a gun?"

"A gun?" Nicholas sounded almost shocked. "You want me to buy a gun because a lawn ornament went missing and a few people went through our trash?"

"I don't care for guns either Nick, but it would make me feel a whole lot better knowing we could defend ourselves if we had to." With that, she walked back into the kitchen.

Nicholas sighed then checked all the locks on the doors and windows.

They were walking Houdini on his leash again. It was warm out, but there was a bit of overcast above their heads. They found themselves on the same street as they had a few days ago where the girl had the lemonade stand and sure enough, she was there again.

"She's back at it," said Christine. "Bet she won't get many customers today." Nicholas nodded in agreement, and they walked on the other side of the street, but that didn't stop the girl from looking up from her coloring book to smile. There was no sign of the father on the porch.

Stopping only to let Houdini pee on a few hydrants and stop signs, they turned onto a street in the neighborhood they hadn't been down before and decided to follow where it went. An elderly woman watered her flowers close by. Houdini led them past the woman's house, but Christine grabbed Nicholas' arm.

"Did you see that?" she asked.

"What?"

"Did you see what was in her yard?" Nicholas hadn't been paying attention and shook his head. "It was my ornament. The one that was stolen."

"The same one?" He looked back at the yard.

"Don't stare," she hissed.

He didn't and she waited for him to say something. "What? You think that old lady stole it from our yard?"

Christine stared hard. "It's the same one, Nick."

"You can't possibly know that. We weren't that close to it, and you know it's possible she may own the same one."

Christine shook her head and continued walking with Houdini.

Nicholas stayed put and looked back at the house; the woman had gone inside. He scanned the yard and a hint of ruby glass stuck out from a bush.

An SUV drove up between Nicholas and the house, blocking his view. He saw the driver was a man wearing a ball cap. For a split second, the driver turned his head and looked at Nicholas, then turned his eyes back to the road as he drove past Christine and Houdini. The SUV turned down a street and was gone. Nicholas thought it looked an awful lot like the man who'd gone through his trash.

"Are you coming or what?" Christine asked. "I think it might rain."

An afternoon shower hit shortly after they made it home. Christine hadn't brought up the lawn ornament again and Nicholas didn't know what she wanted him to do about it. Did she expect him to march over there and take an old lady's lawn ornament out of her yard? Nicholas was not about to make a fool of himself doing that; he'd rather just buy her a new one.

George Herman called shortly after the rain stopped.

Nicholas spoke into the phone. "Hey George, what's up?"

"Hey buddy, how's it goin'?" His voice carried a certain upbeat energy to it that was infectious.

"Not a whole lot. Christine and I walked Houdini earlier and made it home just before the rain started."

"Yeah, it really came down there for a little bit. You got anything going on at the moment?"

"No, why?"

"Well, I'm trying out a new recipe and I forgot to buy eggs. Would you have a couple to spare?"

"I think we got some. Meet you outside in a few minutes?"

"Sure, thing buddy!"

Nicholas found three eggs in the fridge and walked them next door. George was standing in his side yard wearing workout shorts and a tank top that was too small for his portly frame. He was looking up at the sky. "Looks like it might start up again."

"Beats snow, right?" Nicholas handed over the eggs. "Having some guests over or something?"

His gaze left the sky. "I might. Not sure yet. But I found this awesome new recipe for cookies, and I just really needed these eggs. I hate running to the store for one thing and at this time of day it's probably a zoo."

"Yeah, you're probably right," Nicholas chuckled. "Have you noticed anything weird going on lately? Around the neighborhood?"

He gave Nicholas a quizzical look. "What do you mean?"

Nicholas told him about all the peculiar events he and Christine had experienced as of late.

George shook his head. "Can't say that I've noticed anything. I've seen people go through trash before. It's like a weird hobby for some. I'd have to imagine you're going to find some oddballs in any neighborhood. Christine really think that lady stole her lawn ornament?"

"Yeah."

"Sheesh. I don't know man. As far as the peeping toms in your yard, you should invest in some automatic security lights. That'll scare them away."

Nicholas nodded. "I might try that. Well, I'll let you get back to cooking. But let me know if you see anything weird okay?"

"Yeah, no problem buddy." George looked down at the small cartoon of eggs in his hands for the first time and noticed there were only three eggs. Nicholas had already turned around when George asked, "Hey, do you have anymore?"

It rained throughout the night, leaving a fine layer of sparkling morning dew on everyone's lawns. Houdini, needing to be let out, woke Nicholas. Christine didn't wake to his whines, so Nicholas left her sleeping. He let Houdini out and started the coffee machine. Once his mug filled, he stepped outside with it. Houdini was walking circles around the tree, probably sniffing out a squirrel. Nicholas smiled and brought the mug to his lips but stopped there.

There were impressions in the grass.

He walked over to one and looked down. It was a shoe impression. A whole line of them came from the corner of the yard near the fence. Nicholas stared long and hard at them. They were too big to be from Christine and he hadn't stepped foot in the backyard at all yesterday. He walked over to the fence and saw that they kept going on the other side.

Nicholas looked behind him and followed the impressions back through the yard and up to the bedroom window.

"What the hell..."

Nicholas couldn't see much through the curtain, but when he strained his eyes, he could just make out the sleeping form of Christine. He backed up a few steps and then looked around, as if the person who had entered their yard was still around. He looked back down. The shoe prints were very noticeable in the wet mulch.

Nicholas thought about whether to tell Christine about what he'd found. After a minute he used his foot to screw up the mulch. He might tell her, but not right away. He didn't want to send her into a panic. Instead, Nicholas decided he would go shopping.

🦇

Nicholas left right after Christine went to work. Security lights were purchased at the hardware store and once home it took two hours to install one in the front yard and one in the back. He thought it would take longer, but they made them so any moron could install them nowadays. Both were tested and he was happy with the results. The lights would turn on as soon as someone would step within thirty feet. Once done, he went into the kitchen where another purchase sat on the table.

He reached into the bag and brought out a small case, flipped the latches on it, and opened the lid to reveal the pistol.

The nine-millimeter was small in his hands. He hadn't shot many guns in his life, but Nicholas trusted the man working at the sporting goods store and handed over the four hundred dollars. After a quick background check, he was allowed to walk out of the store with the gun.

Nicholas loaded the magazine but didn't put it in the pistol. Instead, he walked into the bedroom and put both items next to each other in his nightstand. Hopefully, he'd never use it.

It just got dark by the time Christine came home from work. She had a sack of takeout in her arms. They ate at the dining room table and talked about her day. "It was a slow for me," she said. "What did you do today?"

"I bought some security lights and installed them in the front and back."

"Really?" She looked somewhat surprised. "I didn't see them come on when I came home."

"I have them set to only come on when it gets dark out. Figured it would deter any old ladies from coming into our yard." He was glad to see that Christine found the comment funny.

They talked, ate, and as time went by Nicholas realized he forgot to tell her about the gun. He decided to hold off on telling her for now. They were having a good time and he wanted to enjoy it.

They let Houdini outside and begun cleaning off the table when Christine said, "Hey, the light came on." Nicholas stopped what he was doing and could see the bright light through the living room curtains. "You hear that?"

Nicholas ran to the window and pushed the curtain aside. In the cone of light, he could make out a hunched figure in the driveway, between their cars.

"Someone's out there." He ran to the bedroom, grabbed the pistol and slid the magazine in before heading to the front door.

"Where did that come from?" Christine asked, concerned. "And what are you going to do with it?"

"From the store. Come stand by the door and be ready to lock it if anything happens." Christine seemed confused but did as she was told. Without warning, Nicholas went out the door.

Nicholas approached the cars. The gun in his hand made him feel better, even if he held it behind his back. He didn't want anyone to see him walking with a gun in plain sight if he could help it. An odd sound came from between the cars where the person bent over a tire. Coming around the car, he saw a man using a lug wrench to take off the rim.

"What the hell is going on?" Nicholas shouted. The man looked up. Nicholas recognized him as the older man with the blue Chevy who had taken the washing machine lid. He was again grimy and covered in grease. The man spun the lug wrench free, pocketing the nut that came with it. Nicholas pulled the gun out from behind him and pointed it at the man. "Put the wrench down and tell me what you're doing."

The man stood up but didn't put the wrench down; he didn't seem afraid of the weapon. Before Nicholas could do or say anything, he saw more people out of the corner of his eye. Details were lost in the gloom of the security light, but it looked to be a handful of people, all walking towards his yard from the sidewalk. Then another group of people came from the left. The man with the wrench stood rock still.

A bad feeling formed in the pit of his stomach and Nicholas ran to the front door and pushed his way inside, almost knocking down Christine. He threw the door shut and bolted it.

"I called the cops," she said, panicked. "What's going on?"

"Quiet!" He heard footsteps on the porch and looked through the peephole. A handful of people stood around on the porch, looking around as if they'd never seen a porch before. One by one, Nicholas started to recognize them as people that lived in the neighborhood. But what were they doing at his house? A figure Nicholas recognized immediately walked up to the porch, pushed his way through the small crowd, and stood right in front of the door.

Nicholas could smell him through the door.

The homeless man looked right at the peephole and grinned. Something was hefted up to the hole. It took Nicholas a second to register what it was. It was the "FREE" sign he'd given to the man.

"What the fuck," Nicholas whispered.

The sign lowered out of view, and the homeless man got so close to the peephole that Nicholas could only see the man's tongue as it rolled around his few rotten teeth. "Do you have any more?" His voice mocked. "You said it was all mine if I wanted it!" The man began laughing.

Nicholas reared from the door.

"I'm scared, Nick." Christine was almost in tears, and he didn't know what to say to her.

It began to sound like a circus outside as they heard more and more voices surrounding their house. Both went to the window and peaked through the curtains. What they saw just didn't make sense. The people of Mammon Estates were everywhere. Their very neighbors! Nicholas saw the man in overalls back to work on his tires while others began to break into the cars, smashing at the handles and windows with various items and tools. The old lady that had stolen the glass ornament bent over Christine's garden and began plucking whole flowers right out of the ground and holding them up victoriously.

Christine was crying. "Why are they doing this?"

"I don't know why they're doing it, but if they try to get in, they'll be sorry."

Just then, the power in the house went out and they heard barking from the backyard.

"Oh my God, Houdini!" Christine ran to the back door. Nicholas grabbed her before she opened the door to run out. "Let me go!"

"Look!" Nicholas pointed out the window. It was dark out now that the lights had lost power, but that didn't stop them from seeing dark forms climbing over the fence line. There were at least fifteen people climbing into their back yard, probably more.

Three of them stood out as the family that had raided his garbage. The teenage boy was first over the fence and before his foot touched the ground, Houdini ran up and bit his calf. The boy let out a wail and fell to the ground as Houdini began tearing and tugging. The mother hopped over the fence and tried and pull Houdini off her boy. She came away with the dog in her hands, while her son wiggled on the ground holding his torn leg. Houdini growled and reeled back and forth in her arms, trying to bite her. The father, wearing the same ball cap as he did in the SUV, stepped up from the other side of the fence and clubbed Houdini over the head with a brick. The dog went limp, and the mother handed him over to the father who took him and began to walk away with him. Nicholas had no way of knowing if Houdini was alive or not.

Christine sagged to the floor and began to weep. Nicholas wanted to hold her and tell her everything would be all right, but he couldn't believe half the things he was seeing. He tucked the pistol in his waistband and managed to pick Christine up off the floor and drag her to the living room where he sat her down.

Red and blue lights began to flash through the curtains and all the noise came to a halt.

After a minute, Nicholas got up and went to look out the peephole. He saw a cop standing with his back to the door. Nicolas looked at his wife. "The cops are here. Everything is going to be okay. We're going to get Houdini back." She looked at him with tearful eyes but didn't say anything. Nicholas unbolted the door and swung it open.

Officer Friendly turned and smiled at Nicholas. "Howdy neighbor. The station got a call from here and I figured since I live on the other side of the neighborhood that I'd come check it out. What seems to be the problem?"

Nicholas was at a loss for words. Hadn't he seen all the people that were outside? Where'd they go? What about all the damage to the cars and yard?

"Hey, you know my kid loved that bookshelf," Officer Friendly said still smiling. "You wouldn't happen to have any more would you?"

Nicholas reached behind his back for the pistol, but Officer Friendly had his out first. A loud ringing filled Nicholas' ears and he felt a white-hot heat in his gut. He fell back into the house.

"*Nicholas!*" Christine screamed and crawled up to him, covering his leaking wound with her hands. The couple watched in horror as the neighbors who'd hid in the yard filed past Officer Friendly and into the house. They started going through everything the couple owned, taking whatever they wanted.

Christine reached for the gun that had fallen onto the ground, but Officer Friendly stomped her hand, then took the gun for himself. "Sorry Miss. You two seem like nice folks, but it's Offering Season and there ain't nothing that can be done about that."

More and more people filled the house until all of the neighborhood had to be in attendance. Within minutes, half the stuff in the house had been pillaged. They were leaving almost nothing behind, and the stuff they did ended up on the floor broken and smashed.

Despite the pain in his gut, Nicholas was conscious of it all, even when the homeless man walked through the door and grabbed up Christine with those frail arms. She struggled, kicking and screaming. The man's skeletal form possessed more strength than it ought to, and he dragged Christine out the front door. Nicholas heard her cries trail off in the night.

George Herman walked in and grabbed the flat screen TV off its stand. "Sorry buddy. I hate to do this to a nice guy like you, but I've got guests coming over later and this would look really nice on my wall. And then there's the Offering..." He looked down at Nicholas with sorrow in his eyes. "I hope we can still be friends." Then he was out of the house.

Nicholas tried to yell, scream, anything to halt the madness, but the pain from the gunshot was too great. A small figure came prancing through the front door. It was the girl from the lemonade stand. She bent over Nicholas and gave him that missing tooth grin. With her hands, she pried open his mouth. He could feel her tiny fingers snag onto his front left tooth and pull. The pain was excruciating. Nerves burst and the tooth loosened up, then came free. She held up her prize with bloody hands and waved it at her father who was standing out on the porch, an approving smile on his face. "Thanks!" she said and ran back out the door.

Nicholas lay bleeding out on the floor. Officer Friendly stood turning the pistol over in his hands, happy with his find. An older man with a cane almost stumbled as he came into the house. He began waving the cane back and forth and it landed on Nicholas' leg. A smile came to the man's lips. He dropped the cane to the ground and bent over, running his hands over Nicholas' face. They found his eyes. "Ahhh, what have we here?"

The man's fingers felt like talons and Nicholas closed his eyes before they sank in. He finally screamed.

The car rolled into the neighborhood and passed the entrance sign.

"Mammon Estates. What does that even mean?" The teen asked her parents from the back seat.

"I don't know, sweetie," her mother said. "But your father and I got a great deal on this house."

The daughter took out her phone and ran a search on Mammon. Her face scrunched in confusion when she saw the result.

Her phone read:

In the New Testament, it's commonly thought to mean money, material, and wealth. In the Middle Ages it was often personified as a deity and sometimes known as one of the Seven Princes of Hell.

3¢
USA
098 SNICKERELLA
MONSTER
VALUE STAMP
THIS IS IT!
CLIP THEM
& COLLECT
THEM ALL!

CRITICAL BLAST PUBLISHING
20¢
A NIGHT AT THE ZALINSKIS'
Damascus Mincemeyer
APPROVED BY THE READING CODE AUTHORITY
WEIRD FANTASTIC WORLDS
CRITICAL BLAST
WHERE POP CULTURE GETS BLASTED
INCREDIBLE STRANGE STORIES
TRAPPED IN A WEB OF TERROR!

WELCOME MAT TRAP When you don't want people annoying you, a simple press of the button and the trap door will dispose of anyone who stands on it, while waiting for you to answer the door.

HEAD KNIVES 100% stainless steal daggers that launch from the top of your head and kill any conversation you find boring.

DIGITAL PUZZLE T-SHIRT Get people's undivided attention when they get engrossed trying to solve the constantly changing puzzles.

HELIUM GAS & BALLOON SET Get away from the day to day grind of your boring life and steal a whole house while the owners are away.

MAKE MINE MONSTERS!

COCAINE FOR PETS When your pets become too excited during mating season and you don't want additional burden of feeding more pets, shot them up with some fine liquid snow and chill them out.

MONSTER VALUE STAMP THIS IS IT! CLIP THEM & COLLECT THEM ALL!

LEARN BLACK MYSTIC ARTS KUNG-FU When you find yourself cornered by Jive Turkey Demons and alternate versions of your bad self, you can always rely on your skills as a High-Kicking, Ass-Kicking Sorcerer of the Black Mystic Arts. CASH ONLY. 6 MONTHS TUITION UP FRONT. NO REFUNDS.

DAMASCUS MINCEMEYER was exposed to the weird worlds of horror, sci-fi and comics as a boy, and thus ruined for life. At one point he drew comics that appeared in Heavy Metal magazine, but now spends his time writing far-out fiction appearing in numerous anthologies, including Fire: Demons, Dragons and Djinn, Earth: Giants, Golems and Gargoyles, Air: Slyphs, Spirits and Swan Maidens, Monsters Vs Nazis, and many more. His first novel, By Invitation Only, is currently with The Rights Factory literary agency. Hailing from St. Louis, Missouri, U.S.A, he can usually be found posting absurd movie games on Instagram @damascusundead666.

When Stuart was a kid, his Grandpa Morty would spend every Friday evening huddled around a poker table with his bowling buddies, a bottle of Miller beside him, cigar between his teeth and a sly smile on his round face. There they'd sit immobile for hours, cloud of foul-smelling smoke infiltrating the adjoining rooms like some B-movie monster, ritually playing hand after hand and grousing about how much the world had gone to shit and how it could all be fixed if only they possessed the authority to do so.

Growing up, Stuart and his brothers had considerable fun at Morty's expense, mocking his knee-high argyle socks and that oiled-back hair that made him look like Ed Sullivan's long-lost twin. *What a bunch of fuddy-duddies,* they'd snicker.

And now, Stuart thought, holy Jesus, now at seventy-two somehow he'd *become* one of those fuddy-duddies, sitting with a clutch of guys who'd make his grandfather seem downright hip. Cigars weren't an issue—his wife Deborah had practically inserted a no-smoking clause into their marriage vows—but the rest could've been cut-and-pasted onto reality straight from Stuart's memories.

His best friend Bruce sat to the left, nursing a Bud Light and a smirk and clad in his usual designer duds: socks-and-sandals, cargo shorts and a Hawaiian shirt so luminous it was likely visible from space. Across from Bruce, Radecker was doing an Oscar-worthy Colonel Kurtz impression, three empty bottles and fifty bucks down for the night, staring at his cards like they were VC snipers ready to pop him from the bush. Hoppy completed the circle, chunky moose that he was, that ever-present Al Capone cap masking a balding dome, aluminum cane leaned against his chair; of the four he'd squeaked out the most cash that night, but his jowly cheeks now wobbled with displeasure.

"Damn it to hell, my hand's dead," he grumbled, tossing his cards down and munching a fistful of pretzels. "How 'bout you, Deck?"

"No surrender, no defeat, Hoppenrath," Radecker chided. "If I'd given up that easily at Lam Son I would've lost more than my leg," he rapped one set of knuckles against his left shin, and a hollow metallic sound answered.

"Here I thought your ex-wife amputated that with a meat cleaver," Bruce cracked.

"I heard it was a hacksaw," Hoppy added.

"Nope and nope," Radecker shot back. "If it'd been up to Edna she would've just ripped it off with those big ole' gorilla hands of hers. Shame she wasn't in my platoon back in '72. Woman could've dismembered an entire NVA battalion all by her lonesome." He glanced at Bruce. "But you wanna talk exes, how many alimonies have *you* paid out? Twelve? Thirteen?"

"Just the two," Bruce rebounded. "And they both *weep* with regret."

"So do *I*," Stuart dropped his cards on the table. "I'm outfoxed this round."

Radecker leered at Bruce. "Just you and me, Goldman," he laid a straight upon the green felt tabletop. "Choke on it."

"*Pffft!* You call that a *hand?*" Bruce slapped down a full house and watched Radecker's mouth delve into a rancorous scowl.

"Well ain't *you* Mr. Las Vegas." Hoppy joked as Bruce counted his winnings.

Stuart groaned. "Dear God, do *not* mention Vegas."

Hoppy cocked an eyebrow. "Y'know, you and Bruce never *did* tell us what happened to the two of you out there. Didn't say much 'bout that movie premiere you went to in Hollywood, either. La la land not all it's cracked up to be?"

"Let's just say I've come to appreciate the virtues of staycations," Stuart replied. "Nice and cozy and *safe*."

"You want safe? I'll give you *safe*—" Radecker reached under his camouflage tactical vest and withdrew an enormous black revolver. "Colt Python. Eight-inch stainless steel barrel. Square ramp foresight. Six 0.57 Magnum rounds. Any crackhead looking to shake down my crippled ass is going to end up one sorry morgue specimen. Take this puppy on your next road trip and there won't be *any* problems."

"Jesus *Christ*, Deck, put that thing away." Stuart nervously hooted, "Deborah would kill me if she knew it was even in the house."

Radecker rolled his eyes, but secreted the weapon into the shoulder-holster beneath his vest nonetheless. "Whatever you say, Starkweather. You saw the shit in 'Nam same as me, but if you wanna pretend the world's a nice, civilized place, be my guest. Just remember, one day you may wish you'd signed up for the Python Protection Plan."

"Speaking of pythons, if you lunkheads will excuse me, I feel the need to drain mine." Bruce announced.

"I could use a break myself," Stuart pushed away from the table.

A dog was barking outside. "Damn mutt's been at it non-stop for half an hour," Radecker complained. "Can't your neighbors shut him up?"

"The Zalinskis?" Stuart peered through the open window to the house next door. "They're on a Caribbean cruise this week. The dog's Kojack. I-I'm supposed to feed him while they're gone. Guess I got so wrapped up in the game it slipped my mind."

"Forgetfulness is the first sign of dementia," Hoppy laughed. "Remind me to never have you look after my fish when I'm out of town, Stu."

"Ha ha," Stuart looked at his wristwatch. It was just past ten; the four of them had been playing for two hours. "Recess break? Pick it up in fifteen?"

"I've got bathroom dibs," Bruce jabbed Stuart's shoulder. "I'll try not to forget to flush."

Stuart followed Bruce from the room but made a left and went alone to the kitchen. Deborah was there, drinking chamomile at the table and thumbing through the latest issue of *Harper's Bazaar*.

"Hey there, handsome," she said between sips. "How's the slumber party?"

Stuart's sigh was crestfallen. "I think I've degenerated into my grandfather, Deb. All that's missing are the argyle socks. It's... *dull*." He remembered Radecker's revolver. "Well, mostly."

"Wasn't that the plan? Stay home, stay out of trouble?"

"I suppose. But it just kinda makes me feel a little, well," his shoulders sagged. "*Old*."

"Awww," Deborah put the magazine down and took Stuart's hand in hers. "Listen, man o' mine. I don't care what any calendar says, you're just as gorgeous and funny and sharp and supportive as the fellow I met forty years ago. True, you also on occasion let Bruce talk you into the absolute *worst* situations imaginable, but if you think about it, gullibility is sure proof of youth. Argyle socks be *damned*."

If Stuart sometimes considered himself a luckless schlep, marrying Deborah more than evened the scales. She was a decade his junior, but the years hadn't rusted her looks or that wonderfully weird witchcraft that allowed her say *just* the right thing at *just* the right time.

Stuart stroked her blonde hair. "How'd I get so lucky to have you?"

"No clue. But you must've done *something* worthwhile in a past life."

Kojack's continued barking drew Stuart's attention away from his wife. "I've got to go."

"What? *Where?*"

He pointed out the window. "The Zalinskis' dog. Haven't fed him since this morning. I completely forgot to do it before the gang arrived."

"*Eek*. Poor thing's probably starving. Need me to come with?"

Stuart shook his head. "Won't take long. I'll be back before you know it." There was a key rack mounted near the kitchen door, and he snatched the spare set Emil Zalinski had loaned him. Prior to stepping out, Stuart faced Deborah again. "Oh, and FYI, Bruce is in the bathroom. He claims it's just Number One, but you can't trust him."

Deborah wrinkled her nose. "Hazmat. Got it. Thanks for the warning. I'll find the Lysol." More seriously, she added, "Be careful out there."

"Like you said, Deb, we stayed home to stay out of trouble." He smiled. "It's just next door. What could *possibly* go wrong?"

The back yard was warm when Stuart walked into the mid-June Michigan night, and without the air-conditioned crispness of the house he swiftly worked up a sweat strolling across the side lawn. The rest of the neighborhood soon came into view, idyllically bathed in the amber glow of streetlamps; all eighty-six houses in Crestview Estates were indistinguishable two-story single-family craftsman-style homes with concrete drives, attached garages, low-pitched gable roofs and tapered colonnaded porches. There was a back patio area perfect for barbecuing, a small lawn that Deborah had transformed over the years into a gardener's paradise and a white privacy fence slicing along the property line on either side.

Bruce lived three blocks down, where Crestview's acreage nuzzled against the outlet mall, in what he all-too-seriously referred to as The Love Hut. Both Hoppy and Radecker resided across town; Hoppy was a widower who lived alone on Lathrop Avenue and Radecker holed up in an apartment situated over Dr. Chau's Chinese Chicken Emporium off 6 Mile Road. Stuart had met them at the senior rec center a year or so before, and despite some initial reluctance enjoyed their company, shooting the breeze, talking baseball and playing darts without the added pressure of trying to impress anyone.

When Stuart rounded the sidewalk to the Zalinskis' side of the fence he saw one of the city's green jetvac sewage trucks parked in front of their house. He'd heard the workers earlier in the day, but once the machinery's noise subsided he'd forgotten about it and was surprised the vehicle remained there at such an hour. The house itself operated on an automatic timer; the interior lights switched on with dusk, and to the unknowing eye it appeared exactly as if someone were home. The Zalinskis were a young family—Emil and his wife Chandra were around the same age as Stuart's own children and their two teenage boys were well-behaved and polite. In the three years they'd lived side-by-side there hadn't been a single neighborly dispute, which made it easy for Stuart to accept the favor to dog-sit while they were away.

Kojack himself abounded with stir-crazy canine energy; Stuart saw evidence he'd spent the daytime sequestration digging holes all over the back lawn, and after re-latching the gate noticed also that Kojack had strategically nudged his empty food bowl into the middle of the yard as if to underscore Stuart's tardiness.

"Yeah, yeah. Rub it in. I'm sorry, all right?" Stuart glibly apologized on his way to the rear door. Kojack, still barking, stubbornly stayed in the yard's dark corner, refusing to heed even when Stuart called his name. After a frustrated minute, Stuart shrugged, retrieved the food bowl and water dish, unlocked the door and went inside.

Like the exterior, the layout within each Crestview home was identical apart from the individual owners' choice of décor. The Zalinski's kitchen was Provencal-style: creamy white cabinetry, elegant marble counters, matte white pendant lights, blue tile and oil-rubbed bronze cookware that lent a warm, aged appearance to the room. Despite the pleasant surroundings, however, a rankling cesspool reek existed now that hadn't when Stuart visited to feed Kojack that morning.

"Yeeech," Stuart's nostrils curdled; he pictured the jetvac truck out front. *Whatever's wrong with the sewer, I hope it doesn't back up into our house next.*

Stuart did his best to ignore the smell; he first filled Kojack's water dish, set it aside, then went to the pantry where the dry dog food was kept. He'd just poured a serving into the awaiting bowl when the packaging split, sending a cascade of Kibbles N' Bits onto his sneakers. Staring at the sudden mess, Stuart groaned, dropped the empty bag and started searching for a broom. In the hallway closet he found one, but by then his stomach was churning. The stench was most potent near the basement door; there were noises from downstairs, too, groaning pipes and creaking timber that stiffened the hairs on his arm.

It's only the foundation settling, you goosey old fart. Just get everything swept up, get the damn dog fed and get home.

Two things happened at that exact moment that made Stuart regret ever leaving his house; the first was the ungodly shriek that penetrated the hall from the basement, followed immediately thereafter by a tremor that shook the walls vigorously enough that family portraits bounced from their nails to smash onto the hardwood.

"Jesus!" Stuart's initial concern was an earthquake; the closet was still partially open, and he braced himself under the door frame. Across from him the basement door juddered, and a fissure opened in the drywall.

What the HELL is happening now? he wondered, and an answer wasn't long in arriving: the floor buckled, splintered and fell away into a yawning black chasm, pulling the basement entryway and a significant portion of the wall with it. Stuart hugged the closet's trim, too shocked to even scream; he'd been terrified as a boy by stories about sinkholes big enough to devour homes whole. Is *that* what this was? From where he huddled he could see straight down into the pit, and...

Something moved. In the blackness he caught the velvet texture of motion; there was another furious crash, only this time the section of hall adjacent the closet fell through, and Stuart tumbled weightlessly into the dark.

Swirling dust scoured Stuart's esophagus once he landed. Absurdly he still clutched the broom, but his bifocals had flopped loose upon impact, and Stuart groped blindly until his fingertips brushed against their wire frames. Above, far above, light streaming through the hole revealed he wasn't in the basement as he'd expected, but further down into a partially caved-in tunnel. The smell was overwhelming, putrescent with decomposition, and Stuart rolled over and promptly puked up the pastrami on rye he'd eaten for lunch.

The shrieking restarted, loud, shrill, and close. Around a bend in the tunnel that tenebrous shape he'd witnessed upstairs lumbered into view, only this time it was larger, each impossible detail boggling his mind: that enormous body, the multitudinous eyes.

Son. Of. A. BITCH. Stuart thought bitterly as the thing closed in. *So much for my staycation.*

When Bruce returned from the bathroom, he was intrigued to find only Hoppy and Radecker perched around the den's card table.

"Stu still isn't back?" He asked.

Radecker shook his head; he had the Python out again, polishing its barrel with a tiny square cloth. "That's a negative, Goldman. I suspect our boy's AWOL."

"Talk about screwing the pooch," Hoppy emptied the last of the pretzels into his mouth. "Stu must be after the world record for longest time taken to open a can of Alpo."

Bruce walked to the window. The dog's barking had stopped, but the neighboring house's lights, so bright earlier, now flickered intermittently. "I think something's wrong next door," he said suspiciously.

"Bruce, you're more paranoid than Deck is." Hoppy snorted. "What, you worried Stu's crossed over into *The Twilight Zone* or something?"

"If you'd seen some of the things we have, you wouldn't say that." Bruce went to the door. "I'm going to check it out."

"Don't get wished into the cornfield," Hoppy cracked, but Bruce ignored him, turned and strode to the kitchen, where Deborah was pulling a spray can of Lysol from under the sink.

"Come to tell me the bathroom's a mess in person instead of letting me discover it on my own this time?" She asked.

Bruce twisted his lips, unsure what to say. "No, I—" *I'm going next door to make sure your dearly beloved hasn't become the plaything to some sex-crazed sasquatch.* "—I just remembered it's past time to take my Lipitor. Left the prescription bottle in my car."

There was mistrust in Deborah's glare. "Isn't a little late in the evening for popping pills?"

"It's some new schedule my cardiologist concocted," Bruce fibbed. "He's a jackass. What can I say?"

"Jackass? Hmm. Sounds like peas in a pod to me."

"Awww, come on, Deb, isn't that a *little* harsh?" Bruce cockily smirked. "Don't tell me you're still mad about me taking Stu to that strip club in Vegas?"

"It didn't earn you any Brownie points, Bruce. Then again, not much does." She waved him away. "*Go.* If you see my husband out there, tell him I'd appreciate it if he doesn't abandon me alone with you goons. I'm not a babysitter."

"No babysitting. Right. Loud and clear." He winked at her before opening the back door. "I'll be sure to let him know."

Outside, the Zalinskis' lights were again unwavering, and self-doubt arose as Bruce rounded the corner. *Maybe Hoppy's right. Maybe I am just paranoid.*

Buzzing flies and that noxious sewage odor hit him the instant he entered the back yard. Bruce hadn't taken two paces before something red and glistening snared his eye; certain he was mistaken, he removed his glasses, wiped the lenses on the hem of his shirt and put them back on, but no, blood cut a crooked path over the patio to the house's wide-open back door, where a golden retriever's fly-smothered upper torso blockaded the threshold, innards uncoiled across the kitchen tile like marionette strings.

Paranoia: justified.

"Jee-zus *Christ*," Bruce gagged. He tiptoed through the entrance. "Kojack, I presume? Sorry to meet your acquaintance like this."

The canine's bottom half was absent; Bruce's primary thought was that an errant bear had stumbled into suburbia for an after-dinner snack, but the eviscerated carcass wasn't the scene's only oddity: a mound of dry dog food sullied the floor, and an inexplicable collection of bloody pitter-patter polka dots led from the kitchen.

"*Stu?*" Bruce ambled into the hallway. "You get a hankering for hot dogs while you were over here or what?"

Silence. It was darker in the hall, draftier and abhorrently malodorous; votive fixtures lay shattered on the hardwood, and he didn't see the floor had vanished into a black void until it was almost too late. Bracing one hand against the wall, Bruce steadied himself, wiped sweat from his brow and shouted directly into the pit:

"Stu? Stu, are you down there?"

This time he heard a reply, too faint to discern any actual words. Bruce was about to shout again when something skittered on the ceiling; looking up, a shadowy form pounced through the gloom squarely onto his back.

"*SHIT!*" Bruce staggered into the opposite wall, screaming, desperate to dislodge his unknown assaulter. The creature was heavy, its hold crushing; when Bruce reached out an investigative hand all he felt were legs, slimy, hairy and bratwurst-thick. Something acrid dribbled into his face, and Bruce choked, spit, then shifted his body into reverse, slamming his weight against the wall so hard his unwelcome passenger screeched. He repeated the action and only then did the thing's grip slacken; Bruce pitched forward, slung the whatever-it-was over his shoulder, then marveled as it swiftly scampered out-of-sight into an adjoining room.

"*Damn it,*" Bruce wheezed; he wanted to pursue the critter, just to learn what had jumped him, but another cry from the hole, louder and clearer than before, diverted his attention.

"Bruce?" The voice yelled: Stuart.

Bruce crawled to the pit's outermost rim. "*Stu?* What the hell are you doing down there?"

A pause. "We need your help, Bruce. We're kinda…
hung up."

"*We?*"

"You've got to help us. Before they come back."

"*They?*" Bruce sucked in a palpitant breath. "What's going
on, Stu?"

"Just hurry up, will you?"

Bruce grumbled, but carefully sat on the precipice anyway.
The structural damage was worse than he'd initially realized—
everything from the closet to the front window was gone, but a
ramp of wreckage existed that enabled him to descend without
losing his footing. A dozen scrapes salted Bruce's shins by the
time he reached the bottom; the tunnel he found himself in
was rank, humid, moldy, ankle-high with mud and
unpleasantly claustrophobic. Nearby was a broken broom
surrounded by footprints. Some were human. Others…weren't.

"Stu?" he called.

An answer floated from the ether: "This way. Follow my voice."

Bruce ventured the tunnel's length; twenty yards in he
stumbled upon more footprints, and more items, pressed into
the muck. A spattered white hardhat. A short pickaxe with a
yellow fiberglass pole. A length of rubber hose and a flashlight.
Taking the pickaxe and the flashlight, Bruce rounded a narrow
curve and was taken aback when the tunnel opened into a vast
domed cavern, its floor covered in bones, walls plastered with
a sinewy translucent weave in which bodies—cats and dogs,
squirrels, raccoons, the odd woodchuck—dangled in various
stages of decay. Stuart was cocooned five feet up, two men clad
in neon-yellow PVC coveralls and safety harnesses suspended
beside him, their heads free but the rest of them wrapped tight.
Shaking off his astonishment, Bruce propped the flashlight

against a boulder and clumsily clamored atop the rock.

"Funny running into you here," Stuart dryly quipped.

"I was in the neighborhood," Bruce hacked at the translucent bindings with the pickaxe. "Something sucker punched me up there. What the hell are we dealing with this time, Stu? Vampires? Zombies?"

"No."

"Demons?"

"*No.*"

"Shape-shifting aliens?"

"NO."

"*What* then?"

"Spiders, Bruce. Gigantic. *Fucking.* Spiders."

"*Spiders?*" Bruce envisioned the skittering creature that attacked him. "I'm guessing a flyswatter's not gonna do it."

He explained the encounter, and Stuart laughed grimly. "That sounds like one of the small ones."

"The *small* ones?" Bruce balked. "How big are the *big* ones?"

The man bound beside Stuart spoke for the first time; he was probably thirty, heavyset with short black hair, glasses and a stubbly beard. "Biggest motherfuckers you ever seen, Pops. King Kong's pet tarantulas on steroids. And if you don't hustle, they're gonna come back an' mash us all into fuckin' pasta sauce."

Bruce frowned. "Who's this clown?"

"That's Devlin," Stuart told him. "The other is, uh, Jarrod, I think. You see the sewer truck out front? It's theirs."

"Been complaints about blockage in this 'burb lately, so we came to take a look, clear the line," Devlin recounted. "Three of us find these huge fuckin' egg sacks pluggin' everythin' up. Never seen nothin' like it. Didn't even know what the hell they were until we started breakin' 'em open…Next thing we know, goddamn eight-legged freaks are all over us, a whole *colony* of 'em. Couldn't get back up top, so we ran this way."

"Wait…you said *three* of you?" Bruce asked.

Devlin's voice quavered. "Paul. He…he didn't make it. Couple of 'em dragged him into a side tunnel. That's when we saw the Queen Cunt herself. Goddamn minivan with legs, squirtin' out eggs like mother hen. The little fuckers took Paul to her like some kinda, I dunno, sacrifice. Drank his insides like a fuckin' milkshake. Jarrod got bit, too. Don't know what shit they shot into him, but he's pretty out of it."

Bruce glanced to the twenty-something webbed alongside Devlin. Jarrod's coveralls were torn and a chunk was missing from one shoulder; his blond head hung low, skin waxy and pale. Yellow spittle oozed from his mouth.

"And here I hoped their bite would give us superpowers," Bruce said. He finished carving through the webs confining Stuart, who dropped awkwardly to the cavern floor. He'd barely started in on Devlin's bonds when a noise echoed around the chamber, like impatiently drumming fingernails, gathering in intensity as the seconds ticked by.

"Oh shit, here they come!" Devlin labored against his cocoon. "Get us down, you dumb old codger!"

Bruce made a face. "Who you calling *codger?* I slept with Cheryl Ladd once, you little punk."

A breath later the webs were severed, and Devlin toppled onto a pile of bones with a pained yowl. "My ankle!" He grabbed at his left boot. "I twisted my fuckin' ankle!"

Stuart shouldered some of Devlin's bulk. Squat shadows scuttled from the passageway at the cavern's far side, fast and fluid.

"Bruuuuce..." Stuart warned.

Sweat greased Bruce's palms while he worked at liberating Jarrod; once he almost lost the pickaxe, but at long last the thickest webbing around the man's midsection tore and the youth slid down the wall.

"*Bruce!* Come *on!*"

Looking over, Bruce saw the creeping figures, closer, larger, and, shit, oh shit, *shit, SHIT,* they really *were* spiders, pouring through the aperture, more than he could count—twenty, fifty, a hundred?—surging ahead on every surface, crawling over one another, jostling for position.

The first reached Bruce as he hopped from the boulder. In the flashlight's beam the arachnid was fully exposed, black, bristly, with a rottweiler's heavy build, its eyes reflecting in the light, legspan longer than Bruce's open arms. For an instant he was frigid with terror as the spider's fangs unfurled, longer than his forearm and dripping with venom. Only a second shout from Stuart broke the trance:

"Bruce, get Jarrod and let's *go!*"

Adrenaline kicked in. Jarrod was inert in the mud, but Bruce knelt, secured one of the sewer worker's trembling arms around his own neck and strained to hoist him up.

They didn't get four steps before the spider leapt, the collision so great it separated the two men. The flashlight went flying. Mud went into Bruce's mouth. When he rolled over the spider was straddling Jarrod; what happened next was gruesome: those hideous fangs sank deep into the muscle of the youth's back, quivering as they pumped digestive enzymes into Jarrod's body. Bruce heard a slurping sound, like a near-empty soda being drawn through a straw, and Jarrod convulsed. Fluids—blood, sputum, bile, God knew what else—poured from every orifice; his eyes rolled back, showed white, then imploded. He was being hollowed out, emptied, withering as his insides liquefied, and the dehydrated husk that remained once the spider's feast was complete resembled less a human being than a deflated, discarded balloon.

A second spider appeared, a third, a fourth. Bruce used the pickaxe as a standing crutch, then pivoted, hammering the tool's tapered point through the soft space of his nearest pursuer's eyes. When the arachnid crashed lifelessly to the mud Bruce wanted to cheer, but there wasn't time; the spider that had drained Jarrod was on him, but Bruce held fast, wedging the pickaxe through its abdomen. Tawny ichor splashed his face as he wrenched the blade free and rammed it in again, peppering the arachnid until it delved into a shivering heap.

More spiders arrived, twenty feet away, ten, five. Bruce backpedaled through the bone-strewn muck to where Stuart shepherded Devlin toward the ramp of debris. Devlin's injured ankle had hampered their progress, and when a spider landed on Stuart, it easily knocked him flat.

"*Shit! Stu!*" Bruce lanced the spider twice through the head, kicked the corpse over and grabbed Stuart's arm. Devlin's bloodcurdling cry reverberated through the chamber then; a pair of spiders had immobilized his limbs while a third throttled his ample gut. Unlike Jarrod's semi-stupor, Devlin was fully cognizant to his fate; Bruce spun to intervene, but too slowly—the spider's fangs already injected their poison, and a mask of knowing horror froze Devlin's features as his muscles seized. The rest was shockingly fast; the man shuddered while his internal organs became jelly, his privates shriveled like burnt sausage and Devlin wilted into a desiccated shell of loose skin and sickly protruding bone. At least the screaming had stopped.

"*Oh my God!*" Stuart shouted. Bruce shoved him forward.

"Run now. Pray to Baby Jesus later. *Move!*"

They had one chance. Up the slope of debris back to the house's main floor, then…what? Phone the police? The National Guard? NATO? Bruce imagined such a call: *Hi, I'm a concerned citizen just letting you know that a thousand ravenous man-sized spiders are running amok in my subdivision. Please send an air strike. Preferably something tactically nuclear. Thanks.*

A rumbling beneath Bruce's feet killed any lingering glibness. He glanced over his shoulder; a monolithic mass blocked the entirety of the cavern's entranceway, gnarled bones from long-consumed prey embedded in its hide, crushing the weaker spiders in its path as it trudged steadily onward.

The Queen Cunt herself, Devlin had said. *Goddamn minivan with legs.*

"That's not a minivan," Bruce refuted aloud. "That's a *bus.*"

Both men scaled the incline. Climbing was more treacherous than coming down had been; the ruins groaned and shifted, threatening to collapse completely the higher they went. Halfway up Bruce's lungs heaved, and his arthritic joints ached; Stuart wasn't faring any better, but neither slowed their ascent. A chance look back showed the spiders at Bruce's heels; he swiped at the closest one, but the pickaxe's handle was slippery and the tool slid from his fingers.

This spider was more guileful, and far stronger, than the one Bruce had fought in the hallway; once it pinned him down there seemed no escape. *So this is how I go out*, he pondered as those over-sized fangs neared. *Guts blended into a smoothie by some juiced-up black widow. At least it'll make for an interesting obituary.*

There was a *craaaaaaack!* and the spider's head fragmented into sudden goo. It was that quick—one instant Bruce was being prepped for dinner, the next he almost suffocated under the arachnid's dead weight. A second shot sliced the air above him, then a third, and two nearby spiders went tumbling end-over-end. Before Bruce could fully comprehend the happening, sturdy hands hauled him from beneath the carcass and into the hallway.

There was always a point in those old westerns when the beleaguered heroes, all hope lost, were on the verge of being overrun by Comanches or Mexicans or desperadoes, and salvation would swoop over the ridge on a storm of charging cavalry hooves, always in the nick of time and to a rousing bugle call.

That's what Stuart thought of Hoppy and Radecker showing up just then, Radecker with the Colt Python in hand, Hoppy brandishing his cane like a Louisville Slugger: a motley sort of cavalry.

Stuart was still disoriented, sitting on the floor where Hoppy had dropped him. "H-How'd you two..."

"Oh, puh-leeze, Stu." Hoppy tutted. "*You* not coming back from the neighbor's house means you've wandered off like a senile old goat. Bruce not coming back means something's physically *wrong*. I was thinking maybe you'd slipped and broken a hip." He cast a disbelieving glare to the hole in the hallway. "Were those things what I think they were?"

A concerto of shrieks arose from the pit. "It's not a litter of angry kittens," Stuart said.

"Kittens wouldn't be any better," Bruce announced once he stood. "I'm allergic to cats."

From below, a thunderous bellow shook the walls.

"Now what in the hell was *that?*" Hoppy asked. Stuart backed up.

"Momma's not happy."

There was a swell in the dark of the hole; spindly black legs curled over the precipice, and before Stuart blinked they were everywhere, walls, floor, ceiling. Hoppy's jowly face drooped into panic when a spider as large as he was emerged in front of him, staring dumbstruck until Radecker downed the arachnid with another revolver shot.

"Fighting withdraw, boys!"

A second spider dropped beside Hoppy, but bolstered by Radecker's bravado, he swung his cane like an executioner's axe, cleaving open the thing's head with one sharp strike. He did the same to the next spider, but a fourth battered the cane away, threw Hoppy off his loafers and moved in for the kill.

Stuart dove, snatched a broken shard of floorboard, and drove the sharpened point into the spider's flank before yanking Hoppy away just as the floor space they'd occupied spiraled into the pit.

Ahead of them, the arachnids obstructed the route through the kitchen. "We're penned in!" Bruce hollered.

"This way!" Stuart ducked into the living room; in the far corner Kojack's lower half hung from a cobweb above the TV, the spider who'd obviously done the deed guarding its grisly trophy with hissing resolve. Radecker raised the Python, fired, and Stuart watched the arachnid's head dissolve to chowder.

"One round left!" Radecker grimly announced.

The living room exited into another hallway; directly across from that a stairway went to the second floor. The other end led to the garage.

"Jiminy Christmas, would you look at this!" Hoppy suddenly yelled; he'd opened a closet positioned under the stairs. Within was a cache of carefully arranged BDSM equipment—latex fetish gear, gas masks, whips, chains and paddles, studded collars, ball gags, handcuffs and rope. Hoppy glanced to Stuart.

"What the hell kind of neighbors *are* these?" He asked.

"Kinky ones," Bruce uncoiled one of the whips. "I always secretly wanted to play at being Indiana Jones, but the wives wouldn't go for it."

Another tremor. Another bellow. From the living room a gray, wolfish arachnid crept into the hallway. Hoppy nudged Bruce with an elbow.

"Now's your chance, Indy."

Bruce inched away from the spider's approach. "Long-legged dames are one thing, but this is ridiculous," he threw the whip down. "I guess some fantasies are best left unfulfilled."

Radecker opened the garage door. "Quit yakkin' and get your asses over here!"

Hoppy stumbled over the threshold; Stuart and Bruce followed, but the spider pursued, ramming into the door just as Radecker secured the lock. There was an aggravated rasp; the door bulged as the spider continuously heaved against it, but the deadbolt, at least momentarily, held.

Radecker flipped on the light. The garage was both orderly and ordinary; an empty space where Emil and Chandra's silver Camry should've been parked, a riding lawnmower, some odds and ends, nothing special. To a needy, imaginative eye, however, it was an armory of possibility.

"Grab what you can. That door won't hold forever," Radecker commanded. He'd tucked the Colt at his waist and sifted through some tools; a breath later he clicked his tongue, went to the corner and slid a 20-gallon propane tank from behind the lawnmower. "God bless Home Depot and backyard grill masters everywhere," he beamed. "I set this baby alight in that burrow and the spider factory will shut down faster than you can say Saigon Sally."

"That's *insane*, Deck." Hoppy blurted out. But Radecker's features were resolute.

"The mission is what matters, Hoppenrath. And our mission is to keep those creepy-crawly commie sons a bitches from overrunning town. We hold the line here or else."

"Easy for you to say," Stuart countered. "But in case you haven't noticed, we're a *little* outnumbered."

Bruce took a shovel leaned against the wall. "If we run the gauntlet past the stairs, we might be able to slice through the dining room into the kitchen."

"That's a big goddamn *if*," Hoppy noted; he clung nervously to a post-hole digger. "What we *really* need is something to clear the bastards out of our way."

Stuart withdrew a gas-powered Craftsman chainsaw from beneath a work bench, 42 cc's, 16-inch blade, probably fifteen pounds. "Got just the thing."

Radecker's weathered face lit up. "Looks like you're our shock trooper, Starkweather. Can you handle it?"

More pounding against the door; the hinges were working loose. "There a choice?" Stuart asked.

"Not any good ones." Radecker drew his revolver once more. "It's like this: on the count of three we open that door. Goldman, Hoppenrath, you cover Starkweather. Once he carves a path, I rush the explosive ordinance to the burrow while you three evac outta here. If I'm lucky, I'll be right behind you."

"And if you're not?"

"Then I'm a crispy fritter." Radecker gulped.

The door started to split. All four men bristled.

"Get ready," Radecker placed a hand on the knob. "One..."

"Two..." Hoppy continued.

"*Three!*" Bruce finished.

The wood splintered before Radecker unfastened the lock; two of the spider's fat legs slithered through the gap. The hinges twisted, broke, and soon the door was in pieces.

"Now, Stu!" Radecker cried.

A small smirk graced Stuart's chin as he pulled the chainsaw's start cord. "I bet Grandpa Morty never did *this*."

The engine's revving rhapsody filled the garage. Ten feet away the spider was almost fully through the doorway, but Stuart's prior fear had fled; he brought the blade down in broad, unrehearsed strokes that redecorated the garage with a coat of bloody slop and left the arachnid's dissected parts sprawled haphazardly across the cement.

"Let's *go!*" Radecker shouted. "Over the top, boys!"

Entrails squished beneath Stuart's feet as he charged ahead. Once in the hall he realized how accurate his earlier concern was—a seething line of marching spiders piled atop one another like a traffic accident, a sea of wiggling, wriggling legs. *Now I know how General Custer felt at Little Bighorn,* he thought.

Swinging the chainsaw, it became impossible to tell where one arachnid began and another ended—they were just a single tight mass of opening faces and slit bellies, and Stuart was quickly slathered in head-to-toe gunk. When one spider landed too close for him to maneuver towards it, Bruce and Hoppy appeared, sweaty and coated in syrupy grime, gracelessly spearing their tools through the arachnid's side.

"Nice of you to join the party!" Stuart yelled.

Bruce impaled a spider with the shovel. "Didn't think we were gonna let you have *all* the fun, did you?"

It was less than a minute since their counter-offensive began, but already the hallway was knee-deep with sticky slaughterhouse viscera. They'd just passed the living room entrance when Radecker screamed; he'd been carrying the propane tank in a bear hug behind Bruce and Hoppy, next he was foundering beneath a trio of arachnids, cursing for all he was worth as they dragged him across the carpet towards the ever-widening pit.

"*Deck!*" Stuart turned, gave chase and caught Radecker's abductors before they slipped into the opposing hall. He heaved the chainsaw's blade through one spider like a lumberjack felling a redwood; before he approached the other two they abruptly abandoned Radecker altogether. Stuart couldn't understand why until the ground rumbled again, worse than ever. The hallway rippled, and from underground the Queen surfaced, a colossal thing of nightmares, tree-like limbs and that multi-eyed head, demolishing the house's construction as it shoved itself upward.

Radecker was already upright, retrieving the propane tank from where it rolled near the coffee table. There was a pressurized hiss once he twisted the knob, and the unmistakable aroma of gas assailed Stuart's senses.

A lunatic grin curved Radecker's lips. "Time to make Charlie some barbeque," he said before blitzing headlong into the hall.

The spiders had formed a defensive ring around the emergent Queen and ten feet from their perimeter Radecker forcefully chucked the propane tank towards them; it landed with a dull clang in a pocket of debris underneath the Queen's cephalothorax and, satisfied, Radecker shouted urgently to the others:

"Fire in the hole, boys!"

Hoppy was first into the kitchen, then Bruce, then Stuart, protecting their retreat until the chainsaw's engine sputtered, wheezed, and stopped. Tossing the power tool aside, he stumbled over Kojack's remains; near the rear door Radecker waved him towards the back yard.

"Go!" He spurred. "Get the hell out of here!"

Until that instant Stuart hadn't wondered how Radecker intended to detonate the propane tank; it was just a fact he'd abstractly accepted. Now, though, he saw Radecker's right arm extended in the direction of the Queen, the Colt's eager barrel given a clear line to the exposed tank and the hypothetical dots connected.

SHIT.

Stuart had just reached the patio when a tsunami of super-heated air enveloped him. The concussive blast twirled his body upside-down onto the grass, breathless and worryingly deaf. An excruciating minute went by until sound returned: the roar of flame, the crackle of tinder, the repetitive bleat of triggered car alarms. When Stuart finally pushed himself up his hand touched something wet: one of the spiders, rent asunder by the explosion, lying beside him in a goopy puddle.

Three yards away Bruce stood, his Hawaiian shirt shred to ribbons, surveying the fallout with bewildered bemusement. Slowly he wandered over to Stuart.

"You okay, geezer?" Bruce asked. Stuart nodded.

"All things considered. Where are Hop and Deck?"

"I'm here, Stu." This was Hoppy's voice; his Al Capone hat was lost and his clothes, like Bruce's, hung in tatters, but beyond cuts and scrapes and missing dentures he seemed uninjured. Glancing past Stuart, he let out a long, wondrous whistle. "Well, I'llllll be. Look at *that*."

Stuart rolled over. The Zalinskis' house was ablaze, its western façade reduced to a bombed-out crater, the Queen's smoldering chunks intermingled amid the smithereens. Something shifted beneath the nearby wreckage, and Stuart was impressed when Radecker's sooty body squirmed free, coughing from the smoke. Once he stood, Hoppy slapped Radecker on the back.

"Deck, you son of a *bitch!* I thought you were a goner for sure."

Appraising the devastation, Radecker smiled. "I told you, Hoppenrath—no surrender, no defeat, regardless of how many appendages the enemy may have."

Awe was in Hoppy's tone. "If I hadn't seen it, I wouldn't have believed it." He glanced at Stuart. "Is *this* the kind of stuff that happens on your road trips?"

Stuart shook his head. "This actually qualifies as a slow night."

The four of them observed the fire a few minutes longer before walking to Stuart's front yard. Each house in Crestview was alive with light by then, and a gawping carnival throng of curious pajama-clad bystanders clogged the street, staring, pointing, taking videos with their phones.

"There goes the neighborhood," Stuart lamented.

The front door opened and Deborah appeared on the porch, sipping a fresh cup of chamomile and dispassionately assessing the chaos before looking at her husband.

"Get the dog fed?" she tartly asked.

Stuart wiped sludge from his forehead. "Not quite."

"Extraterrestrials from an alternate dimension, or something more exotic?"

"Giant mutant spiders."

"Ah. Cute." Wailing sirens made Deborah sigh. "I suppose I should call our lawyer."

"Not a bad idea, honey. Might want to phone your brother-in-law and see if he can post my bond again. If he's not still miffed about last time, that is."

"Will do. No worries." Deborah passed Stuart her cup of tea, then turned to go back inside. "Love you, dear. I won't wait up."

"High time I bug out, too," Radecker proclaimed. The windows of his Jeep Wrangler had been shattered by the blast, but he simply brushed shards from the upholstery, settled in and reversed slowly into the street. "Fighting by your side was an honor and a privilege, gentlemen," he assured them. "Poker at my place next Friday?"

Stuart shrugged. "Sure. If we're out of jail."

After Radecker had gone, Hoppy exhaled a wistful breath. "Mutant spiders. *Damn.* How do you think they got *down* there? Some prehistoric evolutionary holdover? Radioactive waste in the groundwater?"

"One of life's mysteries, Hop." Stuart claimed. "Right up there with how *Bruce* nailed Cheryl Ladd."

"I-It wasn't actually Cheryl Ladd," Bruce admitted. "It was one of her second cousins. But close enough."

Hoppy rubbed his bare head. "What are you going to tell the Zalinskis when they get home, Stu?"

There was a lawn chair Stuart favored when watering the grass that he now flopped into. "Don't know yet. Probably not the truth. I just hope they're insured. What I do know is, after this, I *definitely* need a vacation."

"Acapulco is still an option." Bruce proposed. "Rent a hacienda. Flirt with the *señoritas.*"

Stuart mulled the suggestion. "It'd be our luck to get held for ransom by a drug cartel. But I'm not ruling anything out at this point."

An exhausted silence blanketed the three men. The first tufts of sunrise painted the horizon as firemen arrived. When they began dousing the flames a tiny granddaddy long-leg scampered across the driveway near Stuart's sneaker.

"Not so fast, big guy," he grunted, grinding the thing to paste beneath his sole. Afterwards Stuart nestled into the chair, sipped the chamomile, and watched the new day's oncoming dawn through the night's dying flames.

CRITICAL BLAST PUBLISHING
20¢
APPROVED BY THE READING CODE AUTHORITY
THE MONSTERS NEXT DOOR
All about CRITICAL BLAST and what is available!
WEIRD FANTASTIC WORLDS
CRITICAL BLAST PUBLISHING
WHERE POP CULTURE GETS BLASTED
INCREDIBLE STRANGE STORIES
A SCORE OF SCARES
EDITED BY R.J. CARTER!

THE DEVIL YOU KNOW
edited by R.J. Carter

A short-story anthology of encounters with various incarnations of The Devil, with genres ranging from fairy tale to folk tale, from urban fantasy to science fiction, from comedy to horror. Featuring the works of Jared Baker, Erica Ciko Campbell, Sarah Cannavo, Michael W. Clark, Christopher Cook, Andra Dill, Cara fox, R.A. Goli, Gerald A. Jennings, Kevin Kangas, Daryl Marcus, Damascus Mincemeyer, Steve Oden, Evan Purcell, Troy Riser, Joseph Rubas, Hannah Trusty, Wondra Vanian, Henry Vogel, and K.D. Webster.

THE DEVIL YOU KNOW BETTER
edited by R.J. Carter

The next volume chronicling the meet-ups between everyday people and The Devil himself. Collecting fantastic tales from Mike Baron, .Ravenna Blazecroft, Richard J. Brewer, Hart D. Fisher, L.N. Hunter, Charlie Jones, Ken MacGregor, James Maxey, Tim McDaniel, Damascus Mincemeyer, Lena Ng, Diana Olney, P. Anthony Ramanauskas, Troy Riser, Edward R. Rosick, Nadia Steven Rysing, Rose Strickman, Anna Taborska, Stanley B. Webb and Ray Zacek.

BULLETPROOF: ORIGINS
by Stephen J. Mitchell

Kody Haywood is a freshman at Bannerville High School, struggling to maintain focus. Every day he finds himself getting lost in his thoughts, the hallways at school, or even in conversation. Having a mind that wanders makes him an easy target for the school bully and all-star athlete, Brett Walker.

As his birthday approaches, Kody discovers a genetic change in his body that renders him indestructible. When a mysterious letter from his deceased father arrives on his doorstep, it puts him in the crosshairs of an international terrorist!

GODS & SERVICES
edited by R.J. Carter

When old gods need new worshipers, they offer their divinity for sale. Put a little god in your life with this collection of short stories from authors Ross Baxter, Ira Bloom, Laura J. Campbell, Aristo Couvaras, Jon Del Arroz, David J. Pedersen, Zach Smith, Michael Tierney, and Katherine Traylor.

BROTHERS GRIMM
edited by R.J. Carter

The complete fairy tales of Jacob and Wilhelm Grimm, with over 300 vibrant full-color illustrations and large text to bring each tale to vivid life. These are the stories in their original forms, formatted in an easy-to-read design that will promote faster reading and inspire imagination.

MONSTER VALUE STAMPS
3¢ USA THE BOUNCER 1
3¢ USA CRY BABY
3¢ USA MRS. PLACED 18
3¢ USA 37 WC
3¢ USA CANDY HEAD
3¢ USA LAFFGOBLIN 261
3¢ USA CHUCKLEFIZZ 537
3¢ USA JIMMY COFFEE 99
3¢ USA POTATOE JOE
3¢ USA LENNY THE FIG 335
3¢ SA SLICK VINCE
3¢ USA 527
TY BOY MAD NAIL
3¢ USA NO HEAD 6
MAD MAC M
MRS. PLACED
3¢ USA 57
3¢ USA MOUNTAIN CINDY 613
SMIRKFLASH 830
VLAD
SMIRKROAR 493
WATER GIRAFFE 123

THE MONSTER VALUE STAMP CHECKLIST! (-1-)

- ☐ 001 BOUNCER
- ☐ 002 GHOST WHALE
- ☐ 003 BEAR GOBLIN
- ☐ 004 SPIDER OCTOPUS
- ☐ 005 BEETLE BILLY BOB
- ☐ 006 NO HEAD MAN
- ☐ 007 CRAB NAB JAB
- ☐ 008 BAT-GOD BUNJABIE
- ☐ 009 MAD MAC MANLEY
- ☐ 010 VAMPI VETALA
- ☐ 011 ABAGALE VIPER
- ☐ 012 SPIKE VALARION
- ☐ 013 CRY BABY
- ☐ 014 AQUA-SANDY
- ☐ 015 CRYPTO-DILLY DALI
- ☐ 016 HANGOVER HARPY
- ☐ 017 JINGWEI SLASHER
- ☐ 018 MRS. PLACED
- ☐ 019 HOARIS
- ☐ 020 KALAVINKALI
- ☐ 021 SIREN SALLY
- ☐ 022 ACHELOIS THE PAIN
- ☐ 023 LADY SIL LAMBENT
- ☐ 024 TERP SICHOARE
- ☐ 025 SWAN KNEE SAM
- ☐ 026 CINNAMON KILLER
- ☐ 027 DEVIL BOY BOB
- ☐ 028 MIRACULOUS MAMA
- ☐ 029 COPPER CLAWS LOU
- ☐ 030 THE SLAVIC COOK
- ☐ 031 PRIMORDIAL OOZE
- ☐ 032 VISHNU NOODLE TIM
- ☐ 033 HABA-HABA HILGA
- ☐ 034 HUCK-CHU SNEAZY
- ☐ 035 SNUGGLE PORKY
- ☐ 036 FLUFFY MCTOE
- ☐ 037 WOLFDOG MAN
- ☐ 038 MORTIMER VORTEX
- ☐ 039 XANDER DAYSHADE
- ☐ 040 LUCIUS GRIMRIDER
- ☐ 041 SELENE BLACKHEAD
- ☐ 042 KAEL GRIMSHADOW
- ☐ 043 LILITH BLOODMOON
- ☐ 044 VAL ABSISSY CLAW
- ☐ 045 SELENE DOOMCLAW
- ☐ 046 BUMIE VON GOBBLE
- ☐ 047 GIGGLES MCGLOOP
- ☐ 048 FIZZLE FUZZYPAWS
- ☐ 049 SNICKER DOODLKINS
- ☐ 050 GIGGLES WOBLEWAG
- ☐ 051 FUZZZILLA
- ☐ 052 JIGGLYPUFF SALLY
- ☐ 053 HUMA BIRD
- ☐ 054 QUEEN MOTHER
- ☐ 055 HENRY
- ☐ 056 SIMURGHA
- ☐ 057 TIN FOIL CON
- ☐ 058 SMIRKLORD
- ☐ 059 GROUCHYFANG
- ☐ 060 CHUCKLEBOP
- ☐ 061 GIGGLESWAMP
- ☐ 062 SNICKERWICK
- ☐ 063 LAFFNINJA
- ☐ 064 QUIRKLING
- ☐ 065 GROUCHFIZZLE
- ☐ 066 WITTYWHIRL
- ☐ 067 CACKLEHOP
- ☐ 068 HAHAGLOOP
- ☐ 069 JOKULITE
- ☐ 070 CHUCKLEWHIZ
- ☐ 071 GIGGLESKULL
- ☐ 072 QUIRKBEAST
- ☐ 073 SNICKERFLARE
- ☐ 074 MIRTHPAW
- ☐ 075 DRACUGRIN
- ☐ 076 CANDY HEAD
- ☐ 077 GROUCHSHADE
- ☐ 078 CHUCKLEQUILL
- ☐ 079 QUIRKHOWLER
- ☐ 080 HAHAJESTER
- ☐ 081 JOKUBAT
- ☐ 082 SNICKERSPOOK
- ☐ 083 GIGGLESCRANK
- ☐ 084 CACKLEJINX
- ☐ 085 LAFFSHADE
- ☐ 086 CIY CLOPSIE
- ☐ 087 WITTYFLAME
- ☐ 088 GRINWHISPER
- ☐ 089 QUIRKCLAW
- ☐ 090 GROUCHYWHIRL
- ☐ 091 CHUCKLEJOLT
- ☐ 092 SNICKERGRIN
- ☐ 093 GROUCHOSTEIN
- ☐ 094 QUIRKNINJA
- ☐ 095 GIGGLESSNARL
- ☐ 096 MUMMY MCQUIRK
- ☐ 097 GIGGLESWORTH
- ☐ 098 SNICKERELLA
- ☐ 099 JIMMY COFFEE
- ☐ 100 CHUCKLES DRAC
- ☐ 101 LAFFULA
- ☐ 102 QUIRKULA
- ☐ 103 FRANKENFUNNY
- ☐ 104 ASENA THE BILLION
- ☐ 105 AMAROKIE
- ☐ 106 BUGBEAR
- ☐ 107 FAT LOUIE
- ☐ 108 POUKAI
- ☐ 109 EAGLE EYE ERNIE
- ☐ 110 GARLIC ROOSTER
- ☐ 111 BASAN
- ☐ 112 THUNDER THIGHS
- ☐ 113 WITTYWISP
- ☐ 114 SNICKERCLAW
- ☐ 115 LAFFTANGLE
- ☐ 116 HAHAWHIZ
- ☐ 117 GRINWHISPER
- ☐ 118 QUIRKLING
- ☐ 119 GIGGLESCRANK
- ☐ 120 CHUCKLEQUILL
- ☐ 121 SMIRKPAW
- ☐ 122 LAFFLING
- ☐ 123 WATER GIRAFFE
- ☐ 124 GROUCHFLAME
- ☐ 125 QUIRKCLAW
- ☐ 126 SNICKERSNARL
- ☐ 127 HAHABUZZ
- ☐ 128 CHUCKLEJESTER
- ☐ 129 GIGGLENINJA
- ☐ 130 LAFFPHANTOM
- ☐ 131 WITTYHOWLER
- ☐ 132 QUIRKQUAKE
- ☐ 133 GROUCHBOP
- ☐ 134 SMIRKWHISPER
- ☐ 135 JOKUBAT
- ☐ 136 SNICKERWISP
- ☐ 137 HAHAGRIN
- ☐ 138 CHUCKLESNARL
- ☐ 139 QUIRKCLAW
- ☐ 140 GROUCHYJINX
- ☐ 141 LAFFWHIRL
- ☐ 142 WITTYSHADOW
- ☐ 143 SNICKERHOWL
- ☐ 144 GRINFLARE
- ☐ 145 LAFFSPARK
- ☐ 146 CACKLEBOUNCE
- ☐ 147 JOKUPOP
- ☐ 148 GROUCHYFLUFF
- ☐ 149 CHUCKLEGLIDE
- ☐ 150 SMIRKROAR
- ☐ 151 WITTYFLICK
- ☐ 152 QUIRKCRUNCH
- ☐ 153 FISHWOMAN
- ☐ 154 LAFFQUAKE
- ☐ 155 CACKLEBUZZ
- ☐ 156 JOKUSHADOW
- ☐ 157 GROUCHCLAW
- ☐ 158 CHUCKLENOODLE
- ☐ 159 SMIRKWISP
- ☐ 160 WITTYBEAST
- ☐ 161 QUIRKHOWL
- ☐ 162 SNICKERFIZZLE
- ☐ 163 LAFFQUAKE
- ☐ 164 GIGGLESBOP
- ☐ 165 HAHAFLAME
- ☐ 166 CHUCKLEPHANTOM
- ☐ 167 JOKUKNIGHT
- ☐ 168 QUIRKNOODLE
- ☐ 169 CHUCKLESTEIN
- ☐ 170 DRACUCHUCK
- ☐ 171 GIGGLESMUMMY
- ☐ 172 WOLFIEWIT
- ☐ 173 QUIRKENSTEIN
- ☐ 174 JOKULA
- ☐ 175 GROUCHYPHANTOM
- ☐ 176 CACKLEBLOB
- ☐ 177 SNICKERELLA
- ☐ 178 LAFFZILLA
- ☐ 179 HAHASWAMP
- ☐ 180 QUIRKULA
- ☐ 181 GROUCHHUNCH
- ☐ 182 SMIRKFISHMAN
- ☐ 183 CHUCKHYDE
- ☐ 184 MIRTHWOLF
- ☐ 185 SNARKULA
- ☐ 186 GIGGLESBRIDE
- ☐ 187 QUIRKLAR
- ☐ 188 CACKVAMPIRE
- ☐ 189 GROUCHOBOLT
- ☐ 190 CHUCKHUNCH
- ☐ 191 LAFFLOCK
- ☐ 192 WITTYMUMMY
- ☐ 193 MIRTHRA
- ☐ 194 CACKLEWORM
- ☐ 195 HAHABRIDE
- ☐ 196 SCREAMHAHA
- ☐ 197 GRINPHANTOM
- ☐ 198 CHUCKLEFLY
- ☐ 199 LAFFINVISIBLE
- ☐ 200 GROUCHYBLOB
- ☐ 201 QUIRKYETI
- ☐ 202 CHUCKWRAITH
- ☐ 203 LAFFBOLT
- ☐ 204 SMIRKENSTEIN
- ☐ 205 QUIRKBRIDE
- ☐ 206 GROUCHOBATS
- ☐ 207 MUMMYWIT
- ☐ 208 HAHAMERMAN
- ☐ 209 GIGGLESFLY
- ☐ 210 CHUCKCYCLOPS
- ☐ 211 GRINZILLA
- ☐ 212 JOKSTEIN
- ☐ 213 QUIRKOOP
- ☐ 214 SNICKERBLOB
- ☐ 215 CHUCKLEWORM
- ☐ 216 DRACUWIT
- ☐ 217 LAFFULA
- ☐ 218 QUIRKRAT
- ☐ 219 WITTYMERMAN
- ☐ 220 GROUCHFISHMAN
- ☐ 221 CACKLEPHANTOM
- ☐ 222 HAHAGOBLIN
- ☐ 223 SNARKFLY
- ☐ 224 CHUCKLEYETI
- ☐ 225 GROUCHYSHADE
- ☐ 226 CACKLEWHIRL
- ☐ 227 POTATOE JOE
- ☐ 228 GIGGLESHUNCH
- ☐ 229 JOKVAMPIRE
- ☐ 230 QUIRKGOBLIN
- ☐ 231 CACKMERMAN
- ☐ 232 SMIRKULA
- ☐ 233 LAFFGHOUL
- ☐ 234 CHUCKLEGHOST
- ☐ 235 QUIRKWITCH
- ☐ 236 GROUCHYWOLF
- ☐ 237 MIRTHBATS
- ☐ 238 CHUCKRAT
- ☐ 239 QUIRKBLOB
- ☐ 240 JOKBOLT
- ☐ 241 LAFFWITCH
- ☐ 242 SNICKERHUNCH
- ☐ 243 CACKLEPHANTOM
- ☐ 244 GROUCHOWIT
- ☐ 245 CHUCKLEMUMMY
- ☐ 246 HAHAYETI
- ☐ 247 SNARKWITCH
- ☐ 248 GRINBLOB
- ☐ 249 JOKULA
- ☐ 250 QUIRKHUNCH
- ☐ 251 CHUCKLEPHANTOM
- ☐ 252 LAFFBOLT
- ☐ 253 GROUCHMERMAN
- ☐ 254 HAHAGHOUL
- ☐ 255 SNICKERGHOST
- ☐ 256 CHUCKFISHMAN
- ☐ 257 QUIRKOOP
- ☐ 258 SMIRKWIT
- ☐ 259 GIGGLESRAT
- ☐ 260 CACKLEFLY
- ☐ 261 LAFFGOBLIN
- ☐ 262 CHUCKLEYETI
- ☐ 263 GRINBRIDE
- ☐ 264 GROUCHOWITCH
- ☐ 265 QUIRKULA
- ☐ 266 SNARKENSTEIN
- ☐ 267 HAHAPHANTOM
- ☐ 268 CACKLESWAMP
- ☐ 269 CHUCKHUNCH
- ☐ 270 GIGGLESBLOB
- ☐ 271 CHUCKIE
- ☐ 272 QUIRKSTER
- ☐ 273 GIGGLESNARL
- ☐ 274 SNICKERCLAW
- ☐ 275 MIRTHQUAKE
- ☐ 276 DRACUCHUCKLE
- ☐ 277 LAFFTANGLE
- ☐ 278 GROUCHETTE
- ☐ 279 WITTYWISP
- ☐ 280 HAHAHOWL
- ☐ 281 JOKEMONSTER
- ☐ 282 QUIRKZILLA
- ☐ 283 CACKLINA
- ☐ 284 CHUCKLEBYTE
- ☐ 285 QUIRKSHADE
- ☐ 286 GIGGLESNACK
- ☐ 287 SNICKERTHUD
- ☐ 288 MIRTHQUAKE
- ☐ 289 DRACUFIZZ
- ☐ 290 LAFFNUDGE
- ☐ 291 GROUCHGLEE
- ☐ 292 WITTYZAP
- ☐ 293 HAHACHOMP
- ☐ 294 JOKUBUZZ
- ☐ 295 QUIRKZILLA
- ☐ 296 CACKLEBUMP
- ☐ 297 SMIRKLASH
- ☐ 298 GROUCHYJOLT
- ☐ 299 CHUCKLEFLUFF
- ☐ 300 GIGGLESWIRL
- ☐ 301 SNICKERTHUNK
- ☐ 302 LAFFFLICK
- ☐ 303 QUIRKBOUNCE
- ☐ 304 GROUCHFROLIC
- ☐ 305 WITTYWHAM
- ☐ 306 CACKLEPLOP
- ☐ 307 HAHASQUISH
- ☐ 308 JOKULUXE
- ☐ 309 CHUCKLEZOOM
- ☐ 310 GIGGLESCRUNCH
- ☐ 311 QUIRKROAR
- ☐ 312 SNICKERBEAM
- ☐ 313 MIRTHPOUNCE
- ☐ 314 DRACUGIGGLE
- ☐ 315 LAFFTWIST
- ☐ 316 GROUCHYZEST
- ☐ 317 CHUCKLEGLIDE
- ☐ 318 QUIRKSOAR
- ☐ 319 HAHACHUCKLE
- ☐ 320 JOKUPOP
- ☐ 321 SNICKERBOUNCE
- ☐ 322 GIGGLESWHIZ
- ☐ 323 CACKLEZAP
- ☐ 324 LAFFSPROUT
- ☐ 325 SMIRKPOP
- ☐ 326 WITTYZOOM
- ☐ 327 GRINBOUNCE
- ☐ 328 QUIRKCHOMP
- ☐ 329 GROUCHZOOM
- ☐ 330 CHUCKLEZIP
- ☐ 331 SNICKERSNORT
- ☐ 332 HAHARUMBLE
- ☐ 333 QUIRKTWIRL
- ☐ 334 GIGGLESWHAM
- ☐ 335 LENNY THE FIG
- ☐ 336 GRINSWAMP

WHY WAIT FOR THE LARGE HADRON COLLIDER TO OPEN THE DOOR TO HELL… WHEN YOU CAN COLLECT ALL 666 CARDS AND OPEN THE DOOR YOURSELF! GOULISH HUNTING!

THE MONSTER VALUE STAMP CHECKLIST! (-2-)

- ☐ 337 CHUCKLEFIZZ
- ☐ 338 QUIRKGLEAM
- ☐ 339 GIGGLESNAP
- ☐ 340 SNICKERDUNK
- ☐ 341 MIRTHQUAKE
- ☐ 342 DRACUSIZZLE
- ☐ 343 LAFFJOLT
- ☐ 344 GROUCHGLIMP
- ☐ 345 WITTYZEST
- ☐ 346 HAHACHOMP
- ☐ 347 JOKUSHINE
- ☐ 348 QUIRKZILLA
- ☐ 349 CACKLEDAZZ
- ☐ 350 SMIRKFLASH
- ☐ 351 GROUCHYJOLT
- ☐ 352 CHUCKLEFLUFF
- ☐ 353 GIGGLESPREE
- ☐ 354 SNICKERDAZZ
- ☐ 355 LAFFTWIRL
- ☐ 356 QUIRKBOUNCE
- ☐ 357 GROUCHFROLIC
- ☐ 358 WITTYWHAM
- ☐ 359 CACKLEBOP
- ☐ 360 HAHASQUISH
- ☐ 361 JOKULUXE
- ☐ 362 CHUCKLEZOOM
- ☐ 363 GIGGLESCRUNCH
- ☐ 364 QUIRKROAR
- ☐ 365 SNICKERBEAM
- ☐ 366 MIRTHPOUNCE
- ☐ 367 DRACUGIGGLE
- ☐ 368 LAFFTWIST
- ☐ 369 GROUCHYZEST
- ☐ 370 CHUCKLEGLIDE
- ☐ 371 QUIRKSOAR
- ☐ 372 HAHACHUCKLE
- ☐ 373 JOKUPOP
- ☐ 374 SNICKERBOUNCE
- ☐ 375 GIGGLESWHIZ
- ☐ 376 CACKLEZAP
- ☐ 377 LAFFSPROUT
- ☐ 378 SMIRKPOP
- ☐ 379 WITTYZOOM
- ☐ 380 GRINBOUNCE
- ☐ 381 QUIRKCHOMP
- ☐ 382 GROUCHZOOM
- ☐ 383 CHUCKLEZIP
- ☐ 384 SNICKERSNORT
- ☐ 385 HAHARUMBLE
- ☐ 386 THE WARP
- ☐ 387 GIGGLESWHAM
- ☐ 388 LAFFSPARK
- ☐ 389 CACKLEBOUNCE
- ☐ 390 JOKUPOP
- ☐ 391 GROUCHYFLUFF
- ☐ 392 CHUCKLEGLIDE
- ☐ 393 SMIRKROAR
- ☐ 394 WITTYFLICK
- ☐ 395 QUIRKCRUNCH
- ☐ 396 SNICKERSWOOP
- ☐ 397 JERRY THE NAIL
- ☐ 398 GIGGLESWHIZ
- ☐ 399 HAHACHUCKLE
- ☐ 400 CHUCKLECRUNCH
- ☐ 401 JOKUZIP
- ☐ 402 QUIRKBOUNCE
- ☐ 403 GROUCHZOOM
- ☐ 404 SNICKERSWIRL
- ☐ 405 WITTYWHAM
- ☐ 406 LAFFCHOMP
- ☐ 407 SMIRKPOP
- ☐ 408 QUIRKZOOM
- ☐ 409 GROUCHYZIP
- ☐ 410 HAHAPOUNCE
- ☐ 411 CHUCKLECHUCKLE
- ☐ 412 GIGGLESFLICK
- ☐ 413 SNICKERBOUNCE
- ☐ 414 LAFFSPROUT
- ☐ 415 WITTYWHIZ
- ☐ 416 GRINCHOMP
- ☐ 417 QUIRKTWIRL
- ☐ 418 GROUCHYWHAM
- ☐ 419 CHUCKLEZOOM
- ☐ 420 JOKUZIP
- ☐ 421 SNICKERSNORT
- ☐ 422 HAHARUMBLE
- ☐ 423 GIGGLERUMBLE
- ☐ 424 QUIRKBOUNCE
- ☐ 425 LAFFTWIST
- ☐ 426 SMIRKWHAM
- ☐ 427 CHUCKLEWHIZ
- ☐ 428 SNICKERSWOOP
- ☐ 429 QUIRKFLICK
- ☐ 430 GROUCHPOP
- ☐ 431 HAHAWOOSH
- ☐ 432 LAFFWHIZ
- ☐ 433 CHUCKLEFLUFF
- ☐ 434 GIGGLESNORT
- ☐ 435 QUIRKBOUNCE
- ☐ 436 JOKUPOP
- ☐ 437 CHUCKLEFIZZ
- ☐ 438 QUIRKGLEAM
- ☐ 439 GIGGLESNAP
- ☐ 440 SNICKERDUNK
- ☐ 441 MIRTHQUAKE
- ☐ 442 DRACUSIZZLE
- ☐ 443 VLAD CHAD
- ☐ 444 GROUCHGLIMP
- ☐ 445 WITTYZEST
- ☐ 446 HAHACHOMP
- ☐ 447 JOKUSHINE
- ☐ 448 QUIRKZILLA
- ☐ 449 CACKLEDAZZ
- ☐ 450 SMIRKFLASH
- ☐ 451 GROUCHYJOLT
- ☐ 452 CHUCKLEFLUFF
- ☐ 453 GIGGLESPREE
- ☐ 454 SNICKERDAZZ
- ☐ 455 LAFFTWIRL
- ☐ 456 QUIRKBOUNCE
- ☐ 457 GROUCHFROLIC
- ☐ 458 WITTYWHAM
- ☐ 459 CACKLEBOP
- ☐ 460 HAHASQUISH
- ☐ 461 JOKULUXE
- ☐ 462 CHUCKLEZOOM
- ☐ 463 GIGGLESCRUNCH
- ☐ 464 QUIRKROAR
- ☐ 465 SNICKERBEAM
- ☐ 466 MIRTHPOUNCE
- ☐ 467 DRACUGIGGLE
- ☐ 468 LAFFTWIST
- ☐ 469 GROUCHYZEST
- ☐ 470 CHUCKLEGLIDE
- ☐ 471 QUIRKSOAR
- ☐ 472 HAHACHUCKLE
- ☐ 473 JOKUPOP
- ☐ 474 SNICKERBOUNCE
- ☐ 475 GIGGLESWHIZ
- ☐ 476 CACKLEZAP
- ☐ 477 LAFFSPROUT
- ☐ 478 SMIRKPOP
- ☐ 479 WITTYZOOM
- ☐ 480 GRINBOUNCE
- ☐ 481 QUIRKCHOMP
- ☐ 482 GROUCHZOOM
- ☐ 483 CHUCKLEZIP
- ☐ 484 SNICKERSNORT
- ☐ 485 HAHARUMBLE
- ☐ 486 QUIRKTWIRL
- ☐ 487 GIGGLESWHAM
- ☐ 488 LAFFSPARK
- ☐ 489 CACKLEBOUNCE
- ☐ 490 JOKUPOP
- ☐ 491 GROUCHYFLUFF
- ☐ 492 CHUCKLEGLIDE
- ☐ 493 SMIRKROAR
- ☐ 494 WITTYFLICK
- ☐ 495 QUIRKCRUNCH
- ☐ 496 SNICKERSWOOP
- ☐ 497 LAFFTWIST
- ☐ 498 GIGGLESWHIZ
- ☐ 499 HAHACHUCKLE
- ☐ 500 CHUCKLECRUNCH
- ☐ 501 SLICK VINCE
- ☐ 502 QUIRKBOUNCE
- ☐ 503 GROUCHZOOM
- ☐ 504 SNICKERSWIRL
- ☐ 505 WITTYWHAM
- ☐ 506 LAFFCHOMP
- ☐ 507 SMIRKPOP
- ☐ 508 QUIRKZOOM
- ☐ 509 GROUCHYZIP
- ☐ 510 HAHAPOUNCE
- ☐ 511 CHUCKLECHUCKLE
- ☐ 512 GIGGLESFLICK
- ☐ 513 SNICKERBOUNCE
- ☐ 514 LAFFSPROUT
- ☐ 515 WITTYWHIZ
- ☐ 516 GRINCHOMP
- ☐ 517 QUIRKTWIRL
- ☐ 518 GROUCHYWHAM
- ☐ 519 CHUCKLEZOOM
- ☐ 520 JOKUZIP
- ☐ 521 SNICKERSNORT
- ☐ 522 HAHARUMBLE
- ☐ 523 GIGGLERUMBLE
- ☐ 524 QUIRKBOUNCE
- ☐ 525 LAFFTWIST
- ☐ 526 SMIRKWHAM
- ☐ 527 ALI EAN
- ☐ 528 SNICKERSWOOP
- ☐ 529 QUIRKFLICK
- ☐ 530 GROUCHPOP
- ☐ 531 HAHAWOOSH
- ☐ 532 LAFFWHIZ
- ☐ 533 CHUCKLEFLUFF
- ☐ 534 GIGGLESNORT
- ☐ 535 QUIRKBOUNCE
- ☐ 536 JOKUPOP
- ☐ 537 CHUCKLEFIZZ
- ☐ 538 QUIRKGLEAM
- ☐ 539 GIGGLESNAP
- ☐ 540 SNICKERDUNK
- ☐ 541 MIRTHQUAKE
- ☐ 542 DRACUSIZZLE
- ☐ 543 LAFFJOLT
- ☐ 544 GROUCHGLIMP
- ☐ 545 WITTYZEST
- ☐ 546 HAHACHOMP
- ☐ 547 JOKUSHINE
- ☐ 548 QUIRKZILLA
- ☐ 549 CACKLEDAZZ
- ☐ 550 SMIRKFLASH
- ☐ 551 GROUCHYJOLT
- ☐ 552 CHUCKLEFLUFF
- ☐ 553 GIGGLESPREE
- ☐ 554 SNICKERDAZZ
- ☐ 555 PRETTY BOY LENI
- ☐ 556 QUIRKBOUNCE
- ☐ 557 GROUCHFROLIC
- ☐ 558 WITTYWHAM
- ☐ 559 CACKLEBOP
- ☐ 560 HAHASQUISH
- ☐ 561 JOKULUXE
- ☐ 562 CHUCKLEZOOM
- ☐ 563 GIGGLESCRUNCH
- ☐ 564 QUIRKROAR
- ☐ 565 SNICKERBEAM
- ☐ 566 MIRTHPOUNCE
- ☐ 567 DRACUGIGGLE
- ☐ 568 LAFFTWIST
- ☐ 569 GROUCHYZEST
- ☐ 570 CHUCKLEGLIDE
- ☐ 571 QUIRKSOAR
- ☐ 572 HAHACHUCKLE
- ☐ 573 JOKUPOP
- ☐ 574 SNICKERBOUNCE
- ☐ 575 GIGGLESWHIZ
- ☐ 576 CACKLEZAP
- ☐ 577 LAFFSPROUT
- ☐ 578 SMIRKPOP
- ☐ 579 WITTYZOOM
- ☐ 580 GRINBOUNCE
- ☐ 581 QUIRKCHOMP
- ☐ 582 GROUCHZOOM
- ☐ 583 CHUCKLEZIP
- ☐ 584 SNICKERSNORT
- ☐ 585 HAHARUMBLE
- ☐ 586 QUIRKTWIRL
- ☐ 587 GIGGLESWHAM
- ☐ 588 LAFFSPARK
- ☐ 589 CACKLEBOUNCE
- ☐ 590 JOKUPOP
- ☐ 591 GROUCHYFLUFF
- ☐ 592 CHUCKLEGLIDE
- ☐ 593 SMIRKROAR
- ☐ 594 WITTYFLICK
- ☐ 595 QUIRKCRUNCH
- ☐ 596 SNICKERSWOOP
- ☐ 597 LAFFTWIST
- ☐ 598 GIGGLESWHIZ
- ☐ 599 HAHACHUCKLE
- ☐ 600 CHUCKLECRUNCH
- ☐ 601 JOKUZIP
- ☐ 602 QUIRKBOUNCE
- ☐ 603 GROUCHZOOM
- ☐ 604 SNICKERSWIRL
- ☐ 605 WITTYWHAM
- ☐ 606 LAFFCHOMP
- ☐ 607 SMIRKPOP
- ☐ 608 QUIRKZOOM
- ☐ 609 GROUCHYZIP
- ☐ 610 HAHAPOUNCE
- ☐ 611 CHUCKLECHUCKLE
- ☐ 612 GIGGLESFLICK
- ☐ 613 MOUNTAIN CINDY
- ☐ 614 LAFFSPROUT
- ☐ 615 WITTYWHIZ
- ☐ 616 GRINCHOMP
- ☐ 617 QUIRKTWIRL
- ☐ 618 GROUCHYWHAM
- ☐ 619 CHUCKLEZOOM
- ☐ 620 JOKUZIP
- ☐ 621 SNICKERSNORT
- ☐ 622 HAHARUMBLE
- ☐ 623 GIGGLERUMBLE
- ☐ 624 QUIRKBOUNCE
- ☐ 625 LAFFTWIST
- ☐ 626 SMIRKWHAM
- ☐ 627 CHUCKLEWHIZ
- ☐ 628 SNICKERSWOOP
- ☐ 629 QUIRKFLICK
- ☐ 630 GROUCHPOP
- ☐ 631 HAHAWOOSH
- ☐ 632 LAFFWHIZ
- ☐ 633 CHUCKLEFLUFF
- ☐ 634 GIGGLESNORT
- ☐ 635 QUIRKBOUNCE
- ☐ 636 JOKUPOP
- ☐ 637 CHUCKLEFIZZ
- ☐ 638 QUIRKGLEAM
- ☐ 639 GIGGLESNAP
- ☐ 640 SNICKERDUNK
- ☐ 641 MIRTHQUAKE
- ☐ 642 DRACUSIZZLE
- ☐ 643 LAFFJOLT
- ☐ 644 GROUCHGLIMP
- ☐ 645 WITTYZEST
- ☐ 646 HAHACHOMP
- ☐ 647 JOKUSHINE
- ☐ 648 QUIRKZILLA
- ☐ 649 CACKLEDAZZ
- ☐ 650 SMIRKFLASH
- ☐ 651 GROUCHYJOLT
- ☐ 652 CHUCKLEFLUFF
- ☐ 653 GIGGLESPREE
- ☐ 654 SNICKERDAZZ
- ☐ 655 LAFFTWIRL
- ☐ 656 QUIRKBOUNCE
- ☐ 657 GROUCHFROLIC
- ☐ 658 WITTYWHAM
- ☐ 659 CACKLEBOP
- ☐ 660 HAHASQUISH
- ☐ 661 JOKULUXE
- ☐ 662 CHUCKLEZOOM
- ☐ 663 GIGGLESCRUNCH
- ☐ 664 QUIRKROAR
- ☐ 665 MAD MANDY
- ☐ 666 SNICKERBOUNCE

WHY WAIT FOR THE LARGE HADRON COLLIDER TO OPEN THE DOOR TO HELL... WHEN YOU CAN COLLECT ALL 666 CARDS AND OPEN THE DOOR YOURSELF! GOULISH HUNTING!

THE MONSTERS NEXT DOOR

Edited by R.J. Carter

THE MONSTER VALUE STAMP CHECKLIST! (-2-)

❏ 337 CHUCKLEFIZZ	❏ 393 SMIRKROAR	❏ 449 CACKLEDAZZ	❏ 505 WITTYWHAM	❏ 561 JOKULUXE	❏ 617 QUIRKTWIRL
❏ 338 QUIRKGLEAM	❏ 394 WITTYFLICK	❏ 450 SMIRKFLASH	❏ 506 LAFFCHOMP	❏ 562 CHUCKLEZOOM	❏ 618 GROUCHYWHAM
❏ 339 GIGGLESNAP	❏ 395 QUIRKCRUNCH	❏ 451 GROUCHYJOLT	❏ 507 SMIRKPOP	❏ 563 GIGGLESCRUNCH	❏ 619 CHUCKLEZOOM
❏ 340 SNICKERDUNK	❏ 396 SNICKERSWOOP	❏ 452 CHUCKLEFLUFF	❏ 508 QUIRKZOOM	❏ 564 QUIRKROAR	❏ 620 JOKUZIP
❏ 341 MIRTHQUAKE	❏ 397 JERRY THE NAIL	❏ 453 GIGGLESPREE	❏ 509 GROUCHYZIP	❏ 565 SNICKERBEAM	❏ 621 SNICKERSNORT
❏ 342 DRACUSIZZLE	❏ 398 GIGGLESWHIZ	❏ 454 SNICKERDAZZ	❏ 510 HAHAPOUNCE	❏ 566 MIRTHPOUNCE	❏ 622 HAHARUMBLE
❏ 343 LAFFJOLT	❏ 399 HAHACHUCKLE	❏ 455 LAFFTWIRL	❏ 511 CHUCKLECHUCKLE	❏ 567 DRACUGIGGLE	❏ 623 GIGGLERUMBLE
❏ 344 GROUCHGLIMP	❏ 400 CHUCKLECRUNCH	❏ 456 QUIRKBOUNCE	❏ 512 GIGGLESFLICK	❏ 568 LAFFTWIST	❏ 624 QUIRKBOUNCE
❏ 345 WITTYZEST	❏ 401 JOKUZIP	❏ 457 GROUCHFROLIC	❏ 513 SNICKERBOUNCE	❏ 569 GROUCHYZEST	❏ 625 LAFFTWIST
❏ 346 HAHACHOMP	❏ 402 QUIRKBOUNCE	❏ 458 WITTYWHAM	❏ 514 LAFFSPROUT	❏ 570 CHUCKLEGLIDE	❏ 626 SMIRKWHAM
❏ 347 JOKUSHINE	❏ 403 GROUCHZOOM	❏ 459 CACKLEBOP	❏ 515 WITTYWHIZ	❏ 571 QUIRKSOAR	❏ 627 CHUCKLEWHIZ
❏ 348 QUIRKZILLA	❏ 404 SNICKERSWIRL	❏ 460 HAHASQUISH	❏ 516 GRINCHOMP	❏ 572 HAHACHUCKLE	❏ 628 SNICKERSWOOP
❏ 349 CACKLEDAZZ	❏ 405 WITTYWHAM	❏ 461 JOKULUXE	❏ 517 QUIRKTWIRL	❏ 573 JOKUPOP	❏ 629 QUIRKFLICK
❏ 350 SMIRKFLASH	❏ 406 LAFFCHOMP	❏ 462 CHUCKLEZOOM	❏ 518 GROUCHYWHAM	❏ 574 SNICKERBOUNCE	❏ 630 GROUCHPOP
❏ 351 GROUCHYJOLT	❏ 407 SMIRKPOP	❏ 463 GIGGLESCRUNCH	❏ 519 CHUCKLEZOOM	❏ 575 GIGGLESWHIZ	❏ 631 HAHAWOOSH
❏ 352 CHUCKLEFLUFF	❏ 408 QUIRKZOOM	❏ 464 QUIRKROAR	❏ 520 JOKUZIP	❏ 576 CACKLEZAP	❏ 632 LAFFWHIZ
❏ 353 GIGGLESPREE	❏ 409 GROUCHYZIP	❏ 465 SNICKERBEAM	❏ 521 SNICKERSNORT	❏ 577 LAFFSPROUT	❏ 633 CHUCKLEFLUFF
❏ 354 SNICKERDAZZ	❏ 410 HAHAPOUNCE	❏ 466 MIRTHPOUNCE	❏ 522 HAHARUMBLE	❏ 578 SMIRKPOP	❏ 634 GIGGLESNORT
❏ 355 LAFFTWIRL	❏ 411 CHUCKLECHUCKLE	❏ 467 DRACUGIGGLE	❏ 523 GIGGLERUMBLE	❏ 579 WITTYZOOM	❏ 635 QUIRKBOUNCE
❏ 356 QUIRKBOUNCE	❏ 412 GIGGLESFLICK	❏ 468 LAFFTWIST	❏ 524 QUIRKBOUNCE	❏ 580 GRINBOUNCE	❏ 636 JOKUPOP
❏ 357 GROUCHFROLIC	❏ 413 SNICKERBOUNCE	❏ 469 GROUCHYZEST	❏ 525 LAFFTWIST	❏ 581 QUIRKCHOMP	❏ 637 CHUCKLEFIZZ
❏ 358 WITTYWHAM	❏ 414 LAFFSPROUT	❏ 470 CHUCKLEGLIDE	❏ 526 SMIRKWHAM	❏ 582 GROUCHZOOM	❏ 638 QUIRKGLEAM
❏ 359 CACKLEBOP	❏ 415 WITTYWHIZ	❏ 471 QUIRKSOAR	❏ 527 ALI EAN	❏ 583 CHUCKLEZIP	❏ 639 GIGGLESNAP
❏ 360 HAHASQUISH	❏ 416 GRINCHOMP	❏ 472 HAHACHUCKLE	❏ 528 SNICKERSWOOP	❏ 584 SNICKERSNORT	❏ 640 SNICKERDUNK
❏ 361 JOKULUXE	❏ 417 QUIRKTWIRL	❏ 473 JOKUPOP	❏ 529 QUIRKFLICK	❏ 585 HAHARUMBLE	❏ 641 MIRTHQUAKE
❏ 362 CHUCKLEZOOM	❏ 418 GROUCHYWHAM	❏ 474 SNICKERBOUNCE	❏ 530 GROUCHPOP	❏ 586 QUIRKTWIRL	❏ 642 DRACUSIZZLE
❏ 363 GIGGLESCRUNCH	❏ 419 CHUCKLEZOOM	❏ 475 GIGGLESWHIZ	❏ 531 HAHAWOOSH	❏ 587 GIGGLESWHAM	❏ 643 LAFFJOLT
❏ 364 QUIRKROAR	❏ 420 JOKUZIP	❏ 476 CACKLEZAP	❏ 532 LAFFWHIZ	❏ 588 LAFFSPARK	❏ 644 GROUCHGLIMP
❏ 365 SNICKERBEAM	❏ 421 SNICKERSNORT	❏ 477 LAFFSPROUT	❏ 533 CHUCKLEFLUFF	❏ 589 CACKLEBOUNCE	❏ 645 WITTYZEST
❏ 366 MIRTHPOUNCE	❏ 422 HAHARUMBLE	❏ 478 SMIRKPOP	❏ 534 GIGGLESNORT	❏ 590 JOKUPOP	❏ 646 HAHACHOMP
❏ 367 DRACUGIGGLE	❏ 423 GIGGLERUMBLE	❏ 479 WITTYZOOM	❏ 535 QUIRKBOUNCE	❏ 591 GROUCHYFLUFF	❏ 647 JOKUSHINE
❏ 368 LAFFTWIST	❏ 424 QUIRKBOUNCE	❏ 480 GRINBOUNCE	❏ 536 JOKUPOP	❏ 592 CHUCKLEGLIDE	❏ 648 QUIRKZILLA
❏ 369 GROUCHYZEST	❏ 425 LAFFTWIST	❏ 481 QUIRKCHOMP	❏ 537 CHUCKLEFIZZ	❏ 593 SMIRKROAR	❏ 649 CACKLEDAZZ
❏ 370 CHUCKLEGLIDE	❏ 426 SMIRKWHAM	❏ 482 GROUCHZOOM	❏ 538 QUIRKGLEAM	❏ 594 WITTYFLICK	❏ 650 SMIRKFLASH
❏ 371 QUIRKSOAR	❏ 427 CHUCKLEWHIZ	❏ 483 CHUCKLEZIP	❏ 539 GIGGLESNAP	❏ 595 QUIRKCRUNCH	❏ 651 GROUCHYJOLT
❏ 372 HAHACHUCKLE	❏ 428 SNICKERSWOOP	❏ 484 SNICKERSNORT	❏ 540 SNICKERDUNK	❏ 596 SNICKERSWOOP	❏ 652 CHUCKLEFLUFF
❏ 373 JOKUPOP	❏ 429 QUIRKFLICK	❏ 485 HAHARUMBLE	❏ 541 MIRTHQUAKE	❏ 597 LAFFTWIST	❏ 653 GIGGLESPREE
❏ 374 SNICKERBOUNCE	❏ 430 GROUCHPOP	❏ 486 QUIRKTWIRL	❏ 542 DRACUSIZZLE	❏ 598 GIGGLESWHIZ	❏ 654 SNICKERDAZZ
❏ 375 GIGGLESWHIZ	❏ 431 HAHAWOOSH	❏ 487 GIGGLESWHAM	❏ 543 LAFFJOLT	❏ 599 HAHACHUCKLE	❏ 655 LAFFTWIRL
❏ 376 CACKLEZAP	❏ 432 LAFFWHIZ	❏ 488 LAFFSPARK	❏ 544 GROUCHGLIMP	❏ 600 CHUCKLECRUNCH	❏ 656 QUIRKBOUNCE
❏ 377 LAFFSPROUT	❏ 433 CHUCKLEFLUFF	❏ 489 CACKLEBOUNCE	❏ 545 WITTYZEST	❏ 601 JOKUZIP	❏ 657 GROUCHFROLIC
❏ 378 SMIRKPOP	❏ 434 GIGGLESNORT	❏ 490 JOKUPOP	❏ 546 HAHACHOMP	❏ 602 QUIRKBOUNCE	❏ 658 WITTYWHAM
❏ 379 WITTYZOOM	❏ 435 QUIRKBOUNCE	❏ 491 GROUCHYFLUFF	❏ 547 JOKUSHINE	❏ 603 GROUCHZOOM	❏ 659 CACKLEBOP
❏ 380 GRINBOUNCE	❏ 436 JOKUPOP	❏ 492 CHUCKLEGLIDE	❏ 548 QUIRKZILLA	❏ 604 SNICKERSWIRL	❏ 660 HAHASQUISH
❏ 381 QUIRKCHOMP	❏ 437 CHUCKLEFIZZ	❏ 493 SMIRKROAR	❏ 549 CACKLEDAZZ	❏ 605 WITTYWHAM	❏ 661 JOKULUXE
❏ 382 GROUCHZOOM	❏ 438 QUIRKGLEAM	❏ 494 WITTYFLICK	❏ 550 SMIRKFLASH	❏ 606 LAFFCHOMP	❏ 662 CHUCKLEZOOM
❏ 383 CHUCKLEZIP	❏ 439 GIGGLESNAP	❏ 495 QUIRKCRUNCH	❏ 551 GROUCHYJOLT	❏ 607 SMIRKPOP	❏ 663 GIGGLESCRUNCH
❏ 384 SNICKERSNORT	❏ 440 SNICKERDUNK	❏ 496 SNICKERSWOOP	❏ 552 CHUCKLEFLUFF	❏ 608 QUIRKZOOM	❏ 664 QUIRKROAR
❏ 385 HAHARUMBLE	❏ 441 MIRTHQUAKE	❏ 497 LAFFTWIST	❏ 553 GIGGLESPREE	❏ 609 GROUCHYZIP	❏ 665 MAD MANDY
❏ 386 THE WARP	❏ 442 DRACUSIZZLE	❏ 498 GIGGLESWHIZ	❏ 554 SNICKERDAZZ	❏ 610 HAHAPOUNCE	❏ 666 SNICKERBOUNCE
❏ 387 GIGGLESWHAM	❏ 443 VLAD CHAD	❏ 499 HAHACHUCKLE	❏ 555 PRETTY BOY LENI	❏ 611 CHUCKLECHUCKLE	
❏ 388 LAFFSPARK	❏ 444 GROUCHGLIMP	❏ 500 CHUCKLECRUNCH	❏ 556 QUIRKBOUNCE	❏ 612 GIGGLESFLICK	
❏ 389 CACKLEBOUNCE	❏ 445 WITTYZEST	❏ 501 SLICK VINCE	❏ 557 GROUCHFROLIC	❏ 613 MOUNTAIN CINDY	
❏ 390 JOKUPOP	❏ 446 HAHACHOMP	❏ 502 QUIRKBOUNCE	❏ 558 WITTYWHAM	❏ 614 LAFFSPROUT	
❏ 391 GROUCHYFLUFF	❏ 447 JOKUSHINE	❏ 503 GROUCHZOOM	❏ 559 CACKLEBOP	❏ 615 WITTYWHIZ	
❏ 392 CHUCKLEGLIDE	❏ 448 QUIRKZILLA	❏ 504 SNICKERSWIRL	❏ 560 HAHASQUISH	❏ 616 GRINCHOMP	

WHY WAIT FOR THE LARGE HADRON COLLIDER TO OPEN THE DOOR TO HELL... WHEN YOU CAN COLLECT ALL 666 CARDS AND OPEN THE DOOR YOURSELF! GOULISH HUNTING!

THE MONSTERS NEXT DOOR

Edited by R.J. Carter

www.ingramcontent.com/pod-product-compliance
Lightning Source LLC
Chambersburg PA
CBHW062112290726
48975CB00001B/201